ALL THE CREATURES THAT BREATHE

A NOVEL BASED ON REAL EVENTS

D. DAUPHINEE

KICKING PIG
PRESS

Kicking Pig Press 24 Main Street
Bradley, Maine 04411 U.S.A.

Library of Congress Control Number: 2021925825

www.ddauphinee.com

Book design by Cyrusfiction Productions

Printed in the United States of America

ISBN: 978-0-9863089-2-5 (Paperback)
ISBN: 978-0-9863089-3-2 (E-Book, Kindle)
ISBN: 978-0-9863089-4-9 (Hardback)

For Alberto, Robin, Ed, and John.

TABLE OF CONTENTS

ALL THE CREATURES THAT BREATHE

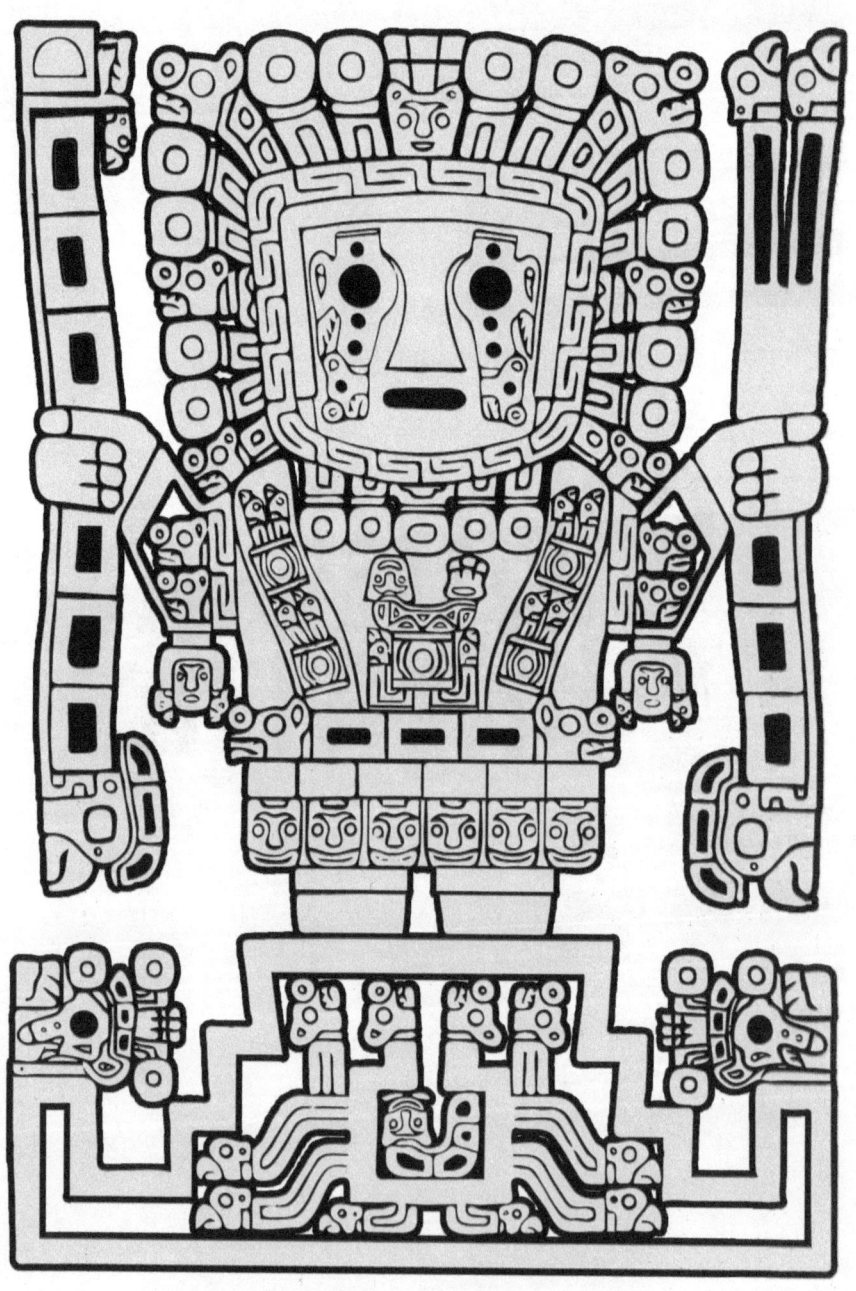

Viracocha, God of Creation

ONE

Veritas

— *October 1985* —

She was bent over, half squatting in the trench, covered in dirt from head-to-toe with smears of dried sweat streaking down both temples. Her T-shirt was riding up, and her hip bones, also dirty, showed above the waistband of her jeans. Flecks of sunlight trickled down through the hanging branches of the tall elms and oaks that framed the Yard. Casey sat on the grass and watched her from above. She glanced up from the trench as she wiped her brow.

"Look at those idiot tourists, rubbing that guy's foot," Claire said.

Casey looked across the Yard. More than thirty tourists were taking their turns, stepping up to the statue of John Harvard — or who they thought was Harvard — and caressing the polished right foot of the figure while another tourist took their photograph.

"Don't they realize it's not even Harvard? It's just some guy."

"Doubt it," Casey replied. He looked back at Claire, who kept scratching at the trench wall.

"Why does that bother you so much?" he asked. "You see them do it every day."

"Because, Case, nobody seems to give a shit about history anymore."

"That's true," Casey said, "but *we* do, and that's why we're covered in dirt and sweat. Anyway, it's just a copycat thing from Verona, where tourists touch Juliet's right breast for luck."

"Did you do that when you backpacked through Europe?" Claire asked. "I can't picture you doing something that cheesy."

"No. Seventy-five years ago, I might have. But I don't believe in superstitions. For me, Europe was all about the architecture — and of course the food. But I *did* grind my heel into the bull's testicles in Milan, just for luck."

The conversation paused while Claire continued to work.

Casey glanced back at the statue. "Hoar," he muttered.

Claire stopped scraping the dirt. She squinted up at him through the thin veins of shadows and sunlight. "Might want to work on your sweet-talkin'."

"No, Sherman Hoar. That was the law student who modeled for the statue — at least for its head."

"Oh, that's right," Claire said, turning back to her work. "Forgot." Head down, she scraped the side of the trench first with a dental pick, then switched to a tiny brush.

As Casey sat on the grass at the edge of the trench, he couldn't help noticing how lovely she was.

Her blonde hair was pulled back into a perfect ponytail, and it had a splendid, natural little flip at the end, almost touching the back of her neck before it turned upward in a sexy curl. Casey knew that her eyes were a lighter blue than most people's, almost ice blue, which gave her an exotic look. Those almond-shaped aquamarine eyes were his favorite feature.

"Is Jack coming tonight?" Claire asked.

Casey snapped out of his trance. "He told me this morning he's planning to."

"I wish he'd find a date," she said. "I worry about his sex life."

"He has one?" Casey asked.

"He's lonely. If he could meet a woman, I think he'd be happier."

"Well, in the meantime, he's got us."

"Is that a good thing?" she asked.

Casey peered over Claire's shoulder into the side of the trench. "What is it?"

"Pipestem. Pass me a baggie?"

Casey and Claire had been together for seven months. They had volunteered for the same dig in the Yard to chronicle the early days of Harvard College in hopes of finding some physical evidence of the school before the fire of 1764. The instant Casey laid eyes on Claire, he had been smitten. She had been standing at the counter in the foyer of the Peabody Museum, going over photographs of some pre-Incan artifacts — Moche, maybe, or possibly Nazca. He had stepped through the door and stopped dead in his tracks. In profile, the young woman before him had the most perfectly shaped body he had ever seen.

He said, "Hello," and Claire turned around. When he saw her eyes, he fell in love.

He held out his hand. "Casey, but some people call me 'Case.'"

Claire shook his hand but let go and turned her attention back to the photographs. "Claire," she said with a subdued grin as she glanced up at the other woman who had been standing opposite the counter. (Casey hadn't noticed her.) It was an awkward meet.

Before removing the piece of clay pipe stem, Claire photographed it in situ and recorded its position on a record sheet (north wall, so many inches from specific landmarks). Then she carefully lifted the artifact from the soil, brushed it off, blew air onto it with a small bulb syringe, and marked a record number with a waterproof marker on the baggie. Then she placed it in a shoebox.

It was getting late. After Claire finished recording the pipe stem, she and Casey covered the trench with tarpaulins. Then they placed the trowels, spoons, waterproof black markers, labels, plastic bags, pencils, some brushes, record sheets, two clipboards, maps, and two small sieves into a canvas gear bag. Casey lifted it, and Claire picked up the two shoeboxes lined with bubble wrap and the few newly found artifacts.

"Let's go get cleaned up," she said. She lightly rubbed Casey's back between the shoulder blades as they started walking.

TWO

"Service to the People."

— *Maoist political slogan*

The following day, October eighteenth was the start of a beautiful day in Lima, Peru. At eight o'clock — the same time Casey and Claire were leaving their flat in Cambridge to go to work at the Peabody Museum — seventy-two-year-old Domingo García Rada, a Peruvian magistrate, walked out of his house on Roma Street in the San Isidro neighborhood and got into the passenger seat of his 1983 racing-green Peugeot sedan. He did not like riding in the back seat alone. He said, "Buenos días" to his driver, Segundo Navarro Silva, as he did every morning.

It would be a busy day for the Judge. He was also the Commissioner for the upcoming Peruvian general elections, for which there was much to prepare.

García Rada opened the morning edition of La República. He was traveling to his office to coordinate the details of the second round of general elections. Segundo surveyed his surroundings, checked the rearview mirrors, and pulled out onto the street.

Less than three hundred yards down the road, they approached the intersection of Burgos Street. Fifty feet before the intersection, a light blue compact car sped from a stopped position and swerved in front of the Peugeot, forcing Segundo to slam on the brakes. Neither of them were wearing seat belts — most mornings, it was an easy, enjoyable ride to the office. García Rada was thrown forward into the dash, smashing his face on the glovebox. Segundo's chest hit the steering wheel hard, knocking the wind out of him. Wincing, he leaned back, grabbed his chest, and tried hard to catch his breath as a bullet popped through the windshield and pierced his throat. His hands moved quickly from his chest to the wound in his neck, and he opened his eyes in time to see more small caliber holes bursting through the windshield.

The third or fourth hole in the glass was made by the bullet that penetrated his forehead, just above the bridge of his nose, killing him instantly. His lifeless body slumped forward again onto the steering wheel as more bullets and shards of glass peppered his head and neck.

Slumped next to Segundo, the sound of gunfire, broken glass flying in all directions, and the snapping sound of bullets flying by his head disoriented García Rada. It was as though he was in a dream — he could hear nothing except the snapping sounds, and he felt light-headed. He stayed down, leaning forward against the car's dashboard. He could not see the eight men and a woman spraying the vehicle with bullets, and he did not see the man light a stick of dynamite and try to throw it under the Peugeot.

The explosive missed its mark and detonated next to the vehicle, rocking it sideways. The blast tossed García Rada to the left, hard against Segundo's lifeless body. He noticed his driver was not moving. Suddenly, the politician's hearing began to return. Something other than muffled gunfire rang in his ears; people were screaming, and he could hear sirens in the distance. Then there was a sharp, severe pain in the side of García Rada's head. He raised his hand to his temple and looked up at the driver's side-door window, which had been shot out. He saw a young woman step to the door. She had hatred in her eyes. She looked straight at him, raised a handgun, and everything went black.

The newspaper articles worldwide would report that the attackers were "Sendero" — the Shining Path terrorists — and that the young woman and four of the male attackers had been captured. All the papers reported that the terrorists were anti-democracy, but after four hours of brain surgery, Judge Domingo Garcia Rada, like democracy, would live on.

In subsequent days and weeks, the news articles would use the attack to unify the people against the communist efforts of the Shining Path.

Those articles, however, would not report what happened to the assailants in prison. Not one newspaper reported that the men were beaten unconscious every few days and that one of them died from head trauma.

The woman prisoner, Alicia Maria Vilca, a pretty young woman from the highlands outside of Ayacucho, kidnapped by the Sendero when she was twelve, was also beaten by the military men and the prison guards but she suffered much worse.

The interrogators wanted to know where the Sendero leaders were living, and they thought it would be easier to break Alicia than the men. After they had gang-raped her several times, and the beatings did not loosen her tongue, a Navy officer arrived to take over the "interviews."

One evening the officer and three guards woke her in her cell, stuffed a rag in her mouth, and dragged her to a room in the prison basement. The guards all covered their mouths and noses with bandanas. The officer did not. The room smelled awful. They ripped her prison uniform off and tied her hands behind her back. She stood, naked and defiant, staring at the officer as he walked around her, touching her breasts and cupping her buttocks. Her eyes closed as she braced herself for yet another raping.

"Soon," the officer whispered in a calm voice, "you will tell us where your comrades are hiding."

The man's voice was low and ominous, and it was at once tranquil yet threatening. She could tell this was going to be different, and she felt the fear wash over her.

The guards threw her to the cement floor and held her down. Two of them kicked her legs apart and held them in place with their boots. The officer loomed over her, brandishing a very small pocketknife with a tiny, triangular razor blade.

He made tiny slices into her areola and nipples. Alicia tried to scream out, but the rag wouldn't allow it. Her shrieks came out as guttural moans. Then the officer incised minor cuts on the soles of her filthy feet and another slice the length of her clitoris.

The young terrorist was now crying, which sounded like choking because of the rag. If she wanted to talk or divulge information, they did not give her a chance. They left the rag in.

The officer motioned to the guards, who lifted her by her arms, almost dislocating her shoulders. They tied her feet together and dragged her by her hair to a spot where they threw a rope over a rafter and hanged her by her feet. As she became airborne, she swung out over a cistern of filthy water with feces in it — human, llama, burro, dog — and urine too. She vomited, and some oozed past the rag at the corners of her mouth and fell into the vat.

She became faint as the pressure in her skull increased.

Then they lowered the rope.

Alicia's head went into the cistern. She writhed and twitched but could not lift her head out of the urine, shit, and water. She again tried to scream, and she was so afraid she urinated. Before she could drown, they quickly hauled her up again. She coughed and snorted light-brown material from around the rag and her nose.

The guards then dragged her back to her cell, covered in blood, vomit, and feces, and tossed her in without any clothes. Her cell was empty, with no bed, no blanket, no toilet. They pulled the rag from her mouth as she gasped and cried.

"In the morning," said the officer casually, "we will return with paper and pen. If you do not tell us everything about your comrades, we will do the same thing again, but you will die. Then we will throw your shit-covered naked body into the Rímac where the eels will devour you."

They left the cell and shut the door.

The newspapers did not report that.

THREE

Friendship

Claire moved into Casey's flat a month after they first made love. Before that, Claire had a South Korean roommate named Seo-yun, who went by "Sue." Sue was perfectly friendly but was so quiet it became unnerving for Claire. By the end of the first week together, a week of exceptional quietude, she wondered if it was going to work out. Claire spent most nights with Casey anyway, so she went about her decision-making empirically; she took progress notes in the third week of rooming together. In seven days, despite Claire trying to carry on conversations and inviting Sue places (which she invariably declined), the South Korean spoke forty-eight words — an average of fewer than seven words per day.

Claire told Sue she had "fallen madly in love." (An exaggeration), and she couldn't bear to be apart from him for one night (a downright lie). She said uncharacteristic things like, "You understand…the heart wants what the heart wants." She cringed as the words came out of her mouth — she hadn't rehearsed that part.

"Anyhow, sorry," offered Claire. "We'll see each other around campus."

Sue blinked but didn't say a word.

Claire smiled and left. As she walked to Casey's apartment, she couldn't help wondering why Seo-yun had chosen to study International Relations.

꩜

Casey felt his heart glow when she showed up at his front door, standing next to a bulging, wheeled suitcase and wearing an overstuffed backpack. He'd hoped for this.

He stood inside the screen door, smiling.

"You going to let me in?" Claire asked.

He pretended to turn serious. "Well, if we're going to do this, there will be ground rules."

Before she could say, "*Just open the door!*" Casey said, "Sex, a minimum once a day during the week, three times daily on Saturday, Sunday, and holidays."

Claire wasn't laughing. "Open the door, asshole."

"Ah, ah, ah," he said, holding up an index finger. "*And,* Thai food at least twice a month."

"Casey Rust Feagin..." Claire's backpack was getting heavy.

Casey opened the door, and she plunked her luggage on the floor. He had tried to play it cool, and he had tried to be funny, but he was damned excited. He took Claire's shoulders in both hands and kissed her hard on the lips. He pulled back, looked her in the eyes, and said, "It's as if the inner dome of Heaven has fallen, and now I am in it."

"You and your poetry!" Claire said as she flopped down onto the couch.

"Not mine, exactly," he said, sitting down next to her. "I'm paraphrasing. *And* I stole it from Jack, who I'm sure was quoting a real poet. Want to talk about it?"

"Not much to say. At first, I thought it would be nice; a quiet roommate would help me study. But after a week or so, the silence was deafening." She reached over and held his hand.

They went to the bedroom and cleared out dresser drawers for her to use. Claire seemed happy to be moving in, and Casey tried hard not to seem ecstatic.

"There's more stuff over at the dorm room," she said. "Can you help me get the rest tomorrow?"

Claire hadn't agreed to Casey's teasing conditions of moving in, but after she unpacked, she consented to his first. Afterward, they called some take-out Pad Thai. They ordered three servings because they knew that sooner or later, Jack would show up.

As they ate, they heard the screen door slam shut.

"What's shakin' kiddos?" Jack asked as he walked into the kitchen.

"Oooh … Pad Thai. Sweet." Casey slid a container across the table to Jack as he sat down.

"Many thanks," he said. He smiled as he popped the top off the aluminum foil plate.

When Casey introduced Claire to Jack, he explained that his friend was "…a complex man, egalitarian in nature, and fiercely loyal."

Claire only saw him as six feet tall and slim. She noticed he had quiet hands, and his forearms were large for his size. He appeared very strong for his size. He had thick, brown hair and wore a trimmed, close-cropped beard under high cheekbones. She liked his eyes straight away; they are very dark and intense, and many women have remarked on them.

But it is his manner that people find attractive. His eyes show compassion, and they always tell the truth. Jack is an accepting person, and he cares silently for people and makes them feel smart and important.

Jack was enjoying the meal.

Claire asked, "Aren't you going to the benefit tonight?"

"Ayuh." (Jack held fast to his Mainer speech whenever he could.)

"Well," Claire finally said, "we're supposed to be at the museum at eight o'clock." (No response as Jack ate.) "Showered," she said. Jack smiled at her, inhaling the noodles and peanut sauce. "And *dressed*," she pressed him. "Do you even have a suit coat here?"

"Yeah," Jack said proudly. "A blue one." Claire shook her head.

Jack always dressed down, even when he tried to dress up. He loved the natural world and came from a long line of lobstermen (fishermen, he called them) and farmers. A brilliant student, Jack was also a gifted athlete. He was the only child of four siblings to go to college, and he would always tell people, "I'm the least smart of the four, but I got the scholarship. It's a lot of pressure." Casey thought his friend might have an eidetic memory.

"Are you guys digging this weekend?" Jack asked.

"I might Saturday morning," Claire said. Casey nodded his head yes.

Jack finished the Pad Thai. He cleaned up his container and tossed the plastic fork into the trash. "Okay then," he said. "I'll see you guys at seven-thirty." As he went out the front door, Jack swung around, facing the couple still sitting at the table. He kicked the bottom of the screen door gently with his heel, and it popped open. He pointed at Claire and Casey with both index fingers and said, "Open bar!" And then he left.

Claire looked at Casey, smiled, shook her head, and said, "He's your friend."

Casey and Claire walked together up the steps to the Peabody. He was light on his feet, and he was happy. She looked stunning in her only "little black dress," which beautifully matched her blood-red choker. She had asked a friend to French-braid her hair, and she wore small, dangling silver earrings her father had brought her from India. They hadn't planned it, but Casey wore a black suit and tie accented by a red scarf.

All the faculty and the grad students from the anthropology and archaeology departments knew that funding for North American prehistory studies was hard to come by. The Ph.D. students and candidates were expected to attend the fundraiser; they had been asked to help set up and schmooze with the wealthy Boston benefactors. The students knew what some of the family names would be: Saltonstall, Lowell, Warren, possibly some Cabots or Emersons. There might even be a Kennedy, but not one of the famous ones. Casey, Jack, Claire, and the other students would have to be engaging, and more importantly, they would have to pretend they were happy to be there, all gussied-up.

The couple stepped into the lobby. It was one of Casey's favorite places. The Peabody is not a large museum, but it houses more than a million artifacts and documents. For Casey, it had an odd feeling of home.

Claire's heels clicked on the checkered Saltillo tile flooring. She waited, holding her clutch in front of her thighs with both hands while Casey checked their coats. She looked around the lobby and thought it odd to feel so excited to be in the museum since she was there almost every day of the week. Claire glanced up the stairs that led to the fifth-floor staff offices and labs and then looked at the familiar inlaid brick wainscoting, which to her always seemed a weird choice given the wide oak paneling of the reception desk. She glanced through the gently arched doorway into the main gallery. The entire length of the hallway in the first-floor gallery is only 174 feet, and at the far end, through the museum's indirect lighting, she could make out fancy-looking people milling around a bar and tables.

Casey returned. "Ready?"

Claire smiled and nodded.

They picked their way through the gallery, past the American Indian displays, the native artwork, and the bison skins painted with light, pastel-looking dyes made from roots, berries, animal fat, and squashed insects. They walked amongst the people in suits and pretty dresses. They passed glass cases with Plains Indian arrows and bows made from ash and sinew and the huge Dakota war bonnet decorated with eagle, hawk, and owl feathers. They found Jack standing at one of the tiny temporary pedestal tables, already nursing a whiskey and ginger. He knew where the little tables would be because he had hauled them down out of storage early that morning and set them up. Tomorrow, he knew he'd have to carry them all back, so he was determined to use one. He *was* wearing a suit.

"You look nice, Jackson," Claire said. She reached up and straightened his Windsor knot.

"So do you," Jack replied. "Buy you guys a drink? I owe you for the Pad Thai anyway."

"Glass of red," Claire said.

"Just a beer," Casey responded.

Jack Beal came from less money than almost every other student at Harvard, but except for the very wealthy students, he was often the only one with any folding money because he worked two days a week at the Museum of Fine Arts. He accepted the job, not for the minimum wage, but because he had a thing for the Impressionists. Jack liked being in their company. He loved them all except for Matisse, whom he thought less inspired than Cézanne, Millet, and Renoir. But Van Gogh, whom Jack called a "Post-Impressionist whack-a-doodle," was his favorite. Before and after his shifts, he would go to one of the museum's six Van Goghs and stand in front of it, sometimes staring for hours. Jack's father, a lobsterman, had watched him do it as a youngster and thought it quite strange, but the elder Beal was okay with it. "Young Jack sees something in those swishy brush strokes and finger smudges," his dad would say when he saw his son staring at Vincent's pictures in art books. "Makes him feel good." He was proud of his son.

As the three grad students milled around the potential benefactors, Claire became bored talking to wealthy people about the legacies of founder George Farnsworth and Frederick Will Halloway, the first preeminent director of the museum. In the 1870s, Halloway changed the Peabody Museum's culture by recruiting students (including women and Native Americans) and sending them with archaeologists to thirty-seven states and countries. When Claire's boredom reached critical mass, she snuck up the stairs to the third floor, where the Andean artifacts were displayed.

When she walked into the hall of antiquities, she noticed Jack standing in front of an ancient-looking sledge encased in a glass case the size of a small car.

Claire startled him. "Didn't take you long to ditch the party." He turned and gave her a light-hearted hug.

"It was getting hot down there," he said. "And I notice you're here also."

"I prefer people who are dead, preferably for several hundred years," she said.

"I think some of them fit that description."

"Don't be scornful," Claire said. "They're just wealthy — and at least they're interested in what we try to do."

Jack smiled and looked back at the display.

"You know why I don't trust some of those rich people?" Jack glanced sideways at Claire and then nodded at the sledge. "He never made it, you know," Jack said. "Peary. He never got to the North Pole. He wasn't even close, and he knew it." Claire looked at the seven-foot-long sledge made from driftwood, walrus bone and ivory, recycled old boat lumber, and rawhide strapping.

"I've heard the story — or read it somewhere," said Claire. "Cook, wasn't it?"

Jack nodded. "Frederick Cook. He was a good, solid guy, and he truly did get close enough for the accepted criteria of the day, almost a year before Peary's folly. And you know what?"

Claire loved Jack's stories, his convictions, and his reasoning. "What?"

"Rich men from New York City, Boston, and even Maine, I'm sad to say, ruined Cook in one of the worst smear campaigns in history. Peary's backers and his fans, men of industry, met behind closed doors as soon as he made landfall back in the U.S. and threw together a plan to claim the pole for him and to discredit Cook. At first, it didn't work. Tens of thousands of people turned out to cheer Cook. There were parades for him. Newspapers took polls, and Cook was favored — *believed* by the public 5:1 over Peary. But the good ole boys in Peary's camp went a step further. If discrediting Cook wasn't going to prove easy (he *did* get close enough to the pole, after all), then they would ruin him financially and socially. And they did."

Now Claire was genuinely interested.

"They even had judges in their pockets who trumped-up charges like profiteering and tax evasion. They got one crooked fucking judge in Wyoming, I think, to send him to jail!" Jack was mildly worked up.

"They ruined him alright," Jack continued, "simply because Peary was driven to be famous, no matter what the cost. He came to think 'discovering' the Pole was his God-given right."

Jack paused and then, leaning on the railing in front of the glass enclosure, turned toward Claire. "What gets me riled about that story is that Cook was the good guy. He was an honest dude. He was kind to the Inuit — he lived with them, hunted with them, and befriended them. He treated them with respect. Peary, on the other hand, was a wannabe aristocrat who thought of the Inuit as inferior. By most accounts from people with him in the Arctic, he did not treat them well."

Jack's forehead became furrowed. "Jesus! Peary brought a handful of indigenous people back from Greenland to be studied! At a *museum!* The poor souls were poked and prodded until almost all of them died from the flu — or some other disease for which they had no immunity.

"Today," he continued, "nobody hears Cook's name in history class. Anyway, it's just my belief of what happened." He paused and added as if an afterthought, "It's stories like his that made me want to teach history, that made me want to come to Harvard. I knew I wouldn't fit in, but I wanted to hear lectures from professors like Steve Williams and Larry Stager.

"Hell, I know none of those people downstairs are anything like those dicks that ruined Cook's name. They all seem quite nice. But the problem is my comfort level. Claire, I have to drink to be around them."

Jack had finished his story. Then he looked at Claire and smiled. "Incidentally, you should know that you look beautiful tonight."

Claire smiled back. "Jack, you always say that."

"Well, Cee ... you know I can't lie." He took a sip of his whiskey and ginger, which was a bit too strong, and he winced, which made him look like he had winked at her. "And you know, I love Casey, but he doesn't deserve you."

"I know he doesn't," Claire said, winking back at him. "But I'm fond of him, so…"

"*And* here he is now," Jack said.

Casey was cresting the top of the stairs. "There you are," he said.

Jack said, "Yup. Here we are."

Claire turned on her heels and kissed Casey on the lips. Jack was still leaning on the railing.

"Oh, God," Casey said. "I hope he hasn't been boring you with that Frederick Cook story?"

"I thought it was wonderful," said Claire, elbowing Jack's arm.

"Stories, Casey," Jack said. "I keep telling you, through diligent science, we're telling *stories*. The story is the thing, and stories are the best delivery system for teaching history."

"Is that why you're always reading things you don't need to read? Like books about art, or, what was the last thing? The childhood of Samuel Morse?"

"Yes!" Jack said. "Don't you see? If I read Van Gogh's personal letters, then I know about his brother Theo and their relationship, and I learn that Vincent wasn't crazy at all — only epileptic and sick. The letters taught me how close the brothers were and what a lovely writer the artist was. Once I learned his story, his paintings told me more. Moved me more."

Casey was only half hearing Jack. He was staring at Claire. And Claire, who was trying to pay attention, said, "I get it." Jack had seen that look on Casey's face many times. "Okay," Jack said. "I gotta see a guy about something." Jack glanced back at Claire and again pointed at her with both index fingers as he turned to leave. "If I don't catch up with you later tonight, will I see you Monday?"

"After my morning class," Claire offered. "At the Monets."

He walked down the stairs as Casey and Claire said simultaneously, "We'll see you shortly." But they knew that they might see Jack downstairs, or they might not; when it came to events or gatherings, he was unpredictable. He came and went on a whim, and he was interested in everything he came in contact with, which occasionally rendered him unreliable.

"Why doesn't Jack date anyone, ever?" Claire asked.

"I have an idea but don't know for sure," said Casey. "I've tried to find that part of him, but he won't talk about it, and I don't push too hard. He's just very private about his love life, I guess. I used to wonder if some girl up in Maine broke his heart." He thought for a moment. "But maybe it was in Wyoming." He offered nothing else.

"Do you think he might be gay?"

"Oh, no," Casey replied. "I see him look at pretty women often enough. Sometimes, he looks for a long time, and he has a longing look in his eyes — almost as if he's in a trance. But whenever I've suggested he should ask one of them out, he would change the subject. Eventually, I got the feeling he was annoyed by my asking, so I've stopped saying anything."

"Well, I think it's sad that one of the most interesting, complex, and diverse men I've ever met doesn't have someone with whom to be intimate. And he's handsome to boot."

Casey rubbed his hand along Claire's back and said, "I guess he's just a private guy about some things."

The couple left the Peary exhibit and walked past the Meso-American artifacts to the Incan and pre-Incan exhibits. Casey's interest in Incan culture was born of Claire's long-held fascination with it.

Claire strolled ahead of him. Her blonde hair seemed brighter in the soft, filtered museum light, and her French braid was made more attractive against her black dress. Beautiful and ancient Incan artifacts were displayed all around them as they made their way to the back of the room.

"I love this floor," Claire said.

Casey studied Native American history of the northeastern United States, with a focus on New England. As a child, he had studied the "Indians" of the colonial period near his hometown of Salem.

"Yes. It's wonderful," Casey said. But he wasn't looking at the displays; he had seen them hundreds of times. He was looking only at Claire, how beautiful she looked in that dress. She was athletic, and Casey loved the curve of the back of her thighs from years of running. Her stomach was flat, and her behind, as always, was perfect. She had beautiful, sassy-looking eyes that always sparkled and small dimples at both corners of her mouth that drove him wild. Her breasts were not large and not small and fit her body impeccably. Casey wanted her.

Claire had settled in front of a sealed glass display that contained several choice artifacts. Like the Peary sledge exhibit, this one also had a brass and iron railing in front of it to keep the public from getting too close. Behind the glass, on a black velvet display, were some Incan jade llamas, a couple of silver brooches, a silver shawl pin, and a turtle shell spoon. But they were all overshadowed by the piece in the middle, a golden, pre-Incan mask. It was only six inches across at the ears but looked heavy. It had a slightly hooked nose, a straight mouth, and a tiny owl protruding from its forehead. The eyes were its most enticing features. They were wide-set and made of inlaid jade with dark, semi-precious stone pupils. More than enticing, its eyes were mesmerizing. The mask was beautiful, and it shone through the room's soft light. It was brighter and more noticeable than everything else, almost as if it produced a faint, glowing light.

"It's Moche, I think," Claire offered. "Certainly pre-Incan."

Casey shook his head only once and said, "Well, it's not Narragansett."

She smiled but wished he would tease just a little less about her interests.

Casey gently touched her neck. He leaned forward and kissed the back of it near her shoulders. Claire closed her eyes and tilted her head to the opposite side, exposing more of her neck. The slight press of his fingers along her back sent tingles down her spine. A nibble on her earlobe and her softly breathed moan made Casey's body quiver.

"Casey," she whispered. "Not here, for God's sake."

"Which God?"

"All of them," she said, breathing hard.

Another kiss on her neck caused her eyes to flutter — the telltale of ecstasy for Claire. She could see him in the glass reflection.

Casey was still behind her. His left hand slid up her side and cupped the side of her breast. The other hand reached down to her right thigh and slid up to cup the bottom of her butt. She felt her heart quicken. Claire knew Casey had lifted her dress, and now her ass was exposed.

"Casey —" she breathed the word more than said it. The bright blue eyes of the golden mask shone behind the museum glass, and though she was excited beyond belief, the eyes seemed to look straight at her. Now, somehow, they looked angry.

"What if Jack comes back?"

"He'll leave."

"What if someone else comes up?" Claire asked. She could feel him pressed up against her.

"We'll be quick," he said.

With that, she looked at the eyes of the mask again and spun around to face him. Both of their eyes widened a bit as they looked at each other.

"'*We'll be quick?*' You certainly know what a girl likes to hear," she smiled as she pulled her dress down and straightened herself. Still breathing hard, she said, "This isn't right. Not here. If you behave, we'll be home in a couple of hours..."

Later, Claire couldn't help thinking about being with Casey while talking with the patrons downstairs. Even standing amid the gentry of Boston, she realized she was still excited. *But people do it in the strangest places*, she thought. *It might have been great*, but she knew it wouldn't have been right to have sex upstairs. And she also knew she'd be home in an hour.

As they hurried down Museum Street to their flat, Claire and Casey were downright giddy. That night, the museum raised over $200,000, and Casey would enjoy the best sex of his life.

As the gala ended, Jack went back upstairs to the Peary exhibit and stared intently at the driftwood and bone construction of the sledge, fuming the entire time. Then, he walked down Divinity Street, crossed behind Memorial Hall, and into the Yard, where he lay on the cold grass under a bare oak tree and gazed at the moon through the black branches. He could smell the dirt from the dig just yards away as he thought about the galaxies beyond the moon and the stars, beyond everything.

FOUR
The Plan

Claire strode up the granite steps of the Museum of Fine Arts with a bounce in her step. It was a beautiful, sunny autumn day. Mondays were slow at the museum, and she knew she would have plenty of space to herself. She smiled at the security guard sitting by the door on his tall chair. "Hello, Robert," Claire said as she walked through the foyer.

"Morning, dear," Robert replied. Claire no longer needed to show Robert her museum pass. She walked straight up the stairs to the second floor, then around the rotunda to the back of the building, and then left through the big hall lined with the Rubéns, Varelas, Vázquezes, and the Vargases with all the human skulls and half-naked saints. She stopped, as usual, to look at Francken the Younger's *"Allegory of Man's Choice."* Her eyes were again drawn to the Monkey King, sitting obnoxiously on his creepy throne while he ridiculed the rich and powerful. She hated that Monkey King. She turned left down the carpeted hall and, as always, slowed to look at the Renoirs, Sisleys, and the Pissarros. But she didn't linger. The three rooms she wanted — her favorite rooms — where the Monets hung were just beyond.

The Museum of Fine Arts was something Jack and Claire had in common; she purchased a pass every year and went there once a week, no matter what else was going on in her life. She would often meet Jack, and they would discuss art at exhibits or in the café when he could find time for a break. Before college, Claire had vacillated between archaeology and art school. She liked creating landscapes with pastels, and she was very good. She had painted one seascape while visiting Jack's family in Maine, of which more than one person had said, "In it, you can smell the sea and feel wind and water."

Like Jack, Claire, too, loved the Impressionists. On one occasion, shortly after they had become friends, she sat next to him on a bench staring at *Houses at Auvers* for so long that she fell asleep with her head on his shoulder. He sat perfectly still for over an hour and let her sleep. When she finally woke, she had drooled down his shirt, and he did not mind.

She lifted her sleepy head, and Jack was looking at her, smiling. She was a little embarrassed but recovered quickly. "How long was I out?"

"Not too long," Jack replied. "Ooh," he said, touching her cheek.

Claire reached for her face. "What?"

There was a red line across her cheek, an indention made from pressure where she rested her face against his shoulder.

"Here," he said, gently rubbing the mark. "It'll go away in a minute."

She looked to see what made the mark. There was a thin leather lanyard around Jack's neck.

"What's this?" Claire pulled on the lanyard while still rubbing her cheek.

Jack lifted his chin and pulled a small, copper-colored stone amulet from under his shirt.

Claire took it in her hand and examined it. It was a little bigger than a quarter and was worn very smooth. A small hole had been eroded through it, which the leather string fit through. Claire looked closer. "There's a 'J' on it."

"Sort of a 'J,' if you use your imagination," Jack responded. "I think that's why Casey gave it to me."

"Aww," Claire chided, "Casey gave you a man gift. Well, I think it's pretty cool."

"It is, actually," said Jack. "It's a Hag stone."

"Yes, I know," Claire said. "They're supposed to ward off evil spirits or something."

"Something like that. Case found it when he was backpacking through northern Germany. Because of the little "J" mark of sedimentation, Casey wanted me to have it, and I've worn it ever since. For luck.

"You know, if you close one eye and peek through a Hag stone's hole with the other eye, you'll be able to see into the Fairy world…but I guess it depends on what city you're in."

"I like it," Claire said. "I know some people think they're powerful talismans, and if it breaks, they believe it has used its power to protect a life."

Jack tucked the stone back under his shirt.

"You know," Jack commented as they walked out of the museum, "I can now technically say that you slept with me."

Claire laughed. "Go for it."

But that time she fell asleep was almost a year ago. Now, as they walked past the same painting, Claire said, "I have to head home." She gave him a one-armed hug. "See you tomorrow?"

Jack smiled, "You bet." And he went out into the hallway. He turned left and glanced as always at the Monets in the opposite room as he walked by.

Claire thought about the paintings and the conversations with Jack on the Green Line to Park Street station and out the Red Line to Harvard Square. She thought about them as she walked across Mass Ave. and through the Yard and past the dig site with the tarps pulled over the sawhorses and then down Museum Street to the apartment.

That evening, as Casey and Claire cooked supper, there was an unusual disquietude. Casey asked her if she was okay twice, and twice she said she was, but he could tell something was bothering her. As they ate, he pressed.

"You going to tell me?" he asked.

"Jesus — there's nothing wrong. And if there was, you know, it's not your responsibility to fix stuff for me. I'm just thinking about something, and I don't even know what it is."

"School stuff?" Casey asked. "Oh, God … *girl* stuff?"

"Don't be a dick. I think I need to go somewhere. Somewhere new, like on a trip."

Casey tried to process it but didn't have enough information.

Claire took a drink of six-dollar-a-bottle Merlot, winced, and said, "I've been studying Andean culture for years, and I've only spent, what … less than two weeks there? And that was two years ago. And before you say anything about my going there for my field studies in two years, I think I'd like to go sooner."

Casey looked at her face. She had his attention.

"What about a trip to Peru in early spring?"

"Spring," Casey said. "*This* spring?"

"Why not? We both have enough money, probably enough for a month, and if Jack can swing it, we can all go, and he can document some of the Andean culture around Cusco. He has mentioned about going to Ollantaytambo a few times."

"When are you thinking?" he asked.

"March...maybe April. What do you think?"

"Well," Casey replied, "I'd have to finish my paper; get some stuff done ahead of time. I'll have to talk to *El Profesor*, but as long as my work gets done and my teaching assignments are complete, I don't think he or anyone in the department will mind. I think Jack will jump all over it if he has enough for a plane ticket. You know him — he won't need much money once he's in the country." He smiled at her. "Hell, we feed him most of the time anyway."

"Jack would be in heaven," Claire said.

They ate their meals almost with an urgency. Their minds were spinning, but they would have the winter to plan. Claire was excited.

⚜

After class the next day, Casey and Claire found Jack in the documentation room in the cellar of the Peabody. He was looking at maps.

Claire spoke first. "Jack, honey ..."

He interrupted. "Oh Lord, what did I do? I've been crowding you love birds, haven't I?

Casey jumped in, "Well, now that you mention..."

"No!" Claire said, mock slapping Casey on the shoulder. "I — we have an idea that we're hoping you'll be up for."

Jack's eyebrows raised. "Lay it on me."

"We're thinking of taking a trip to Peru — the three of us. See Cusco, go to some of the archaeologic sites, take notes, do some hiking. We can even go to Machu Picchu if you want."

Jack thought for a long minute. He was computing. "I can swing it," he said. "But I'll go on two conditions: we don't linger too long at Machu Picchu, and I get to call it an expedition. You know how I like expeditions."

Casey chuckled and pointed his index finger at him. "We can skip Machu Picchu as far as I'm concerned. I know how you hate being where there are too many tourists, but Claire does want to spend some time on the Inca Trail. And a strong 'Maybe' to calling the thing an expedition. We're thinking of hitting all the sites close to Cusco and then spending most of the time in the village of Ollantaytambo, using it as our basecamp."

Jack was smiling and sat back in his chair. He was all-in. "I have enough money," he said. "But we do this; we're taking our fly rods." Jack took a fly rod on every trip, even once to New York City to fish for bass in Central Park.

"Of course," Casey said. "We'll take the rods."

Claire's mind was racing. Five months seemed like a long time, but she knew there would be a lot to do, especially getting their academic affairs in order. "We'll talk to Dr. Maryanne Fitzroy," she said.

"She's Andean culture, right?" Casey asked.

"Since 1967," Claire said. "I've had a few classes with her — and she has had a fair amount of experience with the Sendero Luminoso terrorists in Peru."

"Those Shining Path people?" Casey asked. "Not too worried about them, but we should have the conversation."

Claire nodded. "I'll leave a note in Maryanne's office.

FIVE

Council

The following day, Claire stopped at the Peabody and climbed the stairs to the fifth floor. She walked down the long, dark hallway past the *Reproductive Ecology Lab*, the *Evolutionary Genetics Lab*, and the *Cryo Lab*. She negotiated the stacks of boxes and crates and shipping supplies and took a right turn down the dark hall marked with the sign, *Anthropology Department — Archaeology Program*, and knocked on the office door of Dr. Fitzroy.

"Come in," Fitzroy said.

There is no way to describe Maryanne Fitzroy other than "frumpy," though many have tried. Her neutral-colored brown hair just covered her ears and had no part, and it always looked like she had recently cut it herself. She had a plain, nondescript face except for some high cheekbones, and she had a penchant for wearing a small, black fanny-pack in the front below her belly the entire time she was awake — no matter the setting. She wore a teal green windbreaker in all seasons and all weather, and she never wore it zipped-up. She dressed in simple, department store slacks or jeans and (typically) turtlenecks with Birkenstock sandals, except during winter months when she wore mail-order L. L. Bean boots.

Maryanne Fitzroy was a disheveled, chubby genius with an omnipresent smile, a professional affect, and a settled demeanor.

Claire entered the office. "Good morning, Dr. Fitzroy."

"Morning." Dr. Fitzroy smiled at Claire as she stood up from her desk. "How may I help?"

"Claire Martin," Claire said. "PGY three. I was in your *Ethnographic Research Methods* course two years ago."

"Of course, I remember you. Wisconsin — or is it Minnesota?" the professor asked.

"Wisconsin. Wow, you remember that."

"Yes," Dr. Fitzroy said. "We talked about it — I grew up in Minnesota, near the border."

"I remember well," Claire said, "I'm just surprised you remember a conversation with a first-year graduate student."

"My dear," Fitzroy said, "the students are why I do this." Claire smiled. Dr. Fitzroy motioned toward one of the two captain's chairs positioned in front of her desk, and they both sat down. "What brings you to me?"

"I read most of your papers last year," Claire said. "I know you've been going to Peru since the late '60s. Three of us in the program are planning a trip there early next year, at the end of the semester — not through the school — just on our own. Kind of a gap-year thing but without an actual gap." Claire thought, *Be more professional.*

"We want to spend some time in the mountains observing Andean culture as an independent study and visit some of the lesser-known Incan ruins. Maybe do some backpacking."

"Sounds wonderful," said the professor.

"It'll be myself, Casey Feagin, and Jack Beal, whom I'm sure you know," Claire said.

Dr. Fitzroy smiled, "I do know Jack. He's a lovely young man and one of the most learned students I've met."

Claire looked around the room as the professor spoke. All manner of Andean artifacts and relics were spread throughout it. There were watercolors of Campesinos and mountains. There were artifacts, textiles, jade, and silver figurines on every flat surface. A lovely khipu was in a frame behind the desk (pronounced "KI-poo"). Khipus, spelled *Quipu* in old Spanish literature, are knotted strings used for messages and records. They are sometimes made of cotton, but more often from llama or alpaca fur. Typically, there is one short string from which many longer strings radiate outward like sun rays and have knots tied in each of them. The knots' differing lengths and locations meant something to Incan messengers, accountants, military leaders, and taxmen. This one, in the frame, had strings dyed several colors, and it was impressive. Dr. Fitzroy noticed Claire looking at it.

"There's an anthropologist at Colgate who's starting the definitive work on khipus," the professor said, looking back at the frame. "We'd like to get him here someday. What exactly do you need from me, Claire?"

"We'd like some travel advice," Claire responded. "And any cultural pointers you think would be important. Maybe some contacts or any cautionary things you think might help. I've been reading about the Shining Path communists lately, and whatever you know about them might be helpful."

"All right," Dr. Fitzroy said. "I'll be happy to do that. Talk to your boys and write out your dream trip. First, figure out where you want to go and make a shortlist of your main goals for the journey. Drop it off here. I'll look it over and come up with some suggestions and ideas — there may be some changes, maybe not. But that would be a good starting point."

Claire thanked her and left. She excitedly walked down Divinity Avenue, past Memorial Hall, and crossed the Yard to the Widener Library, where she found three new books about Peru and one specifically about the Spanish conquest of the Inca. Then she went home to Casey.

Jack stayed for supper, and the three students prepared a meal together. Casey was indifferent about cooking, but Jack was interested in it. He had given Casey a shopping list and wanted to try a meal he had enjoyed while backpacking in Arizona two years earlier.

"Mushroom and leek chimichangas ..." Claire said as she chopped some Hatch green chilis. "You sure about this?

"Just you wait," Jack said.

Casey had a Walkman radio earphones on and was listening to a Red Sox game. Jack had found a grocery store in Jamaica Plain that sold primarily Latin American goods and had purchased a can of nopalitos. He chopped them and sautéed them with diced onions, garlic, jalapenos, and tomatoes. While they cooked, Jack and Claire talked about the trip.

"I'm excited to see Cusco and some of the lesser-known sites near there," she said.

"Well, I've been reading about the region and its history. I don't feel driven to go to Macchu Pichu," Jack said, "There are plenty of villages around Cusco, but I really want to spend some time in and around Ollantaytambo. At the Harvard Coop, I picked up Hemming's *Conquest of the Incas,* and I'm flying through it, which is good because it's over 600 pages. Ollantaytambo was kinda the last stand for the Incas."

"That'll be easy," Claire said. "Maryanne mentioned Ollantaytambo and said it would be a great jumping-off place."

Casey pulled down the Walkman's headset. "Sox are up, two-to-one."

"That's great," Jack said, "but we're talking about the trip."

"Oh."

While still chopping the chilies, Claire spoke. "We should talk about the Sendero Luminoso. Should we worry about them?"

Jack looked at her thoughtfully. He moved his head once to the left and then back, winced, and said, "Don't know. Normally, traveling alone, I wouldn't worry. But as a group, I'm not so sure. How active are they?"

"Active enough, in the southern part of the country," Casey said. "I talked to a backpacker friend a couple of weeks ago, and he said he had some interaction with some of them a few years earlier. He was in a village in the mountains, scouting for a water management project while doing some kind of seasonal job. Apparently, the Shining Path blew up a building and burned ballot boxes in the highlands of the Ayacucho Region. He said the terrorists announced they were going to overthrow the government of Peru, and they seem to have a thing for harassing railroads."

Claire said, "This morning at the library, I met a student named Dani from Ecuador. He has Peruvian friends and visits there every year. I started talking about our trip to Peru, and he mentioned that the Shining Path had recently attacked a judge near his friend's home in Lima. They shot the judge in the head killed his driver. He showed me an article in the New York Times about it. Four of the terrorists were caught and arrested. One was a woman. This Dani guy said the terrorists mostly remain active in certain areas in the south of Peru and that the attack in Lima was rare. Maybe we should talk more about it."

"I think we should speak to Maryanne about it more," said Casey. "I also sent a letter off to my friend Jim Bartlett in Lima — he was my climbing partner on Rainier. He's from Colorado but lives in Peru now running guided trips throughout the country and in Ecuador."

"Cool," Claire said. She glanced at Casey. "Are you still close with this Jim guy? He could be a great resource for us. Though I don't think we can afford a guide."

"We still write back-and-forth. Jim's a great guy. He reminds me of one of those nineteenth-century British ex-pat adventurers. Like me, his heroes are Eric Shipton and Bill Tilman."

Claire shook her head. "Never heard of them."

Casey continued. "Super-cool mountaineers, sailors, and explorers in the 1920s and '30s."

Casey was looking down at the plate Jack slid in front of him. The chimichangas looked great, and the mixed vegetables on the side were pretty but looked exotic.

"Yum!" Claire said.

"I know," Jack said, "the veggies are different. My dad would take one look at them and take them out for the trash pandas."

"Trash pandas?" Claire asked. Casey took a bite of the chimichanga and, without looking up and with his mouth full, said, "Raccoons."

While cleaning up after supper, the talk was still about the trip. The excitement was creeping up. Claire said, "So as soon as I hear from Dr. Fitzroy, we'll all three meet with her. She thought it might be two weeks before she has time to sit down with us. In the meantime, let's see what we can find on our own."

"One last thing," added Claire. "We should be sure we all have enough money. I ran some numbers and stopped by Harvard Square Travel and looked up flights. I think if we're careful, we could be in the country for three-and-a-half weeks and get to all the places we want to go for less than $1,500 each. Everybody good with that?"

"I'm all set," Jack said. "Plus, I'll have three more months to save up from the museum job before we go."

"Casey," Claire said, "if we got into a pinch down there, is there a possibility that your dad would help us out?"

"He would," responded Casey, "but I'll have to work it off next summer if he does." Claire and Casey had been worried about Jack having enough dough to go, and they both looked at their friend.

Jack offered, "I don't think we'll have any problem if we all have over $1,500. I bet I could live down there for a month on a lot less than $800."

The three drank some cheap wine and agreed that this was a great idea.

As he walked home in the cool, crisp autumn night, with the collar of his pile jacket zipped-up all the way, Jack thought it was strange how Casey never mentioned the meal, whether he liked it or not. *He was a wealthy kid growing up*, he thought, *probably used to different cuisines.* For Jack, experiencing new foods and new things were marvels. He was looking forward to the trip, and though he had no doubts about Claire's capabilities to cope with anything that might come up, he wondered how his best friend would travel. He knew all about Casey's backpacking trip through Europe, and by the sounds of the trip's telling, he coped with the usual obstacles well enough. Jack knew that he could be comfortable in nearly any environment — except perhaps extreme duress. If trains were missed or simply never arrived, or if no accommodations were available, he knew from experience that he could find a copse of trees on the edge of a meadow and sleep under a space blanket nice and quietly, and with no fire. He felt sure Claire would be okay with that, and she would chalk it up to the adventure.

Jack also knew that all three friends were aware this would be no vacation, and it would be a trip of learning, of experiences beyond just backpacking. He figured his camera equipment and writing supplies alone would weigh about six pounds. *I'll probably need two journals for this trip*, he thought. They would be carrying everything they had on the journey in their backpacks.

Jack was sure of one thing: if you want to find the true nature of a friendship, go traveling together. Preferably backpacking.

SIX

Logistics

One week before Thanksgiving break, the three students visited Dr. Fitzroy's office. Jack arrived first, and he tapped on the open office door. "Hola," he said.

"Come in," Dr. Fitzroy stood up with a smile and held out her hand. "Jack Beal ..."

"Good morning Dr. Fitzroy. Claire and Casey should be here in just a minute."

"Nice to see you," said the professor. "And call me Maryanne, please. I'll tell you, Jack, I read your paper on cultural diffusionism in nomadic sub-Saharan tribes, and I enjoyed it. You could be a writer." She flattered him, and it made him uneasy.

Jack said, "Many thanks." As she started to sit down, Dr. Fitzroy motioned to one of the three straight-backed chairs lined in front of her desk. Jack sat.

"Do you remember our conversations two years ago when you took my class?" she asked.

Jack smiled. "I do. That was kind of you."

"Kind?" Dr. Fitzroy said. "I enjoyed your insight. I remember thinking, 'Here is a young man with a thousand interests — I hope he has focus.'" Jack, still smiling, shifted in his seat. He did not know how to respond. He was relieved when Claire and Casey walked into the office. Dr. Fitzroy stood up again.

"Good morning. Thank you for meeting with us," Claire said as she extended her hand, and the professor shook it.

"My pleasure."

They all took their seats.

Dr. Fitzroy spoke. "I've been thinking about your trip." She motioned to a map laid out on her desk. "I do have some thoughts based on what Claire has told me, but it will be helpful to know what input you're looking for in this expedition. What are your goals exactly? Learning? Adventure? Exploring sites? All of the above?"

"Well," Claire said, "we can get travel information from an agency, things like train and plane details, customs, typical delays, and so forth. But from you, we're looking more for guidance such as any cultural aspects you think might be worthwhile observing, and maybe some connections. We won't be there in an academic capacity, just for our pleasure and edification." She did not mention the terrorist activity in Peru.

Casey finally spoke. "Also, some side trips to any villages you might think worthwhile. We plan to do some hiking and maybe a little mountaineering. And Jack and I'll be taking fly rods — if there's time."

The professor's hands were folded on her desk. "Okay," she said. "Claire mentioned that you'll be visiting Machu Picchu and some other places in the department of Ayacucho."

Claire didn't want to interject, so she did not mention that Machu Picchu was still undecided. Besides, even without traveling to Machu Picchu, they *would* be in the Sacred Valley of the Incas — close enough.

Dr. Fitzroy continued. "I assume you all know about altitude sickness if you're going to be in the mountains, and no matter where you go, you'll prepare for GI issues. Do you have a tentative itinerary prepared?"

"We do," Claire said. "But it's basic. We plan on spending the bulk of our time in and around Cusco and Ollantaytambo, but we're open to any suggestions, even ones that might change the plans completely. We're open to suggestions."

Dr. Fitzroy nodded.

Claire continued, "As Casey said, we hope to do some hiking. With a bit of luck, we can get off the tourist trail. The maps look like it wouldn't be hard to find some remote spots all along the Sacred Valley."

"I see," said the professor studying the map. "You'll fly from Lima to Cusco, of course. From there, you'll have a lot of choices for one-to-two-day excursions into the hills. I'd recommend at least two or three days in Cusco, just wandering around town to acclimatize. There's plenty of history right in town. The archaeologic site Rumicolca is less than a two-hour bus ride from town. I think it was once was an Incan customs depot at one of the entrances to Cusco. And there's Sacsayhuaman just outside of town, which was a fortress or perhaps a retreat for royals back in the day."

The doctor ran her index finger across the map, tracing the route from Cusco up the Sacred Valley, then tapped the town of Ollantaytambo. "Once you get here," she said, "there will be plenty of chances to hike out of town and fish. The Urubamba River always looked to me to be quite a torrent, but I don't fish. I do know that the elevation drops a few thousand feet in less than fifty-five miles."

"You've been to Ollantaytambo?" Claire asked.

"I have," Dr. Fitzroy replied. "There are both taxis and buses that run between Cusco and '*Ollanta*.' The buses take a couple of hours and can be quite painful. Best bet is to hire a taxi through your hotel. Dr. Fitzroy looked almost wistful. "I love Ollanta. It's a pretty town with world-class history, and it sits in a bowl surrounded by mountains very near to the Urubamba River. The architecture is amazing, and it almost seems like you're on the edge of things."

Jack looked up from his tablet. "What things?"

"Civilization." The professor looked straight at him. "Technology, the availability of supplies…even the edge of history. The edge of a myth. I felt like I was on the edge of places unknown to most people." She smiled at Jack. "You'll love it."

"If you want to hike, fish, and absorb some culture, *and* if you have the time, you might consider another trek." She leaned forward and moved her index finger back to Cusco and then slid the digit about sixty miles southeast and tapped another spot on the map. "You could do another less well-known mountain trek that starts from here, in the tiny hamlet of Tinki. If you poke around Cusco, you can easily find a guide to help you with transportation to and from the trek. You'll have to do some research first, but the name of the biggest mountain along the way is Auzangate. A friend of mine climbed it a few years back. It's a beautiful, imposing mountain — over 20,000 feet. My friend is also a fly fisher. He said the trail passes several streams and alpine lakes for fishing. A few of the lakes were stocked with trout many years ago. He told me some of the fish are large if you can find them."

The fish story piqued the interest of Casey and Jack, although neither of the men were trophy fishermen. Jack, especially, could care less if he caught big fish. Casey had picked up the sport quickly after meeting Jack, who had fly-fished the lakes and brooks of Down East Maine since he was old enough to hold a rod. With time, Jack became a gifted caster. As a teenager, he took a bus to Wyoming and guided for two summers.

"Jack doesn't care if he catches fish or not," interjected Claire. "But he's a wonder to watch on a stream."

All four studied the map. Claire worried they were taking up too much of the professor's time. "Well, that's a lot to digest," she said. "Thank you so much for your help. We'll each do some research over Christmas break."

"You're welcome." Dr. Fitzroy folded the map and handed it to Claire. "Take this; I have another." All three students thanked her.

As they walked out of the museum onto Divinity Avenue, they were excited. Even the planning process was going to be fun. "Au Bon Pain?" asked Jack. "My treat."

Walking through the Yard, Jack said, "I met an old alumnus a few weeks ago, and he told me this one story about how students would often yell "*Rinehart!*" as a call to arms. He wasn't sure how it originated, but he said it was kind of a big thing at Harvard for decades. He said it was even a rallying cry for Harvard alumni around the world. I remember thinking, where have all the old, interesting college traditions gone?"

Claire listened to Jack's ramblings. She loved them.

Jack continued, "The old guy asked if anyone still yelled *Rinehart* at football games or rallies, and I told him I had never heard it. He looked a bit sad, so I nudged his shoulder and asked if he'd like to go out into the Yard with me and scream it to see if anyone answered the call."

"Did he do it?" asked Casey.

Jack shook his head. "He just smiled and said, 'No ... that's okay. But I'd like to do that someday, just for old times' sake." Then Jack grinned at his friends.

"What, now?" asked Claire.

Jack jumped up onto a park bench, cupped his hands around his mouth, and yelled as loud as he could, "*RINE--HART!!*"

They looked up at the dormitories, and Claire glanced around the Yard. Jack held up an index finger and waited.

Casey laughed aloud.

Nothing. No reply. Not even a sound. They waited for a moment, and Jack jumped down off the bench, looking a little sad.

Finally, they arrived at Au Bon Pain. "It's getting colder," Casey said as they sat at a tiny table.

Once they had their coffee and croissants, Claire spread the map of Peru on the table, and Jack pulled his yellow tablet out of his backpack once again. He studied the elevations around Machu Picchu, Ollantaytambo, and Mount Auzangate. "If we do go in May, we're going to need good sleeping bags. It could get uncomfortable."

Casey pondered the map lovingly. "I hope so."

Claire said, "Let's agree to have our plans finished by the new year. That'll give us time to get our ducks in a row."

"You know," Jack replied, "I think this trip is just what I need."

SEVEN
Christmas

Jack drove north over the Portsmouth Bridge and into Maine.

He loved the drive to Maine in the springtime, but in winter, it was a chore when everything was grey, and the roads were slippery and punctuated by the hundreds of ancient, black graveyards made more conspicuous because of the lack of foliage. His old truck plodded up Interstate 95. Once past Augusta, Jack turned east onto Route 3 and then north again onto the famous Route 1 to the old lumber shipping town of Bucksport. From there, he picked his way along secondary roads back toward the coast. Finally, five hours after leaving Cambridge, Jack rolled down Tennent's Hill into the fishing community of Stonington. Going easy on the brakes, he wheeled the truck into the gravel driveway of his father's ancestral home.

"Jack!" cried his little sister Lisa. She ran to the truck, and as he stepped down from the cab, she grabbed him around the waist.

"Hi, Honey," Jack said. He rubbed her back with one hand as he pulled his backpack from the truck. He looped one strap of the pack over his left shoulder and started for the house with Lisa still hanging onto his hip.

"She didn't even let you get in the dooryahd," said their mom, Karen, in her thick coastal Maine accent, the "r" substituted for an "ah" sound.

Karen stood in the doorway, wiping her hands on her apron. A wide smile dominated her pretty, angular face. Her fitness, bright blue eyes, and ponytail made her look younger than her fifty-four years.

Jack kissed his mother's cheek as he dropped his backpack in the mudroom.

"Hi, Mom," he said.

"You've lost more weight," Karen said.

Jack smiled at her. "Is Dad out?"

"No, the boat is up for repairs. He thinks it's a problem with the linkage. He's lost five days already. He's down at Lynwood's shop — but he'll have seen your truck ..." She wasn't finished with the sentence when Alton Beal drove into the driveway. "Here he is now," she smiled at Jack. Mother and son and Lisa went to the doorway.

"Jackson!" he yelled as he jumped down from the big, one-ton pickup truck.

"Hey Pop," Jack said. Lisa had a finger hooked into one of Jack's belt loops.

Once Alton was in the door, he gave Jack a big bear hug and then patted Lisa's head. "Hi, Sweet," he said.

"Hi, Daddy," Lisa replied, "Mom said Jack is skinny."

At this, Alton looked in mock seriousness at his son and palpated his chest. "He'll live."

Alton gave Jack a worried look. "The boat's up."

"Mom told me. Linkage?" Alton grimaced and nodded.

In the big kitchen, Jack could smell the sweet balsam from the Christmas tree in the living room. The smell was faint and overpowered by the aroma of baking bread and the loaves cooling on the sideboard. Tired of sitting in the truck, Jack stood and leaned against the kitchen counter. His mother caught him looking at the golden loaves of French bread. She touched his arm. "Not those, but I'll cut you a slice when the ones in the oven are done."

"Where are the guys?" asked Jack.

"They're all at the gym. You know this town and basketball."

Jack smiled and nodded.

"Jack," Lisa said, "come see the tree!" Jack sat on the floor in the living room with Lisa and regarded the familiar Christmas tree. Like every year, it was draped almost beyond the limits of the branches with the same antique or homemade bulbs and ornaments. Many of the decorations had been made by the children over the years. There were wooden carved ornaments in the shapes of stars or evergreens with the child's name and date written on the back. Some were family heirlooms, and each ornament meant something to Karen. She hung liberal amounts of tinsel on the tree because that is what her mother did.

Karen Beal, who stood on traditions, celebrated Christmas with warm, childlike delight. The tree was always hand-picked on the woodlot across the road, and it was cut down with a hand saw and dragged out either by one of the boys or behind the ATV. The family watched the same movies on VHS every year; It's a Wonderful Life and The Homecoming. A few days before Christmas, Alton always made homemade doughnuts from his father's recipe (on an old recipe card was written, "*Use lard, not vegetable oil ... it's the secret,*" in his father's faded script), and Karen always complained that she was the one to clean up the mess. But the tradition never wavered.

Each year, Karen, an exceptional cook, would bake a dozen large loaves of French bread. After covering them with icing, halved red cherries, Paradise candied green cherries, and crushed walnuts, she would have Alton cut and sand pieces of plywood which she'd cover with aluminum foil to deliver the two-foot-long loaves. Then she would carefully cover the bread in plastic wrap and deliver them to those neighbors who had proved neighborly the previous year. The bread was spectacular and was a great incentive throughout the year for the Allens, Pelletiers, Grays, and the Leightons.

On Christmas Day, scores of friends and extended family (some more extended than others) would stop by the Beals home for coffee and doughnuts. They would ask the same things; both older brothers would invariably be asked if they were still playing basketball. The others would hear, "Reading anything interesting, Karen?" "Lisa, are you excited for Christmas?" "How's the boat runnin', Alton?" But Jack would always hear, "Have you dug up anything interesting, Jackson?" (At those holiday get-togethers, Jack never tried to explain the difference between archaeology and his chosen field of anthropology, and on a couple of occasions between anthropology and astronomy.) He would simply smile and say, "Not recently."

The brothers came home smelling of sweat. They snuck cookies from the jar, talked of the goings-on in town, and asked Jack about his studies.

The younger brother, Tom, looked at Jack and said, "I didn't get you anything for Christmas this year because you're a smug college asshole." Then he gave Jack a tight bear hug.

The excitement of Jack returning was too much for Lisa, and she crawled up on the couch and fell asleep.

Karen entered the living room, wiping her hands dry. "Ah, she's down…are either of you in for the day?"

Wade said, "I am. Just plan on doing some reading."

"Great," Karen said, "I'm going to go for a walk — maybe thirty minutes."

"I'll be here if she wakes up," said Wade. "But you know, she takes care of herself better than we all do."

Lisa was born fourteen years after Jack. She was the result of a combination of a new yellow chiffon sundress and a warm, bluebird spring day at the family's summer cottage on Georges Pond and a misunderstanding between Alton and a surgeon in Ellsworth about how soon after his vasectomy he could have relations. (Despite hearing the post-op instructions, Alton left the office believing Vasectomies were instantaneous.)

Tom's secret nickname for Lisa was *Cleveland* — the "Mistake by the Lake."

"Mind if I come with?" Jack asked. "I was in the truck for too long."

"Love it," Karen said as she pulled off her apron. The two walked down the bottom half of Tennent's Hill toward the waterfront. The sidewalk had patches of snow and ice, so Karen laced her arm in the crook of her son's elbow. Everybody who drove by waved to them. They walked past William King Art Gallery and the Harbor Antiques. They skated in their boots on some ice as they passed St. Mary Star of the Sea Church, and Karen leaned her head down to her right hand, still held by Jack's left arm, and made the sign of the Cross with her fingertips.

They walked past the Dockside convenience store where Main Street flattens out and then onto the town pier where the brokers weighed and packaged lobsters. The sun was setting fast, and even the seagulls, looking uncomfortable as they perched on the wooden pilings, feathers fluttering, made the air feel colder than it was, and the approaching twilight mixed with the grey pall that always hangs over the bay on overcast winter days. Jack noticed the pink in his mother's cheeks.

Mother and son left the pier and walked back up Main Street toward home. They crested the hill, and as they entered the long, circular driveway, Jack was happy to see the red lights in the windows. Most people in town put white lights in their windows during the holidays, and a few used blue bulbs, but Karen always liked the glow of red lights.

She said the red in the windows complemented the many-colored lights on the Christmas tree, which shone like a beacon in the big bay window in the front of the house, and she swore it made the home seem warmer — cozier. Jack had seen the lights for twenty-four years but just now noticed that they did seem to make the house look warm.

Christmas Eve and Christmas Day went off without a hitch. The tree did not catch on fire or get knocked over by Lisa's cat. Nobody got sick on too much eggnog, and *this* year was the first Christmas party anyone could remember when Elbridge White did not get drunk and fall into the bathtub and pass out with his suspenders down and his pants undone.

All things said and done, it was an altogether successful Christmas. And when asked how school was going, Jack answered the question — he did not mention the trip to Peru partially because he hadn't purchased his airline ticket and partly to obviate the barrage of questions that were bound to follow.

The day after Christmas, the dust settled, and most of the family hunkered down to relax, eat leftovers, and clear their heads. Wade and Tom left late morning for the high school to play basketball in the open gym where the young adults, the heroes of yesteryear, would try to teach the current varsity players how to pass. "Each generation," Alton said, "had a better grasp of basketball fundamentals than the previous."

In the afternoon, Jack, Lisa, and Karen sat in the living room listening to a homemade tape of Christmas-themed songs: Nat King Cole, Willie Nelson, Eddy Arnold, and Bing Crosby crooned away on the cassette player. Alton sat in the corner at an old, fold-down writing desk tying flies.

"Dad," Jack asked, "can you listen while you tie?"

"Sure can," he said, whip-stitching a knot on a Royal Wulff.

"So, I want to tell you about a plan we've set in action. Casey, Claire, and I are hoping to go to Peru in the spring." Both parents listened intently. Karen shifted in her antique caned rocking chair, and Alton got up and sat in the big leather chair by the fireplace.

"We want to go to some of the well-known archaeological sites and maybe do some exploring...nothing severe, maybe visit some mountain villages that are a bit off the beaten path. And of course, we hope to do a little fishing."

"Well," his mother said, "that sounds exciting. I like both Casey and

Claire, and it was fun having them visit last summer, and I think Claire really liked it here."

"She did. She still talks about going out on the boat with Dad. She has a cute little scar on her hand where the lobster got her."

"That was your father's fault," Karen said. "He knows how hard a lobster's claws can clamp down." Alton waved her off. "She never turned a hair. Claire's a tough midwestern girl, and you know, Wisconsin is the Maine of the west." Karen and her son both rolled their eyes at Alton.

"Seriously, Jack," Alton asked, "Peru…is it safe there?"

"It is, Dad," he replied, not mentioning the Sendero Luminoso terrorists, "it's a lovely country."

"What kind of fishing is there?" Alton had taught each boy how to fish at an early age. Jack was the most gifted, but Lisa picked it up faster than any of the boys had.

"I recently heard that rainbows had been stocked in several mountain streams and lakes in the 1930s."

"Bows…nice," his father said.

"This could be a great trip," Jack suggested. "I hope to get some good photos of the region and take a lot of notes."

Again, Karen shifted in her chair. "How long do you plan to be there?"

"We hope for four to five weeks."

Karen stared at her son, blinking. Jack was the adventurous one of the three boys, and he was the boy bound for travel. His brothers were interested in the world but were also content with the culture in their hometown. Tom and Wade felt that meaningful exploration of the state of Maine would take more than a lifetime.

On the other hand, Jack felt at a young age that the world was there to explore. His interest in how other people live drove him to anthropology. While he was fascinated even as a young boy by the things from by-gone days, he was constantly digging things up around town. He was consumed with the wonder of how the people used the old tools and household items. How were their lives conducted? How did the tools fit into their culture?

"Claire and Casey are committed to this trip?" Karen asked.

Jack nodded. His mother had always encouraged his inquisitive mind, and they shared a love of stories, poetry, and learning. He could see the unavoidable worry in her eyes.

"I have some simple Spanish," Jack said. "Casey doesn't, he took German in school, but Claire speaks it pretty well, I think. Plus, the university is involved with many archaeologic and anthropologic projects in Peru. We're in the process of lining up some contacts down there, and I'm sure we'll be able to work out some local support."

"Well," Karen said, smiling and placing her hands on her knees. "It sounds like a wonderful time." Then she rose from the rocker and started for the kitchen. "Maybe we can help you plan."

Alton slid forward in the big chair, the fire flickering on the left side of his cheek. "What kind of flies do you think they use down there?"

"Not sure they fly fish at all, Dad."

Alton pointed a long, gnarled finger at his son. "You can't go wrong anywhere with leeches. I'll tie you up some Wooly Buggers, olives, and blacks. They'll work; mark my words." He remembered the years before he was married, when he backpacked through Europe and fly-fished everywhere he went, like beneath the Pont Neuf on the Seine where he could only roll cast, gently flipping his fly into the river without the benefit of a typical backcast. He slid back into the chair and gazed into the crackling fireplace. Within minutes, he was mesmerized by the flames and dreaming of his youth.

EIGHT

Commitment

Jack walked down the dimly lit hallway of the Peabody's fifth floor, where old industrial lamps were placed too far apart in wire cages lined the hall. He liked the faint smell of formalin and the musty scent of ancient things as he breathed deeply. Jack loved the fifth floor. He walked past the Paleoanthropology Laboratory, the Reproductive Ecology Lab, the Evolutionary Genetics Lab with the sign saying, "Only authorized people may enter here," and into room number 561.

Claire jumped up to hug him. As they did, Casey leaned forward in his chair and gave his friend a "high five."

"How was the drive?" Jack asked.

"Long," Claire said, "but the visit was nice."

"Your family?"

"They're good. My mother decorated a ficus for Christmas, and dad spent most of Christmas eve on a protest march in Madison."

Jack laughed. "You're mom's fun." He sat down next to Claire. "Case ... everything good at home?"

"No problems," Casey said. "My dad gave us a bunch of his backpacking gear. We can use whatever we need. It's all at the apartment." He paused and said, "Dad was at the hospital on Christmas day trying to piece together a shattered calcaneal fracture."

Jack pulled out his yellow writing tablet, filled with notes, and placed another blank tablet on top of it.

Claire asked him, "How were your mom and dad? Wisconsin holidays are nice, but I can't imagine what Christmas is like in your house in Maine."

Jack beamed innocently; "It was wonderful. The house is always warm and inviting, and it smells of baked bread and pies and balsam at this time of year. You should come for Christmas some year. You'd love it. Mom had an actual balsam tree, though."

"Nice," Claire said. She changed the subject. "So, did anyone have time to check airline fares?"

Casey shook his head. "I didn't. Going tomorrow."

Jack said, "I'm ready to pull the trigger."

Casey nodded in agreement.

"We should try to nail down a date by the end of the week," Claire said.

Casey responded, "We go to Mt. Washington in three days to teach you how to handle climbing ropes and crampons. While there, let's agree on the dates, and we'll buy the tickets next week."

Claire smiled and held up two fists. "I can't wait to climb."

Casey said, "It's more of a hike than a climb. But it'll be a great place for you to learn some of the basics — how to walk with crampons, rope up, and self-arrest. It'll be fun. And it'll be great prep work for Peru if we get to climb down there."

"Still," Jack interjected, "even though it's a small mountain, you have to respect it. Over 100 people have died hiking Mt. Washington, almost half as many deaths as on Mt. Everest. But, that's because of its proximity."

"Proximity to what?" Claire asked.

"People," chimed Casey. "Cities."

Claire nodded.

"To climb Everest," Jack said, "it takes at least a year of planning and more years of training."

"And $30,000," offered Casey, "just for the permit—that's in addition to travel costs and supplies."

"That's right," Jack said. "It's grueling, dangerous, and treacherous, and then there's the altitude, which changes everything. The only people who attempt Everest are world-class climbers, elite athletes, or the uber-rich, and they too have to train and be in great shape. So, think about it; it's a huge investment of time and money for anyone who tries Everest, and they're aware they are assuming a ton of risk. They prepare for years. If they die up there, it's usually because of the altitude, which can lead to people making some really poor decisions."

Claire nodded again, listening intently.

"Exactly," Casey said. "Though the Presidentials are small mountains."

"Foothills compared to the Himalayas or the Andes," interrupted Jack. "Or the Alps."

"They do have some pretty good weather swings," continued Casey. "And Washington is, what, three hours from Boston and six from Manhattan? It's too easy to get to. Each spring, city-folk decide it would be a nice weekend to 'hike Washington,' and they have little or no experience above treeline. They grab a grade school backpack, a windbreaker, and a water bottle and jump in the car. A few hours later, they're hiking the trail from Pinkham Notch Visitor Center at the base of the mountain. Seven hours after they left Boston, they're having a heart attack, or they're stuck to the side of The Summit Cone in a freak snowstorm, and they can't see their hands in front of their face, or it's 50 degrees colder than when they left the parking lot. That's why we gear up like it's a real mountain."

"The weather can be fierce there, even by Alps or Andes standards," Jack started off on a tangent. "The Westerlies, those subtropical winds that flow up the Pacific Ocean and then east, across the western United States in a fairly steady stream, continuously rolling passively over the midwestern states. But land amplifies the flow patterns, and when the winds hit the Presidentials, they are impacted. They increase in velocity and shoot over to the east side of Washington, sort of like when you hold your thumb over the nozzle of a garden hose."

Claire and Casey stared at Jack.

"*Anyway*," Casey said, "it can get windy up there, so bring layers."

NINE

"On Belay"

The three left the parking lot of the Pinkham Notch Visitor Center by nine in the morning. The sky was grey, and they could smell the balsam and the pines, and the sweet scent of cedars wafted into the mix. It was cold enough that the snow squeaked beneath their boots and their noses were already red. They had spent nearly a half-hour at the car getting ready, checking clothing layers, hats, sunglasses, Gore-Tex mittens, water bottles, emergency bivvy sacs, and a mountaineering stove containing a small bit of fuel — just in case. The men strapped ice axes to the outside of their backpacks. This was a training hike for Claire, who loved backpacking but lacked any climbing experience. She was ready first, so she watched the boys organize their gear. They had an air of confidence and efficiency married with a camaraderie that indicated they had hiked and climbed together many times before.

Casey glanced at Jack's gear as he packed the last few items. He spied his friend's compass. "It hasn't snowed for days," he said. "The trail's going to be obvious. But I know you always carry that old compass."

Jack looked skyward and sniffed, then shrugged and carefully shoved the compass into the top pocket of his pack. There were only snow flurries in the forecast, but this *was* Mount Washington.

Casey started up the trail past the Visitor Center with Claire, with Jack following closely behind. In only a hundred yards, they were crunching along the beaten path up the switchbacks. They plodded through the alders, maples, and the birches and were quickly out of sound and sight of the road and the parking lot. They found a rhythm in their steps. The trail steepened, and the cold made them feel tiny, sharp pains in their lungs with each breath. Yet, they warmed up swiftly.

The switchbacks through the trees would widen out over the next two miles on their way to Hermit Lake at the base of Tuckerman's Ravine. The trail would eventually become a steady, uphill grade. Jack and Casey, both athletes, kept a steady, methodical pace that Claire had no problem keeping. Her jogging was paying off. *Casey had been right*, thought Claire; *the snowy trail was a forest highway.*

"I need some water," Casey said after topping a steep section. He and Claire sat on nearby rocks and unholstered their water bottles.

Jack took a knee and looked at his watch, then at Casey. "Exactly an hour."

Casey spat a little water onto the snow. He was almost breathing hard. "Not bad time. Another thirty to the base of the ravine?"

Jack nodded. "If we move along."

"Alright," Casey said. "Let's rest there." And they all rose and started off before any sweat on their backs got cold and chilled them.

Twenty minutes later, Claire noticed the junipers, fir trees, and the tangled little spruces were much shorter. *Getting there*, she thought. The sky began to open into view. After crossing a bridge over a tiny brook called Cutler "River," the trail again turned into switchbacks and steepened before gradually leveling out. It crossed the water again, and after a short section, the Hermit Lake Shelters appeared on the right.

The three continued toward Hermit Lake at the bottom of Tuckerman's Ravine. With the headwall looming above them, there was the building known as "HoJo's," the caretakers' cabin and the outpost for Tuckerman's. Jack and Claire dropped their packs on the cabin's deck while Casey peered into the door window.

"No one home."

Claire said, "Maybe we can squeeze in another practice climb before we leave for Peru."

"I'd be up for that," Jack said.

"I'd love to," Casey replied, "but my paper is going to occupy most every weekend until we leave. I'll try, though."

It was truly a beautiful day. Grey overcast skies were blanketing New Hampshire and keeping the weather calm, and the temperature had warmed almost ten degrees. There were sparse, slow-falling snowflakes here and there, and it was quiet. There were no chickadees, no Jays, no songbirds at all. The kind of winter day in the hills that makes a body feel good to be alive.

They shouldered their packs and continued up the Tuckerman Ravine Trail. The footpath became steeper as they negotiated the Little Headwall to the base of the gorge at a section of craggy boulders. The ravine shot straight above them.

"What do you think?" Casey asked.

Jack looked along the base of the ravine. "I think along there, to the north. There's no route above there for someone to send rocks down on us, and it's pretty steep and is probably as much like the real thing that we're going to find."

"Sounds good," Casey said. They split off the Tuck Trail and headed to the spot along the base of the ravine. Once there, they cleared off some boulders and looked up at an excellent thirty-three-degree grade. Above them was a 100-foot headwall of packed snow. Casey and Jack started pulling equipment out of their packs. They placed a 100-meter climbing rope, three harnesses, a rack of climbing hardware, a couple of snow stakes, and some carabiners on a boulder. Jack had brought three small pieces of an old, retired foam sleeping pad to sit on and some trail snacks. Claire placed one of the pads on a rock and sat.

"Gorp?" Jack asked Claire, handing her a bag of trail mix.

"Gorp..." Claire said.

"Trail mix. That's what everyone in Jackson Hole called it, and now I can't seem to call it anything else."

Claire took a handful of nuts, shaved coconut, raisins, and M&M's. She was staring into her palm and said, "That's odd ... most of the M&Ms are blue ones. Did you eat all the other colors?"

"Actually," replied Jack, "I *may* have taken the blue ones out of three bags and put them in when I made the Gorp because they're your favorites."

"Aw...that's sweet!" Claire was mocking Jack.

Casey separated two pairs of crampons and said to Claire, "Blue ones are your favorites? Why don't I know that?"

Claire and Jack spoke simultaneously; "Good question."

Jack pointed to a section of snow about forty yards above them and said, "Why don't I set up a belay there. I can protect her from above, and you can instruct."

"Sounds good," Casey said. Jack already had stepped into a climbing harness and had his crampons strapped to his boots. He picked up his ice axe, shoved the two V-shaped snow stakes into the belt of his harness along the small of his back, and looped a "rack" — a sling of webbing laced with biners and other equipment — over his head and one shoulder. He slung the climbing rope over the other shoulder. As Casey taught Claire about crampons, Jack walked along the base of the ravine about fifty yards and then started climbing. He worked his way up and then diagonally back toward them across the steep section of the headwall. Jack held his ice axe in his uphill hand but did not use it. He simply kicked steps in the steep snow with his boots. He looked quite comfortable and natural, thought Claire as she looked directly up at him.

Casey held the harness out for Claire to step into. He cinched the belt and tightened the leg loops around her upper thighs. "These need to be tight," he said, "but not so tight they pinch your skin or pull the hair." Claire looked at him with a faux disgust, as though he must be kidding. "Better check," he said, smiling. Before she could say anything witty, he placed three fingers between her groin and the loops and pushed against her vagina with the back of his hand, and she stiffened.

"Oh!" she said with a start. "Very funny. Do you check Jack's harness like that?"

"He does it to himself." Casey straightened up and pretended to be pensive. "Maybe you're right," he said. "Maybe we should get him a girlfriend."

Both grinned, and Casey said, "Okay, focus now. The basics are important." Casey strapped on Claire's crampons and started teaching. "Put these on like this — with the buckles on the outside of each boot, so that if they need to be adjusted, you can reach down and do it easily, even if you're on a steep slope. If the buckles were on the inside of the boot, you'd be reaching across your leg, and it would be easy to lose your balance."

"Got it," she said.

Casey helped her with her boots. "But here's the tough part about learning to walk with crampons; you always have to remember that you're wearing them ... they can do a lot of damage to the rope, which is often around your feet. They can also tear your pants or gaiters. Or skin."

"That's a lot to remember," Claire said.

"Seems so," Casey replied, "but you'll get the hang of them really quickly. When we start up the slope, keep your knees and ankles slightly flexed so that all the points on the crampons bite into the snow. When you traverse a slope like the one above us, keep upright and away from the snow, at an angle to the fall line." Casey looked Claire in the eye, and she seemed fine with everything so far.

"Jack will belay you until you're comfortable. Plus, I'll remind you of all this as we go along." Claire gave him a thumb's up and looked up at Jack, who was now sitting against the slope high above them, gazing across the valley.

"Claire ..." Casey said, "you don't really need crampons to climb this mountain in most conditions; this is simply a teaching exercise. You ready?" Claire nodded and smiled, and she was having fun.

Casey yelled up to Jack. "You ready?" Who yelled down, "Ready!"

Casey hollered, "On?"

"On!"

"Rope?"

Then Casey said, "Step back, Claire. Mind your crampons." Claire carefully took two steps backward and looked up.

Jack yelled, "Rope!"

The coiled rope flung out from the headwall and fell toward them, landing in a loose pile at their feet. Casey picked it up and showed Claire how to tie a figure-8 knot on the free end of the rope. He tied one slowly, untied it, and did it again. Then, he untied the knot and had Claire try. She was good at it, but Casey wanted her to try it a few times to program some muscle memory. She tied five more figure-8's and then looked up at Jack sitting on the side of the headwall, his crampons wide-apart with his boot heels dug into the snow. The rope hung down on a straight line between his legs. He looked comfortable. "We're taking a while," she said, "won't he get cold?" She knew already that he would not get impatient. He never did.

"Don't worry about him," Casey said. "You know Jack; he'll start thinking about things and get lost in it. He'll find something he can learn, sitting there."

"Yeah, I do know. Ever seen him look at a painting in the museum?"

They both smirked and shook their heads.

"All right," Casey said, clipping the figure-8 knot into the belt loop in her harness, "let's head over to where Jack went up the headwall." Casey motioned to Jack, and he waved down to him. Without any further communication, Jack pulled up some of the rope so that there was very little slack between his belay device and Claire. A proper belay was not yet needed. She went first, following in Jack's footsteps. After walking along the base of the ravine — Jack paying-out rope as they walked — they started climbing up the steep slope. In the first few steps, Casey stopped her. He gave her the ice axe and explained how to use it. He looped her right wrist, her "uphill" side, through the circular piece of webbing attached to the head of the axe. Casey then placed her hand over the head of the tool, with the point facing away from her body. With the axe on the uphill side of her body, it helped prevent her from leaning too close to the slope, and it kept her weight over her feet where it belonged.

"The axe is mostly for protection," Casey said. "With this tool, you can 'self-arrest' if you fall…we'll teach you how to do that up above. You're doing great. Notice how Jack is pulling in rope as we get closer to him? That's so if you do fall, you won't drop far, and he'll hold you right where you are. Also, the rope isn't under-foot where the crampons can damage it."

Claire turned her head sideways and nodded. *This is so cool!* she thought.

About halfway to Jack, Claire turned her attention away from the task for only a moment and looked left. The view was gorgeous. Looking east, she could see for miles, even in the overcast. Spinning her body around, she thought she could make out a bit of the Androscoggin River straight ahead, and she could look down into the bowl of Tuckerman's Ravine. Casey gave her a moment.

Before he made his belay on the edge of the headwall, and before Casey and Claire started climbing up to him, Jack had cut out some seats in the snow for them both.

Claire looked beautiful, standing in the mountain's diffuse light in her red Patagonia Storm Jacket, her lovely blonde hair falling in wisps from under her black pile hat. She wore a purple and black scarf that cradled her chin. Her high cheekbones were so pink they looked even more pronounced. *My God,* thought Jack. *She looks so natural.* Just then, Claire turned, ebullient, and with a broad, pink-cheeked smile, she kissed

Jack on the cheek. Both Casey and Jack laughed. Jack pulled on the slack rope, coiling it in the snow.

"This is so much fun!" Claire said. Jack was taken aback by the kiss but said nothing more and waited for Casey to continue. Both men understood — as much as anybody would — her enthusiasm. It *is* fantastic to be in the mountains, and there is an interesting, intense connection between people when they are roped up together, especially for the first time.

"Okay," Casey said to Claire, "you've learned how to walk in crampons, how to tie a figure-8, and about rope awareness. Now we need to teach you how to self-arrest with an ice axe. If we cover these things this weekend and can practice a bit, I think we'll be in good shape in Peru."

"Excellent," Claire said.

"Up high," he told her in full-on teaching mode, "on a big mountain, if you lose your ice axe, you're done for." Casey placed Claire's wrist through the strap on the head of her ice axe, and he cinched the strap firmly around her wrist.

"The idea," he said, "is to stop yourself as quickly as possible when falling. The longer the slide down a slope, of course, the faster you'll go, and the more difficult the self-arrest will be." Claire listened and watched.

"Now, when you start to fall, stay as calm as possible — for these first few tries, Jack will have you. Keep your feet apart, and you *must* roll over prone. You lock the handle of the axe against your chest like this, and if your grip on the axe head is right, the pick will be here, pointing into the slope." Casey demonstrated the axe position. As he did, he said, "See why the hand position on the axe head is so important while climbing?"

Claire could visualize it.

"Plus, it's natural this way," he continued, holding the axe in the self-arrest posture. "And it can't be here —" Casey raised the axe in the same position but higher over his head. "If the axe is too high up the slope while you're trying to dig it into ice or snow, it's possible to lose the axe or to break your wrist."

Claire nodded. These details were basic enough, she thought, but they were clearly important. She held the axe Jack had brought for her in the proper position and committed it to memory.

Casey went over it all again in one simple sentence: "Grab the lower end of the axe shaft with the other hand, stick your butt up in the air, away from the slope and dig the axe's pick and your crampons into the snow and you'll stop." Casey looked down the slope to the base of the ravine, about 100 feet below.

"I'll show you a couple of times, and then Jack will belay you while you try. Now, repeat the steps back to me."

She did, verbatim.

"Good," Casey said.

Jack sat contentedly, patiently, in his belay seat, watching them both. "Anything to add, Jack?"

Jack shook his head. "You want protection?"

"I'm okay here,"

Un-roped, he said to Claire, "Now, watch me."

With that, Casey flung himself off the slope. He shot down like a rocket and tumbled fast, forcibly twisted himself over onto his abdomen, and dug his axe with the ice pick into the slope, and then stiffened up onto his toes. Casey stopped abruptly in a spray of snow and ice. He had traveled only about thirty-five feet down the steep ravine.

"Whoa!" Claire exclaimed.

"It works," Jack said.

Casey climbed back up the ravine. When he got to Claire and Jack, he wasn't even breathing hard.

"Okay…watch again." And again, he flung himself off the slope. He arrested his fall in twenty-five feet this time, and it looked automatic. Again, he climbed back up and again asked Claire to repeat the steps involved to him, and she had it down pat.

"Now, are you ready to try?" he asked.

Claire looked down the slope and said, "You bet."

"All right." Casey checked her figure-8 knot and the locking carabiner, gave a tug on her harness, and nodded to Jack, who had payed out about forty feet of rope on the slope just below. Casey placed both her hands correctly on the ice axe. "The first few times, we'll start in the position."

Claire smiled and said, "You gonna check my harness leg loops again?"

Casey smiled back and said, "Jack's got you. Ready?"

She nodded.

"You got her, Jack?"

"I got her." His belay device was ready. He dug his heels in a little more.

Casey looked briefly at the anchors. Jack sat into the slope for a belay, then said, "Go!"

Claire leaned sideways and fell. Her brain knew she was holding the ice axe correctly, but her white world was spinning around as she tried to roll over prone. *My God, I'm falling fast,* she thought. She was stuck on her side. She forced herself onto her stomach, and the ice axe had never left the position next to her chest. The pick dug into the slope and kicked snow into her face. She pushed her butt up into the air, and the toe points found some purchase in the snow and ice. Suddenly, she stopped. The abruptness of it surprised her. She wiped the snow from her face and looked up at Casey and Jack. They both were smiling. Casey stuck both thumbs up in the air.

Claire pushed herself away from the slope and got her feet under her. She kicked her crampons into the snow one at a time to ensure her footing. The rope between her harness and Jack's was not tight but also not slack. Breathing hard, she called up to the boys, "Well...that was exhilarating!" She looked where their packs were, perhaps thirty yards below. She took a couple of deep breaths and climbed back up the headwall.

"What'd you think?" Casey asked. "You did it perfectly."

"Yes," Claire said, "it worked, but it felt sloppy. I can do it better."

"It was your first time, and it's supposed to be sloppy."

"So, let's go again," she said.

"Jack?" Casey asked.

"Ready," Jack said. "Claire?"

"I'm ready." And off she went. This time, she tumbled around twice before getting into the prone position because her legs were too close together, but she was quicker digging the axe and the points of the crampons into the snow.

Jack, carefully controlling the rope from above, said to Casey, "She's a natural."

"Sure is."

Claire practiced arresting falls for almost an hour. She kept getting better at it, and eventually, she became comfortable. Jack was getting quite cold, sitting in his snow belay seat, but he said nothing. When she climbed back up for another try, Casey said. "Let's call it a day." Claire looked at her watch. "It's not even noon."

"Up for a short hike?" asked Casey.

Jack was ready to move around and warm up. Both he and Claire said, "Sure."

Jack pointed up the northeast edge of the ravine and said, "We can climb here, up and over the headwall and cut across and down through Lion Head."

"Sounds good," Casey said. I'd feel better if we rope up Claire since it's her first time on crampons."

"Ayuh," Jack said.

And so, they did. First, Casey needed to retrieve the packs which were still at the base of the ravine. He slid down the headwall on his butt, using his ice axe to steer and to slow him down a bit. Claire watched.

"It's called a glissade," Jack said. "French for '*slide.*'"

As Casey brought up his and Claire's packs, Jack climbed quickly up and over the ravine's headwall. He set another belay for Claire, and once tied into the end of the rope, she climbed easily over the top.

"That wasn't difficult," Claire said.

"True," Case said. "We ski that sometimes. We're just getting you used to wearing crampons and how a belay works."

From the rim, the three hiked east along the snow-swept alpine meadow. It was a different world than down in the ravine. Here, exposed, there was a strong, biting wind that drove through every crack or crevice in their clothing. They were at what hikers call the Lion Head summit, a craggy outcropping of boulders at the eastern edge of Tuckerman's Ravine. On the lee side of the big boulders, all three hunkered down out of the wind, had a few sips of water, and ate some more Gorp. Jack had brought some hot chocolate in his thermos. Each sipped from the thermos cap, and he sliced some pieces of cheese to go with the gorp.

They had to raise their voices to be heard over the wind. "See how the conditions can change in the mountains?" said Casey. Claire nodded. A tear trickled down her cheek from behind her sunglasses, where the biting wind found its way past the lenses. Casey was almost yelling from two feet away. "If this was a big mountain, say, over 20,000 feet, it can get exponentially worse. *Worse* probably isn't the right word," Casey regarded, "but more dramatic or intense condition changes." Again, Claire nodded, acknowledging that she understood.

As soon as they descended downhill below the Lion Head rocks, they were again out of the wind. The hike down to the parking lot was beautiful. They remained out of the wind the entire time, and large, slow-moving snowflakes alighted on their shoulders and foreheads as they walked. Jack and Casey did not talk much while hiking, so Claire refrained also. She felt an exciting feeling of exhaustion and, what was it, jubilation? Perhaps not jubilation, but she felt a tired excitement. She felt happy for having been in the mountains and happy for having tested herself on the steep slopes.

Within twenty minutes of leaving the Pinkham Notch parking lot, the three tired hikers were sitting on one of the old sofas in the spacious front room of the Wildcat Inn in the village of Jackson. Four minutes after that, Casey had already ordered three cheeseburgers and some locally brewed beer. After the meal, they each planned on drinking some of the hot toddies the inn was known for. There was a fire crackling in the fireplace. Jack rose to look at some of the old photographs on the wall; black-and-white images of loggers, ice harvesters, and natty-looking men and women in the early twentieth-century skiing on Mt. Washington using wooden Telemark skis with leather bindings.

The burgers were excellent, and the beer reminded Casey of Guinness. They talked about Peru. At one point, Claire asked Jack if he had noticed how cute the bartender was. Jack looked over at the bar, and she was lovely.

"I think she might be of Indian descent," Claire said.

"Abenaki?" asked Casey. "Or Pennacook?"

Claire looked disgusted with Casey. "No, *India*. She said her name is Bina."

Both men liked the name. "Bina" is a Mainer's nickname for a carabiner. Jack did not talk to her.

By 9:30, Claire's eyelids began to droop, and she yawned. Casey did not notice, but Jack did and said, "Well, I'm going to read some and then hit the snow." He patted Claire on the shoulder and nodded goodnight to Casey, who nodded back. He walked out the front door.

"Didn't he mean he was going to hit the hay?" Claire asked. "And where's he going?"

"Hmm?" muttered Casey, who also was fading fast.

"Where did he go? She asked again. "He's not crashing with us?"

"Oh," Casey replied, "he's doing the Wildcat Bivvy."

"The what now?"

"That's when you party too late here at the inn and crash in your sleeping bag or bivvy sack out on the snow across the street," said Casey. "A lot of climbers do it to save money on a room. Jack has the money — or he could crash with us — but he likes it. Does it all the time. Sometimes I think he prefers sleeping in weird places, like barns and snow caves. Last spring, he slept in the Yard at school. He got up and went to his flat early in the morning before the maintenance guys showed up for work. Those guys get pissed at homeless people on Harvard grounds."

"Will he be all right?" Claire asked.

Casey looked at her as though he didn't understand the question and gave her a funny look. He and Jack possessed a truly adventurous spirit. Sixty years earlier, they might have been a duo like Ernest Shackleton and Frank Wild. "Don't worry about Jack," was all he said with a trace of a smile.

Jack slowly trudged out of the tavern, snatched his backpack out of the pickup bed, and slung it over his left shoulder. He grabbed the small plastic avalanche shovel with his free hand. He walked across the street and out of the yellow glow of the tavern lights and down the snow-covered ninth fairway of a tiny golf course. The moon cast shadows from the balsams and spruce trees that lined the fairway.

In the tiny bedroom upstairs, Claire and Casey both took extremely short showers and climbed into bed. There was room for Jack to sleep on the floor if he'd wanted, but Casey was glad he was bivouacking. The room was warm, and Claire wore nothing but black and red panties. As tired as Casey was, he was still twenty-five. He wanted to fool around. Claire lay on her stomach. Her blonde hair splayed out on her pillow, and she hadn't pulled the covers over herself yet. *Now*, he thought, *if I could get her to do that self-arrest position…*

He leaned down and kissed the nape of her neck, and she exhaled and smiled. With her eyes closed, she clumsily reached behind her head and patted his hair. Her arm dropped down onto the bed, and she sighed once and fell fast asleep.

TEN

Death of a Lovely

Claire woke Casey to ask what time they were supposed to meet Jack for breakfast. Casey rubbed his eyes. "Eight o'clock," he said.

"It's after seven now," she replied. They both started to dress.

As they packed their gear, Casey spoke. "Claire, honey, try not to push Jack onto women too much."

"God, I don't think I *push* him…it's just that sometimes I think he'd be happier and, if he had someone, perhaps not feel too much like a fifth wheel. Though honestly, I don't know many women who would want to do the Wildcat Bivy."

"I was thinking of the bartender last night. I know you mean well and that you care for Jack. It's complicated with him, is all," he said. "He struggles with female relationships. But I think as time goes by, he'll be all right with it."

"All right with it? All right with what?

"Has he not mentioned Rachael?" Casey asked.

"No. Who's Rachael, an old girlfriend?"

Casey replied, "Listen, I'm probably speaking out of school here, and I don't want to betray Jack's trust; but I'll tell you because I know that you two have a connection, in art and, well, in life I guess. But you must promise not to bring her up to him. He doesn't talk about her. If, and when, he decides to tell you about her, he will."

"Sounds serious," Claire said.

"It is, more than you know."

"I promise not to bring it up. And I do care for Jack, and I want to know."

The look on Casey's face told her that it was dire.

"One night, at the apartment, Jack and I drank Coronas while we re-watched Jeremiah Johnson. We got a little tipsy and started philosophizing and investigating the complexities of modern society. Jack was rummaging through his journals, looking for some tidbit to illustrate a point he was making when papers fell out onto the floor. Ticket stubs, news clippings, bar napkins with poems and sketches written on them, and a photograph, which I picked up before he saw it."

"It was a photograph of a woman," Casey said, looking straight into Claire's eyes. It was a *beautiful* woman." Casey cocked his head a little and said to Claire, "I always tell you the truth."

"I know."

"And she was the most beautiful woman I have ever seen."

"Wow," Claire said. Casey gravely nodded.

"This gorgeous woman was sitting on the ground under a bristlecone pine, its shadows streaking across her white blouse and her dark brown ponytail. She wore a white headband with 'Jackson Hole' printed across it. Her face was perfect — better than any model's. Wonderfully proportioned features: a fine, straight nose and thin eyebrows, she had an angular jawline, and she was smiling. She had perfect teeth, and her smile had a sort of kindness to it. She looked like the kind of woman who would light up any room, and I don't mean just because of her outstanding beauty, but because, and this is weird because I only saw her photograph, in the image I could see a certain quality about her. That sounds strange, I know.

"I finally flipped the photo around toward Jack and said. "Who's this?"

"He was still on his knees, picking up scraps of paper when he looked up. He saw the photo and took it from my hand, sinking back, sitting on his calves. He had a wistful expression. He stared at it for a long time and rubbed his fingers gently across the image, tracing the woman's face."

Casey slowly shook his head from side to side four or five times, looking at the floor. Then he looked up at Claire again.

"He said she was the love of his life and that she had died a couple of years earlier. Then he told me all about her."

Claire's shoulders slumped, she breathed in hard, and she covered her mouth with her right hand. She did not speak.

"You know that he went out to Jackson Hole to guide for a few summers," Casey said. Claire nodded. "The second summer there, he met her. She had tagged along with her uncle for a fly-casting lesson Jack was teaching. He taught her how to cast and stood close behind her, cradling her casting arm in his hand to help her feel the correct tempo. Their bodies were nearly touching, and when Jack told her she was a natural, she turned her head toward his face and smiled, and from six inches away, he said he fell hopelessly in love. He had to work hard to get her to go out with him, but within a month, they were dating. They spent that summer together, and by autumn, both were in love. At eight months, he told me he knew he wanted to marry her.

"She was an all-around outdoorswoman and accomplished skiing, mountaineering, hiking, kayaking, and river rafting. And talk about kindred spirits; she loved the arts. She had a bachelor's degree from Northern Arizona University in Arts Management and worked part-time in Phoenix while chipping away at a Masters. He told me she had produced and directed a modern dance showcase with the Kennedy Center for the Arts. He said she had come home to Jackson to climb and hike for the summer. She ended up really getting into fly-fishing."

"What happened?" Claire asked. She rubbed her throat and swallowed hard.

"When summer ended," Casey replied, "she had to go back to Arizona. They made commitments to each other and vowed to see each other several times during the school year. She was only back at school for a few weeks when she went hiking with some new acquaintances. Apparently, they drove up to Eldorado Canyon State Park in Colorado. They climbed the Yellow Spur there. You can do it without ropes, so they didn't have any technical gear. On the descent, they ran into a rainstorm and had to hunker down and wait it out. After it passed, they tried to down-climb on the wet rock, and Rachael slipped and fell about 100 feet onto a ledge."

Claire gasped and again covered her mouth.

"Amazingly, there happened to be a mountain rescue team training in the area. Jack said they got there in only thirty minutes. She had a head injury, among others. They could not save her life. She died a couple of hours later in the canyon."

Claire was crying. "*Jack...*" was all she said.

"By the end of his story," Casey continued, "Jack was in tears."

"He said to me, 'I *told* her, a month before she left for school, it pays to carry a short rope a few pieces of hardware in case of an emergency or if you get off-route and need some protection. And she was a smart climber. I feel she would've wanted to stay put until the rock was completely dried. She probably just didn't want to be a pain in the ass to the others.'"

"Jesus...Jack," Claire kept muttering.

"Yeah," Casey said. "He went to the funeral. He admitted to me that night that he's never been the same. Not when it comes to women or loving someone."

"She sounds amazing," Claire said. "I'm sure he feels he'll never find someone as good for him again." There was a moment when neither of them spoke.

Then finally, Casey broke the sad silence.

"You."

Claire looked up at him through her tears. She wiped the tears away with the back of her hand. Casey reached over and squeezed her shoulder. She sniffed, smiled, patted his hand, got up, and went into the bathroom.

Jack was waiting at a table, sipping a large coffee, when Casey and Claire arrived in the downstairs tavern. He handed Claire and Casey each a menu as they sat down. Casey asked him, "How'd you sleep?" Claire smiled at Jack from across the table but had a sad realization that she was seeing him differently. She loved him as a great friend. She loved him for the vigor of his mind, his strength of character, and because of his endless wonder. She was disturbed that their friendship was now affected by her knowledge of such a sad tragedy.

"It was...eventful," replied Jack.

"Eventful?" Casey asked.

"I found a nice flat spot among the spruce trees, where I figured the wind had packed down the snow some. I may have had one too many last night." He sipped from the coffee mug. "Anyway, about two o'clock, something made me wake up. I thought maybe a big semi had pulled over for some reason. But when I opened my eyes, there was an enormous, blinding white light. It took me almost a full minute to realize it was a guy sitting there on a Snow Cat, idling, wondering what I was doing laying on his groomed cross-country ski trail. He couldn't back up, so he had to wait for me to collect my gear and move off his trail. I waved as he went by, but he just shook his head at me."

He looked at Claire and Casey as he took another sip and said, "How was *your* night?"

ELEVEN

The Explorer's Club

Claire walked into her apartment. Their living room was a miracle of organization. A two-foot swath of exposed hardwood flooring wound from the front door, through the big open room, and into the kitchen. The boys had pushed the coffee table, couches, and chairs to one side of the room. Spread out over the floor were five large squares of gear and equipment; one square had climbing gear. Another, smaller square had fly-fishing equipment, while another had clothing, and the fourth section had camera equipment and camping gear. The last pile of equipment contained the empty backpacks.

Claire made her way carefully through the room and plunked her messenger bag, student I.D., and keys onto the bar that separated the dining room and the kitchen. Casey and Jack were both on their knees, trying to eliminate any piece of gear that wasn't essential.

Claire said, "This morning, I was thinking again of that assassination attempt on the judge in Lima. Remember? The Shining Path murdered his driver? There was a follow-up article in The Times about it a few days ago. Peru is definitely having troubles."

Jack and Casey scanned all the gear spread everywhere.

"Does this change your mind about anything?" Casey asked.

Jack quickly said, "No."

Claire asked. "What about you, Case?"

He shook his head, still looking at the gear on the floor. "No. Unless the country erupts into full-blown war in the streets, I'm good to go. From everything we've heard, it's not likely to do that."

"I'm glad to hear that," said Claire, holding up three airline tickets. The boys straightened their backs and sat back on their calves.

"Sweet!" they both spoke at once. "Straight through from Miami?" Casey asked.

"No," said Claire, "apparently, we have to fly first to Aruba or Jamaica, then to Lima."

"Shit!" exclaimed Jack. "Which one did you choose?"

"The travel agent chose. She put us through Jamaica."

"How long of a stop-over?" Jack asked. Claire looked sideways at the tickets.

"Hour-and-a-half."

"Damn," Jack said. "Not long enough to walk the streets."

On Friday morning, the trip to Logan Airport was easy enough; each traveler had only one large backpack. Each had a small fanny pack for a carry-on that could later be emptied out and stuffed into the last cubic inch of the backpack or strapped to its outside. In the fanny pack, each carried their passports, a paperback, cameras, lenses, some of their cash, and traveler's checks.

Jack stayed over at Casey and Claire's apartment the night before. They trudged with their overstuffed backpacks up Divinity Street, past Memorial Hall, and through the Yard to Church Street, and caught the Red Line inbound to South Station. There, they transferred to the Blue Line bus that finally took them to the terminal at Logan. The flight to Miami was uneventful and a bit boring. The seven-hour wait in the terminal to board their Fawcett Airlines flight to Lima was painful, but all three took it in stride. Jack watched the bags and read while Casey and Claire walked the terminals.

When they finally could board the Peruvian DC-10, all three friends were exhausted.

When the plane touched down in Jamaica, some passengers started to applaud, and Casey and Jack were taken aback. Claire, clapping, said, "There are a lot of homeward-bound Peruvians on the plane, and clapping upon landing is normal in Latin America."

The hour-and-a-half layover at Manley International turned into three hours. Sitting in the hard-backed plastic chairs in the terminal, Jack and Claire watched passengers from other Miami flights file past. Casey stood and stared out the big window at the tarmac, anxiously hoping their checked bags would not be mistakenly taken off the plane and loaded onto another aircraft bound for who-knows-where. The passengers were steadily changing from European-looking to those with "Indian" characteristics. Claire was right: Peruvians were returning home. Jack, at six feet, suddenly felt tall. Once Casey was convinced the bags had stayed on their airplane, he returned from the window. All three began to feel the excitement that precludes an adventure as everything around them began to change — the language, the shapes of faces and bodies, and passenger's skin tones. The beginnings of the returning Peruvians revealed the blended features of their proud pre-Columbian ancestors with those of their Spanish conquerors: lovely, almond-shaped eyes and high cheekbones framed by straight, black hair. Some had the profiles of those ancestors depicted on pre-Incan pottery over 1,000 years old.

Jack broke the silence in the group, "This Shining Path…I reckon they're nothing to worry about."

"I've looked into it a bit more," Casey said. "They *are* distributed around the country a little, trying to spread their wings, but they're mainly in the south. Remember my climbing friend Jim I told you about, who lives in Lima? I called him last week and asked about them. He said if we're not in the Department of Ayacucho in the south, we shouldn't have any problems. He said our biggest worry should be pickpockets.

Jack nodded.

Claire listened, then finally spoke. "I asked Dr. Fitzroy about them. Maoists, she called them. In Peru. That seems strange to me, but I don't know why."

Once they were underway, the stewardess's worked their way up and down the aisles handing out customs declaration cards and *Tarjeta Andina* — landing cards. It was up to the passengers to provide a pen.

Claire studied the cards. "If we fill these out now, it'll be quicker getting through Customs. Make sure the total of all your gear comes to less than $1,000. Otherwise, you'll have to pay a tax on the overage. On the landing card, just put 'Hiking & Fishing."

In just under fifteen hours after leaving Miami, the plane touched down in Lima. Casey led Claire and Jack to the baggage claim and then to the Customs line for foreign travelers. All three backpacks had arrived unmolested.

Once in line, all three felt a slight apprehension in their chests. If the Customs official was having a bad day, or if he didn't like their looks, he could ruin the start of their trip. Luckily, the official looked their passports over one at a time and waved them through with a tilt of his head.

Outside the terminal, the scene assaulted their senses. Lining the street were cabs and cabbies, beggars, police, pickpockets waiting for their window of opportunity, tourists waiting to be helped out of their cash, and a fleet of VW Beetle taxis.

"What a smell," Jack said. Their nostrils became assailed with the scents of street food, aviation fuel, fish, diesel, and urine. Casey put his hand on Claire's back and guided her off to the side of the terminal entrance. Jack followed.

"Look for a skinny white guy with shoulder-length hair and glasses," Casey said. "That'll be Jim. I'll check on the other side of the entrance." Before he walked away, Casey made eye contact with Jack, who then moved in closer to Claire so that his legs could straddle the backpacks. Casey went to look for his old climbing partner.

"Do you know this Jim guy?" Claire asked.

Jack shook his head and said, "Never met him. Casey and Jim climbed Rainier together, and I think they went to Joshua Tree a couple of times. Case told me he found a home here in Lima, running adventure travel trips for a company out of Boulder. Apparently, he's pretty involved with the mountaineering scene down here, even politics." Jack and Claire fended off the dirty children who were holding out their hands, begging for candy. Jack looked solid and confident as he guarded the backpacks.

Within five minutes, Casey was sliding sideways through the crowd with a gringo in tow. "This is Jim," he said, hanging his left hand on Jim's shoulder. Jim extended his hand first to Claire, then to Jack. Casey's friend looked more like an accountant than a world-class mountaineer except for being thin and appearing fit.

"Glad you all made it," Jim said. "How was the trip?"

"Great, fine," Jack and Claire both spoke at once.

"Excited to be here," added Jack.

Jim pointed his thumb over his shoulder. "I've got a car over here. Got everything?"

"We do," Casey said.

All three followed Jim through the labyrinth of people, who were still waiting for rides or loved ones or were trying to beg for candy or money or were simply hanging out suspiciously. Jack took up the rear so he could watch the other's backpacks, and he carried his pack cradled in front of his chest.

There was a yellow and white 1968 Volkswagen bus waiting curbside for them. The driver jumped out to help with the packs and loaded them into the back of the bus.

"We'll stop by the hotel and get you settled," Jim said, "then we go to the club." Claire, Jack, Casey, and Jim piled into the bench seats of the old bus.

"This is a great VW," Jack said.

"Yeah," replied Jim. "If it starts, it's great." It did. Javier wove through the VW Beetle taxis and the old four-cylinder pickups along Lima's ancient streets. He did not drive like everyone else in the congested city, where red lights are merely suggestions, and pedestrians are moving targets. He drove courteously, which meant it took twice the standard time to arrive at the Hotel Plaza de Armas in the center of town. The hotel was on a one-way street, so Javier had to circle the Plaza before driving up to the hotel entrance. The building was constructed of red sandstone and brick, a remnant of colonial days. Its Andean Baroque façade was ornate, with ornamental designs, arched windows, stone flora and fauna, and two large, heavy carved doors. Javier stayed with the bus while the others carried their backpacks into the foyer. The spacious lobby was beautiful, with oak and teak woodwork and mahogany wainscoting. Jim, speaking flawlessly fluent Spanish, arranged two rooms for the trio. It took no time.

"All set," Jim said, handing Jack and Claire room keys. Why don't you guys freshen up, and I'll meet you here in the lobby? Then we'll go to the club."

"The club?" asked Claire.

"Oh, sorry," Jim said, "I should've told you. The South American Explorers Club. You'll love it. There, we can fine-tune your trip plans, and it's only a block away."

"Sounds great," Claire said.

After washing up and changing clothes, they walked east through the narrow streets perpendicular to the Plaza de Armas. Abruptly, Jim said,

"This is it." There was no sign. The South American Explorers Club was in a nondescript, gray, 1880's structure, similar to the adjoining buildings on either side. Again, the façade was ornate, and this one was mostly intact, but the neighboring buildings were slowly crumbling and in competing states of decay. The building's age and wear were made less subtle in the harsh mid-afternoon light. The large, arched windows on all three floors gave it a regal aspect. Inside, the building breathed a sigh of new life – as though it was proud of both its heritage and its current utility. Claire noticed the long, somewhat narrow entryway. It looked like it may have been an ice cream parlor in the early days, or perhaps a five-and-dime or a haberdashery. Dimly lit, she could see more mahogany wainscoting and that it was elegant. Jim guided the group through the hall to some stairs in the back that led to a big, story-wide landing. There, on the second floor, the building became open and airy. Upstairs had the same dark hardwood floors, but the whitewashed walls made the second floor seem bigger.

For Jack and Casey, this was the stuff of dreams. They were in a foreign country, in an Explorer's Club in its capital city, and they were about to embark on an adventure.

The room was long, spacious, and filled with everything an adventurer — or a *wanna-be* adventurer could hope for. Along the edges of the room and in three corners were old, overstuffed chairs with comfortable, cracked leather or Victorian era crushed velvet upholstery, their colors fading in areas of wear. Some of the chairs were accompanied by ottomans, and each was draped with Andean blankets. In one of the room's corners, next to one of the arched windows, was a large card table strewn with maps and books.

The room's interior had several homemade drafting tables that served as mapping desks. Next to one of the drafting tables were two six-foot-tall cabinets, each fitted with about two dozen drawers only three inches tall. The top of one cabinet held a stack of old National Geographic magazines, and on top of the other were many assorted pieces of camera gear. The cabinet drawers looked to keep maps and charts. The white walls were a miracle of imagery and were plastered with photographs of all sizes. Some were color, some black and white. Claire, Casey, and Jack stood at the top of the stairs taking it all in as Jim walked to the windowed front of the room.

Jim held out his arm. "Welcome to the South American Explorers Club. Look around." Claire and Casey eyeballed the room. They walked along the walls and perused the photographs, paintings, and maps. Some were framed, some not. In one corner, leaning between two bookshelves, were spears from the Amazon. In another corner were two four-foot-long blowguns. Something interesting occupied every corner. The couple walked to the windows where Jim was clearing a place at the table. Jack did not follow; he was facing one of the walls, transfixed, staring at dozens of the photographs. There were several images of Andean condors and of mountains and a half-dozen black-and-white photos of Indian villages in the Amazon. The rest were pictures of people — naked, indigenous people. The faces staring back in the camera direction wore an expression of intense curiosity backed by a tinge of some strange desire.

"Who are these people?" Jack asked. The Indians in the photographs were healthy, and they all had thick, straight black hair, cut in a straight line across their foreheads just above the eyebrows and hung shoulder length. These were not short people, and they looked proud and unafraid, and they looked intense.

Jim got up and joined him at the wall of photographs. "Those are the Mascho-Piru," he said. "A friend of mine from Cuzco took those pictures. The Mascho are uncontacted in the last hundred years, or least, they stay really well hidden."

"But they were contacted a hundred years ago?"

"Thereabouts," Jim said, now looking at the photographs. "When the rubber extraction industry was booming, speculators and harvesters cut huge swaths through their territories in the Manus, in the Amazon Basin. The Mascho-Piru pushed back with spears and darts. The American-owned rubber company employees murdered and enslaved them. A few of the slaves escaped and fled deep into the jungle of the Manus where they've remained in hiding, uncontacted for generations."

"Amazing," Jack said, looking Jim in the eye. "And you know the photographer?"

"Si," Jim said smiling. "And you're going to know him also; he is your contact in Cuzco. You'll meet him in a couple of days."

Jack's eyes flashed back at the photographs.

"You'll love him. His name is Alberto Montero, and he lives in Cuzco, and he is a truly amazing guy."

Jim thought for a moment, looking at the photographs, and then explained, "Alberto saw the Mascho accidentally while on a river expedition in the Manus. These are 'unofficial' photographs. He was not close to them — he was on the far side of the river from them. He told me he was using a 400-millimeter lens. Al is working with anthropologists in Cuzco. He has shown them these photographs. Al's worried that if people start contacting the Mascho, it might be catastrophic for them."

"Quite likely," Jack said. "A common cold could wipe them out."

"Obviously," Jim said. "Let's hope it doesn't come to that."

Jim returned to the table. Jack looked at the photos for another few minutes and then joined the others. They all sat around the little table in the corner.

Claire leaned over, looked out the big arched window, and looked down onto the avenue. Three small children were kicking a misshapen soccer ball held together with duct tape. A young couple walking up the street toward the Plaza de Armas had to sidestep all the scurrying kids. With the mass of five-story buildings lining narrow streets, the afternoon sunlight turns to dusk in a hurry in the city. *Just like in the mountains,* she thought.

As Jim pulled out a map of the southern half of Peru, a beautiful woman about nineteen years- old came upstairs and across the landing. She walked toward the table with a particular air of confidence. The woman was Meztisa, a person of combined European and Indigenous American descent, and she exuded pride. Tall for a Peruvian woman, perhaps 5'10", she had the classic straight black hair and dark, mischievous eyes, but they were eyes that shone with the light of a cultured woman. She approached the table and placed her hand gently on Jim's left shoulder. "Buenas tardes," she said. Jim put his right hand on top of hers and held it onto his shoulder. "Everyone, this is Eliana."

Smiling broadly but elegantly, the young woman shook each of their hands.

"Eliana has been helping me here at the club for over a year," Jim said.

"I have been looking forward to meeting you all," Eliana said. Her English was perfect, better than many Americans, and her thick, black eyebrows offset her high cheekbones and beautiful, white teeth. "I have also been looking forward to showing all of you Cuzco."

"Eliana will be accompanying you to her hometown," Jim interjected, still holding her hand.

"Can I get you all a drink?" Eliana asked.

Jim pointed at Casey. "Pisco Sour?"

Casey nodded exuberantly. Jim had made him try some at a Peruvian restaurant in Seattle.

Then he looked at Jack and Claire. "Would you two like a classic Peruvian cocktail?"

"I'd love one," Claire said. "It won't be my first."

"I'm game," Jack replied.

Jim looked up at Eliana. "Do you have time to join us?"

"For one," she said. Jack was sure that her eyes were actually sparkling.

"I'll be right back," she said as she turned away.

Casey looked at Jim as Eliana walked down the stairs. "Your letters never mentioned her. How long?"

"Almost a year," Jim replied. "She's grown fond of me, I think."

Casey cocked his head to one side, and both eyebrows raised demonstratively. "Well, she's too good for you."

"Absolutely," Jim said. "But don't you tell her." He smiled at Claire. "But don't let her beauty fool you; she's also extremely competent. She fills in as a flight attendant for Fawcett when they need her, but her main job is a translator for the government. She speaks seven languages fluently."

Casey said, "She is lovely."

Jim got up, pulled another chair close to the table, and moved a stack of maps to make room for the cocktails.

Eliana returned with a carafe and a tray of drinks in small European juice glasses. On the tray were some small crackers and some sliced cheese.

"Ah..." murmured Claire. It had been a long time since she had a Pisco Sour.

"This," Jim said, raising his glass, "is a cocktail worth fighting for." All five friends raised their glasses toward one another, and Jim started a toast. Holding his glass higher, he said, "*I cheer a Deadman's sweetheart –.*" But before Casey could respond, Jack replied, "*...but never ask me whose.*" They clinked the small glasses and drank. The taste was earthy, sweet, and tart, and it was lovely.

Jack liked it very much and grinned.

"Oh, that's good," muttered Claire. She wiped her lower lip. "It really is."

"This is *the* classic Peruvian cocktail," Jim said, as the others kept sipping, "but it was invented by an American if you can imagine that." Claire looked sideways at Casey's friend. "It's true," Jim continued, "back in the 1920s, there was an ex-pat named Victor Morris here in Lima, and he owned a bar not far from here. Like most tenders, Morris experimented a lot. One night, he blended a base liquor, Pisco, with lime juice, egg white, and bitters. And, *Voilà!* or perhaps I should say, *ahí está!* Pisco Sours were born. Eliana poured more from the carafe, and the evening, while young, progressed nicely.

"Now," Jim said. "Let's go over this trip you planned."

TWELVE

Preparation

Jim produced a map. It was old, but it would serve its purpose. Casey noticed that the borders of Peru and Ecuador seemed wrong, just as Jim pointed out the ongoing border dispute in the north.

"In the southeast, along the borders with Brazil and Bolivia," Jim offered, "the dubious border markings on the map are not disputes; it's simply because the territory is so remote the cartographers haven't updated the region in half a century."

Jim looked at all three travelers and asked the same question Fitzroy, "What do you want to get out of this trip?"

Casey spoke for the group. "We're not asking for much; just a little archaeology, anthropology, personal exploration, fly-fishing, sightseeing, mountaineering, and culinary experiences. Maybe make some friends along the way."

"Oh, that's all," Jim said. "Well, you're in the right country."

Casey flattened out the map with the palms of his hands. "For starters, we want to be based out of Cuzco, as I mentioned on the phone. We would like to try to see some of the lesser-known ruins in the area. We definitely want to spend some time in the village of Ollantaytambo, and we think that from there, we should be able to make some interesting side trips." He paused.

Jim thought for a moment and regarded the map. "I see…with those towns as your bases; you should be able to do everything you want to do. Doing it all in only three to four weeks might be tough, especially with any mountaineering, but you should be able to do a fair amount of exploring. I have arranged for you to meet Alberto and his wife, Marisol, in Cuzco. They are like a power couple in that city.

Marisol is an artist who paints and makes beautiful pottery. Alberto has made a name for himself as a guide and professional explorer. They are pretty cool people. When they walk into a room, they own it. Alberto would show you around as a favor to me, but I would prefer it if you can pay him something. I'm sure you know how strong the US dollar is here; for $200, he will take you where you want to go for two weeks. For $400, he will take you into the backcountry in any capacity you need, and you could probably retain him for the entire trip."

Claire, Jack, and Casey looked at each other. Casey spoke first, "I can come up with $400."

Jack followed with, "I'll pitch in a hundred dollars if we think we need his help that much."

Jim interjected, "Casey has told me about you, Jack." Jack shifted in his chair. "I know that you're a capable guy and that you'll more than likely want to explore on your own or within your small group, and that's cool. I'm the same way. But if I can make a recommendation..."

"Of course," Jack said.

"I've told Al in a letter about you three already. He is excited to help you because he knows he will not have to hold your hands or help you too much. He is looking at this more as an opportunity to spend time with people like yourselves — folks with many of the same interests he has. I think you'll find he will be more like a friendly host who happens to have a wealth of knowledge about the region than a guide. We just don't want to take advantage of his hospitality, so paying him will be a bonus for him and Marisol. It's hard enough to make a living here in Peru, and two hundred US dollars is way more than many people spend on a monthly mortgage here. So, they would be happy. Maybe give him your extra $100 as a tip at the end."

"Understood," Jack said. "As long as he won't mind us taking some solo side treks if the desire arises."

"No, he won't mind," replied Jim. "Alberto is all about that. You'll see. But he will have an innate desire to help you stay safe, if only by educating you about what to expect wherever you want to go." Jim paused for a moment. He looked at Jack. "It's not so much that I think you guys specifically need a guide, but he would be *the* guy you want to have with you in the unlikely event that you run into the Sendero Luminoso. There is trouble in the hills now."

"That's right," Casey said, "We should talk about them."

"Agreed," Jim said. "What do you want to know?"

The three friends looked at each other, and Claire finally spoke. "How dangerous are they, for starters? And what is the likelihood they will be in that area? I've read they're farther south."

"Okay," Jim said. "They are dangerous, but mostly to villagers and the government officials in the rural areas in the department south and west of Cuzco. The two most common modalities are to set off homemade explosive devices, typically in or near government facilities, or just generally harass, sometimes lethally, the villagers going about their normal municipal duties. Small, Indian villages usually do not have any armament, except maybe tools, so when the Sendero intrude on the village, they definitely have the upper hand."

"What's this group's point?" Jack asked.

"That's a good question," Jim said. "I don't really know. They spout off all kinds of disjointed antigovernment propaganda, but I haven't been able to make sense of it. Nobody has. You'll want to talk to Alberto. If anybody's got a handle on it, it'll be Al."

Claire, Casey, and Jack all nodded in agreement. Casey then turned to Eliana, who had been listening quietly the entire time. "Eliana, we heard about the assassination attempt on the judge last October. What are your thoughts about these Sendero?"

She glanced at Jim and then looked Casey square in the eyes. She regarded him for a moment and then shook her head slowly while she responded. "I live in Cuzco and in Lima, both in parts of the country so far largely unmolested by the Sendero except for that assassination attempt a few blocks from here. I read most of the papers. But I think Jim knows more about them than I do. That sounds bad, I know, but the Sendero are…" she turned to Jim and placed her hand on his forearm, "*Como se dice en ingles, ambiguo?*"

"Ambiguous," responded Jim.

"Yes," said Eliana. "The Sendero are *ambiguous.*" She looked at Jim again, looking for agreement. "I'm not aware of them harming any tourists, are you?"

Jim shook his head. "I haven't heard or read anything about tourists being confronted."

"Okay," Claire said, smiling at Eliana. "Thank you for your thoughts." Eliana nodded.

The carafe was now empty, and Casey said, "can we treat you guys to supper nearby?"

Eliana looked at Jim and half-whispered something in Spanish, and he responded to her. Then Jim said, "we have a lot to do to get ready for Eliana's trip to Cuzco. And tomorrow morning, she is going to make all your travel arrangements to her city."

"Oh, I'd hate for you to have to do that, Eliana," Claire said. "My Spanish isn't very good, but it might get us by. We probably could manage to buy the plane tickets and figure out where to go in Cuzco once we arrive."

Eliana was gracious. "No, no…it is my pleasure. I want to help."

"We've looked forward to this," Jim said. "Eliana will pick up the tickets in the morning, and we will meet you at the hotel at about one o'clock and will go for lunch. There is a good spot near your hotel. After that, you can walk around Lima and breathe it in." Jim drew a small box on the back of the map with the heading "Lima," and inside, jotted down a few choice places to see in the city. "The following morning, you just need to catch a cab to the airport. No problem."

"If you're sure it's no trouble," Claire said.

"None," Jim replied.

Turning the map right side up, Jim took a highlighter from the windowsill and traced the road they would need to travel from Cuzco to several nearby archaeological sites, which he circled with a pencil. In the margins of the map nearest Cuzco, he made some notes. As he wrote *Cross Keys Pub*, he said to everyone at the table, "This is where you will meet Alberto the evening after tomorrow. I'll add his home address and phone number just in case." Still taking notes, he said, "The pub is just off the Plaza de Armas near the center of town. I'll draw directions to it from the Hotel Inka where Eliana has booked you on the back of the map. It's cheap, clean and very nice. Once you get to the hotel from the airport, let them know how many days you want to stay. I'd recommend three or four days there to acclimatize while you make your plans with Alberto and do some sightseeing."

Eliana softly said to Jim, "*Tengo que irme pronto.*" Jim nodded. She then turned to Casey, Jack, and Claire, "I am so sorry, but I have to leave now." Jim folded the map as he and Eliana stood up. He gave the map to Casey. "We'll walk up to the Plaza where Eliana has an appointment, and then I'll drop you off at a nice restaurant that I like if you trust me."

"Of course," Casey said. They all walked down the stairs, through the long foyer, and out into the street. Jim locked the door to the club behind him. As they walked up the avenue towards the Plaza de Armas, Casey mentioned to Jim, "Lima has a particular smell all its own, doesn't it?

"Like many metropolises," Jim said, "it's an edgy city and has its fair share of big-city crime and corruption. It has crumbling infrastructure everywhere except perhaps the wealthiest neighborhoods, but it has a certain charm I've come to love. Its smell? It's sort of a sweet, foul mix of diesel, urine, and when we're fortunate, you get a nice whiff of the fishmeal plant that's north of the city." Jim smiled and patted Casey on the chest with the back of his hand. "One gets used to it, with time."

"If you say so," Casey responded.

Jack predictably said, "I don't mind it too much."

"Course not," Claire said. "You probably want to investigate it; dissect the odors to find out, using some root cause analysis, the origin of each particular smell. But that's why we love you, Jack."

"Just happy to be here," replied Jack. "You know," he continued, "Medieval Europeans believed that foul smells were harmful."

"Oh God ... here he goes," Casey said.

"To me," Jack continued, circling his fingers up under his nose as if sampling the bouquet of a fine cologne, "it fills up my senses."

Jim was looking at Jack with a wry smile.

"You get used to him," Claire offered.

Then Jim, still chuckling about Jack liking the smells of the city, patted Casey on the back and said, "Yeah, you guys are going to have fun here."

In the morning, Claire found Jack staring at a calendar adorned with a Van Gogh print in the lobby corner. A favorite memory popped into her head.

Once, on a day they both were free of studies, he and Claire had traveled to the Museum of Fine Arts in Boston specifically to see some newly acquired Renoirs. They meandered around separately but in the same room of the exhibit. A few minutes later, Claire noticed Jack had left the room. In the adjoining room, she found him staring at the Toulouse Lautrec painting, *Carmen Gaudin in the Artist's Studio.* Claire went back to the Renoirs for a while, then to the restroom, then to lunch. When she returned, he hadn't moved. She walked up to him and looked at the picture. She put her hand on his back and said, "Grabbed you, has it?"

"What a story," Jack said, snapping out of a trance.

Claire looked again at the painting. "She looks so sullen."

Jack regarded the woman in the painting, staring coldly at the viewer with her mussed hair painted in several tones and colors and her unflattering workaday clothes, and said, "Sullen, yes. But she's clearly pissed off."

"That's nothing new — or old," Claire responded. "Models even today get a thousand dollars an hour to look pissed-off and anorexic."

"But it's not a *look* for her," Jack said. "It's real. They're dealing with a lot."

"Like what?"

"Well, the backstory is important. Do you know about Carmen?" Jack asked, nodding at the model.

"No. But I know Lautrec painted a lot of prostitutes and Can-Can dancers."

"He did," Jack said. "But she was Carmen Gaugin. Toulouse-Lautrec met her in the mid-1880's in Montmartre. She became perhaps his favorite muse. He stayed in her brothel for weeks at a time. Some accounts said he loved her. What people usually think about when they look at this picture is the well-known story that they did have a falling-out after she dyed her hair from red, which he loved, to brown. It pissed him off so much he never used her as a model again."

"That's sad," Claire said.

"But they're missing a lot in the picture," Jack said.

"There's more? What am I saying? There's always more to the story with you." She rubbed her hand on his shoulder again.

"First look at her expression, her affect; with work-roughened fingers laced in her lap, she stares out at the viewer with a sullen — you saw it — expression. The life of a professional model was difficult. She was a prostitute, so there wasn't the social stigma of being a model to contend with, but her extra work, her modeling, depended on whether her "look" fit the artist's vision. I see several things here. *One*: I think she knows it's her last time sitting for Henri, or she suspects it. *Two*: What affliction do you typically think of when you think of syphilis 100 years ago?"

"I guess," Claire said, "things rotting off ... noses, fingers."

Jack pointed at Claire. "Right. *Three*: In the background, Henri has painted himself into the picture, half in the frame, half out, like he's truly as inconsequential as he has always regarded himself in life. He's naked, and look closely."

"Oh, my!" cried Claire. "He's hideous and grotesque, and his nose has rotted off. Syphilitic?"

"You got it," Jack said. "The art historians say it's a study of a man Henri painted while apprenticing, and he randomly included it in this picture. Either they've all got it wrong, or they've tried to sanitize the piece. The story in the painting is, to me at least, that Carmen, the love of his life, has given him the boot. He has blamed her for his venereal disease, and she has changed the color of her hair, his favorite feature, just to put him off so perhaps he'll stop *trying*. But money is money. Carmen is sitting for him for the fee, but you can feel the tension. Finally, number *Four*: Henri *wants* the viewer to know that he blames her for his syphilis, though some speculate he caught it from Rosa La Rouge, another prostitute he painted. He paints himself in a hideous rage, nose-less, almost as though he is screaming at her, but even Lautrec might not realize that it was probably truly rage against the life he had been given and the cruelties he had to endure. It's all right there. The poor bastard died less than three years after this painting was done. I read about it. Complications from syphilis and all the absinthe he drank for years. He was only thirty-six."

It was at that point when Claire realized that Jack was different. That he possessed enough energy of the mind that he saw things differently than most people, whether it was a bird's nest, a mountain, the rotation of a basketball in flight, a trephined human skull, or a Toulouse-Lautrec painting.

Now, two years later, she was waiting in a Peruvian hotel, wondering where in the heck their trip would take them.

THIRTEEN

Leaving Lima

J im and Eliana walked into the lobby, right on time.

"How was your morning?" Jim asked.

'Wonderful,' Claire said.

"Excellent. Javier is around the corner with the van." Jim stood up with more maps under his arm. "Ready?"

The lunch at the restaurant was again simple fare and was very good. Casey ordered another Cristal beer saying, "Hair of the dog," and Claire drank bottled water. Jack asked the waitress what sodas they had, and she only smiled back at him, wrote something in her notepad, and left.

"Jack," Jim asked, "do you like Fanta orange soda?"

Jack said, "I guess. I drank it as a kid occasionally."

"Good, because that's what you're getting." Jack realized he was experiencing a cultural moment. "You see," Jim continued, "there are only two kinds of soda in most of Peru; Fanta, and Inca Cola, which tastes kinda like liquid bubble gum.

Jim pulled two small tables together and cleared the condiments off one to open the map.

"They're nuts about Fanta here," Jim said. "They love it. It's like a coveted staple in their diet. Here's an example: In the mountains, there are often rituals with offerings to *Pachamama* — 'Mother Earth.' In ancient times, some of the pre-Incan people sacrificed children, infants, or teens in the mountains. Today, the offerings are obviously not humans but things that are important to the poor Campesinos, like food or alcohol. Even though they are all Christians, many old beliefs still carry on, hence the offerings. But some of the communities these days are converting from Catholic to Protestant. *They* pour their precious Fanta onto the ground when they have their mountain ceremonies instead of offering alcohol. I have an anthropologist friend who calls it 'Fantacide.'"

Jim laid out the small map. It was the southern half of Peru, with Cuzco almost in the center, just as it once was the center of the Incan Empire. The map stretched into the borders of Brazil and Bolivia. He pointed to the town of Ollantaytambo to the northeast of Cuzco and the village of Pisac, a bit farther to the northeast with the mighty Urubamba River connecting them.

Jim traced his finger along the river. "This river was sacred to the Inca. See here; it flows north and west through the mountains." Everyone's eyes followed the blue line on the map. Miles downriver from Ollantaytambo was the tiny village of Aguas Caliente and the ruins of Machu Picchu.

Jim tapped the map over Ollantaytambo. "This was the Inca's last stand. Their Alamo, except they were victorious. It's one of my favorite places in Peru. You have to decide what you want to do, and then like every good trip, let it unfold before you and evolve. Be open to changing destinations as you go along. Is a visit to Machu Picchu of paramount importance to you? Climbing a mountain? Fly-fishing? What have you planned so far?"

All three friends' eyes scanned the map. Jim laid out a pencil, a pen, and a highlighter. Then he pulled out a large envelope and laid it next to the map.

"Perfect," Casey said, smiling again.

"I thought you'd understand," Jim said.

"Understand what?" Claire asked.

"Oh," Casey said. "Bill Tillman, that explorer we told you about, once said, 'Any worthwhile expedition can be planned on the back of an envelope.' Here's our envelope, although I'm sure Tillman meant a much smaller one." At the top, Jim wrote and underscored "*The Harvard Guys Great Peruvian Adventure*."

"Here's where you want to find yourself for climbing." With the pencil, Jim circled a mountain southeast of Cuzco. With one index finger over the mountain and the other over Cuzco, he said, "Nevada Auzangate is only about sixty miles from your base of operations. You can hire a van and driver for about thirty bucks U.S. each way to take you to the village of Tinki — it's a tiny farming community — and start your trek to the mountain from there. I like that climb because it gets much less traffic than the Andes farther north, and it's a haul, almost 21,000 feet. The mountain is also quite significant in Incan mythology. Each spring, a few miles away in the shadow of Auzangate, there is a festival called the 'Star Snow,' which is something to behold. It's one of those events that is part ancient mythology, part Roman Catholicism. Pilgrims come from all over, and it's quite a spectacle, with long lines of colorfully dressed people stringing out across the snowfields. I think it takes place during the Corpus Domini, so you'll miss it."

"I've seen pictures of it," Casey said.

Jim looked at Casey, "I know you like to keep your climbs light and free, but I think it would be better if you engaged Alberto on the climb if he's available. Some of that country is true wilderness, and if you have a problem, God forbid, there's no mountain rescue available. Al would be a good man to have in your corner. And he's just fun to travel with."

"How much?" Casey asked.

"Probably $500 U.S.," Jim guessed. "So, if you engage him for the entire trip, the climb would be included, and you would be covered for whatever you decide to do."

Jack was staring at the map, leaning on his elbow with his chin in the palm of his hand. "All of the routes established?"

"Pretty much," Jim said, "though all the mountains down here have some unclimbed routes."

"Just curious," Jack pondered. "I wouldn't attempt a first ascent with Claire on her first climb, but maybe on another trip...what about fishing?"

"Ah," Jim breathed. "The fly fishing is great all through the mountains. What did you bring for rods?"

"Two five-weight and two three-weight travel rods," Casey said.

"Perfect. You'll have some great fishing. While you're trekking, don't be afraid to try every ditch along the way. Most of them will hold small trout; Rainbows. The little mountain ponds and lakes often hold bigger fish."

"I've heard there were trout stocked here decades ago," Jack said.

"Yup," Jim acknowledged. "In the 1930s, Rainbow Trout were brought from Canada and released into a few rivers and lakes in and around the Sacred Valley. I believe the idea was to create a new source of protein for the impoverished highlanders. The trout thrive all along the Urubamba River Valley, and it's a lot of fun to fish some of those small tributaries of the river. Shortly after these fish were stocked, the Peruvian government began constructing trout hatcheries along the banks of several mountain rivers. More rainbows and browns also entered Peruvian rivers from fish released into neighboring countries. Before that, in the 1890s, steamships made transportation of live fish possible for the first time, and as a result, trout were stocked throughout the South American Andes. Eventually, the Chilean Andes were seeded with trout to make a recreational sport fishery for European settlers."

"Do you think five-weight rods will be too heavy?" Jack asked.

"No," Jim responded, "especially in the Urubamba or any of the other rivers. There's some pretty big water. And you'll have to watch your footing."

"What about flies?"

"I've only fished the Sacred Valley once," Jim said, "and I used tiny streamers and nymphs. That worked pretty well."

"Okay," Claire said, changing the subject, "what about ruins? If we do a climb, it sounds like we're going to have only ten or twelve days to explore ruins, and that includes if we take the trek to Machu Picchu."

"Yes," Jim replied, "that's something you guys are going to have to sit down and figure out. It's all about time constraints. Remember, you will have to acclimatize a little bit in Cuzco if you want to climb Auzangate, and the climb itself will take three to four days, including the approach and descent. I think you guys are going to have to do some math. As I said, either way, you need to build in a little flexibility to the schedule; at least that's what I would do."

Eliana hadn't spoken a word, and Jack noticed it. "Eliana, you grew up here. Do you have any suggestions?"

She sat back in her chair and smiled, and it was a gorgeous smile. "My sister and I would be happy to show you around Cusco while you're there...maybe do a couple of day hikes."

"That would be great," Casey said. "Maybe we could take you and your sister out for a meal."

"That would be nice," Eliana said. "How early can you meet me at the airport? The flights to Cuzco are only a little over an hour, but they travel through the mountains. Quite often, the flights that leave in the afternoon are delayed or even canceled because the weather gets…" She whispered to Jim, "*La misma?*" to which he replied, "temperamental." She continued, "…gets temperamental later in the afternoon. It is better to fly out early."

"Whatever time you suggest," Casey offered.

"If you can be there at six o'clock, that would be best. I'll meet you at the ticket counter, and I'll purchase tickets for you on the left side of the plane, so you'll have nice views of the Andes."

"Six o'clock will be fine," Claire and Casey said together.

It was an early night at the hotel, an evening of short walks, adventure talks, and dreaming of the Incas.

Tomorrow, I will be in the capital of the ancient Incan Empire, Jack thought. And he hoped he would feel something other than altitude sickness.

Like a child on Christmas Eve, he struggled to fall asleep.

FOURTEEN
Cusco Magic & Mystery

In Cusco, Eliana rode with Claire in a separate taxi to the Royal Inka Hotel. At thirty-two U.S. dollars a night, it was one of the finest hotels in which the three friends would stay, but it was worth every penny. Located just off the Plaza d'Armas in the city's center, the hotel was a lovely colonial three-story building built on top of an Incan foundation that reached up almost through the entire first floor. The Incan masonry was left exposed; its polished stones fitted perfectly without mortar 500 years ago. Above the Incan stoneworks was a pinkish-taupe stucco building. The second floor had an exposed balcony the entire length of the building, and the third floor had two small, enclosed patios for single rooms with one enclosed balcony between them. The lobby was tastefully appointed with beautiful tiles, teak and mahogany furniture, and hand-woven rugs. The rooms were clean and white-washed, but the open courtyard in the center of the building was the most remarkable feature; the ground was covered with two-foot square gray tiles swept spotless. The yard had outdoor furniture — four small tables with chairs and an eight-foot-tall water fountain. There were potted palm trees and benches for lounging. Each level above the courtyard was surrounded by ornate balconies where the boarders' rooms were.

"This is a three-star hotel," Eliana had told them, "but with a five-star ambiance."

Casey and Claire's room was on the second floor, and Jack's room was on the second floor on the opposite side of the courtyard. All three hauled their backpacks up to their rooms, and Jack found his room and purposefully did not watch Casey and Claire as they entered theirs. They all spent the afternoon lounging.

Late in the afternoon, the three travelers met Alberto Montero at the Cross Keys Pub, only a half-block from the Plaza d'Armas. It was a cozy, British-style pub with a lovely limestone fireplace. Casey chose seats in the center of the pub at the only table big enough to hold an unfolded map. On either side of the small table were two low couches. Football jerseys from the United Kingdom hung from the ceiling on one side of the pub, and below the jerseys were three official size dartboards. On two walls of the pub were photographs of mountaineering scenes from Peru and Scotland. Opposite them, pictures of exotic birds, the Manus, and the jungles of the Amazon adorned the walls. In one corner, there were two framed photographs, one above the other. The top picture was of a leopard resting and draped over a horizontal tree trunk. Below was a photo of a man in a leopard skin bodysuit, striking a pose similar to the leopards on the same tree trunk.

At first, the pub seemed out of place in Cuzco, but once the group had settled on the couches and were sipping craft-style beers and Pisco sours, it seemed a natural enough setting. It was comfortable.

Twenty minutes later, Alberto Montero and his wife Marisol breezed into the room. Most everyone in the pub knew them both. Alberto was not tall or muscular, but he was handsome and carried with him an evident quality — an affect. He was, for the lack of any better term, *cool*. Marisol commanded the room with a sensual presence but in an understated way. A scarf made of red and gold silk wound around her head. Tied behind the nape of her neck, it trailed its way down her jet-black hair, cascading down to the small of her back. She wore what appeared to be a silk robe tied at her waist. Marisol was a little bit of a hippie.

As the couple floated through the door, the pub became a different place. The atmosphere changed. Alberto walked straight up to their table, smiled a toothy smile, and asked the table, "Casey?"

"I'm Casey." He raised his hand.

"Evening, I am Alberto Montero, and this is my lovely wife, Marisol." She bowed in acknowledgment using only her eyelids. Each person at the table shook hands, but Marisol hugged Casey, Jack, and Claire, kissing each on both cheeks with an understated stylishness.

Casey pulled another chair to the table for Marisol. She looked to be about thirty years old, like Alberto, and she seated herself with an elegant ease. Then Alberto sat down opposite Jack, who was on one of the short couches with Claire.

"Jim and I have talked on the phone a few times about your trip," Alberto said. "It sounds exciting. How are you enjoying Peru so far?"

"Great," Jack said.

"Beautiful," Casey chimed.

"I've been here once before," Claire said, "on a dig two years ago near Huaraz, but I didn't have the opportunity to see much of the country."

"Good," Alberto said, "I still believe your prior experience will help on this journey. Jim told me of your goals. I don't fish, but I think we will find some trout. The trekking, climbing, and exploration will be easy."

"Great," Casey said, pulling out a map. "Jim spoke with us a little in Lima, and he's made some notes on our map. So, we have some ideas. We hope you can help us finalize some plans while acclimatizing here in Cuzco for a few days. We will pay you for your time and effort."

Alberto waved him off. "You can buy Marisol and me a drink, and that will cover planning costs." It was apparent he was helping them as a favor to Jim. "If you want to hire me to help during your trip with guiding or logistics, we can talk about that later."

"Thank you," Casey said. "What'll you have?"

Alberto looked at his wife. "Daiquiri?" She nodded. He looked back at Casey. "One daiquiri, and I'll have an Abbott ale. Many thanks." Casey went to the bar.

"So, you are all archaeology students?" Marisol asked.

"Casey and Claire are," Jack said, touching his chest, "anthropology."

"Ah," Alberto said, winking, "you have come to learn our ways."

Jack smiled and leaned forward to pick up his beer. "I've come to fish, to climb, and to experience the country. If I do that well, I'll pick up some culture along the way."

Alberto liked Jack straightaway.

Casey returned with the drinks.

Alberto raised his glass. "Salud!" They each drank as Case flattened out the map, and both he and Jack produced small journals for notetaking.

Casey held up his drink and made his usual good-luck toast: "*With rue my heart is laden ...*" And Alberto spoke up, "*... for golden friends I had!*"

Claire thought Jack and Casey were going to explode. Alberto knew Housman!

Casey's eyes widened; Housman was his favorite poet. He and Jack grinned as they looked at one another, and then they both made approving eye contact with Alberto, their new best friend and drank the toast.

Al winked at them and said between drinks, "You know, we too have poetry in South America."

To that, Jack sat forward with a serious look and plunked his beer bottle down on the table, almost wetting the map. "Do-you-know-Neruda?"

Alberto waved in the air. "Of course! '*Someday, somewhere - anywhere, unfailingly, you'll find yourself, and that, and only that,*'" Alberto and Jack now speaking together, "'*...can be the happiest or bitterest hour of your life.*'"

Everybody drank to that.

Once they all settled down, Casey started the conversation. "First off, I guess we should ask your availability over the next three weeks."

"Actually," Alberto responded, "I'm free starting four days from now, which might work since you guys want to acclimatize for a few days here anyway. It's reasonable for you to see a few archaeological sites near Cuzco while you do that."

Casey nodded. Pointing at the map, he said, "If we use Cuzco as our base, I think we can do most of what we hope to do." Alberto and Marisol cozied up to the map and looked pensive. Casey drew an imaginary line east-southeast of Cuzco.

"We were thinking about Auzangate, then coming back here and taking another trip to the village of Ollantaytambo, and maybe the classic trek on the Inca Trail to Machu Picchu. I figure all along the trail, we can fish the Urubamba River and some of its tributaries. We'd love to find some water that is likely not to have been fished, if that makes sense?"

Alberto studied the map. "Yes, this could all work. It could work nicely, and we definitely could help you with logistics and streamlining your trip." Alberto tapped the spot on the map on the road outside of Cuzco. "If Marisol was to gather some supplies and meet you here, you could bypass Cuzco on the way back and shoot straight to Ollanta — that's what we locals call Ollantaytambo. It's pronounced Oh-YAN-tay-TAMbo — no 'L's.' It would save you some time, and Ollanta would be a nice place to recover for a couple of days after the climb. Soak your feet."

"That sounds great," Casey said. "Have you climbed Auzangate?"

"Several times. So has Marisol." Alberto put his hand on his wife's back.

Jack finally spoke up. "Is there a *Routa Normal?*"

"Yes," Alberto answered. "Heinrich Harrer first climbed it in the 1950s. His route is the classic. It's pretty straightforward — not too technically difficult — but it takes some stamina to break trail on the summit plateau." All three friends stared at the map.

"Really," Alberto offered, "it is a six-day climb if you're up for it, and - and mind you, I don't know what gear you brought, it requires a *high camp* on day three below a col. The snow there should be stable this time of year. But you'll have to decide if you want to take that much time out of your trip."

Claire reached across the map and placed her hand on Casey's arm. "Do you think I'm ready?" Casey looked over at Jack, who gave him a single nod of affirmation.

"It's a lot for her to take on," Jack said, "but I do think she's a natural."

"Alberto," Casey asked, "could you give me a hand with another round of drinks?" Al jumped up and stepped to the bar with Casey. They ordered drinks, and both leaned on the bar and talked as they waited for the tender. Before they picked up the glasses, Jack saw them shake hands. When they returned, Claire and Marisol talked about Incan art while Jack listened.

As they sat down, Alberto jumped up again. "Mi Amiga!" he shouted.

Eliana strode toward the table with her sister in tow. Everybody greeted them as Eliana introduced her sibling; "This is Maria."

There was awkwardness for more than twenty seconds. Maria was even more beautiful than her older sister, and she was an inch taller than Eliana. She had the same high cheekbones and perfect black eyebrows but much larger breasts which were tastefully displayed by a low-cut yellow cotton blouse. Her smile was world-class. She settled in next to Jack. They all shifted in their seats to accommodate the two ladies.

"Now," Alberto said smiling, "it's a party."

After only her second Pisco Sour, Claire leaned over and said to the sisters, "you're the most beautiful women I've ever seen."

There were stifled laughs at the table, and then Casey said, "All right, no more cocktails for you."

Jack gently leaned over to Maria and whispered, "I must agree with Claire." Maria flinched, blushed, and smiled.

Claire was beginning to understand just how powerful Pisco Sours were. She slumped back into the couch. She looked at Jack and at the blushing Maria. *Maybe Jack will finally get laid*, she thought. Then Claire looked down at her glass. She felt very content. She was in Peru, she was on an adventure, and she was surrounded by like-minded people. *Beautiful* like-minded people and her best friend was finally showing signs of being attracted to someone. She wondered if it was the altitude.

A reasonably solid itinerary was hammered out by the end of the evening, and the trip was shaping up nicely. Jack was confident Claire had the capability to climb Azungate. Still, Alberto and Casey agreed that a circuit trek around the peak would offer enough excitement and satiate their desire to be in the mountains. They would get to an elevation of 16,000 feet.

"We could get up onto some glaciers," Alberto told Claire toward the end of the evening. "If we add a seventh day to the itinerary, we could go as high as you're comfortable with."

"We," thought Claire. Even with the Pisco Sours still kicking in, she put it together; "Oh, good Alberto — you're coming with us?"

"Yes, it's all arranged with Casey. I'm very excited, and it should be a lot of fun for all of us. You will see some beautiful country."

Claire, momentarily forgetting Jack's flirtations with Maria, gave Alberto a quick hug as if to say, *I'm so glad you'll be joining us!* But there was no need to verbalize it.

As they departed the Cross Keys, Alberto said, "So we'll meet for breakfast at your hotel the day after tomorrow for final plans. After breakfast, we will organize supplies, and I'll have the transportation arranged before then."

Each person hugged and kissed cheeks goodbye. After spending much of the evening conversing with Maria, Eliana, and Marisol, Jack walked with Casey and Claire back to the hotel.

🌴

In the morning, Jack sat at one of the little tables in the hotel's courtyard. He drew sketches in his journal of the little birds flitting around the yard while waiting for Claire and Casey.

"Good morning," Casey said as the two walked down the stairs from the balcony.

"Ayuh," Jack replied.

As they devoured the breakfast of fruit, coffee, bread, and potatoes, they decided to hire a taxi to take them to the ruins of Saqsaywaman, a former Citadel on the northern outskirts of the city.

"Are you sure we are pronouncing that correctly?" Casey asked. "*Sexy-woman?*"

Jack said, "I'm sure that's incorrect. It was more melodic when Eliana suggested it last night."

"I don't know," replied Claire. "I assume it's Quechua. I doubt it's 'Sexy-woman.'"

Jack shook his head. "That's definitely not how she pronounced it." He reached into his hip pocket. "She wrote it down on this bar napkin."

Claire couldn't help herself; "Is there a phone number on there also?"

"For Jim's girlfriend? No."

"For her sister," Claire said.

Casey spoke up. "Leave him alone, Darlin'." After a moment of silence, he continued, "This town, it will be a great place to walk around to acclimatize. Speaking of the altitude, I'm definitely feeling it."

"Then why don't we go to the ruins in the afternoon?" Jack asked. "Eliana and I are going to walk around town in an hour. Last night I asked her for a history lesson."

"Oh, damn," Claire said. "I'm seriously too whacked out by the thin air right now, or I'd love to go. I think I'll go back to the room for a few hours to rest. Maybe I'll be able to read."

"I'm totally up for some rest myself," Casey said. "How about we try for a taxi around two o'clock? Jack, meet you here or at the ruins?"

"I'll play it by ear. If I'm not here at the hotel by one o'clock, I'll meet you there."

※

Both Eliana and Maria arrived in the hotel lobby promptly at nine o'clock. They were a vision; both wore stylish state-of-the-art hiking clothes. Jack noticed Maria's Vasque hiking shoes — the brand he preferred. He also saw her black Moonstone Lycra hiking pants that showed every aspect of her athletic form. Standing in the soft morning light, she was gorgeous.

"Are Casey and Claire coming?" Eliana asked.

Jack shook his head. "Feeling the altitude."

"But you are not?" Maria asked.

They hugged each other hello. Jack may have embraced Maria a second or two more than necessary. "I am not. Not yet, at least."

"Okay," Eliana said, "let's go for a history tour." They exited the lobby and crossed the street toward the Plaza de Armas. As they walked, Eliana went into full-blown tour guide mode. "The name Cuzco comes from a Quechua word meaning navel, or center. You see, this city was the capital of the Incan Empire, an empire that started in the 11th or 12th century. At the time of the Spanish conquest in the 1530s, it stretched over 2,600 miles from the northern border of present-day Ecuador south to the center of modern Chile."

"That's amazing," Jack said. He walked between the two sisters. As he listened to Eliana, he realized how lucky he was to walk in such an enchanting city with such lovely women.

"Yes, it *is* amazing," agreed Eliana. "It was, as their capital, their largest city. Some people estimate that there were as many as 200,000 inhabitants."

On both sides of each street were walls of Incan masonry. "This stonework is beautiful," said Jack.

"I agree," Eliana said. "Did Maria tell you last night she is studying architecture?"

"She did," Jack said.

"What is truly amazing," Maria interjected, "is that the Inca did all of this — moved stones that weighed several tons into place without the benefit of the wheel. It is very fine craftsmanship. Most of the joinery of the stones is so tight that you cannot even slide a dollar bill into the cracks. Yet the walls are dynamic; there is no mortar. Instead, the stones were fitted precisely, and some were carved with mortise and tenons."

Jack placed his hand on a wall. These old Incan walls were now serving as foundations or even the entire first floors for many of the Spanish colonial structures. He ran his fingers along the ancient joinery.

Maria proudly continued. "These walls have withstood countless earthquakes throughout the centuries. Do you know that two years ago, Cuzco was designated a UNESCO world heritage site?"

Jack shook his head. "Rightly so."

They crossed another street and walked onto the mall of the Plaza d'Armas.

"Spanish invaders during the conquest destroyed most of the Incan buildings, temples, and palaces," Maria said. "As you can see, they built a new city on top of the remaining ruins."

As they strolled through the old streets, some of them very narrow, some stepped, he came across sticks protruding from cracks in the masonry above the doors and windows of residences. Red rags or bandannas dangled from them. Jack pointed at one as they walked underneath it.

"That means chicha is sold there," Eliana said. "Do you know chicha?" Jack shook his head, and the women giggled. "Oh, you are in for something."

"That sounds ominous," Jack said.

"It is homemade beer made of corn," explained Eliana. "It is not very strong alcohol, but people drink too much of it."

Maria explained, "In the old days, certain women, some say the 'Sun Virgins' — the emperor's favorite females — chewed the corn into a mash and then spit it into a vessel. They would mix river water with it and bury it for weeks to ferment. Sometimes, berries or fruit would be mixed with it. Made that way," Maria's eyes widened, "it was very alcoholic. These days, except for the tiny communities high in the mountains, it's made differently with more modern methods. But every person who visits Peru should try it at least once."

"I will," Jack said, "perhaps later." And he meant it.

Eliana pointed at another red flag across the street. "Now you know where to buy some."

"Jack, do you know that Cuzco is the oldest inhabited city on the continent?" Maria asked. She turned to her sister, *"¿Es lo más viejo en el hemisferio?"* who shrugged her shoulders. "We are not sure but maybe in the hemisphere."

"I believe it." Jack was enjoying the walk, but he felt himself craving oxygen and noticed that the altitude was affecting his ability to focus.

"It is sad," Maria said, "that because the Inca had no written language that we know of, most of what we know about their culture is from the conqueror's *crónicas*."

"Their records," Eliana translated for Jack.

"But they did communicate throughout the empire," continued Maria, "using runners. They were called *Chasqui*. The Chasqui were highly trained and physically fit. They were in charge of carrying the *quipus* — colored strings tied with many strategic knots that could be read and interpreted — or messages and gifts. The Chasqui were important people. They could read the quipus, not just carry them. They were the rock star athletes in the empire."

"They used a relay system," interjected Eliana. "There were roads and rope bridges built throughout the empire just for the relayers. The Chasqui would cover over 80 kilometers a day. They could run from the seacoast to Ollanta or Cusco in three days, carrying fresh fish for the Emperors. Many kilometers apart were relay stations called *tambos*, where the runners would exchange goods, quipu, or information. The Chasqui could relay information from Quito, Ecuador to Cusco in five days."

Jack did the math in his head; *that had to be over 1,200 miles and at altitudes between 6,000 and 17,000 feet.*

Jack sounded it out; "Kee-poo's?"

"Si," Eliana said. "Some of the *quipus* still exist in museums. There's an American archeologist here in Peru studying them, a Professor Burton. He's trying to decipher them — or at least how the Inca used them. Alberto and Marisol know him. They like him a lot...they're friends."

"I know Claire would love to meet him," Jack said.

As they walked through Cuzco's narrow, enchanting streets, occasionally, they would have to walk single-file to let colorfully dressed Campesinos pass. When Maria stepped ahead, Jack's usually inquisitive, practical mind began to wander. He saw her lengthy, black ponytail hanging against her salmon-colored Patagonia jacket. Her legs were beautiful, toned from years of walking the highlands. He couldn't help focusing on how sexy she was. He averted his eyes and tried to focus on some stonework across the street. He felt he was cheapening a wonderful experience. It wasn't that he was an asexual person. Hell, with Rachael, he had been downright concupiscent. They'd made love multiple times every day.

Maria's beauty would take the breath from most men, and although Jack knew he and she had a connection, he also knew he would leave it alone.

But *why* he would not pursue her was what pained him.

FIFTEEN

A Born Explorer

The taxi ride to the ruins of Saqsaywaman took only fifteen minutes and was without the hustle and bustle of the streets of Lima. As they walked along the ancient citadel, all three friends recognized the potential importance of its location. Whoever controlled the fortress of Saqsaywaman controlled the city of Cuzco.

As usual, all three started wandering the site together but soon drifted apart, occasionally meeting up again, each gleaning new knowledge and experience independently. At one point, Claire walked around the end of one of the tall walls and found Jack hugging a massive cornerstone. "You okay, Jack?"

He smiled at her and stepped back. "They're limestone," he said, looking up at the monolith. "That one stone has to weigh, what, twenty, maybe thirty tons? With his affinity for architecture, Casey must be digging this place."

"He's sitting on one of the walls on the far side," Claire said, "writing in his journal. I think we've lost him for the afternoon."

"I ran into one of the tour guides who was having a snack," said Jack, "he was waiting for his group to return. He told me some of these ruins pre-dated the Inca, who came along and built on top of them. He said it was more of a temple than a fort, and like most citadels, it had its own "Temple of the Sun.' He told me that when several of the Conquistadores arrived here to transport gold treasure for the Incan Emperor Atahualpa's ransom, they found rooms filled with large caches of weapons. He also said they found many Virgins of the Sun — chosen, sequestered women who served the temple. The Incas considered the virgins sacred. The conquistadores, of course, defiled them. Some agents of the church they were. The guide said the captured Incan prince Atahualpa had promised Pizarro that his people would fill several rooms with gold and silver to save his life. The rooms were filled, but Pizarro murdered him anyway."

"Yes," Claire said, looking up at the cornerstone. "I've read about it. Not very Christian of them."

"I'm starting to wonder if it was exactly that," Jack responded. He put his arm around Claire. "Let's go find Case."

As they walked along the massive wall, llamas grazed here and there on the grassy grounds. With their parallel parapets progressing up the hillside, the dark stone ruins framed rainclouds in the distance.

His arm still on her shoulder, Jack said, "I know you worry about me … with women." She inhaled quickly to speak, but he stopped her. "It's okay — I appreciate that you care. But, Claire Darlin', I'm good right now. I've got my books and everything in nature, and I've got you and Case. You know I love him like a brother, actually maybe better, but you are my best friend."

"So, you *don't* love me like a brother?" she tried to tease him. As she did, she thought, *what an idiot, he's actually opening up, and I might've just shut him down.*

"No," he said, "I love you on so many levels. I can connect with you and talk to you much more than I can with anyone else alive, except maybe my mom, but that's different." He squeezed her shoulders a little and took his arm away. They walked a few more yards, and he said, "I'm pretty psyched to be here. This is an amazing part of the world. There's an energy here. Do you feel it?"

"I feel the altitude," she said, "but yeah, I feel something, like maybe when I do get acclimatized, something is waiting for me. It's weird."

"There's the boy now," Jack said. "Still writing." They walked around the end of the wall, climbed up the grassy knoll, and backtracked to where Casey was sitting.

"I'm feeling light-headed again," Claire said. "Ready to head back?"

"Sure." Casey was feeling it also. "Just sitting here, it's occasionally hard to catch my breath. Need to keep hydrated."

All three took a nap for an hour at the hotel before finding a place to eat a late supper. They walked from the hotel and found a tiny restaurant called *Machu Pollo*, which was disconcerting because Claire believed that translated to, *Old Chicken*. They ordered a group combination plate of chicken and sausage with avocado and potato slices. There was no more drinking. Each drank bottled water, and Jack tried an "Inca Cola," but the bubble gum taste was too much for him, and he left most of it.

After supper, Casey and Claire were feeling much better, and the better they felt, the more the vibe of Cusco took hold of them. They wished they had more time to meet — as Jack had put it — "the funky ex-pats and archaeology types living here." They would meet Alberto in the morning, and the following day their real adventure would begin. All three were ready to get into the saddle and hit the mountains.

In the morning, Alberto and Marisol came to the hotel's little restaurant at eight o'clock. Al wore jeans and an old, blue pile Patagonia jacket. Marisol again turned heads dressed in a flowing white cotton dress adorned with Incan designs. She always seemed to glide into a room. A construct of knotted strings resembling a quipu hung between her breasts.

Al and Casey pulled two tables together, and the map was laid out. Alberto pulled two index cards out of his jacket pocket. "Okay," he said. "I've got two nice trips figured out, and you guys can choose one, or we can make any variation you want."

The cards were about the size of an envelope, which made Casey smile at Jack. They both thought of Tillman and Shipman once again.

"This card, we'll call 'Trip One,'" Alberto said, sliding it onto the map. "We go from Cusco to do the Ausangate trek, and as I said before, if we add a seventh day, we can probably get up pretty high, weather permitting. After the trek, we can go straight to Ollantaytambo to rest for a few days and then hike the Sacred Valley to Machu Picchu. From there we can take the train back here. That would give you nearly a week around town to relax. I've talked to a couple of archaeologists and one anthropologist whom I know here in Cusco, and if there's time, they'd all like to meet you."

"That's a great trip," Casey said.

"It is," agreed Claire.

Jack stared at the map.

Alberto replaced the card. "This is 'Trip Two.' It is a bit more adventurous — a bit different. We can call it tailor-made for your chosen fields."

The friends were intrigued, and Jack leaned forward.

"On this trip," he continued, "the first half is exactly the same, and after the Auzangate trek, we take the bus to Ollantaytambo, but then the itinerary changes. We don't go to Machu Picchu; we save that for another trip. Now, as you can imagine, almost everyone who travels to the town of 'Ollanta' uses it as a staging area for their hike to Machu Picchu. All the normal trips lead west-northwest out of Ollanta toward Machu. *But*, if you are game, I thought of something interesting. Instead, we could do one of two things; we go to Ollanta as planned from Ausangate and hike east-northeast into the Cordillera Urubamba and explore some of the remote Campesino communities. I have a friend in Ollanta who was a bonafide explorer in the sixties. He has told me stories of subsistence farming villages where the people have never seen a gringo. If we climb far enough, we might experience something like that."

Alberto paused while they took it all in. "If we choose that option, there might be something special. My friend in Ollanta — his name is *Cauac* — has told me for years about a village high in the mountains where no one goes. It's a two-to-four-day hike just to get close. He has heard they practice the old ways there, and they're very protective. Cauac said back in the late 1960s, a photographer was hanging around Ollanta and got wind of the place. He geared up and tried to find it. He said the guy stumbled back into town three weeks later with no camera gear, a broken arm, and a wild look in his eyes. He wouldn't talk to anyone or let anybody treat his arm. He just slept by the river that night and got on the first bus out of town. Other people I know in Ollanta have corroborated the story. Cauac sort of knows where it is; on the far side of the Cordierra Urubamba before you drop down into the Rio Paucartambo valley. Very remote. Also, I can tell you that any of the streams you would cross on the way will have fish in them and that those fish have never seen an artificial fly."

Jack and Casey stiffened their backs, looked at each other, and sat back in their chairs. They both had the same look on their faces; then, they looked back at the map studiously.

"I realize that's a lot to think about," Al said, "and some of it may even seem crazy, but this is a wild, crazy part of the planet."

"You implied there's a variation to Trip Two?" Jack asked.

"Yes," Alberto replied, "that's a bit more straightforward. Whereas on the first part of the trip, you'll be in the highlands, meeting Campesinos, I thought it might be a good variety to take a week-long trip into the Manus, into the Madre de Dios."

"The Mother of God," Claire said.

"Si," Alberto replied. "The department was named after the Rio Madre de Dios."

"Where the Mashco-Piro tribe is," Jack offered.

"You know of them?" Al seemed surprised.

Jack shook his head. "Only the photos on the wall of the Explorer's Club in Lima."

Alberto had forgotten that Jim had some prints. He smiled his wide, toothy smile and touched his chest. "I took those photographs!"

Jack nodded approval.

"We could spend a week traveling upriver in the Manus. That way," Al looked at Jack, "anthropologically, you'll be able to observe and interact with both the Andean highland culture and the Amazonia. We might not have enough days to get that far up the river where the Mascho are ... or *could* be. They move around, and no one knows exactly where they are at any given time."

"Alberto," Claire said, "these are two amazing trips. Tough to decide. Personally, I'm game for any version." She motioned to Casey and Jack. "It's your first time in Peru, so whatever you two want to do is good for me. I'll be coming back anyway for fieldwork."

"I think you're right," Alberto said, looking at the map. "They are fine trips. I also think you will love the Auzangate trek. You know..." Al's tone became more reverent, "it will be something of a privilege for you all. Maybe you can think of it as a pilgrimage. You will experience more than just beautiful natural wonders. The mountains there, called *Apus* by the locals, are considered sacred beings at the center of ancient Andean spirituality."

"Well," Casey said, "I think we should try to commit right now. Otherwise, we could be up all night trying to decide."

"I agree," Al said, "because if you can, here and now, I can perhaps answer any questions you might have. For instance, your gear. You are geared for climbing and trekking. If you choose the Amazon, we'll have to re-evaluate your clothing and gear — and what vaccinations you've had. Whichever trip you choose, I'll need tomorrow to arrange everything.

We can leave the following day."

"Now?" Casey asked Jack and Claire. Both nodded, but neither said anything. Then they all studied the map.

Finally, Jack spoke. "I must confess, I feel strangely drawn to the Amazon. I don't know why. But that could be for another trip. I'm also intrigued by the idea of exploring the country north and east of Ollantaytambo — did I say that correctly?" Alberto nodded. "I like the idea of hiking the road less traveled. I don't know about a 'lost community" high in the mountains like some sort of Shangri La but exploring tiny farming communities where nobody goes and doing some fishing sounds pretty good to me." He looked at Casey, who was deep in thought. "Unless you want to do Machu Picchu."

Casey didn't say anything.

"I guess," Claire said, "truth be told, I'd rather stay in the Andes than the Amazon. I've been reading about Ollantaytambo, and I've been excited to spend time there. If we go to the Amazon, we won't see that city. But, as I said, I'm up for anything."

That helped. Casey had already eliminated the Madre de Dios. "Okay. Now that you've both weighed in, we can say no to the Amazon."

"Okay," Alberto said. Putting one index card in his pocket.

The three friends all looked at each other. Then, Casey looked up at Alberto and said, "You'd think this would be easier."

"No, this is good. I offered to help plan some potential world-class trips, and in ten minutes, you've made progress."

"Do you have a suggestion regarding us choosing Macchu Pichu?" Casey asked.

Al cocked his head to one side and grimaced. "Two of you are archaeology students. You would like the citadel, but you all seem like the type of people who, like myself, are interested in exploring. There's no more exploring at Machu Picchu."

There was another moment of silence.

"Here's a thought," Alberto said, "after Ausangate and once we get to Ollantaytambo, the logistics don't change a lot. If we strike out into lesser-known territory, we just buy food, put on our boots, and walk out the door."

Jack wondered if Al knew he had again quoted the legendary mountaineer Bill Tillman, who famously said, "*You can start an adventure by strapping on your boots and stepping out the door.*" Then again, Alberto might be Tillman reincarnated.

Al continued, "If you decide late in the game to make the trek to Machu Picchu instead, I can make the arrangements in a day. There's talk about the government regulating the hiking traffic on the Inca Trail to Machu Picchu and getting permits in advance, but we're a few years away, I think."

"I like that," Casey said. "It gives us some flexibility and allows the trip to evolve as circumstances arise, which is more our style."

"Excellent," Alberto said. "Tomorrow, we can pack and buy some supplies. I can meet you here in the hotel lobby after breakfast, say, nine o'clock, and we'll go to the San Pedro Market. As far as transportation goes, I'll get a private minibus, called a *colectivo* here." Alberto handed Casey the remaining postcard. "On the back of the card is an estimated dollar amount for food and transportation."

"We'll be ready," Casey said.

"Before I go, how are you all feeling with the altitude?

Casey, Claire, and Jack all looked at each other.

"Claire and I got whacked when we got here," Casey said, "but we seem better today."

"No problems yet," Jack said.

"Good," Alberto said. "Cambridge is, what, forty feet above sea level? We're at about 11,000 feet here but the Ausangate trek averages over 13,000, and there are two passes over 16,000. Luckily, you've got a month in Peru, so we'll have plenty of time to acclimatize if any of you get altitude sickness. If anyone gets it severely, I've got some Diamox ... we just have to make sure there are no existing liver or kidney disease or any drug allergies. And that none of you are pregnant." He pointed at Casey and Jack.

Both said, "All clear."

"You guys are all fit, and you've had a few days here in Cusco to acclimatize. If we take it slow for the first two days, I'm sure you'll be fine."

The whole decision-making took less than an hour. Claire spoke only a couple of times, as did Jack, but they gathered a wealth of information.

Later, as they spoke about the trip at bedtime, Claire told Casey how excited she was to be in Cusco. But Casey had already drifted off to sleep.

She looked over at him. It had been a long time since they'd made love. *He is in expedition mode,* she thought. She was fine with that.

The walk to the San Pedro Market was a pleasant one. From the Plaza de Armas, they walked south along Calla Manta, past the Incan stone foundations, past Plaza San Francisco, and through the stone archway to the market. The closer they got, the more street vendors and ladies in traditional layered dresses there were. They sat next to the street selling dried fruit, nuts, popcorn, and fabrics. There were tiny local shops nestled ever-closer together selling all manner of things. With Alberto's dickering help, Claire bought a pretty alpaca sweater for $12. She loved it. "It'll be a nice layer in the mountains."

At the market, their senses were taxed. The colors, the humanity, the smells of food cooking in stalls, and the din of people speaking in Quechua and Spanish and vendors playing music struck them head-on. Alberto had brought three large cloth shopping bags. He purchased a bag of nectarines and two bunches of bananas, oranges to make juice with, and some frozen chickens. Al found some small bags of spices. He also picked up small quantities of local fruit, like *lucuma,* which has a hard, green outer shell and soft yellow flesh with a dry texture and sweet flavor, that's often likened to a mix of sweet potato and butterscotch. There were also *granadilla,* a sweet passionfruit, and *chirimoya* (custard apple) which is dark yellow. World traveler Mark Twain had called it "the most delicious fruit known to man."

Alberto worked from stall to stall, buying avocados, tomatoes, and potatoes. Because Al was doing the purchasing, the prices did not fluctuate to *gringo prices.* The market was a marvel of supply. You could get anything and everything at the market or within a block of it. For sale were pens, kitchen magnets, lighters, key rings, bottle warmers, dolls, and cigarettes. Chicha beer could be found under some of the stall's tables if one dug a little. In one stall alone, you could purchase shoes and potatoes, bottles of Inca Cola, tablets of yellow-lined paper, and carburetor kits for either Ford or Chevy trucks, "no matter the year."

With the market shopping finished, Alberto parted ways. He

was off to arrange the van, he told them. "Be ready early tomorrow morning," he suggested. "We'll leave your hotel by six-thirty."

They said their goodbyes, and Casey waited for Alberto to get about thirty yards away before telling Claire and Jack, "Oh! I forgot something I wanted to ask him," and jogged after Al. Jack and Claire watched them speak for only a minute until Casey returned.

"I had wanted to ask him about the Sendero if they are active where we're going."

Claire said, "Last Christmas, my dad told me to be careful of them, but except for that assassination attempt in Lima in April, I haven't heard anything. What'd he say?"

"He said there hasn't been any history of them harassing anyone where we're going on this trek. He also told me he was planning on giving us a briefing on the five-hour drive to the town of Tinki, where we'll start the trek."

"Sounds reasonable," Jack said. "You worried about them?"

Casey weighed that for a moment and said, "Not with Al there. I think he can handle anything you throw at him. You know, I just believe that old saying that *chance favors the prepared mind.* We'll know more tomorrow."

SIXTEEN

"Remember the Apu"

T he friends were packed by five-thirty and in the lobby, ready to go by six in the morning.

The Colectivo, outfitted with two full-sized spare tires and a homemade luggage rack on top, stood parked in front of the foyer. Al had hired an "outdoorsy-looking" driver named Alonzo. There were four bench seats in the back, and one in the far rear had been permanently removed to make room for gear stowage. Everybody was ready to go.

As they loaded their gear into the back of the van, Jack and Alberto looked at Claire and smiled.

"What?" she exclaimed. Alberto quickly looked away and positioned the gear to keep it from jostling around. Jack didn't. He kept up a wry smile.

"What?!" she said again to him.

"You look really cute in your adventure outfit, that's all."

"Shut up," she said, also smiling.

Casey grinned at them as he walked past. "She does, doesn't she?"

They all got into the van, with Alberto in the forward bench seat directly behind Alonzo. Opposite Al was Jack, with Claire and Casey in the seat behind. All three friends carried fanny packs with their money, passports, and cameras.

The drive to the tiny hamlet of Tinki felt longer than five hours. Some stretches of the road were macadam, some were under construction, and some were paved. Within an hour, the massif Ausangate and its neighboring mountains could be seen looming on the horizon through the windshield.

Alberto motioned to them and reiterated, "Remember the *'Apu,'*" he said, "are how the locals often refer to the mountains, but in the old days, Apu also was the name given to powerful mountain spirits. The Incas also used Apu to refer to the sacred mountains themselves. Each mountain had a unique spirit, with the spirit going by the name of its mountain domain. Because of your chosen fields, I'll explain more about the mythology over supper one night if you'd like."

The van ambled along about forty miles per hour. Alberto pointed ahead. "Up here, we're going to pass through the small town of Urcos. There's a beautiful lagoon there that holds trout. If you don't have any fishing luck on the trek, we could try here on the way back. But you'll have many opportunities to fish over the month.

An hour-and-twenty-minutes later, the van rolled into the village of Tinki. Each person unfolded themselves from the vehicle, plunking their feet onto the dirt parking spot. Tinki was a traditional Andean village with less than a dozen buildings.

"This is where we meet your arriero and the horses," Alberto said.

Casey and Jack looked at Claire; "*Arrieros* are muleteers ... burro drivers, she said. "Or, in this case, horse wranglers."

"I'll go find him," Alberto said.

Everyone stretched and walked around. Casey and Claire strolled through the alleys between the farmhouses. "This is strictly an agricultural community," Claire said. She held her hand above her eyes to shield the sun and scanned the countryside. "I don't see any Incan stonework."

Jack was already wandering around the village with his camera. He had a disarming, genial way about him, and he seemed to exude kindness and compassion. People who typically did not want their photograph taken or might want to charge a fee often *asked* Jack to take theirs — no charge.

As he walked around the back of a tiny farmhouse, he almost stumbled onto a Quechua woman weaving a sarape on a loom. She was plump or appeared so because of the many layers of clothing she wore, and on her head was a peculiar hat; it looked like an upside-down pan, embroidered with a multi-colored cloth, and fringed for its entire rim with short, dangling pieces of gold yarn. She was sitting on a colorful blanket on the ground. Her loom was constructed of a piece of Rebar driven into the ground, some sticks, and a short section of thin PVC tubing.

"*Buenos días,*" Jack said.

The woman smiled, blushed, and shyly replied, "*Buenos días.*"

Using the few Spanish words he had picked up from his walk around Cusco with Eliana and Maria, Jack asked, "*¿Puedo tomar tu fotografía?* The woman seemed embarrassed but nodded approval. After taking a few photos, Jack bowed forward on the grass. Leaning on the knuckles of one hand so that she might look up at him, he made the eye contact he was searching for and said, "*Muchas gracias.* He made her smile again, and once more, she blushed. Then he left.

He walked to the front of the stuccoed cement house where Alonzo had parked the van. Alberto and another man walked up the road leading two horses. Casey, Claire, and their driver had all the backpacks unloaded and placed off the road on a grassy spot.

"All set," Alberto said as he and the arriero swung the horses by their bridles around so they were abreast of the packs. They were nice healthy horses. One had a sawbuck saddle, and the other had a western saddle with a cleverly built rack made out of more PVC pipe with large, empty canvas bags hanging from it.

Claire, who had ridden some in her youth, looked at the improvised saddle.

"Everyone," Alberto said, "this is my friend Pedro. He will tend the horses and help with setting up and breaking down camp and with cooking."

The friends greeted Pedro and shook his hand. Pedro was tall for a Peruvian. He had a tattered Carhart jacket, an old felt sombrero with the brim permanently turned up in the front, and he had a sparse, black mustache that did not meet in the middle but turned down around both corners of his mouth. He looked very much like someone who might have ridden with Pancho Villa.

"And this boy," continued Alberto, patting the first horse's head, "Is *Sucio.* He likes to take dirt baths — and that one is *Perezoso.* He needs encouragement sometimes. Now, you guys are climbers, so you're used to carrying your packs, but these horses can carry up to 250 pounds. One of these pack bags has my and Pedro's gear, along with the mess kit and cooking tent. Casey, the gear list you gave me had tents enough for you three, sleeping bags, and such, so we should be all set. I recommend you lighten your loads a lot, and Pedro will pack your gear in the saddle-pack bags. Put it all in separate piles, and he'll keep it that way. You'll each have your horse-pack bag, and your backpacks should feel lighter than daypacks."

Each friend did as Al suggested. They kept out camera gear, fly rods, water bottles, a small first aid kit, snack food, and hiking poles. Before long, Pedro was ready.

The packs were indeed light, and it felt good. They were underway, and it was not yet noon.

This was it. Pedro went ahead with the horses, and Claire, Casey, and Jack followed Alberto on a wide dirt road out of the village. Dry fieldstone walls two feet high lined both sides of the road. The brown rolling hills on the landscape, dotted here and there with sparse conifer trees, gave way in the distance to the serrated white peaks — the *Apus*.

"Look at those hills," said Jack, pointing his trekking pole at the glacier-covered peaks in almost every direction. "I'm getting pumped." They passed a simple sign that read, *Upis Alto* with an arrow. A trail left the road heading southwest toward the mountains. It was slow-going, and no one wanted to rush and run the risk of getting altitude sickness.

Once they were outside of Tinki, alpacas seemed to be everywhere. Grazing a few hundred yards off, a herd of several dozen of the camelids watched the group through shaggy, Ziggy Stardust hairdos. "Did you notice they all had this little shit-eating grin," said Casey, "like they know we're idiots?"

"They might be right," Jack said.

They were in the puna now, a diverse grassland ecosystem that exists above treeline and below the permanent snowline. Assemblages of cushion and mat-forming species of grasses characterize the puna vegetation. None of the varied grasses grow very tall. The alpacas seemed to have plenty to graze on. Several birds flitted about the camp. Jack noticed two finches and a couple of tunnel-dwelling miner birds nearby.

The stark, lovely agricultural landscape was put into perspective by the big, open cobalt-blue sky stretching across the horizon. Within a few hours, stopping only to drink water, the group walked past a few adobe farm buildings at the hamlet of Upis. Pedro was just beyond the buildings, with a camp set up next to a little stream. There was a large, square mess tent, and nearby were two tiny one-person tents. The saddlebags were off the horses and placed on a tarp on the ground. The horses, which were not hobbled, grazed forty yards away. Some cement block outhouses stood a short distance away, and next to the stream were two cement-lined thermal bath pools to soak in if desired.

"I'm not too sure about soaking in there," Claire said, staring into the greenish-brown water in the hot springs.

"*I'm* sure," Casey said as he walked by. "It's a big, fat, no."

As Alberto walked by carrying a duffle bag, he said, "You are in the true valley of Ausangate now."

Looking up the valley a few miles from the campsite, the approach to the mountain climbed straight up from the valley floor, and it appeared ominous but climbable.

As soon as the tents were set up, Jack approached Alberto. "Al, do you think there might be fish in this stream?" Alberto shrugged. "Don't know — but I do know there are trout at tomorrow's campsite in Pucacocha Lake."

Pedro was nearby. He heard enough of the conversation while getting his pots and pans out of the saddlebags. "*Trucha*, si ... si." He waved at the stream, smiling. "*Trucha*."

"He would know," Alberto said. He walked over to Casey, who was kneeling while looking for some piece of gear. "Want to try it?" pointing his thumb over his shoulder at the little stream.

Casey squinted up at him. "I'm going to check on Claire when she comes out of the outhouse and find out what she wants to do. I'll join you if I can."

Jack's tent and sleeping bag were set up and ready, and it was only mid-afternoon. He looked up at Ausangate's pure white glaciers and snowfields framed nicely by intense, blue skies. In the half-light of the valley floor, the stream hurried through the treeless plain on its way to lower valleys where it would pause to irrigate fields before feeding the driving, wild rapids of the Urubamba River.

But here, the stream's milky, silty water was glacial runoff, and since they were above treeline, only pampas grasses were lining it where insects could live. At 9,000 feet, Jack hadn't seen any insects. *But there must be some insect life,* he thought. Jack removed his 3-weight rod from its aluminum tube and prepared to fish. He took two tiny fly boxes from the top compartment of his backpack and put them in his shirt pocket.

He held the rod and the leader in one hand as he walked to the stream. He looked into the chalky water and saw no fish. He kicked up no insect life as he walked through the tall grass. Jack got down on all fours in the pampas on the bank and rubbed his hand through the grass.

Sitting in her camp chair, Claire looked up from her journal. "Is Jack okay?"

Casey glanced over at the stream. "He's looking for insects. He's always looking for something." Alberto heard Casey and, while chopping an onion, watched Jack. Al was beginning to enjoy his new friend.

Jack finally found a few insects, but not many. This was easy fishing. There were no trees to snag his backcast like there were in Maine, and there were no other fishermen to negotiate with for the choicest water like in Wyoming. There was only the stream, his friends nearby, the mountains, and the sky.

He reached into one of his fly boxes and took out a tiny Wooly Bugger, a fly that can be fished like a streamer, which simulates a bait fish — or fished dead drifting like an insect in its nymphal stage of development. He had two 'buggers' that were white.

After walking beside the quick-moving stream, he found where it made a slight turn in the valley floor, creating a deep, cut bank. On the inside of the bend, there was some slightly slower moving water, and it was shallower there. Jack spied a seam between the fast-moving current and the slacker water where fish might hold.

He crouched low and made a few false casts and then let the fly drop upstream above the seam. The fly quickly sank, and Jack looked down to collect the fly line dangling from his reel to start stripping in. As he did, he felt resistance — too soon. *Damn ... I've snagged bottom already.* He raised the rod tip to try to free the fly from the rocks, and as he did, a squirming, tiny fish flew into the air. It surprised him, and the fish flipped toward him, and Jack caught it against his belly. Not six inches long, it was a silvery trout alright, without any of the colorations he was used to seeing. It must've taken the fly as soon as it hit the water. Jack looked at it for a moment, bent down, and released it. It shot off into the bend pool very quickly. He looked back at the campsite. He was glad nobody had seen that. It wasn't very elegant.

Again, he stepped up to the bank, and keeping his elbow tucked to his side and his casting wrist straight, he made another cast. This rod was very light, and casting even a small streamer fly was a chore. He casted to the same spot. This time he stripped line quicker, and immediately he could feel the tugs…one, two, three times. On the third time, the rod tip stayed bent, and another fish was hooked. Again, he simply lifted the fish out of the water. It was the same size as the first, and they were small. He caught and released four more, and when he looked back at camp, Casey and Alberto gave him two thumbs up.

After an hour of catching small trout in such a pristine place, Jack was contented and walked back to camp. *Those little trout were so eager,* he thought, *I wonder how many artificial flies they've seen. None?*

There was a hearth in the center of the camp, in front of the mess tent. Alberto had thought to strap some lightweight nylon camp chairs to one of the saddles. Jack walked up to the others lounging in the chairs. They were reading, and each wore headlamps that were not yet turned on. There was still just enough daylight to read by, but they all knew how quickly the light would disappear in the mountains. Jack started taking down his rod to stow in its tube.

"That looked like fun," Casey said.

"I love it here," replied Jack while reeling in the fly line.

"Any size to them?"

"No, maybe six or seven inches, but they were fun on the small rod."

"We probably won't need the bigger rods until we hit the rivers," said Casey.

Jack nodded.

As evening gathered over the little valley and the mountain was put to bed, the group was treated to a fine meal of tea, cheese, and a Peruvian version of a chicken stir-fry with potatoes and fried plantains and some excellent Chilean Merlot. As it turned out, Pedro and Alberto were excellent cooks.

The supper conversations revolved around climbing and fly fishing. Pedro cleaned up when the meal was finished, and Jack insisted on helping, confounding the Campesino a little.

Once settled around the little campfire, Alberto held court.

"We did not get to talk about the Sendero Luminoso on the bus, as I promised," he said, "and I want to honor that and put any concerns you have to rest.

"It is quick and easy to say that we are in no danger here or when we are in and around Ollantaytambo. There have been no deaths by the

Sendero in these areas, but there have been a couple of minor incidences near the Inca Trail last year. They stole a few items to show who was boss, but no one was harmed. Honestly, I know they exist in Cusco and the hills outside Ollantaytambo. The question always is, are they active?"

Then he asked, "What do you know about the movement, in basic terms?"

There was a hesitation while the three friends decided who would answer, then Casey said, "Not a lot. They're some sort of Maoist terrorist group who have killed some people and set off some bombs. I read it started at a university."

"That is correct," Al said. "The Sendero — better known in the States as the Shining Path — are difficult to explain. They were started by a university professor in Ayacucho about fifteen years ago, along with a few followers. He taught philosophy. His name is Abimael Guzmán and his followers call him 'Presidente Gonzalo.' He studied Marx and Mao. At some point, the professor went nuts and started a revolutionary communist party. They organized and slowly armed themselves. Five years ago, they started the armed struggle by blowing up some ballot boxes in a tiny village near Ayacucho. It didn't take long for things to get very dark."

"Good Lord," Casey said.

"You're on the right track," Alberto said. "A friend of mine who's a secondary school teacher in Ayacucho told me Guzmán got caught up in the Liberation Theology that's been an interesting religious and political movement in Latin America for years."

Alberto stirred the fire with a stick as the group hung on every word. "The Shining Path's goal was to overthrow the state by guerrilla warfare and replace it with a new democracy. They believed that by establishing a dictatorship of the proletariat, inducing a cultural revolution, and eventually sparking a world revolution, they could arrive at full-blown communism. But, there are two major problems."

"Let me guess," offered Casey, "corruption?"

Alberto winced for effect. "Sort of. Or maybe simply ego." He paused for a minute. "Or insanity. The first problem is their message. There doesn't seem to be one. Yes, communism and creating a classless state, but the people they detain, terrorize, and even torture are typically remote village officials or community elders who are often illiterate. Its ideology makes violence an integral part of this goal — and the more violence, the better. But so far, they mostly harm the poor peasants. It makes no sense. They don't try to educate or convert or even persuade. Their tactics are brutal."

Alberto stirred the fire again, and tiny sparks sprayed into the black sky like hundreds of fireflies disappearing into the darkness.

"The bottom line is no one seems to know what their plan is should they take over."

"So, they're just power-hungry thugs at this point," Casey said.

"That might be oversimplifying it a bit," Alberto offered, "but not much. Not now. It's as if they've tasted blood, and they can't turn back."

"That brings me to the second problem, which is bad." Again, Al paused.

"We want to hear it," Claire said.

"Alright. I will tell you. I have friends all over the country, including archaeologists and anthropologists, French, Peruvian, British, and American. These people, as you know, are often out in remote areas like this." He waved his arm at the valley. "What I find interesting is that the Sendero recruit a lot of women. When one thinks of Latin American insurgencies or rebellions, they're typically a 'boys club.' Not so with Sendero. They try to recruit very young girls — often orphans or bastard children and indoctrinate them to Maoist teachings. They even have an anthem, which calls for a 'purifying river of blood.'

"I have met some of these young women," he continued, "and I feel like for some of them, the deep love they feel for the rebellion, as melodramatic as it sounds, is the first real love they've ever known. But my friend who knew Guzman at the university told me he would *never* see women — revolutionaries or otherwise — as equals. He will direct them, and he'll let them worship him."

Alberto thought for a moment. "There are many stories that may be inappropriate to tell now on such an enjoyable trip like this, and in a beautiful place such as this."

"It *is* beautiful here," Jack said. Everybody took a deep breath.

Alberto rose from his tiny folding camp chair. "It's time to find a pillow. Easy on the wine until you're sure you are acclimatized."

"Already corked," Casey said. "Good night."

SEVENTEEN

Highland Devils

While the friends were setting up their tents in the shadow of Ausangate, northwest of Cusco, about forty miles away, fifteen-year-old Theresa Pacari and her twelve-year-old sister Alessa were walking home from tending their small herd of goats. They kicked stones along the dirt road and sang songs, and twice little Alessa tried to trip her sister with a wispy stick she carried.

"Stop it!" Theresa cried, "It's not going to make me fall, and it's only annoying."

Alessa, bored, giggled. As she did, the plastic strap on her tiny sandal snapped, and she walked out of her shoe. She stopped and picked up the shoe. "Help me, Alessa," she called.

Theresa stopped and shook her head. "Mother will be mad at you."

Alessa looked like she might cry.

"Let me see if I can fix it," Theresa said. They both sat on the high grass embankment beyond the gutter that lined the road, and the older sister looked at the broken sandal.

As Theresa tried to stretch the plastic strap into the buckle, a pickup truck came quickly around the corner. It stopped next to them. A woman was driving, dressed in black, and a young man leaned out of the passenger window.

"What's wrong, girls?" he asked.

Theresa shielded her eyes from the sun and responded, "My sister has broken her sandal. She will have to walk the rest of the way barefoot. She has done it before."

"How far do you live?" the man asked. His Quechua speech was not perfect.

Theresa pointed in the direction the truck had been traveling. "About ten minutes's more walk."

The man spoke with the woman driver and opened the door. "Hop in the back, and we will give you a ride."

Theresa was hesitant, but she was tired. These were adults, and she did as she was told. She helped her sister up and walked to the back of the truck. The man lowered the gate and helped first Theresa and then Alessa into the truck bed. There were tarpaulins, a chain, and some buckets in the bed.

"Sit there, against the back of the cab," the man pointed. The girls scooched forward in the bed. As the gate slammed shut, Theresa turned and saw the man was in the truck bed with them. He reached out and grabbed her sister, and as he did, the tarpaulin flung open, and another man sprang out and grabbed Alessa. Both men put a hand over the girl's mouths and muffled the screams. The woman driver jumped out of the cab, hopped into the bed, and tied the girls' hands and kicking feet with rope. Then, she stuffed dirty rags into each of their mouths. The girls were still thrashing their legs and trying to scream.

The sisters could hear the men and women barking orders at one another in Spanish. They tied the sisters together, back-to-back with another length of rope, tight enough that they could not thrash about. The rope hurt. The men threw the tarpaulins over the girls, and they could feel the truck lurch, first forward, then reverse, as it turned around in the road, and then it drove fast in the direction from which it came.

Alessa and Theresa, frightened nearly to death, wondered what had just happened to their world. When the girls did not show up at home, their father went looking for them. He knew where they would've been walking. As he hurried down the dirt track, he looked up and down the vast valley below and down the road that led to the river. The girl's father had only once been down the dirt road as far as the end of the valley. He glared toward the highway that disappeared from the valley to places unknown. Places outside of his valley — the only place he had ever lived and ever been.

His feet kicked up dust in the road when he stopped abruptly. At his feet was a tiny plastic sandal with a broken strap. Then he saw the truck tracks where they turned in the road. He picked up the sandal, stared once again down the valley toward the highway below, and ran as fast as he could for his village.

EIGHTEEN

In the Shadows of Ausangate

In the morning, Jack was up before anyone else, or so he thought. He stepped out of his tent, stretched, and combed his fingers through his hair. He noticed Pedro doing something strange in the grasses about fifty yards away. He was standing in the meadow next to the stream. Every few minutes, Pedro turned both his arms skyward and held his hands above his head for a moment. The morning's first light backlighted him. As Jack walked toward him, he could see a little bird fly off across the stream. When he got closer, Pedro heard him and turned and looked at Jack, smiling. He motioned to Jack to come to him. Once he did, Pedro bent over in the grass and felt around. He stood up with a tiny bird — it looked to Jack a relative of the sparrow — cradled gently in his cupped hands.

Pedro whispered to Jack, "*Frío. Mucho, mucho frío.*" He started blowing warm breath into his hands. The bird's head began moving back and forth. "*De la noche.*"

He breathed on the bird a few more times while holding it close to his chest. Pedro breathed on it once more until it started to struggle, then he lifted his clutched hands above his head and opened them, and the little bird flew off. It landed a few dozen yards away in a sunlit place.

Pedro smiled at Jack and motioned for him to follow. They both bent down and found another bird, curled into a tiny ball in the grass. He nodded his head for Jack to pick it up, and he did. Jack followed the same procedure, and as he clutched the bird close to his body and breathed on it, he could feel it come out of his semi-hibernation or frozen stupor — first moving almost imperceptibly, then gradually a bit more. When Pedro gestured, Jack lifted his arms, opened his hands, and the bird flew off. They found two more frigid sparrows, and it was lovely to see them flitter off into the morning sun and through the steamy columns of fog lifting off the stream.

Jack patted Pedro on the back, and they walked back to the campsite.

Claire awoke early as soon as the sun slanted through the cracks between the mountains. She got up and walked behind the tent to the outhouse. When she returned to the camp, she noticed Jack was already up. Claire looked around and stopped dead in her tracks. There he was, in his little chair with a board across his lap. He was bent over, peering into a small microscope. She loved her friend. Everything he did interested her. She snuck up on him.

"I hear you there," Jack said, not looking up.

"I can't believe you packed a microscope," she said.

He looked up at her with a Cheshire grin. "Look," he told her. He slid another chair close to his. She sat down, and he lifted the piece of wood that made the small worktable, being careful not to upset the microscope. He set it on her lap. She bent down and looked into the eyepiece. It was an insect, unlike anything she had seen. Its body was like a segmented worm — its segments translucent and held together with black bands. It had a strange black head, oversized for its worm-like body with a tuft of odd cotton-like material.

"What is it?" she asked.

"It's a Chironomid. A midge pupa. I seined the stream just now and caught a bunch of these. The adults look like mosquitos, but they don't bite."

"I'm guessing the big part that looks like a head is actually the thorax?"

"Bingo. The whitish tufts? Any guess?" asked Jack.

"Embryonic wings?"

"Nope. Good guess, though. They're gills."

"Really?" She looked back down the eyepiece lens. "I still can't believe you packed a microscope. But it is really cool."

"It's old," Jack said, "made in 1919. It took me a long time to get one like this, one that's not brass, which is too heavy. This one's quite light, but still, I had to eliminate two camera lenses so that my pack wasn't too heavy."

Casey rose from the tent, stretched backward, bent forward, and grasped his ankles, cracked his neck, and ran his fingers through his hair. "I'm not surprised you brought that microscope." He walked over and squeezed Claire's shoulders.

"Morning," she said.

"What'd he find?" Jack gave Claire the time to respond. She thought for a moment and said, "*Chrono ... Chromo ... midge pupae.*"

Alberto came over to look and thought the insect was beautiful. He called Pedro over, who laughed when he saw the bug. "*¿Allí?*" he asked, pointing at the stream.

"Si," Alberto said.

Pedro smiled. "*Gracias.*"

"I doubt any trekkers have offered for Pedro to look into a microscope," Al offered.

After breakfast and when the camp was broken and packed, Alberto gathered everyone around. "This is just the beginning of the trek. Yesterday's hike was just to get us into the mountain valley. Before we start out for 'Camp 2,' we always make an offering to the *Apu*."

"The people who live here," he nodded to Pedro, "believe the Apu mountain spirits also serve as protectors, watching over their surrounding territories and protecting nearby Inca inhabitants as well as their livestock and crops. In times of trouble, the Apus were called upon through offerings. They believe the spirits predated humans in the Andes and that they are constant guardians of those who inhabit this area."

Pedro understood what Al was up to and looked stoic.

"Usually, small offerings such as chicha beer and coca leaves are common. In the old days, in desperate times, the Incas would resort to human sacrifice."

Al reached into a paper bag. "We're short on humans, so we'll offer these coca leaves."

Al asked everyone to take three leaves for the Apu and some for themselves and to hold them in front of their faces. Then he said, first in Quechua, then in English, "*Receive from my hands the coca that comes from the lower valleys, a symbol of the return of water, born of your snow each morning with the sun's warm light and returned each night converted into a river of stars Willcamayu.*"

He made a tiny bed on the ground from everyone's leaves along with some peanuts, candy, lima beans, and a small piece of bread. Then he lit it afire. After it burned down, he finished the offering. "We don't have any chicha." So, he used the next most coveted Peruvian beverage, a bottle of Fanta.

After the offering in English, Al whispered a short prayer in Spanish and finished by making the sign of the cross. Then he winked at Casey and said, "It's good to cover your religious bases."

Pedro wheeled away and led the horses up the valley toward Ausangate, its glaciers now bathed in the brilliant morning sunlight. In single file, the others started walking, and Jack stepped in behind Alberto.

"In your offering," Jack asked, "'the river of stars,' *Will-come-maru* ... is that the Milky Way?"

"Willcamayu," Al said. "You got it, the Milky Way. Did you see it last night?"

"Couldn't miss it," Jack said. "Beautiful. It was as if I might bump my head on it."

"Had you ever seen it that brilliantly?" Al asked.

"I have," replied Jack. "There's this place in Maine, Washington County, and it's very rural. I go fishing there every year, and on some nights — especially in autumn — it seems you can reach up and scoop some of the stars out of the sky."

"On our last day of this trek," Alberto said, "before we hike back to Tinki, we'll be in the tiny village of Pacchanta. There you'll get to interact with some of the local Campesinos. You'll get to observe them. I already trust you not to be — I can't think of the English word — *pushy* and to be respectful."

"Thank you," Jack said. "I've already learned that to be a professional voyeur one needs to be subtle."

"A professional voyeur?" Al asked.

"An anthropologist."

"Makes sense," Al said.

As they started up the valley trail toward the mountain, Jack eased his pace until he was the last in line. He lagged back more, as though he was hiking into the valley for the first time *alone*. He thought about the small ceremony a few minutes earlier. These are spiritual people, he thought, living in a spiritual place. Jack saw the little clouds of dust rising from the trail with every step he took. They were caught by the morning breeze and blown away from the path. He had a strange feeling that they were the dust of the ancient ancestors of the peasants living in the valley. *Perhaps they were preparing to protect us,* he thought, *sent here by the spirits.*

Al caught up to Casey. "This evening, we'll be camped along Lake Pucacocha. I have seen fish caught in that lake. Maybe you and Jack will have some luck."

As he strode away, he continued, "If the Apus are happy with us."

NINETEEN

In Jack's World

A few hours into the second day's hike, the group approached Pas Arapa Apachita; at over 16,000 feet, it was the highest pass they would traverse on this trek. The trail became steeper, and everybody seemed to be acclimatized. Though they were hiking slowly near the top, none complained of headaches. On top of the pass, they stopped for a water break. The 20,945-foot summit of Ausangate loomed in front of the group.

"Man," Casey said, still breathing hard, "it's *right* there!" Jack was arriving but still out of earshot.

"Will he be disappointed about not climbing it on this trip?" Alberto asked.

"No," replied Casey. "Jack's not a 'peak bagger.' He's much more interested in walking into a new country. If the new country is in the mountains, that's great. If it's up high, all the better. I'm the same way. If you ask him, he'll tell you that he's just happy to be here — and in this company."

Casey thought for a moment, then offered, "Jack's love of the mountains isn't about scaling them. It's more of a love of the natural world."

Jack meandered over the final rise to where the others rested. He lowered his pack carefully onto a rock, lest he damage the packed microscope. He sat down next to his backpack and opened his water bottle.

I wonder what else he has in there, Claire mused.

"We were just talking about how much you love being in the mountains," Casey said.

Jack said nothing. He shrugged his shoulders as he drank from the bottle.

Casey went on. "I explained how neither of us are 'peak baggers.'" No one spoke, and there was a moment when it seemed the others were waiting for validation from Jack.

Jack drank again and finally chimed in. "I agree with that. For me, it's more like I have always been drawn to wild places. To exploration —to explorers even."

"Like Tillman and Shipton," Alberto said.

"Yes," Jack said, "and others." He looked to his left, straight up at the summit of Ausangate, so close it seemed you could touch it. "See there," he continued, "that is a magnificent mountain. Is it calling me to climb it? No. Do I feel an urge to 'conquer' it by climbing it? Surely not. But mountains are wild places and always have been. Even these days, it's possible to get up into the mountains and find rock and ice untrodden by humans. And *that* draws me. I love the wild emptiness of the hills."

"Here, here," said Casey. *That was a lot of words for Jack*, he thought.

Alberto smiled and nodded. He liked these three clients very much, and he was enjoying himself and was beginning to feel bad about accepting Casey's money. But he and Marisol needed the money, and making a living in Cusco was a challenge.

Claire watched Jack. With each passing year, she became more aware that she knew no one like him.

To Claire's, Casey's — even Alberto's surprise, Jack kept speaking.

"Take the offering this morning ... I totally get that. From the earliest times, probably in prehistoric times, mountains have been regarded as mysterious. Our ancestors looked upon them with fear and awe. Gods, dragons, devils, the spirits of the damned dwelt on their inaccessible summits ready to wreak vengeance on any daring intruders." He paused. "But we small band of intruders have made an offering. The *Apu* will protect us." He took another swig of water.

"Or not," he said, smiling at Claire.

He rose and put his backpack on, and the others followed his lead.

As they started down the other side of the pass, Claire thought about Jack's words. She felt better knowing he was okay with not attempting the climb on this trip.

Before descending very far from the barren, featureless pass, the hikers could see the landscape behind and in front of them. From high on the pass, it was easy to appreciate that they were circumambulating Ausangate in a counterclockwise loop.

The group worked their way down a switchback trail. They could see quite far down the new valley, but Pedro and the horses were still not in sight. Ausangate was the tallest peak in view, but beautiful, glacier-laden mountains surrounded them in every direction of the compass. It was gorgeous. The thin air was not bothering the hikers. A stunning glacial lake came into view as they rounded one of the switchbacks. It stopped Jack and Casey in their tracks.

"I bet that's less than an hour away," Casey said. Jack nodded. The men picked up their pace.

At the lake, Claire and Alberto were waiting for them. Jack and Case had been alternating, taking up the rear to not push the pace too fast. They both had some experience hiking at altitude. As it turned out, Claire was a beast, setting a faster pace than most would. Perhaps too fast.

The lake was a deep sapphire-blue, in a treeless valley surrounded by blades of golden grass flickering in the taut mountain air. Set deep beneath the towering peaks, the mirror-smooth water reflected the glaciers and the crags above. The treeless shoreline around the lake was more of the spongey, matted vegetation and was fissured in many places by past spring runoffs.

"Hola," Alberto said as the boys walked up. "This is the lake where I've seen fish caught. We've made good time today. We don't *have* to get off this plateau before three-thirty, but if you don't, you'll have to hike down to the camp with your headlamps, so I'd say you'll have a couple of hours to fish if you want to."

Both Casey and Jack were grinning and already opening their fly rod tubes.

"We'll watch for a while and then head down. Pedro asked me this morning if you catch any over fifteen centimeters, please bring them to camp, and he will cook them for us."

They looked as excited as little boys getting ready to go on a fishing trip with their fathers and uncles. Both men rigged their rods.

Like on the stream at the last camp, there was little insect life, and they could find none. They walked along the shore a short way and saw no fish, but that didn't mean they weren't there. The lack of insect life helped the decision-making.

"Streamers," Casey said, staring into the blue lake. "If nothing hits, then chironomids, I guess, but that'd be difficult to fish from shore. With such little forage, they must be largely piscivorous."

Both fishermen inspected their tiny tackle boxes. They each chose small streamer flies that might look like very young rainbow trout. They purposefully chose one dark fly and one light-colored one. They split up and started fishing about fifty yards apart. They did not get too close to the shoreline but first fished the water near the bank. Neither had a bite. They moved farther along the shoreline. Walking gingerly on the spongey ground, Casey stepped closer to the edge. As his foot pressed into the vegetation, something caught his eye: a flash, a streak in the water. *A fish*, he thought. It darted from under the bank to deeper water. He made the quietest whistle and got Jack's attention. He held his hand vertically in front of him and waved it to resemble a fish's tail, motioning it out into the lake. Jack nodded and stared harder into the water. He did not see any fish.

Casey made a few casts in the direction the fish went. Nothing. He tried several different stripping speeds; still nothing. He let his weighted fly sink longer before retrieving, and still nothing. He decided to move along the shore. As he walked into the shadow of one of the many surrounding peaks, he suddenly could see into the shallow water better, and five or six fish were holding about ten feet from shore. Fish always appear smaller in the water, but these looked ten to fifteen inches long. These fish did not dart away. They simply swam slowly into the deep. Casey stepped back out of sight and payed-out some fly line. He crouched over slightly and effortlessly made three false casts, then let the fly hit the water. Casey let it sink for an eight-count. He decided to retrieve the lure with short, interrupted strips so the fly would imitate a small, struggling baitfish. *Trigger a predator response*, he thought.

On the fourth strip of the line, he had the hit. It felt heavy, but he couldn't tell the size. He whistled again for Jack to announce he had a fish on and looked in his direction, and Jack smiled at him from eighty yards away. His rod was also bent.

Casey's fish pulled hard for a small trout. He stripped it in and, having no net, had to hoist it (as Jack called it) onto the grass. It was about ten inches long. It was not fat, but not skinny. It looked to be a nice, healthy rainbow. Its spots were lovely, and the color on its sides was almost non-existent, only the slightest tinge of pink. Casey removed the fly and called out to Jack.

"Keep a few for Pedro?" Both anglers stringently practiced catch and release. Though Jack always said he had no problem occasionally harvesting a fish for a meal, he couldn't remember the last time he killed one, and he hated doing it.

"All right," Jack called back. "Eight, then, if we get 'em."

The water disturbance in the small lake from the first two fish being caught instigated a feeding action. The boys had fish on with every two or three casts. They were in Heaven. All of the trout had the same silvery coloration. Two of Jack's were quite large — over fifteen inches. Too large, he thought, for the pans he had seen Pedro using, so he released them. He kept fish in the seven-to-ten-inch range.

When he had five fish on the bank, Jack called to Casey. "How many do you have?"

"Three," he replied. As he spoke, he had another fish on the line.

"That's eight!" Jack yelled. Casey nodded.

The boys caught and released fish for another hour. Some were very good-sized for their small, three-weight rods. Each took photographs of the other holding some of the bigger fish, with the jagged, glacial peaks looming straight up from the tiny lake. Before they broke down their rods to pack them away, they set the timer on their cameras and posed together, each holding one of the dead fish.

Jack strung the fish through the gills and out the mouths to carry them down to camp. They sat on a big rock next to their packs. Each drank some water as Casey looked at his watch. "Three-thirty," he said, taking his headlamp out of his pack.

"Right." Jack also found his headlamp.

As they drank, they looked at the lake and the tall peaks. Neither one mentioned the incredible beauty of the place. This was what they were both meant to be doing. Casey became strangely melancholic. He and Jack were unique friends — he understood that. The many times he had spent tied to the end of a rope with him had solidified that. All the times he had trusted him with his life and with Claire's life had created a remarkable bond. And right now, at this moment, he was so happy to have shared such a unique fishing experience with him. He suddenly was revisited by an old familiar feeling from his youth, that as an only child, he had always been missing something: the kind of love and loyalty that only siblings can share. And here, finally, he recognized that he and Jack shared that kind of bond.

Jack was staring up at the mountain that shot up from the far side of the lake. Jack always seemed to be thinking, and Casey always let him. But this time, maybe because of the poignant moment they were experiencing, he asked him, "What's on your mind, bro?"

Jack didn't hesitate for a second. He spoke as if finishing the thought, "I was thinking how Rachael would have loved this place."

Casey lowered his head. It had been a mistake to ask. Jack's voice sounded different, quivering almost.

"She was very spiritual. And there's *something* about the Andes. I tell you, I can feel it. I don't know about the Apus, but you can feel the spirits here — everywhere — even in Cusco. It seems like there's magic around every corner. Even in the soil. She just ... she would've liked it."

Casey saw that Jack's head was down. He did not know what to say. All he could do was let him know he was with him. He reached out and gently squeezed his friend's shoulder.

They strapped on their packs, and Casey picked up the fish, and they walked down the trail.

TWENTY

"Put off Thy Shoes"

The hike down from the lake was not strenuous. There was only one trail, so the boys knew they were on the correct route, but the terrain increased again in altitude. They passed three more tiny glacial lakes.

Finally, Casey stopped and looked around. He had been walking in front and wanted Jack's input. "Alberto mentioned more lakes, but it looks like we must have to go over another pass before we drop into camp."

"Si, señor." Jack's state of mind had apparently leveled out. "This is right. If you look at a map of the trek, we're just wheeling around Ausangate, keeping the mountain on our left shoulder."

That's my guy, thought Casey. *Confident and competent, and keeping things simple.*

Another pass, another descent, and another lake, this one bigger and at the far end of the valley. In the waning light, Casey and Jack could make out the campsite in the valley below. They could see next to a winding stream the big, square red-and-green mess tent, the horses, and the four small mountaineering tents.

In an hour, they were walking into camp with thirty minutes of twilight to spare.

Pedro, Alberto, and Claire rose to greet the fishermen. "*Muy buena trucha!*" said Pedro, putting out his hand for the fish. But Jack could see that Pedro was already busy starting supper, so he held the fish back.

"It's okay," Jack said. "I can clean them." Pedro looked perplexed. He was the cook, arriero, and camp cleaner, and that was the order of things. He looked at Alberto.

Al put his hand on the confused Pedro's back and said, "*Dice que está feliz de limpiarlos por ti. Estos no son clientes normales.*"

Pedro nodded twice to Jack, smiling. "*Si. Gracias. Buena pesca,*" and went back to cooking.

Al looked at Jack. "The only things he's used to seeing clients clean are their hands and teeth. I told him you guys aren't our normal trekkers."

"Well, not normal is good, I guess," Casey said. "Thanks for setting up the tents, whoever did it." Alberto held out his hand at Claire, who bowed her head. "She's very strong at altitude. A good hiker." He was not being condescending — only stating a fact

Jack took the fish to the stream, a few yards downstream from the camp. He took the knife of his Leatherman tool and, one-by-one, he made an incision in each fish's belly from the anus to the head. Using his fingers, Jack pulled out the guts, stomach, pancreas, roe, and gills and tossed them into the water. He ran the blade's tip along the spine to cut the clear tissue that covers the bloodline that runs along the spine. He scraped most of the blood away from the backbone and then used his thumbnail to remove the rest of the clotted blood, swishing the flayed-open fish in the icy water. Then he gave them to Pedro.

As he handed the fish over, something caught his eye in the distance, at the very foot of the mountain. "Alberto?" he asked. Al walked to him, and Jack pointed along an escarpment about 1,000 yards away. "More alpacas?" Jack asked.

"*¡Buena fortuna!*" he said. Pedro was bent over a cooler and looked up. "Vicuña," Alberto said. "Seeing them is considered a good omen."

Alberto again went into guide mode. "The camelid family in South America is made up of four animals: the llama, alpaca, vicuña, and guanaco. Most in this area are alpacas. Llamas can be found at lower elevations like in and around Cusco, and the Guanaco can be found farther south in Argentina. The most reclusive are the vicuña. A vicuña scarf can go for tens of thousands of dollars, as it's the softest and warmest of all the wools. They are, as I said, a wary species that don't take well to domestication. Yes, spotting one is good luck."

Claire did not sleep as well as usual. She thought it was because of the

elevation. She rose early and marveled at how beautiful the mountain peak was. She had only seen this vantage in the dim light of yesterday's dusk, but now it was bathed in an intense, bright morning light that shone in colors of vivid yellow, salmon pink, and blood red. It was the same as the alpenglow one sometimes sees in the mountains when the last hour of sunset lights up the peaks in sharp, varying colors while the valleys are still in darkness. Claire looked around the camp, and Jack's microscope was again set up, this time on top of a crate. Then she saw Jack standing a hundred yards from camp, his hands in his jacket pockets. His breathing tossed little clouds of vapor into the air. He was standing in the mountain's shadow, staring at the alpenglow.

When she walked up and stood next to him, he smiled at her but didn't speak. He looked back to the peak. He knew there were only minutes of the light show left, and she remained quiet also.

Finally, he spoke. "Do you remember when we were sitting in the Museum of Fine Arts, looking at paintings by Jean-François Millet?"

"Yes," Claire said, still staring at the mountain light.

"In 1875, when van Gogh entered a room at the Hôtel Drouot and saw Millet's pastels for the first time, he wrote to his brother Theo; *"'I felt something akin to; Put off thy shoes, for thou standest on holy ground.'"*

Claire turned her gaze from the mountain now bathed in orange, black, and yellow to Jack's face as he said, "That's what this feels like to me."

Claire turned back to the mountain and breathed deeply.

Claire put her arm around Jack's waist, and he bent his head sideways onto her brow. And they watched the sun come up. It bathed the rest of the valley with warming light as it rose, but the alpenglow on the glacier was no more.

It was a beautiful moment that Claire knew she would not forget, like so many moments with Jack.

Casey and Alberto were now up and waved to them as they walked back to camp arm in arm.

"van Gogh was such a drama queen," Jack said. She laughed, let go of his arm, and gave him a playful shove.

The group had developed an efficient routine for breaking camp and starting their day. Soon after Pedro again left with Sucio and Perezoso, Alberto spoke with the friends. "Today, we'll hike over our highest pass

— Palomani, a bit under 17,000 feet. Watch your water and speed. Take your time." He looked at Claire and tilted his head toward Casey and Jack. "They've both been higher, but that doesn't mean this time they won't be affected by the altitude. You're doing well. I'll check with you all at the top of the pass, and we'll either take a break there and hydrate or keep moving."

As they left the campsite, nearby herds of alpacas, looking like long-necked sentinels, grazed in the cool morning mist. The pampas grasses seemed taller in this valley, and the vicuñas were nowhere to be seen. All three friends felt acclimatized, but each experienced shortness of breath as they slogged along at the higher elevations. They were far above the grasses and tiny lakes where people had stacked dozens of cairns that made the barren landscape look otherworldly, yet they made good time. Alberto was waiting for them at the top of the pass. They sat and drank water and snacked on fruit.

Al pointed to the southeast, "Those mountains are Mariposa and Caracol." He trained his eyes on the breathtaking mountains. "This is often a good place to spot condors, but I don't see any now."

Casey, Claire, and Jack drank their water, staying silent.

Alberto looked at each traveler. "No headaches?" Each shook their head. "Dizziness?" Again, they each shook their heads.

Al thought for a moment. "Claire, do you still ride horses?"

"Not since high school," she replied.

Then he asked, "Jack, what type of camera film do you shoot?"

Jack squinted into the sun and looked at him. "Kodachrome 64."

Jack knew what Al was doing — he and Casey had done the same before with hikers they had come across — checking for any confusion.

Casey touched Claire on her arm. "You good?"

"I am," she said. Case looked at Jack. He seemed steady as ever.

It was just an exercise. They were all fine. Al was checking because he knew they resided at sea level. Once their breathing slowed and steadied, Alberto asked, "All set then? In an hour, we'll be down lower." They rose to put their packs on, but each stopped to take a few photographs first. Then they moved on.

The lower they went, the better they felt. Once the team had picked their way down the trail to the valley, they continued along a new stream. It was bigger than the streams they had been camping alongside. It was the Jampamayo River. The trail followed the river downstream through the green valley of Finaya Pampa. Finally, they crested a rise and saw a tiny farming hamlet surrounded by many herds of alpaca. The river ran through the center of the small collection of mud and brick buildings.

Alberto turned and said, "This is the village of Jampa. We will camp two more hours beyond it, but if you want to stop and talk to the people or take photos, that is fine. They are very friendly."

Dry rock walls surrounded only a few buildings, and the only people in sight were what appeared to be a man and a boy tending some alpacas far off in the distance. They walked the final two hours to where Pedro was waiting for them.

Jack and Casey decided to fish the river once the tents were set up and the sleeping bags were unrolled. Casey walked up to Claire, who was in her camp chair. She was changing the film in her camera and getting ready to do some journaling.

"You've been wanting to learn," he said, "this would be a great time."

She smiled, clapped shut her journal, and jumped up. Jack was already fishing next to camp. Casey and Claire walked to the riverbank just twenty feet downstream from their friend. Casey explained the workings of a fly rod, how it is mechanically different from a spinning rod. He told her how the line works to cast the lure and showed her some flies in a small box. He explained what the flies imitated and how to tie one onto the end of the leader, which he called the tippet.

"There's nothing to it," he told her, "the rod will do most of the work."

Casey showed her how she needed to get out a certain amount of fly line before starting to cast. He explained that she would have to keep her wrist straight and rigid and that when she extended her forearm, the rod's flex would shoot the line forward. He started with a roll-cast. He knew that she would only have to cast the fly about twenty-five feet to catch a fish in this water. He stood behind her and slightly to her left. He reached around to her front with both hands, with his right hand on hers holding the cork grip and his left hand holding the line where it came off the reel. Then he guided her arm in a slow casting motion. Backward, with the rod tip just past vertical and then down — not quickly, but deliberately, the line shot forward.

"And again," he said to her.

She brought the rod back up to the 'past vertical' position again and then forward.

"Too fast." He whispered in her ear. "That's what everyone does at first. Try this trick; when you bring the rod back to the top, say 'Ausangate' before starting the forward cast."

She did. It worked perfectly. The rod tip flexed, loaded the line, and shot it forward, and it landed farther out onto the water and laid out straight. It looked like one of Casey's casts. Or like Jack's. But when Jack cast a fly, it looked like poetry. She'd heard people say that when she watched him fishing around Boston.

Casey was still standing behind and up against her. She was always sexy, but now, she was fly fishing, making her even sexier. He could feel her butt with his pelvis, and he momentarily forgot about the lesson. He felt himself move a little. He couldn't help it. He looked around for Jack. He had moved upstream, away from them, and Casey could see he had a fish on. A small one.

Casey placed his left arm on Claire's belly, and in the middle of a practice cast, he leaned down and kissed her neck. It tickled, and the line fell into a heap at her feet. She recoiled from the tickle and looked in Jack's direction.

"Case!" she half-whispered. "Not now. It's wide open here..."

"I know," he replied. "But we haven't fooled around on the whole trip."

"I'm sorry. I've been so tired after the hiking, and I think the altitude hasn't helped."

"Yeah, I get it," he said.

"Come to think of it," she fibbed, casting the rod again, "I don't think I've even thought of sex the entire time we've been in Peru. Like I said, sorry."

"No, you're always beautiful, and you shouldn't feel sorry, ever."

Claire grimaced first and then mockingly smiled at him. She needed a shower, and she did *not* feel beautiful. She only felt happy to be where she was. And she had a sense of being very alive. The grimace told Casey she just wanted to fish.

Casey backed away and gave her room to cast on her own. "Try again and slow everything down."

She brought up the rod tip to the top of the backcast, stopped, and said aloud, "Ausangate," then pushed her forearm downward. The line automatically shot through the guides and fell over the water about twenty-five feet from shore. The leader unfurled at the end of the cast, and the little streamer fly gently touched down on the surface. "Perfect!" Casey said.

Claire was loving it. "Why didn't you teach me this earlier?"

"I thought Jack might teach you," he said. "I'm a decent fly fisherman, but Jack is a maestro. It's like the rod is part of him." He looked in Jack's general direction. "He'd be the best to learn from."

"I like that you're teaching me," she said. "Jack will help me later if he wants to."

"I'd have to ask him to," Case said. "I know him. He'll feel that it should be me teaching you, even though I'd love for you to learn from him. You'd be a better angler for it. He's funny about decorum sometimes. I've seen him cling to it, yet he can be a blistering nonconformist if he feels something is wrong or if the mood takes root."

Suddenly Claire shouted, "Oh! I think I have one!" She did. The current caught the line and swung it across the stream, pulling the leader and fly behind it. A trout had followed closely and then slashed at the fly and was hooked.

"What do I do?!" She held the rod, and she grasped the line near the reel in her left hand.

"Run the line under your right index finger," Casey said. She did. "And lightly pinch the line against the rod." She did that.

"Now, without pinching the line too tightly, strip the line with your left hand."

Claire stripped a little too quickly, but the fish was hooked well and did not come off. Once she had stripped the line four or five times, Casey said, "Now lift him up to the bank."

Claire swung the rod tip, and the fish flew out of the water onto the spongy grass.

Alberto had seen what was happening and ran over with Claire's Nikon.

"Your first fish on a fly!" Casey exclaimed.

Alberto said, "May I?" Holding up Claire's camera.

"Of course! Thanks," said Claire.

Alberto wound the film forward, looked to see that it was on an 'automatic' setting. Casey gave Claire the twelve-inch trout, and she held it in front of her waist while he stood next to her, smiling for the camera.

"Let's let him go," Casey said. "He's been out of the water too long already."

Claire kneeled at the water's edge and carefully let the fish go. It did not swim away at first but rather finned in place where she released it until it was resuscitated. Then he slowly swam into the depths. Claire watched him go and then looked upstream for Jack.

He was in the same spot but was now squatting in the pampas grass while he watched her fish. Jack's reel was on the ground in front of him, and the rod leaned against his shoulder. His arms rested on his knees, and his hands were folded in front of them. He unclasped his fingers and gave her two thumbs-up. He was smiling, and his smile told her he was proud of her. Of course, Claire already knew that.

He was always proud of her.

TWENTY-ONE
The Trek

Claire, as usual, was one of the first to rise the following day, but Jack was already up at his makeshift table/, looking into his microscope. She unfolded a camp chair and sat down next to him.

"Good morning, Doctor Pasteur," she said.

Without looking up from the eyepiece, Jack grinned and said, "Bonjour..."

"Now, what are you examining? It's not an insect."

Jack continued to look through the eyepiece and adjusted the focus. "Alpaca dung."

Claire shook her head. "Anything remarkable I should look at?"

Jack sat back in his chair and looked off across the valley. "Nope. But it was worth checking. So, you've got your first fish on a fly rod under your belt. Did you love it?"

"I did," she replied. "Case said I ought to have you help me get better."

"Did he?" He smiled and looked at the ground. Then he looked at her, squinting in the morning's first light.

"What?" she asked

"Your hair."

"What about it?" she brushed her hair back with her fingers to see if it was a tangled mess. "I'm sure it's a sight."

"Yes," said Jack. "It truly is."

It was her turn to squint at him as if to say, *what the hell are you talking about?*

"This early, yellow light, it's almost the same color as your hair, but it's not. The light is blending with it, and, well, it's beautiful." He was

staring at her with an intensity she was unfamiliar with. If anyone else
— *anyone* else — did that, it would creep her out, but she knew Jack's
honesty, and she knew his intensity was genuine. He was, she well knew,
a seeker of beauty and knowledge. Jack continued admiring the light
mixing with her blonde hair.

"Jackson Beal," she was being playful, at a loss for being anything
else, "do you want to touch it?" She smiled mockingly, flicking her
ponytail at him.

He looked away and, with a single, deliberate, slow shake of his head,
said, "Nope."

"No?" she continued to play with him.

He looked back at her, smiled, and said, "No. Because I'm afraid if
I do, I might not be able to stop." She impishly punched his shoulder.

There was the unmistakable sound of a tent flap being unzipped.
Casey stuck his head out and teased them both, pretending to be angry
with his friend. "You want to switch tents with me, Jack?"

Jack craned his neck back in Casey's direction. "We can do that?"
Casey gave him the middle finger, then brushed his hand several times
through his hair and yawned. He got up and headed for the outhouse.
Claire laughed.

Pedro and Alberto walked up the trail from the direction they had
traveled the day before.

"I didn't realize they were already awake," Jack said.

"Good morning," Alberto said. He had binoculars around his neck.
Pedro waved to Jack and Claire.

"Pedro saw some vicuñas this morning," Al said, "but they have
vamoosed. We stopped at one of the campesino's homes that we walked
past yesterday." He turned to Pedro and gestured to him, "*¿Los huevos
todavía están bien?* Pedro reached into his pockets with both hands and
pulled out, three at a time, a dozen eggs.

Alberto rubbed his hands together. "He's going to cook some
Peruvian omelets."

"Al," Jack asked, "*Como se dice en español*, 'May I help with breakfast?'"
Alberto nodded. "*¿Puedo ayudarte a preparar el desayuno?*"

Jack started to sound out the words. He tried three times and almost
had it when he asked Al if he would simply ask Pedro.

"Let's try it together," Al said. It was a chore, but Jack finally said it well enough that Pedro replied, "*Si, si!*" Casey and Claire watched Jack and Pedro communicating with hand gestures. Pedro's two words he knew in English: Fanta and bathroom didn't get in the way of Jack's desire to learn some Spanish. It was no help that Pedro's first language was Quechua, not Spanish.

But they made it work. Pedro was able to communicate that the trick was to cook the omelets over low heat, and that it was tricky to do over a camp stove, *and* that it was better to flip the omelets like a crepe before folding them.

In the end, the breakfast was terrific. The omelets stuffed with cooked potatoes, tomato, mild cheddar cheese, onion, and mild peppers were filling. On the side were avocado wedges and sausages.

After breakfast, Jack insisted on helping Pedro clean up before breaking camp. Before packing, Claire, Alberto, and Casey reclined in their chairs and enjoyed some stout coffee. Al leaned back and sideways in his chair, observing Jack and Pedro washing dishes, putting away cooking gear, trying their best to communicate, and laughing. He turned back in his seat, facing the couple. "Another first for Pedro. I think he's enjoying this trip." Then he changed the subject. "This is an easier day, and it'll be a good day for wildlife watching and photography."

Once on the trail, the group followed a stream down the valley. Within a couple of hours, they were hiking along the shores of yet another glacial lake, Ticllacocha. Jack took up the rear of the group. Hiking deliberately and slowly, his feet were still kicking up the dust of the valley's ancestors. Pedro and the horses, as usual, were quickly out of sight. Eventually, the grade of the trail began to steepen. The terrain became quite rocky, and often, Alberto, who was leading the group, had to stop and kick or pick up rocks that had found their way onto the trail.

Three hours into the hike, they passed a few farm buildings. Again no one was outside —or perhaps they were behind the buildings or rock walls. Claire stopped to take photographs. A short distance past the buildings, the trail became steeper.

"We're approaching *Q'ampa Pass,*" Al shouted. "If you watch along the skyline on either side of the trail, you might spot some *vizcacha* — small animals similar to chinchillas." He caught his breath, then called back once more. "They're actually from the raccoon family!"

Claire looked at Casey proudly. "Trash pandas."

A few hundred feet from the top of the pass, the group stopped for lunch. Each set their packs down and found a rock to sit on while eating sandwiches Pedro had prepared and wrapped in wax paper. There were Peruvian candy bars, dried fruit, and oranges. As they ate, the white peaks looming above them seemed closer and more intimate because of the intense mountain light. Claire took a bite and reached out her hand toward the mountain as if trying to trace the craggy slopes. The closeness and size of the mountains were breathtaking. So was the altitude. They were at nearly 16,000 feet. But they were all acclimatized now, and there were no headaches.

As they rested and looked around them, Alberto pointed to the northwest. "That's Apu Salkantay," he said, "loosely translated, it means, 'savage mountain.'"

Casey was peeling an orange. "I was going to ask you what peak that is. It's beautiful. Have you climbed it, Al?"

"Twice," he replied. "Ausangate is more difficult, I think."

"And does Marisol still climb?"

"No," Alberto said. "I tried a few times to get her into it when we were younger, but she would rather paint a mountain than climb it."

There were no condors, which Jack wanted to see, but as they started over the pass and down to the new valley, they did see another small group of vicuñas far off in the distance. Alberto pointed and said, "Vicuñas! Good omens are showered upon us." And he kept hiking, never breaking stride.

As the team hiked down the trail, the scenery remained the same — spectacular. None of the friends tired of seeing the rolling hills of brown and green dotted by small herds of alpacas or the tiny, phthalo-blue glacial lakes or the steep, white peaks looming from beyond the foothills. They were hiking downhill, lower in altitude, into slightly colder air. The trail eventually leveled out and they were walking down the middle of the valley floor. An hour later, they had almost caught up with Alberto. A few hundred yards ahead, they could see him as he approached the tiny village. Casey looked at the altimeter on his backpack strap: 14,500 feet above sea level.

"That must be Pacchanta," he said. "Saw it on the map this morning. The last stop before getting back to Tinki." This trek had been perfect, and none of them wanted it to end. Though Jack hadn't had the time to try to interact with the Campesinos much, Casey and Claire knew he would have plenty of time for that over the next three weeks while they explored various archaeological sites.

All three looked ahead at the beige and whitewashed cement buildings. This was no tiny hamlet; there was infrastructure. Most of the buildings were two stories, appointed with brightly colored doors and window frames. Casey counted at least thirteen houses. As they approached the town, they found Alberto waiting for them. He was leaning back against a rock wall with his pack still on.

"Welcome," Al said. "We'll take a break here. It is a special place. Let's go to a spot up the road, and we can make a plan for the day."

In Pacchanta, locals were visible everywhere. They smiled and waved as the small group walked by.

"Do they all know you, or are they just happy to see us?" asked Claire.

"They know I'm from Cusco," replied Al waving to a man pulling four alpacas, "and they are very used to travelers and trekking groups. There's Pedro."

They had walked through the town in less than a minute, where Pedro was sitting on a plastic chair drinking a Fanta. Sucio and Perezoso grazed nearby. Their cargo had been unloaded, and both horses were tied to large boulders with a long, thin string — a reminder not to wander too far.

Here the pampas grass was taller and the valley greener. Like seemingly every tiny village in the Andes, a stream flowed next to the town. About fifty yards from Pedro, there were two cement-lined hot springs.

Al looked around the village. "I think it would be fun to rest here, take some photos and maybe walk around the hills, then catch the taxi to Tinki."

Casey turned to Alberto, "Sounds good." Claire and Jack agreed.

"It's noon now," Al continued, "so I'll arrange a taxi for about three o'clock. We can eat lunch first, and then I'll introduce anyone who wants to meet my weaver friend."

Alberto turned to Pedro. "*Van a tomar el taxi desde aquí, amigo mío. Podemos descargar su equipo.*"

Pedro nodded once and jumped up from the plastic chair. "*Sí, sí ... está bien.*" He began organizing each traveler's bags.

"He's checking to make sure nothing of yours got mixed in with his gear," Al said.

Jack picked up the small plastic bag of dirty clothes belonging to the three friends. "I have room," he said and stuffed it into the bottom compartment of his pack. The others packed the rest of their gear, and Pedro re-packed the horses. Once finished, Claire, Jack, and Casey simultaneously turned to say goodbye to him.

Casey whispered to Al, "May we tip him?"

"Of course. That would be nice for Pedro. He's a good man. But he knows you and Claire are a couple, and he won't want to accept any from Claire."

Claire heard what Al said.

Casey walked up to Pedro, but Jack intercepted him and added a wrinkled twenty-dollar bill to Casey's hand. That made it sixty dollars U.S. He shook Pedro's hand, who thanked him and tried to discreetly place the bills in his pants pocket. He smiled broadly, saying, "¡Gracias Gracias!" Jack gave him a slight, brotherly hug and then shook his hand and said, "Thank you for the birds." To which Pedro simply said in halting English, "Good."

Then Claire jumped forward, opened her arms, and said, "Will he accept *this*?" And she gave him a big hug goodbye.

Pedro, embarrassed, waved his hand at all three and said in poor English but with a charming genuineness, "Good people." Then he shook Alberto's hand, pulled himself up into the saddle, and said to him, "*Hasta el próximo viaje.*" And rode off with a wave, pulling Perezoso behind him.

Al turned to Casey. "You gave him sixty dollars?"

Casey nodded. Alberto reached down and snaked his arms through his pack straps. He bent his knees and almost jumped, lifting his body, trying to let the pack settle down onto his hips. The others did the same.

"That's kind of you," Al said, "he can feed his family for two months with that."

"We can stash our packs at the hostel. It is also a restaurant. Believe it or not, they make a pretty good pizza."

"I'm in," Jack said.

Three backpacks were leaning against the wall outside the restaurant door. Claire, Jack, and Casey leaned theirs on the opposite side of the doorway. So did Al.

The room was lit only by two bare bulbs, powered by the village's generator. It took some time for their eyes to adjust. All four waved to the three trekkers — like themselves, two men and a woman about the same age — who were sitting at a small table in the center of the room.

"*Hallo!*" they all said.

They were definitely European, Czech, maybe? Polish?

"Hi," Claire and Jack said. Claire jumped in with both feet and sat down at the table next to them. "Are you all Czech?"

"Oh! No!" they were pretty demonstrative and giggled at the end of their response. "We are from Poland."

Casey leaned in and nudged Jack, whispering, "Trekking Poles."

Jack tried not to smile in case the hikers overhead him but failed.

Alberto returned and leaned in between Claire and Casey. "I know you're not picky, but they will put all manner of things on a pizza here if you let them. Even potato. So, if you're okay with it, I'll get two big pies to share with something close to pepperoni."

"Perfect," they all said at once.

Al ordered the pizzas at the counter and asked that they try to send word for a taxi. Then he sat down with his group.

"Alberto," Claire said, "this is Antoni, Jan, and Maja — from Poland."

Al shook hands with the men but gave Maja a brief hug. While they waited for the pizza and for the Poles to finish theirs, Claire asked, are you starting a trek or finishing?"

"No," said Jan, who seemed to be the leader. "We just climbed Ausangate the day before yesterday."

Jack and Casey spun around in their chairs. "How was it?" they both asked at once.

Jan's English was perfect. "It was epic. We had good weather, and the snow was very good. Very stable. It was an excellent climb."

"That's good," said Casey. "Did you use the Normal Route?"

Jan shook his head. "No, the Shield Route. It looked a little more fun, with some nicer snow and an ice wall."

"I could see that route from the valley," Casey said.

"You are climbers also?" Jan asked.

Claire spoke up. Pointing at Al, Casey, and Jack. "*They* are." All the Poles nodded in acknowledgment and a shared affection for climbing.

"Where are you next?" Al asked the group.

"We are going to see the Machu Picchu," said Jan, "and then to the Cordillera Blanca."

"Beautiful," replied Alberto, "another climb?"

"Yes, Alpamayo."

Alberto stared at Jan without blinking. "You are all very good on ice then?"

"Yes … good enough, I think," said Jan, smiling. He knew all about the nearly vertical 450-meter ice wall. "We have been training for the last two years just for Alpamayo. Ausangate was a warm-up because we want to experience Machu Picchu, and it is close by."

Alberto nodded. He looked at Casey and Jack. "Are you familiar with Alpamayo?" Both men shook their heads. "It is the most beautiful mountain in this hemisphere, in the most beautiful range."

Jan and his compadres agreed. "It truly is."

The pizzas came, and Al was right — it wasn't bad, but the sausage slices on it were unidentifiable. Al guessed Llama, maybe alpaca. After the pizzas and several Crystal beers, the groups separated.

"So, maybe we see you in Cusco or Ollantaytambo?" offered Jan.

"We hope so," Claire said. Antoni's and Maja's English was not as good as Jan's, but they all said goodbyes and shook hands.

When Al, Claire, Casey, and Jack left the hostel, they made plans to meet back for the taxi at three o'clock.

Casey wanted to walk upstream from the village and try for a few trout, and Claire wanted to wander around and take some photographs. "Jack," said Alberto, pointing, "you're with me." Jack took his journal, a pencil, and a camera out of his bag.

Jack followed Al around to the back of the hostel and up a short slope to a yellow, two-story building with a bright green door. He knocked on the door, and a little boy with a runny nose opened it. "*Buenas tardes, ¿está tu madre en casa?*"

"*Si.*" said the boy, "*Ella esta en la parte de atras. Puedes caminar.*"

"She's around back," Al translated for Jack, and with a wave to follow, they walked around the building. A woman was weaving, and except for a different hat, she looked exactly like the woman Jack had seen in Tinki almost a week ago. She was sitting on a woven blanket on the ground working at her loom, and she was leaning back on a strap around her waist, just as her ancestors had done for centuries.

"This is Maria," Alberto said. "She is a very good weaver. She is considered an artist."

"Buenas tardes," Jack said. Maria smiled at Jack and whispered "Buenas tardes."

Alberto told Maria that Jack was a student in the United States and interested in her textiles and techniques. Al knew if he suggested that Jack was interested in her life, culture, or customs, then Maria might be more receptive to his questions.

"*Si, si,*" Maria said. She continued to deftly work the colorful fabric on her rudimentary but incredibly efficient loom.

Alberto started to educate. He had been thinking on the trail about what he wanted to teach Jack, whom he had come to like and admire.

"Weaving is so much more than a commercial activity. It is a reflection of Andean and Amazonian communities and is a way for the world to understand them," he said. Al gestured with both hands at the loom. "This activity shows their understanding of nature, its uses, their ways of living, and their rituals. It is a knowledge that is passed on from generation to generation, and that knowledge doesn't limit itself to the art of weaving. It is also about learning the different techniques used and the exotic plants to dye the wool. Wool that is obtained from the alpacas that live here."

Al watched Maria work with incredible speed and precision. "The people who live here mainly make a living from agriculture and alpaca breeding. Women like Maria take the wool harvested by the men and boys to weave rugs and tunics. Before it is spun, the wool is dyed with natural colorants, including one that is present in the cochineal insect. Are you familiar with that insect?"

"No," Jack said, "but with that name, I'm guessing it has big ears — or crawls into people's ears?"

"I don't think so," Al said. "Its name comes from the Latin '*coccinus,*' meaning scarlet-colored. But it's an interesting bug. It's a scale bug that lives on plants, sucking the moisture and nutrients out of it."

"Like aphids?" Jack asked.

"But much bigger. In Peru, they are scraped off plants, mostly the prickly pear cactus, and then dried and crushed to a powder. It sounds simple, but it's quite a process."

"Interesting," Jack said, fingering a piece of red alpaca wool. "I remember the Irish monks who preserved literature during the Dark Ages used inks made from crushed insects to color and illustrate copies of precious manuscripts and books, like the Book of Kells."

Jack wrote something in his journal, then spoke to Maria with his best horrible accent, which was getting better thanks to some help Pedro had given him; "¿Puedo tomar tu fotografía?" Maria smiled at him and nodded.

"She only speaks a little Spanish," Alberto said. "Her first language is Quechua, and I speak it well enough to communicate."

Jack took a half-dozen photographs.

Al continued teaching. "For Quechua people, the act of weaving is both social and communal. She's working alone right now, obviously, but sometimes the entire extended family gathers outside as the looms are set up, the weavings uncovered, and work begins. For many hours during the dry season, the family members weave, joke, and talk while also keeping an eye on children and animals. The young girls start out making belts and rope and then graduate to more intricate and larger textiles. Eventually, they master the difficult task of leaning back with exactly the right tension to create straight rows and even edges. These Quechua women place the stories of their lives into textiles, communicating and preserving important cultural traditions. The textiles, and through verbal stories, are how their memories are most vividly remembered. Textiles are very important in their culture. Infants are swaddled in the softest alpaca blankets, and the weavings are used for every piece of clothing throughout life. When death comes, Quechua people wrap their loved ones for burial in their finest cloth, the conclusion of a life with a connection to textiles. Even the rope used to keep the burial shrouds closed is made of alpaca fibers."

"What is the tool she's using to push and pull the fabric in the weaving?" Jack asked.

Alberto asked Maria in Quechua, but they responded to each other in a mix of Spanish and Quechua. "Wichuna." Maria pointed to her shin.

"It's made from a llama's leg bone," Al said.

Jack and Alberto watched Maria weave for a while. *She is an artist*, thought Jack. After some time, he asked Al to thank her for her time.

Alberto did. "I'll ask her if there is anything else she would like you to know. Maybe we can get a little cultural insight."

He asked her, and she surprised him. She spoke to Al, who looked genuinely touched.

"She wanted you to know that here, because of Ausangate, we all exist. Thanks to Ausangate, there are plenty of animals and food. We give him offerings, and he gives us everything in return."

"Wow," Jack said, as he wrote feverishly in his journal.

"Yeah," Al said. "Wow."

The taxi was on time, and the ride to Tinki was uneventful. The afternoon sun poured through the van's windows, and though the friends tried to take in the scenery, they soon all became sleepy. Claire felt sad about leaving the mountains and the valleys behind. But she looked forward to a shower and a bed.

Two days later, in Cusco, there were a few days of relaxing, shopping, and sightseeing. Alberto spent time with Marisol, and Eliana had returned to Lima. Claire and Casey walked the city streets, but Jack did so alone. They planned to meet for an early supper on the third day and decide where their adventure would take them. Alberto had recommended a restaurant within walking distance of the hotel, and Marisol accompanied him there.

The Inkazuela was in an old colonial building that had been constructed on top of a foundation of polished Incan ruins like so many structures in Cusco. Its saffron-colored walls, fireplaces, soft lighting, and simple furniture gave it an air of understated elegance.

Al and Marisol were already seated when the friends arrived. There were hugs and kisses all around. "Everyone rested?"

"Yes," Claire said.

"And acclimatized nicely after that trek," Casey offered. "Thank you again for that."

"It was my pleasure. You guys are a joy to hike with."

Marisol spoke up. "Alberto seems to have enjoyed that trip very much. I'm glad you liked it also. Ausangate is a magical place. Did you feel it?"

All agreed they had. Claire leaned forward to Marisol. "None of us will ever forget it." Marisol smiled broadly.

Alberto leaned close to Jack, who had sat down next to him, "Speaking of beautiful, I saw Maria two days ago as she was taking Eliana to the airport. I think she hoped you would call her. I wondered if she might be here tonight."

"Oh…" Jack said, not sure what to say. Then he whispered into Al's ear, "*I'm afraid my heart belongs to another.*"

"So sorry," replied Al discreetly, "I did not know. To me, you seemed to be, I don't know, unattached."

Jack whispered again as the others at the table conversed separately, "No worries. *I* am free, but my heart is not." He reached behind the chair and patted Al on the back to reassure him that he was okay. Alberto knew it was time to drop the inquiry. He hadn't known about Rachael, but he could sense Jack's life was more complicated than it appeared.

Claire spoke up to the group at the perfect time. "Al, don't you think it's time Jack and Case tried *cuy*?"

Alberto smiled. "Ah! Yes, it is time! I recommend a Chilean merlot with it."

"What is *kwee*?" Jack asked.

"Guinea pig," Claire said, and she showed him on the menu.

"I've seen that written but didn't know what 'cuy' meant." Jack was unfazed. "I'm game."

"I'll try it," Casey said, who almost always ate chicken because he genuinely preferred it over anything else.

"Both Casey and Jack?" Alberto asked. He pointed his menu at Claire. "And you also?"

Claire, studying the menu, shook her head. "I have my eye on something else."

Alberto looked at Casey and Jack again. "Fried or roasted?" Both thought roasted sounded better. "Then would you like me to order for you?"

"Sure," they both said. And they agreed on a local IPA to go with it.

When the meals came, Casey stared for a minute at his plate. Yup —

there was a hairless, roasted guinea pig, complete with head, ears, teeth, and toenails still intact. It came with potatoes and salsa on the side, and Jack was still unfazed.

Alberto said, "Salud," and everyone lifted their glasses. When Casey picked up his fork to try the cuy, Al said, "No, no … no fork. That's why your server brought you both extra napkins."

Casey pulled on a piece of meat along the spine, and it separated easily. He looked at it and popped it into his mouth. He then looked at his best friend, already chewing and smiling. Between chews, Jack said, "Kind of a cross between rabbit and turkey. Not too shabby." The salsa that came with it was delicious. *Salsa criolla*, Alberto had called it.

Al asked Casey and Jack if they had tried chicha beer yet.

"Not yet," replied Jack, but Maria and Eliana told me about it. Casey shook his head as he gnawed on a tiny leg. He was still thinking over the guinea pig thing. Jack liked it, but it wasn't much of a stretch for him. He grew up in Maine hunting small game and was used to eating rabbits, partridge, and deer. Once, when he and his brother Wade shot a squirrel, their father made them clean, cook, and eat it. It wasn't horrible, but they didn't shoot any more of the rodents.

Casey asked Alberto about the chicha.

"It is not technically beer, but people call it that," Alberto said. "If it is made traditionally, like in the old days, the corn is chewed and moistened in the brewer's mouth. The enzymes in the saliva activate the starches, which then break down into fermentable sugars. The beer is ultimately boiled, which leaves it sterile and germ-free. Usually, these days, they add strawberries. The berries give the brew a lovely purplish-pink hue making it look deceptively pretty and innocent for a beer with someone's spit in it. It smells like pure strawberries, and the taste is surprisingly refreshing, dry, and a bit spicy. And the flavors become more complex as the beer warms up to room temperature."

"If you try some," Al said, "remember to go lightly. It can knock your socks off." Al thought for a moment and said, "I remember guiding a group down the Inca Trail a few years back. One of the guys — a photographer — did not drink enough water each day, and I had to keep on him. We stopped in the village of Pisac to go to the big open market they have there every Saturday and Sunday. We had hiked a long way that day, and when we got there, everyone in the group separated to shop for souvenirs. After a few minutes, I spotted him sitting on a bench from across the plaza. He had been dehydrated, and he was drinking a big tumbler of chicha. Before I could get to him, he saw something to photograph, stood up, and placed his camera to his face. I couldn't get to him in time to catch him. He passed out and fell forward. He never even lowered his camera. He smashed the ground, shattered his camera lens, and broke his nose. He had an awful cut across the bridge of his nose."

Al paused in remembrance and said to the friends — grinning, but in a serious voice, "Respect the chicha."

The meals were enjoyed, the three friends got to know Marisol better, and plans were made for the next two weeks. It was decided they would, as initially planned, depart the next day for Ollantaytambo and use that town as their base for the remainder of the trip. Marisol would accompany them to Ollanta to visit friends who owned a hostel. Alberto would introduce them to some of his contacts there.

"Knowing you as I do now," Al said, "I think you would like very much to talk to my friends in Ollanta…one of them is a teacher who is a local historian and is very learned about the Inca. In fact, he is working with an American archaeologist attempting to decipher the Incan quipu. Do you know of the quipu?"

"A bit," Claire said. "We've talked about them."

"The other guy I want you to meet is the elder I have told you about. He has spent a lot of time in the backcountry in the highlands on the side of Ollantaytambo, where no tourists go. He has seen villages the government doesn't even know about. From an anthropologic or exploratory point of view, I don't know…it could be interesting."

Claire, Jack, and Casey were visibly excited at the prospects before them. This was shaping up to be a true adventure. There were blind corners ahead.

On the way back to the hotel, everyone felt good. Jack walked on the narrow sidewalk behind Claire and Casey, who were holding hands. Claire's blonde ponytail was glowing from the incandescent streetlamps that also lit the smooth, polished, two-ton Incan stones that lined the footpath. She walked with a certain beauty. She always did. Casey had lost a few pounds on the trek and strode like the natural athlete he was. They made an attractive couple.

"Guys," Jack said. "I'm going to stroll around the plaza to walk-off supper. I'll see you bright and early."

"Remember," Casey responded, "the van will be there at nine o'clock. We'll be packed and having breakfast at eight."

Jack gave them two thumbs-up and walked into the night, in the opposite direction of the hotel. Claire and Casey watched him go, and they saw him stop and face an ancient Incan wall. He rubbed his left hand over the stones and felt the tiny cracks.

TWENTY-TWO
The Urubamba

The van ride from Cuzco to Ollantaytambo was like all others they'd taken in Peru; exciting and sensual, full of sights and smells and wonder. The outskirts of Cusco were some of the poorest sections of the city. The farther out of town, the more agricultural the landscape became with brown, rolling hills for miles. As they drove slowly around some of the road's sharp corners, Jack got good glimpses of the farmers. They had the same bent backs and sad faces worn by the wind and sun as the farmers he saw in the Midwest of the U.S. and in the potato fields of Aroostook County, Maine.

An hour and a half from Cusco, the van stopped in the dirty, depressed town of Urubamba, only a half-hour from Ollantaytambo. For the last part of the ride, the terrain changed dramatically. Ollanta's elevation is 2,000 feet lower than Cusco. Claire pointed out the roiling, brown Urubamba River. This valley was much more beautiful than the land around Cusco, which sits in an enormous amphitheater surrounded by small mountains. Here, the land was green and fertile-looking, and there were trees — tall trees and beautiful plants and wildflowers.

"Are those eucalyptus?" Jack asked.

"They are," Alberto said. "They were brought here from Australia in the first half of the twentieth century. You probably saw some in and around Cusco."

Jack nodded. "They're pretty."

"This is my favorite Peruvian town," Alberto said. "You three, I think, will like it. It has an interesting history." The friends were all ears as the van bumped along.

"Around the mid-15th century," continued Al, "the Inca emperor

Pachacuti conquered and razed Ollantaytambo. The town and the nearby region were incorporated into his personal estate. He rebuilt the town with great, ambitious construction projects and filled the valley with gardens and farms. He built terraces and irrigation systems all up and down the Urubamba Valley. The town provided lodging for the Inca nobility, and the terraces on the steep hillsides were farmed by *yanakuna*, the emperor's retainers. A hundred years later, during the Spanish conquest, the last Incan leader standing was Manco Inca, who was a puppet leader installed by the Pizarro brothers. But he was so mistreated he escaped and started a rebellion. The Inca laid siege to Cusco. After almost a year, Manco retreated to Ollantaytambo."

Alberto pointed to the steep hills farther up the road. "The fortresses they built here offered Manco good protection, and he had the high ground, as you will see, and plenty of food and resources. In 1536, Pizarro sent an expedition to Ollanta to kill or capture Manco, but he defeated the Spaniards in one of the only campaigns when the Incas won the day. But Manco didn't think he could defend the city indefinitely and fled the valley to a more forested site called Vilcabamba — sometimes called the Lost City of the Incas."

"Did he live in hiding?" Casey asked.

"For a while. Three years after the battle at Ollanta, the Spaniards captured Manco's sister-bride, Cura Ocllo — his queen, and brutally murdered her. Legend has it that she effectively resisted being raped, so they tied her to a stake and shot arrows into her until she died. Manco led a guerilla war in the cloud forests near Vilcabamba, but that's when things get a little confusing. There were rivals within the Incan *and* the Conquistador ranks. Some Incas were loyal to Manco, some to Pizarro, some to his Spaniard archenemies. Eventually, factions of one group murdered Manco in the fortress city of Vitcos, about a four-day hike from Machu Picchu. Then, all the guys that killed Manco were quickly killed by another faction. It must have been a confusing time."

"And dangerous," Claire said.

Alberto nodded. "Indeed. And now we have a Maoist death cult roaming the countryside bent on starting a world revolution. It never ends."

Casey nudged Claire and pointed out the window. "I didn't notice on the map the elevation of Ollanta," he said, "but it's got to be lower. You can tell by all the fruit trees and wild roses growing everywhere."

The van eased around a switchback as it dropped into the village. Ollantaytambo was much smaller than Cusco. There were about 350,000 people living in Cusco, only about 8,000 in and around Ollanta. The driver rattled the stick shift, ground into first gear, drove to the far end of the square and took a right toward the river. This *was* an interesting town; the streets were paved entirely with well-worn cobblestone, and the Incan stonework was more prevalent and impressive than even in the oldest parts of Cusco.

Most of the streets were narrow alleyways. The larger *avenidas* were often divided down the middle by a stone-lined ditch that resembled a millrace. At one end of each road, a trough with bubbling water feeding it from underground, like an artesian well. Patacancha Stream tumbled down from one of the steep hills and rolled through town. Its current stayed steady despite so much of its water being siphoned off into dozens of irrigation ditches or canals.

As the van picked its way to Alberto's friend's hostel, children of all ages skipped by and smiled, waving enthusiastically at the passengers but asking for nothing.

The driver worked his way to the edge of town, where the van lurched to a halt in front of a long, brown adobe wall about six feet tall, punctuated by a single green door. Its hinges were made of thick leather straps nailed to the door and frame. Alberto jumped out onto the narrow lane and stretched his legs. After unloading the last backpack, Jack joined the others admiring the scenery. Homes lined the lane on the same side of the hostel, each overlooking the Urubamba River valley on the opposite side of the road. The valley extended between the mountains as far as they could see, and it was green, lush, and scattered with groves of tall trees and cultivated fields, The river was lined with beautiful terraces, and it went on for miles. Paralleling the lane for its entire length was one of the canals, but here it was six or seven feet wide and looked big enough to hold trout. Directly across from the green door in the adobe wall was a little bridge that crossed the canal, and on the valley side of the bridge was a flower garden with outdoor furniture, including four tables and reclining chairs. Rhododendrons, roses, and salvias surrounded the garden. The flowers and the rose bushes made a border between the garden and adjoining acres of silvery-green cornstalks.

In the canal, thirty yards downstream, teenage girls were washing their hair. Each tossed down their shiny black hair and gently scrubbed it with soap. They took turns bending over the stream while their companions poured water over their heads to rinse their scalps.

Jack stood next to Claire and Casey and said, "Shangri la, much?"

The van drove off, and Alberto, standing next to them, said, "Let's dump our packs in the rooms and have a light lunch. Then we'll show you around town."

Inside was an inviting courtyard surrounded by a second-floor balcony. The courtyard was similar to the one at the Royal Inka Hotel but more artistic and rustic.

Immediately all three friends felt connected to the hostel. Jack walked into the courtyard and looked up at the simple balcony adorned with hand-painted tiles and the curly wooden railings. He took it all in and said, "*This* is my kind of place."

A pretty young woman in a black t-shirt came out of the kitchen and said "Hola!" to Alberto and Marisol. They each embraced her, and Marisol kissed her cheeks.

Alberto turned to the three travelers. "This is Benita. She and her parents own this place." They all shook hands. "Welcome," she said in perfect English. "You five will be the only guests for the next week. Think of this as your home."

"Your English is excellent," Claire said, "almost no accent."

"Benita was a foreign exchange student for a year in Frederick, Maryland," said Alberto.

"That's right," Benita said. "Alberto helped set that up for me." She looked at Marisol; "Mama said you'd be here about now, so I've prepared some lunch. Can you all choose the rooms you want while I finish up?"

"Oh, that's very kind of you," Marisol said. "Of course, we'll show them the way."

Al and Marisol led the way up the stairs in the opposite corner of the courtyard from the kitchen. Small bedroom doors lined the balcony, and each was ajar enough that the group could peer in. Al and Marisol knew the place well and offered to take the first double. "The next two are the best rooms," Marisol said, "and there is a single at the far end."

"That'll be me," Jack said, squeezing by the two couples.

The others smiled at him, and Marisol offered, "From what Alberto tells me about you, I think you'll like the room." Jack smiled at her and tossed his head back. He could hear Al say, "Come down to lunch when you're ready."

Marisol had been correct; it *was* Jack's sort of room: there was a single bed, a tiny dresser, framed maps, and shadow boxes with insects and butterflies on the walls, and opposite the balcony door were French doors cracked open to let in the fresh air. They were held from swinging open by a small loop of cord made of alpaca fibers. He smiled at the thought that he could now distinguish between a llama and alpaca wool.

Jack plunked his pack onto the bed, opened the French doors, and stepped out onto a little iron balcony that hung over the most exquisite garden. It had a chair and a small end table big enough to set a book and a beverage. Looking easterly beyond the garden, he saw the massive ruins on the steep hill at the edge of town. *They're very close*, he noted. The balcony was only big enough for one person to recline. There was a window-box the entire length of the balcony's railing filled with red geraniums and tiny white and yellow impatiens. Jack looked into the garden below. *Marisol wasn't kidding*, he thought. *I love it.*

Jack unpacked a few things, changed his shirt, took his journal and camera, and went downstairs. He was the last one down. He sat next to Marisol. "You were right. It's a perfect room for me."

"I can't wait to explore this town," Casey said.

"After lunch," Alberto recommended, "let's take a stroll, relax and get the vibe of Ollanta. It definitely has a vibe, and Marisol says it has magic."

"It does. You'll see," Marisol replied.

She seemed to be looking directly at Claire, who said, "I love it here already."

Benita brought out rice and corn, fruit, and some small pieces of chicken that had been pounded flat and fried with salt, pepper, and garlic. The roasted potatoes were purple. Everyone made room on the little table for their plates, and Al made Benita get herself a plate and join them.

"I guess I might as well just say it," Jack said. "I'm staying. Here, in Ollanta. I'm never leaving."

"Harvard grad-school is a not correspondence program." Casey said, "It'll be hard to defend your thesis from here."

"You're no fun," Jack said. "It is a great place, though. I can feel it."

"That's the magic," Marisol suggested.

Claire breathed in. "I can't tell if it's the eucalyptus or the fruit trees I'm smelling, but I like it."

Jack leaned back and breathed deeply. He could smell the eucalyptus mixed with the freshly turned soil in the fields. He had been joking with Casey about staying in Ollanta, but he felt better at that moment than he had since his days with Rachael in Wyoming. He felt lighter. *I could be happy here*, he thought.

After a day of walking throughout the town and an evening stroll up the 200 carved stone steps through the ruins on the hill to the Temple of the Sun, the group separated and found their suppers. Alberto and Marisol were off to visit friends who lived in town, and Casey and Claire discovered a fine restaurant on the city's north side. At the same time, Jack found a small café near the hostel where, from an outside table, he could watch the comings-and-goings of locals and tourists as they crossed an old wooden bridge that spanned the Patacancha where it tumbled through downtown on its way to the Urubamba. Across the street, two buskers were playing a soulful rendition of Simon & Garfunkel's *El Condor Pasa* on zamponas — Andean pan flutes. He washed down his veggie burger with three Crystal beers and jotted in his journal:

A woman named Carla approached me in the ruins, high on the hill. I think she may have been an off-duty tour guide who was bored. She reiterated something Al had said about the city — that the temples and storehouses on the mountains had been built by a civilization before the Incas ... perhaps a greater civilization. Their temples, residences, and storehouses made of massive stones were later incorporated into Incan cities. Were they Chavín? Moche? No one knows. If only they had had a written language. Maybe someday someone will figure out how to read the quipus, and they will tell us. Then again, perhaps all they'll say will be things like, "Pisac was taxed two houses of grain but gave up only one ... do I kill the Headman?"

I love this place.

After supper, he wandered around town and took photographs. In the narrow labyrinth of stone-lined alleys, he found myriad subjects to shoot; ragamuffin children running and playing in the streets, extremely aged, toothless people who might've been only sixty, scores of busy little guinea pigs scurrying around the dirt floors just inside the open doors of all of the tiny homes he passed, and the ruins on the hills that seem to loom over the town wherever one went.

At dusk, exhausted, he finally found his way back to the hostel. Benita was sitting in the courtyard, reading. Each smiled and waved, and Jack thought about going to her to make conversation, but he was too tired. In his room, he placed his camera and fanny pack on the dresser. He felt obliged to open the French doors and gazed out onto the garden one last time for the evening, then plopped down onto the bed. He put on his headlamp and opened a paperback by Jim Harrison.

Claire and Casey could hear him moving around through the thin wall that separated their rooms. Casey was puttering, organizing his pack. He looked at Claire on the bed. Having just showered, she was wearing only her black panties and bra. She laid on her back on top of the bedding with her left forearm resting on her forehead. *Jesus* thought Casey. Her right hand was rubbing her normally flat tummy, which now revealed the musculature of her abdomen. After all the trekking, she had a six-pack.

"I think I've lost weight," she said.

Casey climbed onto the bed and laid on his side next to her. He placed his hand on her belly and lightly touched it, his fingers going top to bottom, stopping at the top of her panties.

"You look beautiful," he said. Claire smiled and tilted her head back, and closed her eyes.

Casey's fingers made broader strokes, feeling the lines of her muscles and cupping her hip bones. He felt her thighs. They felt stronger, more toned. He leaned down and kissed her neck, and she flinched. It felt good, but she hesitated. His hand slid to the inside of her thigh, and her right hand grasped his wrist. He looked at her, and she opened her eyes.

"I wouldn't want Jack to hear."

"Seriously?" Casey asked. He was hard as a rock.

"These walls are paper-thin," she said.

"Really," Casey said, "at some point, we actually have to make love." She was looking at him strangely. He spoke again, with less conviction, "Right?"

I think it would be hard for him to hear something," Claire said. "I worry about him — he seems so lonely sometimes."

Casey rolled over onto his back. "Honey, you know he's smart, right?"

She nodded.

"And handsome…"

"He is," she said.

"And interesting?"

"Yes."

"And funny?"

"Yes," she said, "he's all of those things."

"Then you agree he could probably have any girl he wanted?"

"I suppose. If the girl is interested."

"My point is," he continued, "since Rachael, I think he's choosing to be alone. Look at Maria. She would be a "10" in any country (Claire hated that talk); gorgeous, smart, elegant, and she was clearly interested in him. But not Jack. He's the one guy who wouldn't exploit her. He's bigger than that. He's *better* than that."

"Well, I think he's struggling," said Claire. "I think he'd like to find someone to love again, and as his best friend, I think it's your job to try to talk to him about it, to help him air it out."

Casey shook his head. "I love you, but you don't understand — I mean, you do, but you don't understand *us* — Jack and me. See, we connect on a different plane than most blokes. If he wanted to air things out, then I'm the one he would talk to. But he won't. I let him live his life the way he wants. I don't put any pressure on him. If he needed me, I'd climb any mountain, cross any desert for him. But if he doesn't ask, then *as* his best friend, it's my job to let him be."

Claire shook her head at him but tried to understand. She heard him, understood the words, but she was a woman. She loved Jack also and wanted to help him, maybe even nurture him, though she couldn't visualize someone keeping up with him long enough to nurture him. A nurse, perhaps, if he was ill or injured. *Jack is more of an artist,* she thought, *meant to be left on his own, learning life through nature, history, and experiences. But Casey's wrong.*

She sensed Casey's frustration. She pushed herself toward the foot of the bed so that her face was level with his hips. She slid her hand up his thigh and touched him.

"You *must* be quiet," she whispered as he combed his fingers through her hair.

🕷

After breakfast the following day, Alberto and Marisol breezed into the courtyard. Marisol always seemed to breeze in and out of places. She was buoyant. Benita was already sitting with Casey and Claire. Alberto bent down to kiss Benita's cheek, and she offered it to him. Al seemed like an uncle to her. He pulled up two more chairs.

"Where is Jack?" he asked.

"He left a note saying he went fishing," Casey said. "We would have gone with him if he'd asked."

"I don't know him outside of the trek we made," Alberto said, "but he seems to separate easily. Is that normal for him?"

"It is," Casey said, "for as long as I've known him." Marisol interjected, "I think Jack has a fan in Alberto." Al smiled and poured her some coffee.

"I like him very much," Al said. There was a pause in the conversation as everyone sipped their coffees and breathed in the Ollanta morning air.

"I think I can explain my affection for Jack if I should call it that; when I was about your age," Alberto said, looking at Claire and Casey, "I went to school in the states. The American University in D.C."

"Did you?!" Claire asked. "My dad went there."

Alberto lifted his coffee cup into the air. "Go Eagles." He smiled. "Yup, I attended the School of International Service. I thought I might be a diplomat or something someday. Anyway, after my second year, I ran out of money and had to take a year off. I studied global environmental politics, and one of my professors got me a job with the Bureau of Land Management, counting wild donkeys throughout the Southwest. It was amazing! I traveled throughout Arizona, southern Colorado, New Mexico, and Utah looking for burros. I had a truck and expenses, but to be honest, I just backpacked and camped all through those states tracking and recording burros." Alberto pretended as though he was telling a secret. "The truth is, I think I was counting the same burros over and over." Everyone chuckled.

"I wondered how you spoke English so flawlessly," Claire said.

"I found ancient ruins," Al continued. "I met amazing people living in the middle of nowhere, befriended Hopis and Navajos, and saw some of the most stunning landscapes on earth. I lived off the land for over a year, seeking beauty, and I felt like I saw more than one man's share of beautiful places."

Casey tried to make the connection. "Yes. I could see Jack doing something like that."

Al shook his head slightly, suggesting, *no, that's not it.* Then he looked Claire square in the eyes. "During those years, I carried an antique microscope to see beyond the things that were obvious, beyond the things that were right in front of me."

Marisol said, "My...I thought I was the poet in the family."

Claire looked back into Alberto's dark eyes for a few long seconds and then down into her coffee. *I can see that* she thought *Jack and Al are kindred spirits.*

"Anyway," Alberto said, "as I mentioned yesterday, today is a day for you to explore and to fish. Tonight, I've arranged a meeting with my acquaintance, Gregorio. He is the elder I've told you about and the one who knows the backcountry from here to the jungle — the Amazon. He's also the local expert on ancient Andean culture and rituals. He will know about any Shining Path activity in these valleys if it exists. He has many stories."

"Excellent," Casey said. "What time, and where?"

"He wants us to pick him up at his house at six o'clock. We'll look at some maps." Al grinned at Claire and Casey. "His stories," he said, "... you just wait."

Then he thought for a moment and looked more serious. "His stories are free, and they are true," Al said. "Sometimes, he can be a bit blunt, but you are scientists. You'll not be offended, and Gregorio will not hold back."

TWENTY-THREE

Ollantaytambo and the Baker

Gregorio's house was on the edge of town. Alberto, Marisol, Claire, Casey, Jack, and Benita walked to meet him promptly at six o'clock. Benita had asked Al if she could go because she hoped to go to college in a year, and, realizing there was a slight possibility she might not return to Ollantaytambo, she wanted to hear the stories.

"Gregorio knows everything that goes on in this valley," Alberto said as they walked through Ollanta's streets. "In his younger years, in the 1940s through the '60s, he guided both anthropologists and archaeologists into the mountains and over into the Amazon. No amateurs, and no tourists. That was Gregorio's rule, only professionals. He didn't want people ruining remote cultures or stealing artifacts."

"A man with vision," Jack said.

"Yes," replied Alberto. "He is highly respected, and he is on the Council for Indian Communities in the highlands. The Sendero are harassing and murdering villagers in communities all over south-central Peru, especially people in positions of authority. But they leave Gregorio alone."

Upon arrival at Gregorio's, they learned that he owns a bakery with his wife, Beatriz. Their home had a wooden floor covered with old linoleum, which was quite elegant compared to many Campesino's homes, especially in the countryside.

"They bake loaves of large, round pita bread," Alberto offered, "which neighboring children sell for them at the railroad station and in the plazas. They have only one son who used to do the selling for them, but he left home years earlier to find a better life in Lima. I know their son. He did not find it."

Gregorio was sitting, waiting on a wooden bench in front of the house when they arrived. He saw Alberto and rose from his perch.

Alberto greeted him in his charismatic way. "*Señor Quispe! Es bueno verte mi amigo!*" Gregorio was genuinely happy to see Al. They shook hands, and he kissed Al and then Marisol and Benita on the cheek. Alberto introduced Gregorio to the three friends. The village elder bowed slightly and shook their hands, except for Claire's. He reached out with both arms, grasped her shoulders, and kissed her on both cheeks. Claire rolled with the manhandling graciously.

Alberto would translate, and if Gregorio slipped into Quechua at times, Benita would help. The patrón waved them into the house to meet his wife. With Alberto's help, Gregorio proudly introduced his wife Beatriz, who had to be thirty years his junior. She was plump and had a regal face, and her enormous smile showcased a complete set of teeth. She stood at her stove and smiled and bowed. Claire, Casey, and Jack nodded and waved.

The main room had a table in the middle topped with a homemade propane stove. There was an earthen, wood-fired Incan-style oven for baking in one corner. Shelving filled with cans and jars were nailed to every wall, and in the entire room, there was a single photograph: A calendar image of the Pope positioned above the squares of days.

The room was a miracle of odors. The smell of the bread mixed exotically with aromas wafting up from the basement, where sheep, llamas, a cow, and guinea pigs were kept. Gregorio directed the group to look out the only window in the room and see its view straight up the hill at the famous ruins.

As he walked by, Jack squinted through the darkness at the calendar and Papal image. It read, December 1959. The picture, permanently nailed to the wall, was of Pope John XXIII, who died in 1963. A closer look revealed pencil marks on most of the days. The entire second week of that December, twenty-six years earlier, had a line through it with the words, "*Profesor de Yale... Madre de Dios.*"

After the tour of the home, Gregorio led the group out the door and around the back of the house. They walked across another narrow alley to a vacant lot next to a cornfield. There was an assortment of chairs and benches and a long, rickety picnic table. There they all sat. Casey unfolded his map of south-central Peru that had Cusco in the center, and it included Ollantaytambo and the Sacred Valley and its surrounding area. Each traveler took out their journals.

Gregorio spoke first, then Alberto translated. "He asked, 'What would you like to know?'"

Gregorio sat dignified at the table, his hands folded in front of him as if in prayer.

Each friend looked at the other.

"I'll start, I guess," Casey said. "I suppose I'd like to know what his experience is in the highlands in terms of very remote communities, and what does he know about the Sendero Luminoso in this area? In other words, how safe is it to travel outside of Ollantaytambo?"

"Okay," Alberto said. He turned to Gregorio and translated Casey's question. The elder statesman of the valley thought for a moment. Then he spoke, with Alberto translating every third or fourth sentence: "Yes, yes...I understand. The Sendero Luminoso are lost souls. They are very violent also. They live among us but are only active in certain places. The Sendero try to recruit people as other counterinsurgency groups have always done. They usually abduct people, often uneducated people, and bombard them with lectures... 'Mao says this... Presidente Gonzalo says *this...*' They always have large posters showing Guzman dressed in a suit and an open shirt with no tie. He always looks better in those posters than in real life.

"Then they give the poor peasant a red book with the inscription, *Develop the Popular War Serving the World Revolution.*' If the peasant can't read, they read it to him or her – they recruit a lot of females. Red flags with a black hammer and sickle are always hanging in their camps. They tell the recruit that Presidente Gonzalo (Guzman) thinks about important things day and night more than they ever could. The lectures become more like religious chants, and the females – the Senderistas are made to recite over and over, *'We give our full submission to the greatest living Marxist – Leninist – Maoist on earth, our beloved and respected Presidente Gonzalo; the chief and guide of the Peruvian revolution and the world proletarian revolution teacher of our Communist Party. We submit to the scientific ideology and the infallible ideology that illuminates our path and minds. We give our submission to the world proletarian revolution. We will cross the river of blood to victory!*'"

The three friends sat in silence. Jack was writing as fast as he could. He looked up at Casey.

Alberto whispered to them, "Told you he knows his shit."

Through Al, Gregorio continued. "These recruits have to pledge to give their life and blood for the revolution. No compromises. Destroy in order to create the New Democracy of Peru. In the end, it's a gamble. If the recruit does not do it, sometimes they let him or her go. Sometimes they kill them. They like to recruit people they think can be useful – people with large farms or disconnected people who maybe have no family, like young orphans or teenagers who seem to have lost their way. They are big targets for recruitment."

All three friends jotted down notes.

"Who is the *antropólogo*?" Gregorio asked.

Jack lifted his pen in the air. The patrón looked at him.

Alberto again translated Gregorio's words to Jack; "If you want to work here, especially in southern Peru, you have to understand that you may witness violence. And you have to be prepared for that. They probably teach you this in school, but I worked with an anthropologist thirty years ago who told me she had been a student of a German professor who made her and her fellow students undergo psychoanalysis before starting their fieldwork. She told me that she thought it was invaluable if she or her fellow students were confronted with situations of violence.

"There also is..." he looked at Claire and Benita, then lowered his eyes and stared at his folded hands "...there is much rape. And the Sendero train women to be hit squads. Killers."

It should have rattled them, but Benita and Claire seemed unfazed.

Gregorio continued with Alberto's voice trailing behind his words. "Guzman... Presidente Gonzalo, as he likes to be called, is a pseudo-intellectual. What makes an intellectual become a revolutionary? Maybe you students know, not me. Perhaps he became angry over some social conditions around him, but from what I hear, his God-like status is dangerous now. Very dangerous. No one can argue or disagree with him.

"Now they are setting off bombs, shooting innocent people, or terrorizing them. They kill people's dogs in the middle of the night and hang the carcasses from streetlights, which was a traditional Incan warning, only they hanged them from trees, of course. They show up in tiny villages with machine guns and pistols and set up mock trials as though they are the authorities. They put some village council members or officials on trial for some made-up offense and then shoot them dead. Sometimes the Sendero stone them or light them on fire while still alive. The government isn't handling it well. They, too, have their military hit squads. They're killing people who are not Senderos! They send soldiers to take five or six suspected people — or people who they think know who or where the terrorists are — up in a helicopter. They tie their hands first. They go thousands of feet in the air, usually over a part of the jungle, and start interrogating them, one at a time. An ex-soldier told me about it. He had been a hardened soldier who had been in battle, and he was weeping as he told me. He said the poor Campesinos in the helicopter who knew nothing were crying. They had never been off the ground except on a horse or burro. They urinated themselves. They went down the line one at a time, and if they didn't tell them *something*, they pushed them out the open cargo door. On his last mission, my friend said they got to the last farmer who had just seen his friends pushed out — murdered. Out of desperation, he gave them names of people who might know something. The soldier wrote down the names and said 'Gracias' and sat back down in the helicopter. Then the superior officer in charge kicked the man in the chest and sent him to his death anyway, while he and some of the other men broke into laughter.

"That was it for my soldier friend. He wanted out. He couldn't sleep. He paid one of his friends in his outfit who he trusted to smash his right hand while on patrol and broke the bones. Then he threw himself off a small cliff. Not one big enough to kill him, but he broke a few more bones and was mustered out of the army. He drives a taxi now in Cusco. He had to learn to work the stick-shift with a deformed hand, but he's doing okay."

Gregorio shook his head. "I don't know what the answer is to the Sendero Luminoso, but a new man is running for President, Alan Garcia. He's young, energetic, democratic, and looks like a big Latino Kennedy. His campaign is based on anti-corruption, and maybe he can do something about the Sendero if he gets elected."

There was a pause. Gregorio didn't know what else to say about the Shining Path at the moment.

"I guess the other question is," Casey said, "what can he tell us about any remote or unique societies or communities in the highlands, or maybe in the Amazon?"

Gregorio regarded his question. He looked gravely at Alberto, who tried to soothe him; "Señor Quispe...they are simply interested in the unknown, for their edification..." Alberto knew not to speak down to him. "I know them, and they are true explorers at heart. Whatever provisions you put on your guidance will be adhered to." Alberto blessed himself.

"There is a place," said the elder, "but it is difficult to find. The people who live there are a mix of gringos, pure-bred Indians, and Mestizos. They live by their own rules. I do know that they still cling to some of the old Andean rituals. I do not know if they're friendly to outsiders. But these are only rumors. Some people say that place existed long ago and that now bad men are living there. Who knows what the truth is?"

Casey and Jack looked at each other. They did not think to look at Alberto for his reaction.

"It is on the far side of the highlands," Gregorio continued, "only a few kilometers from the Madre de Dios Reserve. The village is up steep trails into the sky. Most days, the clouds hang just above it. The land beyond this place the Incas called *Antisuyu* — the unconquered Amazonian jungle on the eastern border of their empire." Gregorio seemed to relish the telling of the old times, his face becoming stern and his copper brow more furrowed. "Antisuyu is a land of true beauty and potential danger. The people who live there still fiercely hold fast to their culture and traditions and resist any government interference. They like to be left alone, out on the edge of the old empire. If you get lost or hurt over there, you're on your own."

Casey asked Alberto, "Please ask him how far it is and if he could show us on a map." Gregorio answered, and Alberto turned to the friends.

"He says it's not on a map, but he could draw it for you. He says it is about sixty-five kilometers from Ollantaytambo, straight...as the condor flies. If you go by road and then hike, the trip one-way will be over 100 kilometers."

Casey was writing in his journal. The three friends sat in silence, digesting the idea.

Gregorio spoke directly to Alberto. "*Es muy difícil y puede ser peligroso. Especialmente en estos días.*"

Alberto translated what he said, "It is very difficult and can be dangerous. Especially these days. I don't know if the Sendero are out there. Just because there's no news about them in a region, that doesn't mean they aren't there."

"Has he been there?" Casey asked.

Alberto asked the question, and Gregorio shook his head. "No, but I was very close once. I saw the village from up on a mountain that looked down on it. I was maybe four kilometers away."

"But he didn't go down?"

Again, Gregorio shook his head. "No…something didn't feel right, so I left."

Gregorio slid the map in front of him. He indicated he needed something to write with, and Casey gave him a pen. He took it with gnarled fingers that spoke of a life of toil and started tracing along the road southeast toward Cusco. About five miles out of Ollanta, the route diverged onto a road that led northeast. It went through a village called Amparaes and then petered out before reaching the tiny town of Calca. He then drew the line up a drainage through the mountains to the east, and on the far side of the mountains, he stopped. There, he made an 'X.'

Viewing the map upside down, it looked to Casey like the 'X' was about thirty degrees north-northeast of Ollanta. "That's doable," he said half aloud.

Through Alberto, Gregorio pointed the pen at Casey and said, "You should know, some people think it is bad luck to go to this place."

"Ask him why," Casey said.

Alberto asked, then translated.

"He says it is a superstition. He said about fifteen years ago, a traveler like yourselves heard about this place and went there. He had left a bag with some things in it in his hotel here in town, saying he would pick them up in a week. He never returned for them. After more than a month, we had a council meeting — right here at this table about what to do with it. We had contacted the authorities in Cusco, but they never sent anyone and said they had no correspondence about a missing person. So, we decided to open the bag and look for any name or address for a person to write to. It had personal things. A small camera, a candle lantern, sunglasses, an unpunched train ticket to Aguas Calientes dated the day he was supposed to pick it up, and six rolls of exposed camera film. There were a few other things, but I can't remember what they were. We decided if no one contacted the hotel about the bag in another month, we would have the film developed."

"Did you?" Casey asked.

Al asked Gregorio, then told the group, "He says they did. Just a lot of tourist photos. From the clothes in the portraits, they could tell that he had been to Ecuador and Guatemala. He said some of the photographs would have been special for the traveler but to no one else. He doesn't know why he never came for the bag, and no one ever came looking for him. I suppose his people did not know where in South America he was when he disappeared."

Gregorio kept talking. "Five years later, there was another trekker that came through. He was looking to get away from civilization. He said he was a photographer, and I believed him. He carried a lot of camera gear. He was traveling with his dog, which is a bit unusual here. He heard about this place also and decided to go to take pictures. A week later, a man I know from the village of Calca rode a horse down this road," he pointed at the map to a spot north of the town of Ampareas, "until he found a car. He drove the car here to get medical help. The horseman was frantic. He said there was a gringo in his village who had rabies. We sent our nurse and a traveling physician in a truck to Calca as fast as they could go. When they got there the man was dead. He had been tied to a post at the edge of town. The doctor said it looked like rabies, alright. The dog had been shot.

The doctor and nurse interviewed villagers who said the man had come back from the mountains a few days earlier but had camped out of town, and they didn't know he was sick. His own dog had bitten him. When some boys found him, the dog was frothing at the mouth and wouldn't let anyone near him. Apparently, some farmers shot the dog and brought the man into the village, hoping to get him to Cusco. But the man went berserk. He was throwing up, screaming, and fighting them. He went crazy. He tried to bite people. So, they tied him up. By the time help arrived, it was too late."

"Wow," Casey said. "Did anyone investigate it?"

Gregorio nodded. Again, through Alberto, he said, "They sent police. They found his campsite and collected his things. All his cameras were smashed, and there were no film canisters anywhere. They took the body to Cusco. I heard some people from America came and got him."

"So, you see," Gregorio continued, "there are superstitions about this place."

"Well," Casey said, stiffening his back and sitting back on the bench, "that's a lot to think about." He looked at Claire and Jack, who was still writing in his notebook. "Do you guys have any questions?" Claire shook her head. She rested her chin in her hand on bended elbow, staring at the map.

"No," said Jack. "We'll have to talk about logistics, though."

"Al," Casey asked, "could you please ask him if he has any stipulations for us if we try to go?"

Gregorio thought about that for a long time and looked at each of the three friends. Then he said, "Perhaps if you choose to go, you should take someone with you. But I am too old."

Then he looked at Alberto with a worn and weary face. "Tell these students," he said, "maybe they should take the train to Aguas Calientes and visit Machu Picchu instead, but I know they won't."

TWENTY-FOUR
No Return

They left Gregorio and walked back to the hostel. There was so much information to digest; they skipped supper. On the way, Jack walked next to Benita. "That was a lot for you to take in," he said to her.

"I like stories," she said, shaking her head, "and not all stories are happy ones." They walked a few more steps, and she said in reasonably good English, "I wish *I* could go to the exploring with you all."

Jack smiled and said, "We'll tell you stories about it when we get back."

At the hostel, the group pulled two tables together and talked about what to do. Casey had the map out again and retrieved his compass from the room. He laid it on the map. "Yup," he muttered, "thirty-two degrees." Alberto was studying the map with him.

"Are you up for this, Al?" Casey asked.

Alberto looked at Marisol, who indicated with a knowing look that whatever he wanted to do was fine with her. She knew her man. Casey had retained him to help out for the month, and she knew a hike like this was right up her husband's alley.

"I'm game," he replied.

Casey looked at his friend. Jack cocked his head to one side and sat back in his chair. "You wanted adventure," he said to Casey. "But we're not taking any sick dogs."

It was decided everyone would sleep on it, and in the morning, they would decide. That would give the team the afternoon to get provisions for more than a week of backpacking and for Alberto to arrange a ride to the drainage south of Colca. They all went to bed early. Jack tried to read by the light of his headlamp, but he could hear Claire's voice through the wall and took a blanket out onto the little balcony, closed the French doors, and tried to sleep in the chair.

As usual, Jack was awake first in the morning, and Alberto came down to the courtyard shortly after, looking for coffee; and Jack had already made some and poured him a mug.

"Up for a morning walk?" Al asked.

They took their coffee and were careful not to let the old, green courtyard door squeak too loudly and walked down the dirt road along the adobe wall. The rows of corn in the valley opposite the road abruptly stopped where a large field had been plowed by oxen the day before. There was a sweet smell of earth in the air. Tiny puffs of steam rose from the new, dark furrows into the early morning sunlight.

"It's late in the season," Jack suggested. "Must be planting a cover crop."

"Yes," Alberto said, "it's a type of clover. You know farming also?"

"Not much. Most locals in Maine do some vegetable gardening, but it's an agricultural state. You can't drive too far without passing a farm, especially in the northern half. Plus, I worked on a farm for a summer job while in high school."

Jack squinted in the bright sun and looked at the contoured furrows. "I watch the people work, and they don't seem to mind it, yet they are *so* poor."

"Sadly, they are," Al agreed. "Only ten years ago, there was a potato blight, and people in the highlands were starving. I heard stories of infanticide. There are rumors that some peasant families even today sell their adolescent children to wealthy families in Lima. I have a policeman friend in Cusco who went undercover a few years ago and drove to villages trying to buy a couple of children but was driven away. So, they may just be rumors. Still, one hears stories about children going missing from the villages. But, it's always girls."

After making a few lefts, Jack and Alberto circled the town and again approached the hostel. Al pushed open the green door, and Casey and Claire were sitting at a table. Casey was writing in his journal.

"Buenos días," they both said. Alberto and Jack had only just sat down when Benita came to ask if they had had breakfast.

"Only coffee so far," Jack said, smiling.

"So," Casey said, "We should start by making a list of what we'll need to take with us."

"Then we're going?" Jack asked.

"Oh, right. Sorry," Casey said. "What's the consensus?"

Jack looked at Claire. "Which do you want to do? Go to Machu Picchu, or explore east and north?"

"I'm good to explore," she said, knowing full well the other three were pretty excited to see what was around the bend. She was starting to understand the allure of blind corners. "Just promise me, if we find something of archaeologic significance, we don't just push on — even if it takes a day or two to do a survey of the site, or maybe do a simple surface scatter analysis?"

"You're so hot when you talk science," teased Jack. She smiled as she threw her napkin at his chest, which he deftly caught without blinking his eyes.

"Okay," Casey said. "Al, if you could arrange the transportation to the drop-off point, we can meet after that and buy food." Al nodded. Casey examined the map. "Question: How do we find transportation back to Ollanta?"

"That's the hard part," Al said. "There are a few options. We'll try to arrange a ride to meet us at the drop-off place, but we might have to walk about nine miles back down the road to the village of Choquecancha to hire a pickup driver." Casey again studied the map.

"Another option," continued Al, "is to wait by the side of the road and try to catch one of the cargo trucks traveling by. They appear almost daily, coming from the mining camps in the mountains or from the Amazon farther north and east. It's a rough ride, though. We'd be packed into the truck bed under tarps with thirty or forty peasants who won't like us being there. And the huge cargo trucks won't have shocks. Or, we could hike all the way back, adding twenty-seven miles on foot. *Hard* miles."

"Well," Jack said, "as appealing as the cargo trucks sound, I vote for arranging for a driver from here to meet us down the road. We can build in an extra day or two for exploration, and if we get out of the mountains early, we can hang out in camp and do some fishing."

Casey asked Alberto, "Should we bother with climbing gear?"

"I don't think so. It'll add too much weight, and we can skirt any part of the route that's exposed. I'm taking trekking poles, though." Al thought for a moment. "Actually, why don't you each bring a harness and a few carabiners. I've got a light, seventy-five-foot rope, and I can bring that just in case. Any extra gear you don't want to bring, we can stash here. Benita will make sure it's safe."

"What about food for ten days?" Casey asked. "If it's a tough slog, we will want to keep the weight down some."

"Yes," Al said. "I've made a list of a few things to get here in Ollanta, but I should make a run to Cusco this afternoon for some dehydrated mountaineering food. There's a place I can buy some, and I have at least a dozen packets at home — it's expired, but it's hermetically sealed and dehydrated. It'll be fine to eat."

"I'll go with you," Casey said, "and I'll pay for the food packets and the driver to Cusco and back."

Alberto handed the local shopping list to Claire, and Benita brought the breakfasts.

"Benita," Alberto asked, "are you busy this afternoon?" She shook her head.

"Would you mind going shopping with Claire and Jack for a few groceries? Neither of them has any Quechua."

"I would like that," she said.

"Good. Lastly, do you have a water filter?"

Casey raised two fingers.

"Excellent. Bring them both

"Okay, then. I'll pick up some white gas for your mountaineering stoves. We'll be here by ten o'clock in the morning, and I'll have the driver ready here at the hostel by noon. It's only between sixty and eighty miles to the drop-off point, but it'll take almost four hours. We'll camp just off the road tomorrow night and head out early the next morning." He paused for a moment, staring at the map. "I don't know if we'll find anything like a strange town or unmapped ruins, but this will be fun."

"You know," continued Alberto, "very few white people have gone where we're going. With the slightest re-direction into the mountains from this route, perhaps you'll be the first."

Casey and Jack exchanged looks, and their eyebrows raised with the slightest grins. They were excited. True exploration, this was what they were built for. Claire saw their exchange and felt the same.

Everything looked good. Spread out on the hostel's bed was everything Casey would carry for the next ten days. He considered the gear one more time. Into a canvas bag Benita had loaned him, he placed the crampons, his rack of carabiners, and other climbing gear — everything he thought they would not need. He rolled his and Claire's harnesses into a ball with four locking biners and shoved them into the recesses of the lower compartment of his backpack, next to the tent he and Claire would share. He repacked the backpack and leaned it in the corner of the room. Then, Claire picked up her bag and dumped everything on the bed.

"Al's meeting me at the square in twenty minutes," Casey said. "You all set with this?"

"I am. I'll take the bag down to Benita when I'm done."

"Good. Okay then, I'm off. See you tomorrow." He gave her a quick kiss.

She nodded. "You'll have fun with Al and Marisol."

It took Claire almost an hour to pack for the trip, leaving as much space as possible for some of the freeze-dried food packets.

There was a full moon, so after an early supper at the hostel, Claire and Jack decided to take a stroll along the Urubamba River, mostly because Jack liked the sound of "*A stroll along the Urubamba.*" The moon was full and was just climbing over the steep mountains to the east — the same mountains they would traverse the following day.

They walked along the stone-lined trail above the rushing river just as thousands of generations of ancient Incas and those who came before them had. The plodding moon washed the valley with its soft light and cast grey shadows from the rose bushes and the tall succulents. On the terraces above them, the foliage of the cornstalks and the shimmering leaves of the eucalyptus trees seemed dreamlike and were made more silver by the bright moonlight. Below, the river was either brightly lit or black in shadow, and the rushing current sounded louder than in daylight.

After rounding a bend in the trail, Jack stopped in his tracks and grasped Claire's hand a short distance from town. She stopped. He strained to listen and held an index finger to his lips. They stepped off the trail onto the grass, and he let go of her hand. They could hear voices. Jack crept closer, and Claire followed. Was it the Sendero Luminoso, holding a clandestine moonlit meeting? Or something less menacing? One of the voices was female. Gregorio had said the Shining Path recruits a lot of females. Claire and Jack edged along the trail and came close to a clearing. It was full of teenagers from town. The two observers were slightly uphill of the clearing and found a spot under a Pisonay tree where they could observe the youths.

Jack whispered, "It's not voyeurism if your field is anthropology."

Claire nudged him with her shoulder and whispered back, "You keep telling yourself that."

There were several boys in one group and a half-dozen girls in another. They were intermingling and giggling. One girl would ask the group of boys something, and one at a time, they would answer. Each boy's response would elicit either "ooh's" or "aah's" from the girls or giggles and laughter.

Claire, sitting very close to Jack, leaned even closer. "I think I know what this is," she whispered.

"Teenagers out having flirtatious fun, just like back home?"

"Maybe," answered Claire, "but when I was in the field near Huaraz two years ago, Dr. Fitzroy told me about this behavior — if it's the same thing. She described a sort of sexual-intellectual play that would get physical."

Jack looked back at the group of teenagers, and the game looked innocent enough to him.

Claire continued, "Groups like this would congregate outside of their communities and have 'sex quizzes,' the riddles were always asked by the girls and were always sexual in nature. It was a way for them to test the knowledge of the boys. Each girl would directly offer a riddle to a boy she was interested in, and he had one shot of getting laid if he answered correctly. If the boy couldn't answer the riddle, he was laughed at and scorned by all the girls. If he could solve the riddle, he and the riddler would go off into the bushes and have sex. For the adolescent boys, the stakes were high."

"Remarkable," Jack said, looking back at Claire.

"It gets better," she said. "The object was to have as many partners as possible."

"Man," Jack said, "I thought last year's movie *Footloose* was edgy. All they wanted to do was dance."

Jack looked back into the clearing. There were fewer teenagers. Two of the girls left the party, and two others reached out and took the hands of two of the boys. The couples walked in different directions out of the moonlit clearing, and suddenly it was empty.

Jack smiled and raised a finger and trained his ears. It was faint, but they could hear adolescents moaning over the sounds of the rushing river below. "Truly amazing," he said.

He looked back at Claire, who faced him. Her blonde hair and her ice-blue eyes looked different in the moonlight. They looked more beautiful than ever, which Jack had always thought would be impossible. He was happy to be with her, on that night, on the banks of the Urubamba. Jack did not look away, as he usually did. He wanted to memorize this moment and hold fast to it for the rest of his life. For some strange reason, he did not care if he made her uncomfortable, staring into her incredible eyes. He wanted this memory. Badly.

Claire did not look away, not for a long moment. It was almost as though she understood his desire and wanted to give it to him. They were less than twelve inches from each other. There came the moment when they would either kiss or turn away, and Jack turned his head toward the empty clearing. Then Claire lowered her head. There was a long, awkward minute.

Finally, Claire spoke. "Honey, I know about Rachael. Casey told me a month ago when we were in New Hampshire."

Jack looked at the ground. *Why was she bringing up Rachael?*

"I understand why you can't love another person," she said. Jack quickly looked at her. *Oh Lord,* she thought, *I've overstepped.* But she continued anyway.

"I get it," she said. "It's just — I think you know I care about you." Claire's eyes widened as she said, "A lot. And it hurts me to think that you must feel lonely at times."

He interjected and stopped her talking. "Claire...Darling..." he took her hand in his and held it firmly. "This is very difficult to say. I will always hold a special place in my heart for Rachael, but I *am* in love. Have been for a long time. That's why I cannot date other women."

Claire waited for him to finish, but he didn't. She was confused. She could tell by his voice that he was in pain telling her. She lifted her other hand and held his left hand in both of hers to comfort him. She looked at his bowed head out of the corner of her eye. She saw on Jack's face — the strongest, toughest, the most intellectual man she had ever met — a look of total defeat and resignation. Then, in the silver light of the moon, she saw a tear roll down his cheek.

Then she knew.

"Oh, God!" she threw her arm around him and, with her other hand, pulled his head to her chest. "Honey...I never had any idea. I'm *so* sorry."

The wave of emotions that came over her made her ill. She had to suppress the feelings and push them down to some hidden place. She rocked Jack in her arms, and he wept. She knew Jack, maybe better than anyone. She understood that he would be incapable of loving someone halfway. If he loved her, she knew, he must've been in agony for a long time.

"How long?" she asked.

Jack tried to collect himself. He put his arm around her, lifted his head, and wiped his eyes, and took a deep breath. "When Casey introduced us."

Claire moaned and looked down.

"It's okay," he said. "I can handle this. I suppose...I guess it feels like I should've told you a long time ago, or maybe never. It's just that Case; he's like a brother to me."

"No," Claire said, "you did the right thing, not going away." They both sat in stunned silence for a while, each trying to analyze the moment.

"Here's the thing, Claire; my love for you is never going to go away. But I can live with it. I have been doing that for a long time now. Casey and I are close — he's my climbing partner — but you're my best friend. I think you must know that. Telling you how I feel might've been a mistake, but right now, it feels good that you know."

Claire was confused about her feelings. They still had their arms around each other. She had known for two years that there was much she loved about this man. She also knew that she and Casey did not connect on many levels. And, she knew that with Jack, his love for anyone or anything would be unconditional. Claire also knew that right at that moment, in his arms, she felt safer, more herself, more loved than she ever had. The realization came on her like a storm, and she thought it odd that she was not surprised by her feelings — that she felt so comfortable and that without the slightest analysis of her feelings, she was utterly convicted in her affection for him.

"Jack, Honey..." she gently cradled his cheek in the palm of her hand and turned his beautiful face toward hers. "I think I love you too."

He only stared at her in disbelief. He waited for her to say, *as a friend.*

But she did not say that. Instead, she continued, "But we can't do this here, not on this trip. We have to get home. We'll talk to Casey together after we get back to school."

Jack's head began to swim. He was overcome at once with unspeakable joy and profound sadness at the prospect of hurting his friend. Claire could see that. She kissed him on the cheek and said, "Allow that I know him differently than you. I think he will be all right."

Jack nodded, trusting her.

Jack was an emotional wreck. Claire controlled the situation. She knew what to do, and she knew she wanted to be with him.

"I want to make love to you more than anything in the world right now," she said, "but we can't. It's strange, but I know my heart belongs to you, and it's really fucking weird." He touched his forehead to hers.

After a long moment, she continued, "How does this sound? We will finish the trip as planned. I will stay with Case for now, but we will not be together physically. You and I will talk when we get home, pick a time, and tell him. Then, we'll go on a date." She gave him a gorgeous smile, and he knew then what he had always known; that he wanted to spend the rest of his life with her.

"Yes," he said. He effortlessly lifted Claire, and she sat facing him on his lap.

There, under the silvery, moonlit branches of a Pisonay tree, he kissed her.

Their lips, their mouths fit perfectly together, as if pieces of a puzzle. As if they were always meant to be together. Jack's hands move tentatively at first, unsure if this dream was happening to him and unsure how much Claire would allow. She felt solid and soft, and warm to his touch. He kept waiting for her to come to her senses and pull away. But she did not.

Instead, Claire's hands moved over him confidently and aggressively. She wanted to know he was wanted. She held his face in her hands and felt his tongue. *My god,* she thought, *he is beautiful.*

On cue, they both jumped up and stripped off their clothes. Jack stopped for a moment, staring at Claire. Her body was now bare and lit by the silver light of the moon. She looked iridescent, and she smiled at him.

Jack shook his head once and said, "This is the most beautiful thing I've ever seen."

"*This?*" she said laughing, "Well, this wants you to kiss it again."

He smiled back at her and embraced her. As they kissed again, both were breathing nearly to the point of hyperventilating. Jack felt Claire's bare belly and breasts against his skin, and just that—only that almost brought him to orgasm. He had never known how much he always wanted her. But he knew now. She pulled him down on top of her onto their pile of clothes. There was no boyish fumbling. Now their entire bodies were fitting together like pieces of the puzzle, and when he was finally inside her, she took a long, deep breath and opened her eyes. As they moved together effortlessly, she stared through glazed pupils up through the branches at the sky. The waving leaves, scintillating in the moonlight, backed by the Milky Way and dampened from the mist of the Urubamba's rapids, looked like a million tiny fireflies flitting about in the night.

Jack was so moved he nearly came to tears. Claire came first, then Jack.

Then they held each other tightly, engaged in their mutual love and happiness. Their joy and love for each other in that afterglow offered a defining moment. A moment they would never forget. A joyful moment they each secretly hoped would sustain them through the gut-wrenching guilt that was already starting to wash over them.

In Cusco by mid-afternoon, Alberto took Casey to the house of a friend who had a black-market operation in his basement selling camping and trekking gear, and it was a going concern. Al introduced the marketeer as "*My friend*" but did not give his name. He was a gringo, an ex-pat whom Casey guessed to be French.

Most of the gear was well organized and stacked throughout the basement. It was purchased, the friend told Casey, from people returning from treks or mountaineering trips. Perhaps they were headed to entirely different travel venues and didn't want to carry them or ship them home from Peru. Casey reckoned that some of the gear had been stolen at bus or train stations or from the airport. And everything was dirt cheap.

Casey and Al started rummaging through huge, lidless cardboard boxes lined with plastic. They started pulling out packages of 'freeze-dried' mountaineering food. Not only were there the American classics from Backpacker's Pantry and Mountain House (Jack's favorite), but there were many brands from European companies the boys hadn't tried. Casey first separated twenty small breakfast packages, then twenty dinners. Each meal was supposed to feed two people. On the bus, Al had told Casey that they would be able to supplement the climbing meals with fruit and potatoes along the way if they were lucky.

The freeze-dried meal packages weighed nearly nothing but were voluminous. They would have to be split up four ways in each person's pack. Forty packages of meals cost twenty-two U.S. dollars, and Casey was happy to pay for it. A pair of sunglasses caught his eye on a shelf next to some books. "How much for the Vuarnet glacier glasses?" *Those would be $450 in the states*, he thought.

"Feefty doll-airs," said the marketeer. Casey picked them up and looked at them. They were in mint condition, and the temples were adjustable, so they always fit. The marketeer was looking on another shelf. "Forty?" Casey asked. They obviously once resided in some poor sap's stolen backpack.

The marketeer turned around and produced another pair that were equally as nice. "How a-bout 'Seeks-ty doll-airs' for two?"

Casey's father had snuck an envelope with $600 extra dollars where he would find it in his backpack. It was meant to finance some of the extras on the trip, but he hadn't used much—only his own money so far, and he had plenty left. He was buying maybe $900 worth of technical sunglasses for sixty bucks. "Deal," he said.

As they walked back to the far side of town to Alberto's home, Casey pulled out the second pair of glasses and handed them to Al. He took them and looked at them. "Very nice," Al said, who then tried to hand them back.

"A gift," Casey said.

"These are not for Claire or Jack?" Al asked.

"Jack has a pair I gave him for his birthday, and Claire has a good pair already. These are for you. You've been an amazing help."

"But you've paid me for the month," Al said.

"Not enough."

Al shrugged his shoulders and smiled sheepishly. "Well. Then thanks. I'll cherish them."

Alberto and Marisol's house did not disappoint. Set into one of the sloping hills on the edge of Cusco, it was built atop an Incan foundation. The doorway into the ancient lower half of the house had distinctive trapezoidal shapes seen in many Incan ruins. As Al unlocked the door, Casey asked, "Was it hard to retro-fit a modern door into this?"

"It was," Al said. "I had to get some help with the carpentry."

Inside, Al turned a light switch. It was one of the coolest rooms Casey had ever seen. Incan artifacts and fabrics were everywhere. In the corner was a wood-fired pizza oven. This was a serious den. There were two couches, two big, well-worn leather chairs, and a coffee table that looked like a free, horizontal section of Incan stonework. Casey pointed at it. "Is that ..."

"It is," replied Al. "A stone lintel. It took me a whole day, a modified dolly, and four friends to move it in here." Just like at the South American Explorer's Club in Lima, each corner of the room held bookshelves with Amazonian blowguns, spears, and arrows leaning against them. Large beams overhead supported the rest of the house. A staircase next to the pizza oven led upstairs.

Marisol called down the stairs. "Are you two hungry?"

Al looked at Casey, who said, "I could eat."

"Whatever you have," Alberto called back, "and maybe a couple of Pisco Sours?"

Casey crashed on one of the couches downstairs. Al had made a small fire in the pizza oven for a bit of warmth. He lay awake under an alpaca blanket after the light was turned off and watched the orange flames dancing off the old Incan stone wall. His mind wandered. *I wonder who lived here, 500 years ago?*

He was excited about the trip ahead. He finally fell asleep.

TWENTY-FIVE

The Expedition Begins

The taxi deposited the two men at the town square in Ollantaytambo the following day. They walked the few blocks to the hostel carrying the bags of freeze-dried food packets. By noon, everyone was packed and ready. The van Alberto arranged for was an old, retired ambulance. The lights no longer worked, but they were intact. The word "AICNALUBMA" was written in big letters on the grill. When it drove up along the adobe wall where Jack and Claire were waiting, Jack said, "Well, that's disconcerting."

Alberto slapped Jack on the back and said, "The four-wheel-drive will come in handy."

The drive to their destination followed the route back to Cusco for a few miles before splitting off to the east in the direction of the Amazon and then north. The ambulance bumped along the dirt road for an hour before turning east again into the remote mountains.

Alberto turned to the three friends. "Heading into the Laris Tribe country," he said, raising his voice over the van's grinding gears and rattling chassis, "the 'Wolf Clan,' these people were once Incan by birthright." Jack looked out the window at the same terraced, gorgeous mountainous country they had been seeing for the past two weeks. Then he noticed the hooks on the vehicle's ceiling for hanging intravenous bags. There was also a broken valve with the word, *Oxígeno* written under it. Twenty minutes later, they passed through the tiny farming community of Lares. The van neither slowed down going through the town nor sped up. In less than five minutes, there seemed no sign of civilization.

The road was getting rougher. There were long sections where the dirt tracks had been washed out in past rainy seasons, and potholes were more like craters. Occasionally, everyone but the driver had to get out of the ambulance to lighten its load and direct the driver through or around the enormous ruts. The trip they were on now felt different. Perhaps it was the road's condition. This was not a road for carting touristas but for prospectors, miners, and farmers. The landscape varied from mile to mile, from fertile green valleys to high plateaus and mountain cloud forests to steaming jungle. After an hour of bumping along at twenty miles per hour, they came to Choquechancha, the last village before their drop-off point.

A mile outside the village, the van passed six tiny stone houses next to the stream.

"*¡Espere! ¡Sostener!*" Al suddenly snapped, and the driver quickly pulled off the road. In front of one of the homes, there was some sort of celebration. Jack couldn't think of any Catholic holiday it could be. Two men were playing zampoñas, and a third was lightly whacking his thumb on a small drum. There was a table set up outside, and a small girl was dutifully sitting atop it in a white dress that looked like a Christening outfit.

"It's a *corte de pelo*," explained Al, "a cutting of the hair ceremony. Jack should see this." He motioned for all of them to follow him out of the ambulance. "Another anthropologic moment," he said to Jack as he exited. Al got out, waving and talking to the family as he walked toward them. The others waited by the van. Claire and Jack waved and smiled when the family members looked across the road at them. Alberto shook some hands and waved the travelers over.

"I told them that you are good students who appreciate the way of life here very much. I asked if I could involve you for a few minutes to explain the *corte de pelo*. They are very honored for you to participate."

The family of Campesinos seemed truly happy to accommodate the travelers.

Alberto translated as usual. "The little girl's name is Eisabel. She is three-and-a-half years old, and this is her first haircut." Eisabel was cute but looked very glum. "Sometimes this 'cutting of the hair' ceremony is done at the time of the baptism, but some clans wait a few years more."

"Please tell her that her dress is beautiful," Claire requested. As she said that, Claire reached across the table and patted the frills along the hem of Eisabel's dress and the little girl recoiled. Her mother and some of the other women laughed and explained to the girl what Alberto said to her — probably in better Quechua than what Al was speaking. The child tried to smile.

A large doily lined an earthen bowl, and as celebrants cut locks of hair with shears, they deposited them onto the doily along with Inti notes. Five or ten Inti notes were only a few U.S. cents. Alberto asked if the students could participate, and Claire, Casey, and Jack took turns with the shears. Eisabel was so terrified, they each carefully snipped only the smallest tuft of hair. They each put into the doily a couple of U.S. dollars, which was quite a boon. Jack put up an index finger to the girl and ran back to the van. He returned quickly and placed an old St. Christopher's medal around her neck. Eisabel looked down at her chest, grasped it, and flipped it over a few times, admiring it before giving Jack a big smile ... her only smile while they were visiting.

"You do have a way with the ladies Jack," Claire said.

"Little ones," he said as he patted down Eisabel's chopped-up hairdo. She smiled at him again.

The family offered food and chicha beer, but Al explained that they didn't have much time and had to leave. The family was very gracious. Before they left, an old man grabbed Claire's hand in a slightly intoxicated attempt to dance, and Claire followed along the best she could.

As they were all getting back in the van, Alberto said, "That was interesting. You all were the first gringos to ever visit their home. This celebration is more like a ritual for them, kind of a 'coming of age ceremony.'"

Claire asked Jack, "You just happened to have an extra medallion?"

"I actually can't remember where it came from. I found it in my pack yesterday while I was rearranging things."

Ten minutes down the road, Alberto said, "Notice we are up in the highlands here — we are looking down steep slopes, but do you feel the oxygen?" He breathed in demonstratively. "We are more than 1,000 feet lower than Ollanta." The van was descending a steep grade to a stream. "Twelve more miles," he said. Every eighth-mile, the road made a hairpin turn on a switchback as they closed in on the stream.

"I hope the brakes are good," Claire said.

Alberto turned to the driver, "*Ella dijo que espera que los frenos sean Buenos.*" The driver leaned sideways, straining to hear Al. Then he laughed and responded. Al turned back to Claire with a shrug, "He says the brakes are fair. I told him they're overrated."

This was lovely green country. The road, which probably should not be referred to as a 'road,' paralleled a beautiful stream. It was lined with tall eucalyptus trees and several other conifers. Like all others in the Peruvian highlands, this stream was rushing and strewn with thousands of boulders, but it was not as milky from glacial run-off as most others. To Jack and Casey, it looked very "fishy." Occasionally, a small stone house with a thatched roof could be seen on the hillside, but this valley was very sparsely populated. Wherever there was a house, alpacas could be seen grazing the steep slopes. The road crawled up the eastern edge of the valley. There was a steep mountainside to the right of the road, with occasional drainages depositing small rivulets across the road and down to the stream and valley floor.

About an hour past the last farmhouse, the van pulled into a wide spot in the road where one of the drainages emptied into the valley. The old ambulance lurched to a halt. Here, another tiny rivulet trickled out of the drainage and crossed the road.

Alberto and the driver spoke while the packs were unloaded. Al called a 'huddle' and explained that the driver would be back at this spot in nine days. "If, for any reason," Al explained in both English and Spanish, translating as he went, "we are not here on the ninth day, he is to return two days later. If we are not here by then, he is to inform Gregorio to organize a search party."

The driver repeated everything back, and Al wrote the instructions down on two pieces of paper and gave them to the driver to take to Gregorio and Benita. He put the name of their hostel in Ollantaytambo on the top of the note. A shake of the hand and the driver was gone.

Casey laid out the map using his backpack as a low table. They all could identify the drainage they were in, and they could see the stream that paralleled the road. Alberto placed a compass on the map, and Jack made some notes on the margins, including some compass bearings and a back azimuth. He noted the same bearings in his notebook and memorized them. The road they were on ran north/south. Even if the map was lost, they could get out as long as they had a compass.

They were ready.

"Let's get out of sight of the road and make camp," Al said.

The drainage they had to climb would be steep in places and hard to negotiate. Fortunately, thousands of trails in the highlands had been cut through the hills by animals and shepherds for as many years. Just to the right of the brook, Al found an alpaca trail and started up it. It wasn't without obstructions. A tangle of vines, yucca, and wild rose branches veiled the trail and slowed the pace. Al stopped near one of the wide shrubs lining the path. "This is called a polylepis," he said, pulling a branch that was clinging to his forearm, "They're in the rose family, and there are over twenty species here in the Andes."

Great, thought Casey. He was interested in everything Al wanted to show them but was already breathing hard. *Keep going, brother*. They hiked about twenty minutes more before finding a level spot next to the tiny spring, where there was enough room for three small mountaineering tents.

"What do you think?" Alberto asked. "There's water to filter, and if you want to fish, it's only twenty minutes back to the stream."

"Perfect," Casey said. Jack and Claire agreed.

All three tents were erected in fifteen minutes. Jack and Alberto pushed and flipped four good-sized boulders in front of the tents to sit on and built a stone hearth.

"Want to try the stream, anyone?" Casey asked. He was already pulling his fly rod out of its aluminum protective tube.

Jack waved him off. "I'm good here, I think. Want to do some writing."

Claire wanted to relax for a while.

"Okay," Casey said. "I reckon I'll be about an hour-and-a-half, maybe two."

Casey strolled back down the rough trail, fly rod in hand. Jack immediately began collecting firewood. Alberto foraged and found some *chirimoya* (the 'custard apple' Mark Twain was so fond of). "I can't believe our luck," he said as he carried four of the strange fruit. The overlapping scales gave them the appearance of scaled dinosaur eggs. "This is pretty high for chirimoya."

An hour from the early sunset that always occurs in the mountains, Jack had a small fire going on the stone hearth and was ready with a pot of spring water to boil. When they were ready, they ate their first freeze-dried meal. While they waited for suppertime and for Casey to return,

Al, Claire, and Jack reclined against the boulders and read or wrote in their journals and shared the sweet, creamy white flesh of two of the chirimoya. Alberto couldn't help noticing when he saw Claire and Jack smiling at each other. He buried his nose in the Jim Harrison paperback Jack had given him.

Casey arrived back at the campsite. It got cold quickly. Jackets were donned, and everyone huddled close to the fire as the water boiled.

"Bro," Casey said to Jack, "you should have come."

"It was good?"

"I caught a few," replied Casey, "but the water was much easier to fish and clearer than the other streams we've tried here. It reminded me of Montana spring creek fishing, except these fish were smaller."

"Maybe we'll find a lake higher in the mountains," Jack said.

The following day, plodding one foot in front of the other, the group followed the drainage up, up, and up. After four hours, the vegetation started to change. The trail petered out, and the explorers simply stepped anywhere that looked like sound footing. They walked around boulders and through the short tufts of pampas grass, and occasionally there would be thirty or forty feet of alpaca or goat trails that traveled in the correct direction. The little spring became braided, flowing down in many places from the glaciers above. At what seemed like a mountain pass that leveled out somewhat, the group stopped and ate lunch.

Jack looked around. Behind, they could see the valley below. *We must have gained 1,000 feet in elevation*, he thought. He looked to the east, where shorter mountains spread out for miles.

"We are on the eastern edge of the Andes now," Jack said. "There doesn't seem to be any civilization anywhere."

Casey pulled out the map. They could see off into the distance in the direction of Gregorio's 'X.' All that lay before them was a lovely landscape of mountains, valleys, ravines, glaciers, and indigo skies. They saw no signs of buildings and homes and not even a plume of smoke.

"We must be over 14,000 feet," Alberto studied the map. "It looks like if we keep on this pass and try to push to the north a little, we'll be on a good track to descend into the next valley. The next range of mountains is not as high." Al tapped the deep green of the Manus that lay beyond the next mountains and smiled at Casey. "There be dragons."

Casey folded the map and placed it in a pocket built into the belt of his backpack. Jack took a few photos, and everyone drank more water.

Jack noticed Claire had sweated through her t-shirt. "Drink more," he whispered to her. She nodded. *That's how half my sentences will be with her now*, he thought. *In whispers. How odd this is now.* He knew that pretending normality was going to be difficult. It went against every fiber of his being, and now when interacting with Claire and Casey simultaneously, he felt physically ill. Twice Jack told Casey that he was struggling with the altitude — he wasn't — he was just struggling with life.

Jack was already wondering if the angst he lived with before when he loved Claire secretly was easier. At least he knew who he was then. He wasn't always comfortable with his life, but it was easier than this. Now, everything was different.

"Ready?" asked Al.

Packs were hoisted, and off they went. The boost of energy from the hydration was a big help. The foursome traversed the pass and followed it to the north. Alberto stopped just before it started to descend a few feet of elevation. It was getting a bit narrow. He looked back at Casey, who turned to Jack. It was not a goat or alpaca trail but instead a naturally forming ledge of rock and scree that wrapped around the small mountain they had just climbed over. The gravel-strewn ledge was about four feet wide now, not wide enough for two people to pass comfortably while wearing backpacks, but not narrow enough to warrant rope protection. To their right was a 1,000-foot drop. Casey didn't have to say anything to Jack, who stepped close to the edge and leaned out enough to survey the terrain past Alberto.

Casey then yelled back to Claire, "You comfortable with this?" She was breathing hard but nodded. Jack shook his head and called to Casey. "We're good."

Alberto proceeded without using the rope.

The gravel ledge followed the mountain around to the north for a thousand more feet before widening into a scree field that resembled a rockslide down the mountain. They skirted the edge of it where the descent was more manageable and picked their way through large boulders until they got lower where the walking was easier. Again, there were goat and alpaca trails each hiker could choose to follow.

"I'd like to get down into the valley for the next camp, if we can," Alberto called out. "Three more hours, I think."

As they hiked, the valley below looked similar to all the others in this part of the Andes. It was green, with meadows, tall trees, and shrubbery, and had a river or stream running through it. But in this valley, they could see no town or village.

꙾

As they reached the valley floor, Claire could feel it in her legs. They were tired. She tried to walk normally, but they were getting increasingly wobbly. She tried to ignore it. *No complaining*, she thought. She guessed the river was another quarter mile farther into the valley. That's what Alberto seemed to be trying for. She was slowing. The walking was easy now, but Jack stayed with her. The trail they were following was wide. Alberto and Casey were in sight but far ahead. Neither had looked back.

Jack came abreast of her and touched her hand. "Only a short way now. Are you feeling it in your legs?"

"Yeah," she said.

"I could see it in your gait. Know what it is?"

Claire shook her head. "Not in good enough shape?"

"Nope," Jack said. "Electrolytes got away from you."

As soon as he said that, she knew he was right. That's precisely what she felt like. "I'll drink more as soon as we get to where they want to camp."

"Good. And I've got something for you that'll help a lot," Jack said.

Forty minutes later, they found Al and Casey beside the stream. Casey had his shirt off and was wringing it out. Al was already unpacking his tent.

"Quite a hike," called out Casey as they approached. Claire dropped her pack next to a boulder big enough to sit on and plopped down onto it. Jack already had his pack off and water bottle out. He poured a little packet of powder into it, recapped the bottle, and shook it up. The water turned pale yellow. He handed the bottle to Claire, and she drank a few ounces even though it was quite salty. Then she handed it back to Jack, got out her water bottle, and drank some more. She felt better almost immediately.

Casey walked up to her as he pulled on a dry shirt. "You okay?"

"Just got a little dehydrated," she replied. "Jack gave me something that's helping."

It was late afternoon. Once Claire felt better, she realized she was getting chilled in her wet shirt. She rummaged through her pack and stood up with her back to the men, and took off her sweat-soaked t-shirt and sports bra. Al and Jack saw her but paid no attention. On an expedition, things are different. Modesty is often irrelevant. Alberto was obviously a man of the world. Casey had seen her naked hundreds of times, and Jack — he just might be her soul mate. Claire wiped herself down with a terrycloth towel and put on a dry shirt. She didn't bother with a dry bra. In new clothes and with the electrolytes kicking in, she suddenly felt fantastic.

"Might want to bring your towel and some dry socks down to the stream," Jack said. "Feels good to soak your feet." Jack walked over to the stream with his towel. Claire watched him and smiled to herself. He had a way about him — it was hard to explain — like everyone seemed better for knowing him. He was kind-hearted, and he could talk to babies and dogs in his normal voice, and they understood him. And the more she thought about him, the more she realized he had always loved her. How could she not have seen it? And the more she thought about it, the more she realized that maybe *she* had always loved him also. She watched him as he found a flat rock next to the stream to sit on. She smiled as he peered closely into the mud and gravel among the rocks. *Looking for insects*, she said to herself and thought it was cute that the ground got his attention, and he started looking around as though he'd lost something before finally sitting on the rock and soaking his feet. She had the strangest urge to go over and rub his feet for him, which she thought odd because she was grossed out by feet.

Jack walked over to Alberto as he was setting up his tent, said something, and went back together to the flat rock by the stream. Claire and Casey exchanged glances as they watched Jack point at something with a stick. Al looked first upstream and then down the valley.

Casey got a small fire going. He put a pan of water on to boil, and when Jack and Alberto returned to the campfire, he held up two packages of dehydrated meals; "beef Stroganoff, or lasagna?"

"They will taste the same," Alberto said, smiling.

"Probably," Casey said, reading one of the packages.

As the boiling water reconstituted the meals, Alberto spoke. "Jack found tracks by the stream. Some were sandaled, and some were barefoot," he said, "Campesinos. But some were booted."

"Hikers?" Casey asked.

"I hope so," Al said, with the slightest trace of concern clouding his eyes. "Or it might be Sendero."

The three friends sat in silence.

"I wasn't going to mention anything," Al continued, "but I suppose we should prepare our minds, just in case. If we do meet up with them, stay calm and smile confidently, like you're not upset to see them. I will tell them the names of two Sendero I know in Cusco and explain that you are science teachers interested in and sympathetic to their cause and even that you are happy to meet them. That might be the best chance for them not to assault us."

Casey said, "Sounds reasonable."

Claire spoke up. "What's that from?" She was pointing north, up the valley. The others spun on their rocks and looked. A thin plume of white smoke spiraled into the sky before bending eastward.

Alberto looked back at their campfire. "Our fire is small. Good…not much smoke."

He stood up, as did everyone, and looked up the valley at the smoke. "About an eighth of a mile."

"Another campsite?" Casey asked.

"Maybe, but too big, I think. Might be a farm up there." Al thought for a moment. "We're exploring, right? I think we should investigate that. Find out who it is."

"We can't walk into a campsite at dusk," Jack said. "Wouldn't do that even in Wyoming. Puts people on edge."

"Right," Alberto agreed, "after we've struck camp in the morning. We'll be cautious. Maybe they won't shoot us." He looked at Jack, Claire, and Casey with a wry smile, and with the tiny fire lighting up his handsome Latin face, he said, "Exciting, isn't it when it all gets real."

The three friends grinned.

"We'll see," said Casey.

TWENTY-SIX

Shangri La

After breakfast, when everyone was packed, Casey called them together. "Alberto, only you speak Quechua, and though we three can be friendly and engaging, would it be wise to go meet these people — if they're still there — with our packs on in case they would rob us? Maybe ditch the packs and just go in without them until we know?"

"That's a good thought," Al replied. "If we backtrack from here about fifty yards and then parallel the stream up the valley toward the smoke, from the slopes, we should be able to see down onto the stream. If we find them, we can decide about hiding the packs. If it's a farm, we'll be okay."

"Sounds good," Casey offered.

They did exactly that. In only thirty-five minutes of walking up the valley through bushes and cacti and skirting eucalyptus trees, the friends came to the edge of a meadow. The scene was idyllic. The plume of smoke was again in the sky, pampas grass and wildflowers sprouted everywhere, and there were six or seven stone and thatched houses sitting in the shadow of a pure white glacier. The picture was framed by the blue morning sky, with wispy white clouds hanging close to the glaciers. Alpacas grazed next to the stream.

Standing in the trees at the edge of the meadow, Alberto said, "We're good," and started to walk.

"Just a moment, please," Jack said. Al stopped. Jack's camera clicked four or five times. "Thanks."

All four approached the houses, with Al whistling a tune loudly. Alberto held up one arm, almost like a Nazi salute, and called out,

"*Wuynus diyas Allin p'unchay! Wuynus diyas Allin p'unchay…*"

Three Indian women came to a doorway and pulled some children into the house. They were frightened. One of them looked like she was afraid for her life and waved the back of her hand, motioning the group to the right of the buildings. All four looked in the direction of her gestures and saw two men approaching. Al again called out 'Good morning,' in Quechua; "*Wuynus diyas Allin p'unchay.*"

Both men gave Al a salute and said, "Good morning."

The oldest man, about thirty years old, was the only one who spoke. He told Alberto his name was Enrico. He was barely five feet tall and was clad in a bright red wool poncho, a handwoven red-and-black breechcloth, and a *chullu* — an alpaca woolen hat with earflaps. He wore homemade rubber sandals. Jack looked at the sandals and recognized the rubber on the soles. They were from an automobile tire.

Alberto was relieved to find Enrico could speak elementary Spanish, and they could understand each other quite well. Everyone sat cross-legged on the grass in a circle and talked. Enrico introduced his companion, Benito as his brother-in-law. "Seventeen people are living here," Enrico told Alberto, "and everyone is related."

He told the group that they grew what they could and took turns once every month to make the two-and-a-half-day trip to Choquecancha for supplies such as kerosene and matches. A few times a year, they sent several men at once with raw wool and textiles to sell. "Some members of the clan have never been off the mountain," he told them. He explained that there were other small communities like this throughout these mountains and that while there were no roads, every valley had trails that lead in and out to various villages. He waved his hands and told Alberto there were trails over the mountains, to the east and west. "The trails have been here since the old ones."

Alberto nodded. "Inca trails."

Casey pulled out the map and asked Alberto to show Enrico and Benito exactly where they were on the map. Al knelt next to the Campesino men and pointed to a spot in the valley. "You are here, he told them. "You are not on the map!"

Enrico looked at the valley and mountains on the map from different angles and then tapped the spot, nodded, then laughed, and said, "*Si, si…Bueno.*" Not on the map. That's just how he wanted it. Everyone smiled at that.

"Interesting," Jack said.

"What is?" Claire asked.

"He could only visualize where his village *should* be on the map when orienting it from the north."

Al asked Enrico if they had any trouble or experience with the Sendero Luminoso. Neither men knew what that was. "Guess that's a no," Alberto said. He went on to tell them what the Shining Path terrorist group was, and the farmer clearly did not understand what it was all about.

His only question was, "Why do they want to control other men's lives?"

Al translated, and the four travelers all stared at the grass. That was the perfect question.

Alberto said in Spanish, "Friend, I am very glad those bad men haven't bothered your beautiful village." And patted him on the shoulder.

Enrico thought gravely about the Sendero for a moment and, in lilting Quechua, said, "Maybe they don't know we are here. Maybe they are using the same map as you."

Alberto asked Enrico if he knew of a settlement to the east, in the last mountains before the Manus. Al pointed his arm east-southeast, aimed up another drainage.

"I think there may be," he said. "About two kilometers downstream, there is a rock dam across the stream where we sometimes net fish. We have seen people cross there and go up the arroyo slightly to the north. But they never come up here, and they never say hello."

Al gave him back the map, and he turned it upside down. He pointed to a drainage. Up the drainage and slightly on the other side was the 'X' he had drawn. Gregorio had been accurate.

"They may live there," Enrico supposed, "we do not go over those mountains."

Al asked if the three friends were the first gringos that had visited.

"In my lifetime, yes. But I have heard of another. Would you like to meet Benito's grandfather? He is the one who will know."

With that, all rose and followed Enrico to one of the houses. They left their packs where they lay and brought only cameras and journals. As they followed Enrico, Alberto spoke to the others in a soft voice, "This is a real privilege."

Each house had a small garden plot with rough stone walls where pigs, chickens, guinea pigs, and sheep were kept. There were stone cooking huts with oversized roofs that resembled mushrooms standing alongside the houses. Benito stood next to the door of one of the houses, and Enrico motioned that this was the elder's house. All four friends entered the building. The house, having only two small windows, was dark inside, and it took time for their eyes to adjust. The dirt floor was blackened from generations of animal urine, spilled kerosene, the blood of slaughtered rabbits and sheep, and was as hard as concrete from thousands of footsteps. In the corner was one good-sized bed covered in a mass of dirty blankets. Sitting at a small table in the middle of the room was an elderly man, sitting straight-backed in a plastic chair. Against one shoulder, he secured a large staff, the top of which was wrapped with ornate pounded silver.

"This is Apurimac," Enrico said.

The old man held out his hand and gave each traveler a feeble handshake. Alberto, through Enrico, explained who they were and how honored they were to see his village and speak with him. Apurimac did not seem too excited.

"Would it be rude to ask his age?" Al asked Enrico. Al thought he looked 100.

Enrico shook his head, smiled, and asked the *alcaldes*. Alberto translated what they came up with, "Between eighty and eighty-five years old."

Alberto, Enrico, and Apurimac convened.

"He knows of another gringo that visited many years ago, who had a group of men with him," Enrico said. "He says he was only nine or ten years old. I myself barely remember my father talking about it."

The friends were all doing the math in their heads. "Was he a prospector?" Al asked.

"No," translated Enrico, "he was an American teacher, looking for the houses of the old ones."

Al digested the response and translated it. Jack looked at Claire, and she whispered to the room, "*Bingham?*"

"I didn't think he came this far north or east," Jack said, "but possibly."

They spoke and visited for a few minutes more through the four-way translation before Alberto made a ceremonial farewell. Outside, Claire and Jack took a few photographs before the group donned their backpacks. After waving goodbye, the four walked back along the stream to find the rock dam and footbridge.

"Did you notice all the women stayed in the houses?" Claire asked as they hiked. "Were they afraid of us?"

"The men probably wanted them kept away from Jack's rugged good looks," teased Casey.

Alberto chuckled, and Jack mustered a mock laugh. Jack glanced at Claire, who looked back at him and made a face as if to say, *I could see that.*

ᛉ

Two kilometers ... Enrico was about right. Ten minutes past their previous night's campsite, they came to the rock dam. It looked old. Everywhere they went in this land, there was evidence of life before the Campesinos, the conquistadores, and the Inca. And the evidence suggested advanced life. In Cusco, Casey had stood in wonder at the architecture and remembered reading that when Pizzaro's brother and a contingent of conquistadores first marched into the city, all the temples were sheathed in gold. The city shimmered in the mountain sunlight. He could imagine how magnificent it must have looked. *They built all this,* he thought, *200 years before the Massachusetts Pilgrims were living in thinly built wood-framed houses, freezing in the winter, starving, and killing each other for being witches. Who was more civilized?*

Standing at the rock dam, the group looked across the valley. The drainages between the mountains on the other side were obvious. One was directly opposite the dam. Al pointed to another, just to the north. "That's the one on the map," he said. "Casey, may I look at the map?" Al removed the compass from a small pocket in his backpack strap. He took a reading and wrote a heading on the map and made a small line across the stream where they stood. "This is the heading back to the dam from the base of that drainage," he said. Jack jotted it down in his notebook.

The day before, the group had gained and lost several thousand feet of elevation and had hiked through several different biomes; deciduous forests, high pampas plains, alpine, and jungle. In the Andes, trekkers can hike for an hour, see completely different flora, and feel they have changed seasons.

Claire's thighs and calves were a bit sore from the hike over the mountains the day before, but once they started across the valley toward the drainage, her legs loosened up, and the pain subsided. Casey seemed to be walking slower, but that might have been because Alberto, walking ahead of him, was constantly trying to find a path. It had been evident on the far side of the rock dam, but now it was ill-defined as it wound through the shrubbery and the eucalyptus trees.

After more than an hour of picking their way across the valley floor, Al stopped for a water break. He had worked hard to stay on the compass heading for the base of the drainage.

"I think," he said, "since we spent so much time at the farming community this morning, we'll probably only get a short way up the drainage before we have to make camp."

They were headed up the east side of the valley. Casey looked up at the mountains for a point of reference and said, "It'll be a nice sunset."

Al looked at his compass and continued. They passed the first drainage, keeping it on their right. As they headed up the second drainage and started gaining a few feet of elevation, they knew they were approaching the mountains — the last mountains before dropping down into the Amazon Basin. The hiking was as good as it gets; mountain vistas, a beautiful valley, and since Al had not been in this particular valley, each was exploring new country. And the terrain was easy. There were still clumps of grasses here and there, but it was intermingled with agaves and prickly pear cacti. Paths through the trees and boulders became easier to find.

By mid-afternoon, they had made their way into the first few thousand feet of the drainage. The sloping terrain quickly became very steep. Another small stream trickled out of the drainage, and they followed it up. Al stopped for a drink where some boulders offered places to sit and rest. Each dropped their packs and got out their water bottles.

From the boulders, the friends could look down into the valley. They could see parts of the same stream they had camped next to the night before. Jack looked up the valley but could find no traces of the stone houses they had visited early that morning. He could see no smoke. Al pointed across the valley to the mountains on the far side.

"You can see the pass we crossed yesterday," he said. He glanced down at the compass. "It's right in line with the heading for the rock dam."

"Al!" Claire called from a few yards away.

He jumped up off the boulder. Jack and Casey followed him. Claire was sitting next to a wild rose bush. She was buttoning her shorts and looking uphill. Holding her buttons with one hand, she pointed with the other. "Steps."

She was right. Clearly, she had stumbled onto a section of the old Inca trail system. Not only was it paved with stone almost eight feet wide, but at spots, there were steps carved in the trail.

"Amazing," Alberto said. "There are sections of the trail found all over the Andes each year. You just found one, Claire."

"So cool," she whispered.

"You peed on it," teased Casey. "Pretty disrespectful."

"Map, please?" Al asked.

Al marked on the map precisely where the trail section was in the drainage. He looked up the mountain. "This may lead to one of the guard towers. We *are* on the eastern border of the old empire. I think we should follow this, obviously, instead of following the stream. Besides, this trail likely parallels the water anyway."

They each donned their backpacks and cut over to the trail. Hiking up, it seemed as natural as could be. Some of it was over-grown. Along the stream, there had been no sign of travelers. But here, on the old Inca trail, stones were worn smooth in places from decades of sandaled foot traffic.

They pushed up 500 feet, then another 500, and 500 more. Everyone felt the altitude because of the steepness of the drainage. It was exciting to be hiking an Incan trail. It was four in the afternoon. Once Al found a flat spot big enough for three small mountaineering tents, they stopped for the night. They had a commanding view of the valley below. The stream below looked tiny now, a slender, silver snake meandering down the center of the valley. Little brown meadows punctuated the green vale, and the fertile fields offered grazing for the llamas and alpacas, and from so far away, they unveiled a sense of life. As they set up their tents and gathered dried twigs for a small campfire, Al reckoned they had only about 1,000 more feet to the pass at the top of the trail.

Their tents were only thirty feet off the trail. Again, they rolled some boulders to sit on, and again they built a small hearth and boiled some water.

"It's remarkable," Casey said between bites of beef stroganoff, "that if you get really hungry, these freeze-dried meals are pretty friggin' good."

As they sat around the tiny campfire, Jack asked, "Al, I notice that the locals in the small villages or farming communities dress differently everywhere we go. Is it simply a matter of local pride or a statement of individuality?"

"Probably both," Al replied, the firelight flickering in his dark Latin eyes. "It is said that the first Inca ordered the dresses of each village to be different so that his officials might know to which tribe an individual belonged."

Casey asked Al, "Do you have Quechua in you?"

"Of course." He paused. "Our history in Peru is sad. We suffered greatly at the hands of the Spaniards, but like many South Americans, we are mixed blood."

"Take the last great Inca, José Gabriel Tupac Amaru II. His story underscores the brutality of the Spanish in the old days. Do any of you know about Amaru?"

"Just that he led a rebellion," Claire said.

Casey replied, "Not my area of study."

Jack shook his head.

"He was one of the last descendants of the original Incas," Alberto said. "You might have seen his bust in Cusco. The Spanish rule had become more oppressive over the 200 years since Pizarro. The Bourbon reforms in the 1700s were meant to gain more control over indigenous subjects by placing a greater tax and labor burden on them, among other things. It was particularly bad for the Quechua-speaking people of Peru. Amaru was a man born into wealth not far from Cusco and educated by the Jesuits. He led a rebellion in the late 1700s to demand changes and reforms within the structure of colonial rule in Peru. But it quickly evolved into something more. Some of his rebels wanted to overthrow European rule and regain something like restoring the pre-conquest Inca empire. They wanted an egalitarian society based economically on the Inca communal agricultural system, without racial divisions or rifts between the rich and poor. They tried to overthrow the forced labor in mines and factories.

"But the rebellion didn't last long, less than three years. They captured Amaru and his family, along with some of his captains. The Spaniards put them in big sacks and then dragged them through the streets of Cusco behind horses. They forced the Inca and his wife to watch as they cut out the tongues of their young son and Amaru's uncle and then garroted them. Then they made him watch as they did the same to his wife. But the Inca's wife's neck was too slender, and the iron collar was not small enough, so the executioner beat her and strangled her with a rope instead.

"Then, after watching his family executed, they sentenced Amaru to die by having four horses pull him limb from limb. When the horses failed to do it, the executioner adlibbed. He disemboweled Amaru and then beheaded him. They then quartered him and sent his body parts to principal places in the colony to be displayed. All records of his lineage were burned, and his twelve-year-old son, who had also been condemned to die, was instead sent to Spain and imprisoned for the rest of his life."

Alberto stared into the fire. "In our veins runs the blood of the conquerors and of the conquered. The people still haven't forgotten what they did to that Incan family."

No one knew how to respond to that.

Jack thought back about the last few weeks. He thought about the strange, magical feeling he felt at different locations where they had walked. He thought about the dust of the ancestors; they were not his people, but he was beginning to understand them.

TWENTY-SEVEN
A Grand Discovery

The morning was frigid, and the nylon flies that covered the tents seemed crisp and crinkled as if there had been a frost. As they ate their re-constituted scrambled eggs, Jack said, "I can't wait to see where this trail goes."

"If it goes anywhere," Casey said, blowing on his hands.

Jack's mind wandered to Kipling ...

"Till a voice, as bad as Conscience, rang interminable changes
On one everlasting Whisper day and night repeated -- so:
"Something hidden. Go and find it. Go and look behind the Ranges ..."

They hiked up to the pass in an hour. At the top, there was no Incan watch tower, no ruins at all. The stone-lined trail simply stopped.

"Well, that was anticlimactic," Casey suggested.

"No archaeologic finds," Alberto confirmed, standing at the edge of the pass staring eastward, "but I wouldn't call it anticlimactic."

Below the friends stretched a different drainage descending to the east. More beautiful Andean countryside lay before them for a mile or two at the base. On both sides of the drainage were terraces that held tiny lakes and lagoons and deciduous trees, and their leaves shimmered in the wind. They were not man-made terraces but rather old lateral moraines, tell-tales of an ancient glacial retreat up the mountainside. But farther east, beyond the mountains and the foothills, everything changed. There was a dark green mass of vegetation as far as the eye could see, like an endless, dense, plush carpet of foliage. It went beyond the horizon; east, north, and south. It was the canopy of a vast rain forest. It was Amazonia, and it was breathtaking.

"The old boundary of the Incan Empire," Alberto said. "I wonder how many people get to climb over a mountain pass and see it like this?"

Jack glanced over at Claire. She was standing by herself, and she looked beautiful. She wore her backpack well, and with her hands were on her hips, she was taking deep breaths of clean mountain air. Her blonde ponytail was lit by the sun, and she was looking out over the jungle canopy far into the distance. He walked over to her. Together they watched the slanting late morning sun light up the Amazon rain forest. Clouds of mist floated here and there as far as they could see, revealing where there were bodies of water hidden in the mystic places below the rain forest canopy.

For two days, Jack had been thinking that perhaps telling her how he felt — how he had always felt — and their making love had been a terrible mistake. Now, everything was different. How could he continue to act normally? For the hundredth time over the past two days, he tried to shake the feeling.

But now, this magnificent view temporarily pushed those feelings aside.

"Not too shabby," he said.

Claire laughed softly, leaned sideways, and nudged him with her shoulder. Casey stepped up next to them.

"What's that?" Casey was pointing below, along the north side of the drainage.

Several plumes of smoke were billowing up from the foothills. Alberto stepped forward, and all four stared at the smoke.

"Civilization?" Casey asked.

"Let's hope so," replied Alberto.

"Everybody still up for this?" Al asked. Each person nodded. Alberto looked back at the smoke. "I think it's just another tiny farming community. It's too high in the hills to be a drug operation. They tend to prefer jungle areas, and it's easier to stay hidden by the canopy and harvest the cocoa leaves that grow down lower.

"We've come this far," Casey said.

"Let's mark this pass on the map also," Al said, "these points on the map will be our breadcrumbs."

⚜

The descent into the drainage wasn't as easy as it looked from above.

There was no more ancient Incan trail to follow, only boulders the size of automobiles with cacti growing in between them. An hour into the downhill hike, there were animal trails that were easier to follow. After three hours, Alberto stopped to take a compass reading.

"We'll soon drop low enough that we won't be able to see the smoke." In fact, the smoke was already gone, but Al had marked the spot on the landscape by a bald rock face in the vicinity. He calculated the compass heading from the bottom of the ravine.

Halfway down the rocky drainage, another tiny stream had formed from a spring, and the group stopped to filter water into their bottles. The lower they got, the easier the walking became. After four-and-a-half hours of hiking from the pass, the group was clearly near the bottom. The terrain had leveled out somewhat, and the cacti and alpine shrubbery gave way to pampas grasses and wild roses. Before long, they were back among the trees, and animal trails were everywhere. They stayed near the stream, which was bigger now. It was early afternoon.

After another hour of plodding downhill, they entered a beautiful, temperate valley of gentle, natural pastureland interspersed with copses of trees. Alberto guessed the altitude of the plateau was about 5,000-feet. On the opposite side of the valley, they knew the plateau would drop down into the Manu.

Al stopped and looked back up the ravine. "We are near the bottom now," he said. "I think we should camp here, near the stream, and start exploring in the morning." He looked to the north. "Maybe skirt along the slopes of these foothills and look around. If you all agree."

There was never any reason not to agree with Alberto.

They all searched around until Casey found a pleasant glade within sight of the stream. A big log from a queuña tree was lying in the open spot that would make a nice bench seat, along with a few boulders already in place to sit on. Once settled and with a fire heating water for their packaged meals, Jack, Claire, and Alberto sat on the log writing in their journals. Casey sat on his sleeping pad on the grass, leaning back against one of the boulders. He was pretty close to the fire, and with his arms crossed on his chest, he closed his eyes. He looked very comfortable. Alberto unfolded Casey's map on his lap. "You know," he said, "we're only about four-and-a-half miles from the border of the Madre de Dios Department. Too bad we don't have about six more day's rations."

Everyone was knackered. Jack was the last one to bed. His mind was racing. He never felt so alive as when he was exploring. In another life, he would've endeavored to do it professionally. Perhaps he could still have a life of adventure while seeking the beauty of life in the world of anthropology. But, what of Claire? They had had one evening to talk. *One*. What did that accomplish? Perhaps ruin his life and maybe Claire's? And Casey's? What had he expected? *That's right*, he thought; *I hadn't expected anything because I never intended for her to know I love her. Now, I've ruined it between her and Casey — and probably between her and myself. The first chance I get, I've got to fix this.*

Jack's guilt was battling his desire, his common sense, his everything. *No matter what happens*, he rationalized, *be her friend. Be her best friend.*

⚐

The group awoke, dressed, ate breakfast, and struck their camp like a well-oiled machine in less than an hour.

They went over the plan for the day and marked their spot on the map. Another breadcrumb. It was decided they had rations enough to spend two full days searching for the community or whatever else they might find. Then they would return to this spot and retrace their steps to Ollantaytambo. Alberto took one of the empty foil freeze-dried meal packages and stuck it on a branch next to the stream.

They topped off their water bottles, checked their compass heading, and hiked northward, skirting the foothills and the edge of the plateau much like they had days before when they found Enrico's hamlet. As they walked, Alberto kept an eye peeled. He thought *I don't believe those plumes of smoke yesterday were more than a half-mile from last night's campsite.*

There were fewer trees at the elevation they were walking. Agave, wild roses, and thorny bushes grew. But occasionally, the impenetrable undergrowth gave way to lovely little meadows that looked perfect for grazing. After an hour's walk, Al noticed llama droppings. A bit farther and there were sheep droppings. For Al, that sealed it. Farmers were somewhere in the area.

Just then, everyone heard a noise. It was a 'clack,' or a muffled bang as if someone had dropped something. All froze in their tracks, and Alberto looked back at the friends and pointed in the direction of the noise. They were in-between groves of thickets. Staring in the direction of the noise, he could see the top of a tall eucalyptus. He motioned the others to come to a huddle.

"I think we should do as before," he said, "and stash our backpacks when we find the place in case they are thieves."

All three nodded in agreement.

"Also," Al continued, "We should talk about something else. I believe it is just another farming community, but there are other scenarios; drug producers, Sendero Luminoso, or people who have moved into the highlands from the Manus."

"We understand that," whispered Casey.

"I do not want to sound melodramatic," Alberto said, "but we are on our own here — nobody knows where we are. There is no hospital for many miles. Not even a road."

"What are you thinking?" Jack asked Al in a hushed voice.

"I think two of us should approach first without Claire to find out their intentions."

Alberto looked intently at Claire. "If they are Sendero or drug people, it could be worse for you." Al shook his head. He did not like saying that, but it had to be said.

"No," Claire said. "We're all together here. I can handle whatever." She thought. *I'm an educated, grown woman. I'm capable.*

Al stayed silent.

Casey finally spoke. "Now, wait a minute. Let's think this over. Maybe Al's right. Hell, he's always right." (Casey knew that she would not argue with that.) "If not just for your safety, maybe you and I should wait out of sight for everyone's safety, to guard our belongings, or to go for help if needed." He paused, and everyone in the group thought about that. If they needed help, it would be at least three days to get to a village with police or medical assistance, *one way.*

"Let's say it right," Casey suggested, "help might be a week away."

Casey stood up straighter. "It's not melodramatic, Al. It's smart. Claire and I will stay and guard the gear. If it's good there, you and Jack can tell them you have two companions at a campsite in the hills. After a short while, if we're invited to stay, you can come get us. But we should agree on a timeframe before we come looking for you … two or three hours."

Everyone agreed on the plan.

Al took a compass bearing using the tall eucalyptus tree as a reference point. They wound around through thickets of shrubbery and through places where they needed to pull apart vines and thorny entanglements simply to take a step. "Watch your step," he said to the others. They found themselves making their way through a very rocky place. There were huge boulders on all sides. Breathing heavily, Alberto whispered, "We must be walking through a huge ancient rockslide from the mountain." After about twenty minutes of hard going, Alberto, sweating, pushed aside several branches and took a big step down onto a boulder. He could barely see through the vines. As he stepped, the weight of his backpack threw him slightly off-balance, and he reached out with his right arm to try to catch a branch or a root — anything to keep him from falling. He grabbed a heavy vine, but it broke under his 160 pounds. He swung down, his body spinning to the right, and he slammed into one of the ten-foot-tall boulders, but not very hard. It was awkward, not dangerous. Al smiled at the rest of the group and gave them a 'thumbs up.' He found his footing and kept going, pushing more vegetation out of the way.

A moment later, he looked back at the friends as he pulled on more vines and whispered, "Whose idea was this?" But his face had the look of a man who would not want to be doing anything else. Everyone smiled back. Al had the machete with him, but it remained attached to his backpack because there was not enough room between the narrow stone walls to swing it effectively.

Claire was the third hiker to pass where Alberto had spun around. She reached out to her right and put her hand on the boulder for support. Something made her stop. The feeling was familiar, like when a strange smell transports you to a childhood memory, and the peculiar smell and the memory click in your brain, and more recollections pile in. It all turns into some fond, profound remembrance.

She rubbed her hand over the vertical stone. It was smooth. She faced the boulder and started clearing away more of the vegetation. Little rose thorns pricked her hands and made them bleed, but she did not notice and kept ripping away vegetation. She had indeed felt that texture before, in Cusco and Ollantaytambo. She stood in awe, staring at the rocks and the cracks between them.

Claire spun around 180 degrees to the boulder on the opposite side of the crevice and started clearing vines and branches.

Alberto and Casey were twenty feet ahead in the gully between the boulders, waiting for her to catch up, and Jack was stymied behind her. Jack waited patiently for her until she stopped flailing, then she put her bloody hand on her forehead and turned to him with an enormous smile. It wasn't a smile so much as a shit-eating grin.

She motioned for Casey and Al to come back. They started pulling themselves up the narrow passage toward her.

"Seriously?" Jack asked. Claire looked at him, breathing hard and still smiling. He started clearing brush from the boulder closest to him, only inches away.

Casey and Al retraced their steps up the "trail" to where Alberto had nearly fallen. "What?" Casey asked.

"It's not a rockslide," she said, "and they're not boulders. They're walls."

"What?!" Alberto asked, feeling the wall and an exposed joint. "Not here…"

She was right. They were not squeezing through boulders from an ancient rockslide; they had been in a narrow passageway between two building walls. And they were Incan, or maybe earlier.

"I cannot believe this," Al exclaimed but in a hushed voice. "We are miles past where we know the eastern border of the empire was. Hell, we are at the edge of the Antisuyu. I wonder what the scale of this settlement is?"

They continued down the passageway and along the route. Al began to notice that the rocks they had been walking on were actually carved stone steps, covered with vegetation. He had missed a step before, and that's how he had lost his footing. Cognizant now of their surroundings, they recognized it when they emerged from between the two walls. A clearing opened up, and they looked around. It was not difficult for their four explorer minds to see what was there: four more tall walls and rows of smaller buildings. They were standing in what had been a street. Alberto looked at his compass. The narrow street where they stood traveled precisely north/south.

Alberto held his hand out to Casey, palm up. He did not have to speak. Casey returned the map. There was an Incan stone on its side in front of one of the walls. Al cleared off the leaves and moss and unfolded the map onto it. Using his compass, he and Casey carefully plotted out exactly where they were and marked the spot.

Jack and Claire were looking around. One of the walls had a dihedral window, too small to poke their heads through. Claire tried to analyze the layout of the buildings. She looked over at Casey and Al, still examining the map and checking each other's math.

"We're on a bench," she said to Jack. "This was once in front of someone's house. Some woman had her loom set up there, or her husband sat here, drunk on chicha, watching children playing." She spread out both arms. "This is a courtyard. Or was."

After a few minutes, Alberto folded the map carefully so that the new site was in the front. That way, they could easily make amendments to their markings. He handed it to Casey.

Al put his hand on Claire's shoulder. "You know, you've made an incredibly significant discovery." As the gravity of the discovery set in, they were overwhelmed. Each realized that as students, they may have discovered a site that could make a career. Claire tried not to get emotional. They each hugged, glanced around, and tried to decide what to do next.

"How does this change things?" Al asked. The three friends looked at each other.

"As I see it," Casey suggested, "we have only two or three days to explore this and try to map it as well as possible. We have a seventy-five-foot climbing rope with us. We can use that with the compass and map this site pretty accurately … unless it covers acres. Or we can push on and try to find the community."

Al shook his head. "Ruins weren't even in my mind. I'm always looking out for them but stopped thinking about them since I thought the valley on the other side of the mountain pass had been the limit of the empire. The Incan frontier."

Claire wanted Alberto's opinion before offering her own. "I know what I think," she said, "but what do you recommend?'

"Personally, I think this is too important. We need to survey and map this as best we can. But I also think people are living close to here. Maybe you and Casey could stay here and explore the site and start measuring and taking notes while Jack and I explore the surrounding area."

Everyone agreed.

"For now, this would be a good time for a bit of lunch while we collect ourselves."

The packs came off, and all four couldn't help strolling around what was likely once a little neighborhood square. After about a half-hour, Al and Jack got ready. They loaded their fanny packs with camera lenses, a camera body, some water, a notebook and pencil, and a few survival tools. Jack grabbed his compact binoculars. Only Al had brought a machete, which he left behind for Casey and Claire.

"You have your own compass, correct?" Al asked Casey.

"I do," he replied. "And Claire has hers."

Alberto nodded. "Okay. The compass headings are written on the map next to each pass and campsite. We'll be back before dark."

Al and Jack each wrote down the bearings, and Jack nodded solemnly at his friends. No words, nor hugs, were shared. Then he and Al turned and walked away.

TWENTY-EIGHT
Into the Antisuyu

The country opened up as they walked downhill, keeping the eucalyptus treetop in sight. Al and Jack still walked among ruins, though now the ancient foundations were more spread out. As the treetop got closer, the two men began walking more stealthily. Al noticed how quietly Jack moved through the brush. The more he did it, the more impressed Alberto became. Jack moved effortlessly and without a sound. Al tapped him on the shoulder, and Jack stopped. He whispered in his ear, "how is it you can move so quietly through the bushes?"

Jack whispered back, "I grew up hunting back home. Honestly, the forests in Maine can be much denser than this. You learn as a kid."

Al nodded. "I think we're close. You are quieter. You lead."

Where they could, they crept along next to bushes or stone walls. They moved downhill for another ten minutes when Jack froze. Al stopped right behind him. Al could feel his heart pounding ... in fact, he could hear it.

Jack did not move a muscle. *It is just a farming community*, he thought. He stayed frozen, and then as his heartbeat quieted, Alberto knew why. He could hear voices.

Jack slowly began to move. He stayed crouched and pointed to his eleven o'clock position as he crept forward. There was a short stone wall about twenty yards ahead. It was not quite two feet high. Jack typically wore his fanny pack in front to have easy access to camera lenses, but now he spun it around to his backside. He held his binoculars in his hand with the lanyard still around his neck so it wouldn't drag in the dirt. He began to crawl on his belly and elbows to the rock wall. Alberto did the same.

They reached the wall and could hear the voices clearer now. Jack slowly lifted himself to look over the wall, and so did Al. They both quickly ducked down again. It took less than two seconds to know that this was not a Quechua farming community. They were only about seventy-five yards away from the first few buildings. Jack found some stones about the size of footballs and carefully, slowly placed them atop the rock wall about eight inches apart. He and Al were out of sight of the people, and he wanted to keep it that way. He amended the top of the wall so he and Al could make some observations, and the tops of their heads would fill the spaces between the rocks they had put in place.

They peered over again.

This time they looked through their binoculars. What they saw looked like a ramshackle camp more than a village. It was situated among more Incan ruins, but the ancient houses were not being lived-in and had not been built upon. They were being used for stables for horses, mules, and burros. A good-sized stream flowed across the plateau's edge next to the camp and then cascaded down to a large river a few thousand feet below the sloping landscape.

"That's how they're moving supplies," Alberto whispered, "by the river. I couldn't see any water from up on the pass."

Then both men quickly ducked back down again. A man had stepped out to the edge of the village. He had an assault rifle across his chest, its sling around his neck. Al and Jack looked at each other. Al was shaking his head. Jack did not need him to speak. Al's eyes told him what he was thinking; *I've got you into this, now we have to get out of here.*

Jack placed an index finger over his lips and took out his journal.

He wrote: *No more talking…they might have dogs.*

Alberto nodded. Then Jack wrote, *If they are Sendero, we'll need to report this place. We need to observe for a few more seconds.*

Al's eyes widened to say it would be dangerous, and they must be careful.

They looked through the binoculars again. Jack would look, then make notes, and look again. There were big tents and shacks, and the tents had homemade camouflage pulled over them. They were laid out in two rows, about forty feet apart. That's all they could see of the construction from the rock wall. Jack could see that he and Al were just beyond the south end of the compound. Jack quickly made a drawing of what he could see of the camp. He drew the course of the stream and the river. He wrote down an estimation of the width of both.

Within a minute or so, another man walked out, brandishing what to Jack looked like an AK-47. He had the weapon slung around his shoulder so that it was hanging on his back, the rifle butt pointing skyward. As soon as the second man stepped into view, another armed person did also — but this was a young woman.

Jack continued to write: *All dressed in black — all armed w/automatic weapons.*

Then, both men were stunned. What they saw next made Alberto physically ill.

Between the two men and the young female emerged seven women from the compound. They were being driven out of the camp by yet another armed man. They were completely naked and tied together by a single rope looped and knotted around each of their necks. Each woman had straight black hair. The women were all in their teens or early twenties, but one of them was so young she had no visible pubic hair.

Jack and Alberto looked at each other with furious eyes. Jack looked again through the binoculars. The man herded the women down to the stream and made them each climb into the frigid water. He yelled at them and threw a bar of soap into the stream. Each woman would squat in the icy water and wash herself. The youngest one slipped on a rock and fell entirely in with a shriek. When she did, the rope tugged on the other's necks, and they all tilted like dominos and fell into the water. The youngest was underwater for too long, and they could hear one of the other younger girls scream, "*Alessa!*"

The others helped the young one up just in time. When the girl who had screamed the name tried to comfort the littlest one who was crying inconsolably, one of the guards yelled at her, threw a rock, and struck her. The older one winced and cowered but still helped the smallest one stand up in the water.

Jack was incensed. He stiffened, and Al could hear the dirt move under his legs. Al quickly reached out and took hold of Jack's sizable bicep to reiterate his need to stay hidden. Jack hunkered down and wrote in the notebook. *Human Trafficking?*

Al took the notebook. With shaking hands, he wrote, *I think so. I've heard they take women as sex slaves.*

The guards seemed preoccupied with watching the women as they washed their genitals. When the female guard turned and left, Alberto, shaking, took hold of Jack's arm a second time and motioned that they should sneak away.

Again, they crawled on their bellies from behind the rock wall. This time, they kept creeping for a greater distance for fear of being detected. Jack was worried about dogs. He thought, *if they have dogs in the camp and if they catch our scent or hear us in the trees — we're dead.*

They did not hurry. They slithered in the dirt until they were on the far side of some trees. They pulled on each other, still afraid to speak. Both men lifted themselves enough to sit against a large boulder. Both were covered in dirt and breathing hard. Their elbows were bleeding. Jack turned to try to look back in the direction they crawled. He could see nothing except the tracks in the dirt where they had dragged their bodies. Jack again motioned with his finger, suggesting they still not speak. He pulled out the notebook. *Must get to C & C and get away at least a mile—but we must remain calm. I will write a note to them now, so it is ready.*

Alberto nodded and gave a "thumbs up."

He prepared the note for Casey and Claire.

They were behind many bushes and shrubs and several stone walls. Here, they could walk in a crouch. Jack wrote one more note: *Step where I step when you can. Don't step on sticks.* Again, Alberto nodded.

Jack was extremely stealthy. He took his time, moving among the trees, boulders, and bushes as if he were stalking a deer. He took care where he placed his feet. Often he bent down and carefully removed sticks and twigs. About 400 yards from the Sendero's compound, Alberto tapped Jack on the shoulder and stopped. He looked at Al, who was taking a compass bearing. Using a wave of his hand, he let Jack know to adjust their direction … a bit farther south. Jack nodded and corrected his line of travel. Five minutes later, they were getting close to the ruins. Still, they felt the precariousness of their situation. Do the slavers have people patrolling the hills? Pickets somewhere?

Al rechecked his compass and made a slight correction. Two hundred yards later, they were walking less crouched and were quietly moving along a tall, overgrown Incan stone wall. It was a wall they recognized. Jack and Alberto hurried now and burst into the open area between the ancient houses where the backpacks were stashed. "Stay together, Al," Jack whispered. They moved between the ruined buildings, frantically looking for Casey and Claire.

As they rounded a large stone wall, Claire yelled, "Jack!" Alberto and Jack spun around and saw Claire and Casey up a slight rise, measuring between two buildings.

Casey also started to call to them when Al and Jack simultaneously raised both hands in a gesture to stop. Casey said aloud, "What's wrong, Jack?" Both Jack and Alberto gestured more emphatically for them to stop talking.

The frantic men fell upon Casey and Claire, and Jack shoved the prepared note in front of both their faces:

There are VERY bad men not far from here! Prob Sendero. No more talking. They will kill us if they find us, or worse. Use notebook to communicate until we get a mile from here. We must move NOW!

Jack looked as though he had tears in his eyes; they looked wild, more mad than scared — but frightened also. Neither Casey nor Claire had ever seen him look like that. They had never seen anyone look like that. Claire read the note and cupped her hand over her mouth. Casey was pissed, and if he was scared, he wasn't showing it. He kept scowling and shaking his head while looking intensely through the ruins and the trees toward the plateau. Jack and Al took their friends by the arms and, holding their index fingers over their lips, pulled them to where the backpacks were. Once they were sure Casey and Claire were following, they let go of their arms and ran to the packs. They pulled them on and started up the trail between the ruins that they had come down less than two hours earlier. Now, Alberto led, thrashing through the briar and the brambles.

Suddenly, they could hear the baying of a dog from the direction of the camp! Between the howls, they could hear men shouting in Spanish.

"They've heard us!" Al said.

Jack smacked Casey on the shoulder. "It's a Sendero camp. Go! I'll take the rear."

Al nodded. There was no time to discuss it. Jack pulled the machete out of its sheath attached to the side of Al's backpack.

"Now!" Jack ordered.

The three friends ran up the slope in the direction they had come.

Jack looked around and grabbed a stick about five feet long and an inch-and-a-half in diameter. He quickly hacked and whittled a sharp point onto the thicker end, making a rudimentary spear. Jack thought he might be able to fend off a dog with it. He ran after his friends as the dog's barking got closer. He could still hear the men shouting orders to each other.

He started shaking.

He swiftly arrived at the narrow, steep passageway between the two ancient Incan walls where Alberto had stumbled earlier. His friends had already made it up through the overgrown steps. He was glad of that. He hoisted himself as quickly as he could up the precipitous shute. He pulled himself up the last section where the corridor was narrowest, and at the top, he turned around. The dog was closer. The animal had put some distance between himself and the men. He could hear their voices. They were following the barking.

Jack pulled some of the branches free from the walls and cleared the area around his feet and shoulders. Now he could swing the machete overhead. He knew what he had to do. He had to take out the dog. Hopefully, only one animal was coming for him. It was his only chance, and this was the only place where he would have the advantage. He pulled off his pack and tossed it farther up the path in his escape route. Then he readied himself. He positioned himself at the very edge of the top step, which was more than three feet above the next lower step. Jack knew the dog would have to leap up from there when he came at him. The dog was growling now and getting close. The voices were still far away. The walls were close — less than four feet apart. Jack would only be able to swing the machete from directly overhead.

He took a stance with his feet shoulder-width apart, the right foot slightly in front of the left. He bent his knees. He readied himself. He held the spear with his left hand a bit behind his left knee, set for an underhand, forward thrust. The machete he held with his right hand, holding it high over his head.

He was no longer shaking. He took long, deliberate breathes.

The growling was combined with heavy panting, and he could see the attack dog approaching the shute. It was a large pit bull, sprinting straight for him in a mad, mindless pursuit. It was locked onto Jack's face, and he could see the desire in the animal's wild, red eyes — it was dying to rip into the trespasser's flesh.

Up the overgrown steps it flew without slowing down and straight up the steps. Jack tightened his muscles and widened his eyes. The dog opened his jaws wide as it leaped up the final, tall step. At the last second, as the dog was airborne, Jack thrust the spear forward into its belly as hard as he could. There was a loud, sharp squeaking yelp as the stick gutted him. The momentum of the dog's attack meeting the leverage of the spear held the animal in midair for a long second, which was enough time for the machete to descend onto the back of its neck. Jack felt it hit bone. Gravity pulled the dog to the step below. As it fell, Jack held on tightly to the machete, and it pulled from the spine. The wounded animal slid off the spear, covering the tip in blood. It lay prostrate on its side between the walls. Its body paralyzed, it continued to bare its teeth and snap its jaws, its guts protruding from its midsection.

Quickly, Jack turned and threw on his backpack. He picked up his weapons and ran toward his friends.

Jack sprinted up the slope through the wild roses and the prickly pear cactus. Even on the run, he could see the footprints left by his friends. He ran with his spear in his left hand and the machete in his right. He tried to hold the cutting-edge of the knife facing away from his body like his father had shown him how to walk while carrying an ax. His heart was pounding, and he tried to pace his breathing, but his expirations and the noise of his feet hitting the ground drowned out every other sound. If the men were still behind him, he could not hear them.

Like Hawkeye in Last of the Mohicans, he ran as quietly as he could. He felt himself gliding through the undergrowth. For a moment, he wondered if he should not lead the evil men away from his friends. He made a snap decision. Still, on a dead run, he made a sharp turn to the right, to the north, farther up the slope but away from the drainage where he knew Alberto was leading Claire and Casey. He did not try to run quietly now. Jack pushed and thrashed his way through the roses and the bushes straight up the mountain. After a few hundred yards, he felt his legs getting tired. His feet felt like blocks of cement. The altitude was getting to him.

Jack ran until he found a few huge boulders the size of small buildings. On the far side, he stopped. He wanted to bend over and rest, but he forced himself to stand up straight to better catch his breath. His chest was heaving, his body soaked with sweat.

Once his breathing slowed a little, with his head and heart still pounding, he climbed up the backside of one of the rocks. He peeked over the top and could see far down the valley. There was not much tree cover, and it resembled Texas hill country — sparse and pretty, in its way, but somehow uninviting.

He could see them.

Three men dressed in black were combing the slope above the ruins. All three had apparently come up the shute where he had killed the pit bull. Without the dog, they were searching blindly. Jack watched as a man crossed over his footprints several times. They can't track, he thought. They suck. That will help.

They were still a thousand feet below him. Since they were making such slow progress, Jack knew he could make it over to the drainage to the Southwest and hook up with Casey and the others. He circled behind the boulders and stealthily headed for an outcropping of rocks he chose as a landmark. He broke off a branch from a bush and tried sweeping the dusty dirt behind him. *Wonder if this works?* He thought. Whenever he could walk on rocks, he did.

In twenty minutes, he was in the drainage they had traveled down earlier that morning. He recognized some of the terrain, and it comforted him. He thought he was likely uphill from his friends, and he was right. He worked his way down, stepping carefully from rock to rock. After only a minute, he stepped out from a small ledge, and there was Casey, poised and looking wild-eyed at him. He was holding high a large piece of wood in his hands, raised like a Louisville Slugger.

Casey twitched as he recognized Jack, who ducked, but Casey caught himself and did not swing the club. He lowered his weapon and hugged Jack. Casey whispered in his ear, "Strong work."

They looked at each other with expressions that said, "*That was nerve-wracking.*"

Alberto emerged from the undergrowth with Claire. Both hugged Jack.

"We heard a scream," whispered Al.

"That was a dog dying," Jack responded.

Jack's face looked different. All three friends looked at the bloody spear and machete. Casey reached over and squeezed Jack's shoulder. Casey knew his friend loved dogs.

"I could see only three men," Jack said. "They are not hunters. I saw them only a few minutes ago. I think they'll spread out and keep looking for us. The only thing I'm sure of is they want us dead. If they can't kill us, they know they will probably have to move their camp."

Everyone nodded.

"Plan?" asked Casey.

Jack sputtered. "I think Al should go up to the pass with Claire and get out of this drainage. Near the top, they can hide among the rocks, and you and I can follow behind as the rearguard."

Again, all three nodded in agreement.

"Al," Jack continued, "can you manage two packs?"

"Yes."

"Good. That will give us more mobility if we need it. Go now. We'll try to stay 300 to 500 yards behind."

Claire kissed both Jack and Casey on the cheek as Al put on his pack and picked up Jack's, looping one of its straps over his left shoulder. He was carrying a lot of weight. Then off they went up the drainage.

When they were out of sight, Casey said, "You've seen them; what do you think?"

"I think if they spread out like they seem to be doing, we can take one of them out easily enough. We are up high, and we can choose the ground."

"All right then," Casey replied.

Jack picked up Casey's club and quickly whittled a sharp point on his thick end while Casey put on his pack.

"Let's find a vantage point," Jack suggested. They quietly made their way up the drainage, following Al and Claire's footprints.

TWENTY-NINE

"Can you do it?"

Casey and Jack crept slowly up the arroyo. They occasionally stopped and listened for any voices from below. Jack had finally caught his breath, but both their hearts were pounding.

Casey looked at Jack with strained and intense eyes.

Jack made eye contact with the same strained face and said, "I know, me too."

Neither man had any military experience, but at least Jack had spent his youth hunting and fishing in the Maine woods. And both were very smart — that would have to do in this life or death moment.

They passed through two huge boulders that framed the path. The rocks were more than twenty feet high and were only five feet apart. Jack stopped.

"This would be a good place," he said.

"For what?" asked Casey.

"To see what we can see." Jack looked all around. "And if there's only one man in this drainage, we can ambush him here."

Casey also looked around. He did not want this. Any of it. He was of a mind to simply try to outrun them. But Jack was already on the uphill side of one of the boulders and was scrambling up it. Casey slipped off his backpack. He climbed up the rock, following Jack.

At the top, they could peek over and see straight down the drainage. "Damn, I forgot," said Jack.

"What?"

"My binoculars. I put them on the ground where I fought the dog, and I left them. They would be handy right now."

Casey winced. "Mine are in my pack, with Alberto."

Both men surveyed the drainage and the sloping valley below. There was a movement far off to the left — to the north. One of the Sendero (if they were Shining Path) was skirting the higher slopes, traveling in the wrong direction. That was good.

"We're out of range for him," Jack reckoned.

Suddenly there was another movement, straight down below in the drainage. The man was moving slowly. He would look at the ground and then up at the top of the mountains. Then he would look downhill behind him, toward his camp. It seemed he did not want to continue.

"If he comes up here," Jack whispered, "we'll have to fight him."

Casey stared down at the man, about 700 feet below them.

Jack looked over at Casey. It was cool in the mountains, but beads of sweat trickled down his temples and forehead, and one dripped off the tip of his nose. Jack thought for a moment. *This was not Casey's temperament. Maybe I can fight him alone.*

"Can you do this, Case?"

Casey wiped his brow with his shirtsleeve, looked at him, and nodded.

"It will be easier with two of us," Jack offered, "but if you're not okay with fighting, you can go now to catch up with Al and Claire. I'm good. I'll have the element of surprise."

Casey was stunned. Here was the gentlest soul he had ever met, who almost wept if he felt he injured or overplayed a trout, and who regularly took the time to talk to animals. And now he was offering to fight some heavily armed man on his own using a stick and a machete.

"No," Casey replied. "I'm with you."

They looked down the drainage again. The man was still coming, very slowly. He appeared to occasionally see some footprints, and he would stop each time he saw a print and then glance down the drainage.

"I bet he's thinking of going down to get his compadres," Jack whispered. "If it occurs to him to fire his rifle to signal them, we're fucked."

The man turned again and looked up, straight at Jack and Casey's position. Then he continued up the path. He was close enough now that they could see his scraggly beard, and they could make out that he was carrying a holstered sidearm in addition to his rifle.

"Well," Casey whispered, "what do you want to do?" He looked again at Jack's bloodstained machete, and his stomach turned.

"This is the best spot," Jack whispered back. "One of us stays hidden here, behind the boulder. The other goes uphill about thirty yards and waits until that prick is here, where he'll have to pass between these big rocks. The uphill one of us will show himself for a split second and takeoff, hopefully before the asshole can squeeze off a shot. When he steps out from between these boulders, the other one clocks him hard with the club. If we can knock him out, we'll take his weapons and his shoes and beat it hard for the pass."

"His shoes?"

"Yup," Jack replied. "Without them, when he comes to, it'll take him forever to get down these sharp rocks to gather his comrades."

Casey breathed hard. "I'll do it."

"Which?"

"Club him."

Jack looked at him. "Are you sure, Case? You can do it? As far as I know, you've never been in a fight."

"Not since grammar school, when I pushed Kevin Hamm down in the playground for being too rough with a girl I knew. But it doesn't matter. If these guys mean to kill us, fuck 'em. Besides, I'm a better batter than you. I'll do it."

Casey held his stick and waggled it as if it was an actual baseball bat. Then he nodded at his friend.

"Okay," Jack said, "once he sees me, I'll double back down the gully and help you."

The two friends looked over the boulder. The man in black was inching toward them, and now he was only 100 yards away. A football field. The man would take a step, look in every direction, squint back at the ground, and take another step.

Jack patted Casey on the back. He did not look quite as frightened as a few moments ago. They quietly climbed down the back of the rock and onto what they were using as a trail. They decided where Casey would stand in ambush. It was a good spot. Hidden from view, he would be able to see the trail below and would know when the man was getting close. When the time came, he would take one step and swing the club. Casey examined the ground to be sure his footing would be adequate and that he would have room to swing the club. Jack watched him as he took a couple of practice swings.

Jack squeezed Casey's shoulder. "You bat better lefty anyway. You got this, Case."

Jack looked between the boulders down the slope and couldn't yet see the man. He turned and started up the gully to his hiding spot but suddenly stopped and turned back, facing his friend. "Would this not be a good time for a *Casey at the Bat* reference?"

Casey gave him a wince followed by a serious "what the fuck?" look.

Jack tried to encourage him. "It'll be fine. Hit him hard, once, back of the head. Knock him out, and we'll be on our way."

Casey watched Jack scramble up the drainage and disappear around a bend about forty yards uphill. Once his friend was out of sight, he peaked downhill through a crack in the boulders. He still could not see the man hunting him, but he could hear him. He could not be far — Casey could hear small rocks and pebbles moving on the ground underneath the trafficker's feet. *I don't know what he is*, Casey thought, *trafficker, drug runner, Sendero...who gives a fuck.*

Case looked down at his hands. They were shaking. His breathing was too fast. *Jesus, he thought, get a grip. You can do this.*

As he stared at his hands on the club, sweat dripped onto his wrist. He looked through the crack again.

There he was!

Thirty feet below him was the man in black. He was looking up at the drainage, past where Casey lay in wait. Case looked straight at his eyes. He did not look as scary as expected, except for the Kalashnikov. He wore a black t-shirt with some sort of insignia where the breast pocket should be and black fatigue pants. His rifle was unslung.

Casey's eyes were drawn to the Sendero's eyes, and he could not look away. The man was young, a few years younger than himself, perhaps twenty-one years old. He was not menacing looking at all. He was Mestizo, and his eyes looked like the eyes of the kid who would rather be playing football. He had rather large ears, and Casey could see straight, close-cropped black bangs just below the brim of his baseball hat.

He doesn't want to be here either, thought Casey. The kid in black was also sweating.

The Sendero took a few more steps in Casey's direction. Casey leaned back against the giant boulder. He glanced up the drainage. There was no sign of Jack. He suddenly felt very alone and exposed, even though he knew he was well hidden. He could hear the Sendero's steps much clearer now. Casey leaned to the side and peeked through the crack again. The man had covered some ground. He was only fifteen feet from the boulders, only twenty-five feet from where Case stood in hiding. Casey could see everything on the boy; the beads of sweat and the dirty fingernails on the hands clasped around the stock of the rifle. He saw the young man's sturdy boots. He noticed scratches on the Kalashnikov's forward arching magazine, and that its stock was made out of plastic, instead of wood.

Casey leaned back against the rock again. This was it. He looked up the drainage one last time, then he looked at the ground. It was good; no rocks in his path of attack, nothing to impede him. *When the Sendero steps past me*, thought Casey, *he would have to turn more than 120° to his right to spot me. If his focus is up the drainage, there would be no reason for him to look behind.*

As he inspected the dirt at his feet, he heard a distinct noise — breathing!

The young man had reached the boulders. Casey raised the club, up, up, quietly, and got into his stance like a batter. He trained his eyes where the Sendero would be forced by the boulders to step out.

Suddenly, there was a subtle noise up the path! It was Jack. Casey saw him by moving his eyes to the right of the drainage while keeping his head turned toward "home plate." Jack casually walked across the path from left to right and kept moving.

The man saw him all right.

Casey heard the tinkle of metal as the man raised the Kalashnikov. He could hear the rifle's safety click off. He listened to the muffled sound as the man leaned against the far side of the same boulder he was hiding behind. Casey's heart started pounding. He felt it would explode out of his chest. He heard the crunching of pebbles as the man took a step closer, then another. Then Casey could see the rifle barrel pointing up the drainage, protruding beyond the two boulders. He expected the man to creep slowly, as he had been, but he must've been excited by the sight of Jack. The exhilaration of the hunt was getting to the Sendero. He did not proceed with caution. He stepped forward deliberately and with a quickened cadence. It was happening fast!

Two, three steps, and the man was just past the boulders. The rifle was against his shoulder, ready to fire, and he was advancing in full combat mode.

After a fourth step, the man cleared the boulders. Casey re-gripped the club, adjusting his hands, his fingers opening and closing, cascading one after the other in sequence on the bat handle. Then he took one step with his right foot — a good stride — and his hips and back exploded forward, throwing his hands at the back of the Sendero's head.

It was a good swing.

The club snapped forward, traveling about sixty-five miles-per-hour, and made perfect contact with the base of the Sendero's skull.

Crack!

Casey extended his arms in perfect baseball form. The sound of the club hitting the young man was sickening, and it sounded very much like when one hits a hollow log with a stick.

The Sendero's head snapped forward, and his neck flexed like a whip. He never made a sound, not a grunt or a moan or cry. He fell straight ahead onto the rocky path driving the barrel of his rifle into the dirt. His legs were extended and rigid behind him as he lay prone on the ground, and his right leg twitched in tiny spasms for a few seconds and then stopped.

At the end of the swing's follow-through, Casey reared back in a stance to strike again, but he did not have to. The man was not moving. As Casey loomed over him, staring at the rigid body, he could not tell if he was breathing. Casey straightened up, wiped the sweat from his brow, and became nauseous. He lowered the point of the stick to the ground and leaned on it. Casey was getting dizzy. As he reached up to wipe more sweat, Jack jumped from the side of the trail and almost landed on the body. That's what the kid looked like now, a body.

"Is he breathing?" Casey asked.

Jack knelt and placed his hand on the man's back. Then he looked up at his friend, and he nodded but with a sideways cock of the head as if to say, "*Barely.*"

Jack grabbed the Sendero's rifle and pistol. He pulled off both of the boy's boots and tossed them about fifty feet to the side of the drainage. Then he stood up.

"You okay, Case?"

Casey nodded. "Yes. But ... is he alive?"

Jack knelt down again. He partially rolled the man over. There was blood. A lot of blood. Casey thought he could smell the metallic odor. "It looks like he broke his nose when he hit the ground," Jack said. "There's still bleeding from it, and he's got a pulse, so yeah, he's alive." Both of the Sendero's eyes were grotesquely protruding as if they were popping out of his head. Jack did not mention the eyes to Casey.

Casey was still nauseous. He lunged to the side of the trail and vomited. The boy on the ground was still motionless.

Jack glanced down the drainage, and no one else was in sight. He kept one eye on the Sendero and patted Casey's back, who then wiped his cheek with his sleeve and stood up. He tried not to look at the boy. Jack was being patient; he knew Casey needed to collect himself.

Holding the Kalashnikov and the machete, Jack tucked the still holstered pistol into his waist belt. He had tossed the bloodstained spear into the rocky terrain next to the drainage.

"We should go," Jack finally said. "Are you okay?"

Casey nodded, looking stunned.

"You lead," said Jack. He wanted to keep an eye on his friend, plus if Casey was in the lead and pathfinding, it might give him some focus, and perhaps it would take his mind off the past few minutes.

And off they went. As mountaineers, they knew better than to run – though they wanted to. Casey kept a fairly and slow deliberate pace. They would save their energy and would run later if they had to. As they picked their way up the rocky boulder-strewn drainage, every five minutes, they stopped, trying to catch their breath, and surveyed the view below. Casey's heart was beating hard, and the excursions from this heavy breathing made it difficult to keep the landscape below from bouncing in his vision.

"I don't see anything," Jack said.

"Me neither." Casey pondered as he caught his breath. "I don't think the others — you said there were two more — are in this drainage yet. But they will be eventually, and when they find our guy, they're going to come for us hot and heavy."

"Agree," Jack replied. "We have to get up to the pass as soon as possible. We still might not be safe then, but it will be our best chance."

Both men again looked downhill for any movement and any sign of life at all, and there was nothing.

They carried on.

As they crested the pass two hours later, where the terrain was much more open and exposed, they saw Claire and Alberto step out from behind some boulders. The two had watched Jack and Casey work their way up the drainage. They were walking abreast, and both could hardly pick up their feet. Their heads were bent forward, and both were very weak. They looked up when they saw Claire. She ran to them and threw her arms around Jack. He held her with one arm and used the other to hold the Kalashnikov, which was slung over his shoulder out of harm's way. Seconds later, she composed herself and gave Casey a big hug. "I'm so glad you're both okay."

"We're all right," Casey said. His voice seemed different, more serious.

"Are we still in danger?" Alberto asked

"Yes, we are," Casey replied. "We must keep moving, as far and fast as we can go."

"I'll find a branch," Jack said, "try to brush away our tracks."

Al shook his head. "Don't bother. If they know we hiked up this drainage, they'll know where we are, and we're headed. Putting distance between us … that's more important."

Jack and Casey nodded in agreement.

Al said, "You can tell us all about it when we find a safe place to camp." Alberto could not know that would be the last thing either man would want to do.

The group began picking their way down the west side of the pass toward safety.

They skirted the steepness of the mountains to their right and kept moving south. When they came to one of the open meadows they had traversed earlier that morning, Alberto edged around it, trying to stay as hidden as possible. In only four hour's hiking from the ruins, they found their last campsite. Al pulled the foil wrapper from the tree branch next to the stream and stuffed it into a pocket.

"Pssst," Claire whispered. She motioned for the group to make a huddle. In a circle, their heads close together, she asked, looking at the rifle, "Somebody want to tell us what we're dealing with?"

"We found a Sendero compound," Jack said, breathing hard. "Well, they might not be Sendero, but they are evil people." He could see Claire still glancing at the gun. "We took this off one of them."

"That was the smoke we saw from the pass," whispered Alberto. "They were all heavily armed. Automatic weapons. They either had sex slaves or are trafficking women. We got about seventy-five yards from the camp. Jack's right. They're bad people … very bad."

"What's the plan now?" Casey asked. He looked through the trees down the slope in the direction they had retreated from.

"For now," Jack whispered, "get the fuck out of here. *Quietly.*"

"I don't believe they knew we were there, watching them," Al said quietly. "As far as they probably think, we were just messing around the ruins. I think if we can make it over the pass by dark, we'll be okay."

"Then let's go," Casey muttered. Each hiker got out their trekking poles and started up the trail. Again, their minds told them to hurry, to scurry up the steep ravine, but experience told them otherwise. Alberto found the old Incan trail and set a fairly slow, methodic mountaineering pace.

The foursome plodded slowly up the trail, one foot in front of the other. As Alberto thought about the Kalashnikovs and the sad, frightened faces of the girls washing themselves, his pace quickened. He had to be disciplined, he reminded himself. It was at least a two-and-a-half-day hike back to the road, and he must set a reasonable pace.

Late in the afternoon, they reached the pass at the top of the ravine where they could see for several miles. Claire was tired, so was Jack, and Al looked exhausted also. The emotional toll combined with the steep ascent had taken a lot out of them all. The four scanned the ravine and the plateau below for any signs of life — for any movement.

"I think we're out of the woods," Jack said in a normal voice. "Strong work Al. Everyone." Al nodded and reached out and patted Jack on the shoulder.

"Yes," Alberto said. "I think we are safe now. But we must still be careful. I agree that they did not detect us at the compound, but remember Enrico down in the valley told us of people who are not friendly who come up this trail from the village of Choquecancha. While I think those people down there (he nodded his head in the direction of the Sendero) get in and out by the river, we must assume that the people who Enrico saw on this trail were also with the bad hombres."

"River?" Casey asked.

"There's a stream that runs next to their compound that flows into a river down below," Jack said. "It's navigable."

"We all need to decide what to do about this," Alberto said.

"We report the ruins to the university in Cusco," Casey replied, "and the Sendero to the authorities."

"Of course," Alberto said. "But we must think it out. Have a plan."

Casey and Claire looked at him. Jack was scanning the ravine with Alberto's binoculars. He understood what Al was saying. Jack lowered the glasses and turned to Claire and Casey. "Al cannot be a part of it," he said. "It would be too dangerous."

Casey nodded, trying to comprehend the gravity of that.

"But this is a great archaeological find," Casey said. "You're a big part of it."

"You don't understand," Alberto explained. "If an expedition goes there to excavate, the government will obviously find out about the illegal compound. I've stayed neutral so far with the Sendero in Cusco. If I'm connected even a little to that compound being raided, Marisol and I will be killed."

"But you said you have acquaintances in Cusco in the Shining Path," Casey said, "wouldn't they be able to help you?"

Al looked at him. "This isn't a gang turf-war in Boston," he said, "it is a revolution. Our acquaintances who smile and speak with us … they'll be the ones pulling the trigger."

Casey grimaced and seemed to have a sharp pain. Somewhere.

"It would be nice being part of the discovery of the ruins," Al said, trying to console Casey. "It would give me some street-cred in the archaeological community in Peru — it might even help get some guiding gigs in the future." He looked at Claire. "Maybe someday, when the revolution dies down, you could write a paper and include me in some small way. That would be nice."

But inside, Casey was in turmoil. He couldn't shake the idea that maybe he killed that kid in the ravine. His shame was boundless. He would not talk to Claire about it, though she tried to get him to, and he even avoided talking to Jack about it. If the boy did die, where did he stand morally? He knew he'd have to carry that weight forever, but would karmic justice hit back at him at some unexpected point in his life?

No matter how many times he told himself those Senderos meant to kill them all, he could not stop the guilt. His remorse was so severe it made him nauseated.

Casey welcomed it when Jack broke his train of thought when he said, "I think we should keep going until almost dark and camp somewhere off the trail."

With that, the friends shouldered their packs and started down the west-sloping ravine toward Enrico's valley. They made it only a couple thousand feet down the ravine when darkness made them stop and camp for the night. They felt uncomfortable being camped so near the old Incan trail. A warm fire would have been nice, but they made a cold camp that night.

That first night on the homeward trail was an early one, and everyone was confused and exhausted. Both Al and Jack slept fitfully. For most of the night, Casey was trying not to cry. Jack especially had difficulty. His head raced between thoughts of the terrible scene he had witnessed and the things he had done and thoughts of Claire — who was sleeping only two thin layers of rip-stop nylon away — *and* with the nagging thoughts of losing his closest friends from the fall-out of his love for her. He laid awake, staring into the blackness of the roof of his tent. *What is certain?* he thought. *If Claire breaks up with Case when they get home, and she and I start dating, I've lost him as a friend. But then what? If I cannot make her happy, then I've lost them both.*

They were the same thoughts Jack had had for the past four days. Toss on top the transient feelings of fearing for his life, the dog killing, what they'd done to the Sendero boy, the anger about the stolen girls, and the emotional toll was nearly unbearable. And what to do about those girls? *Fucking Sendero.* Jack thought about their dilemma all night. By morning he had it figured out — what to do about Al's predicament and what to do about his own.

At breakfast, hardly anyone spoke. Still running a cold camp, they made no campfire and used the small mountaineering stove in an out-of-sight place. Everyone knew how to break camp efficiently, and when it was still early, they were on their way. The trail was easily remembered from the day before. Alberto went quite far ahead in case he met anyone coming from the valley below. He would at least be able to communicate with them. But no one came. By midday, they were down in the valley. By early afternoon, they had crossed the valley and the rock dam. They re-filled their water bottles and decided to hike upstream the short distance to Enrico's family farm. The friends agreed they were safe now, so they dug a hole near the campsite, photographed the rifle and pistol, and buried them. They were all happy to be rid of them.

Enrico stood high on one of the escarpments behind his house, watching a small herd of llamas. When he saw the travelers, he bounded down to greet them, and they did not want to alarm him, so each put a smile on their face.

"¿*Como estuvo tu viaje?*" Enrico asked.

"Our trip was ... tiring," Alberto replied in Spanish.

Casey and Jack tried to look normal, so they wouldn't frighten the farmer.

The foursome dropped their packs on the grass and plunked down next to them. Alberto tried to make small talk, and he did not see any reason to alarm him or make the Campesino's family fearful. Still, perhaps Enrico *should* be worried about the terrorists living in the next valley. Benito again came out and joined the conversation, if only physically. He had no Spanish.

After twenty minutes of chatting and Alberto thanking him for his hospitality two days earlier, he broached the subject.

"Enrico," he asked, "have there ever been any missing people from your valley?"

"Missing? No ... no missing people." He spoke to Benito, saying something in Quechua. Then he turned back to Al. "Benito was in Choquecancha a month ago. While he was there, he heard people saying two girls were missing from the town. Since then, we keep our women in the houses as much as possible." Enrico's omnipresent smile was now missing. He looked at Alberto with a serious and curious expression. He did not have to say, *why do you ask?*

"Those people you see occasionally crossing the rock dam and traveling east, over the mountains — they may be normal people, but it might be best if you keep your distance from them."

Enrico looked at the grass. He reached down and plucked a blade, broke it into short segments, and tossed it back onto the ground. He looked sideways at Al. "Si," he said, nodding his head. It was apparent that this simple man, wrestling a living out of the land in his beautiful valley, was sad that such a thought could invade his tough, idyllic family community.

Al was saddened that Enrico's affect had changed. He mentioned again how thankful they were for his hospitality and what a beautiful farm he had. They cordially went their separate ways.

⚘

When the group returned to the rock dam, Alberto stopped again. From there, he could see far down the valley. He surveyed the vista with his binoculars. He also scanned the trail they had taken over the mountain to the ruins and the evil compound, and he saw nothing.

"Casey, may I look at the map?" Alberto asked.

After close study of the chart, Al said, "We need to alter our plans." He pointed to a spot on the road on the far side of the mountains to the west. "Here's where the driver is supposed to meet us, but we are more than two days early. He tapped on the town of Choquecancha, ten miles south of the rendezvous point. We have to get here to get a ride back to Ollanta. I've been thinking of a plan for reporting the Sendero camp without my name getting involved. It involved you three taking a bus from Cusco to Ayacucho and report it there, but now that there may have been two girls missing from this village, it changes things. If they were in that group of naked girls in the camp, maybe someone could rescue them before they are moved somewhere where they'll never be found."

"Any guesses where they might take them?" Claire asked.

Al shook his head. "Another Sendero camp maybe, to be sex slaves. Or possibly sent to a Brazilian logging or mining camp in the Amazon to be prostituted. Those places are lawless."

Not one person spoke.

"Well," Alberto finally said, "we have to decide how to get back to Ollanta…we can go back the way we came over the pass and down the drainage and then walk the ten miles down the road to Choquecancha, or we can try following the trail down this valley that Enrico's family uses for supply runs and picking our way by map to the town."

Casey exchanged glances with Jack and then spoke up. "I don't care about finding a route down this valley and across the mountains south of here. Normally I'd rather explore a new route, but I think we all need to deal with this and then decompress, so I vote for the known route we hiked to get here." He looked at his watch, which prompted the others to do the same. It was three o'clock in the afternoon, and they had maybe two to three hours of hiking time left.

"It wasn't too bad of a hike," Casey continued, "and I think we can get to that town tomorrow evening if everyone's feeling all right." Casey was starting to think more rationally.

"Agreed?" Alberto asked.

Everyone was comfortable with the plan. Each friend shouldered their pack and left.

As they walked to the west, each person knew that the plan would evolve and that the next few days would be trying.

THIRTY

Flight

The hike over the mountains was strenuous but uneventful. They negotiated the exposed narrow ledge before the summit without difficulty. Even though it was higher than the one the day before, the pass near the summit was a welcome sight. At the top, Jack looked east, down into Enrico's valley. He peered across at the mountains beyond. He felt a strange familiarity with the country now. He could not see the stream that wound down the valley, but he knew it was there. Jack could picture certain sections of the trail that led up the ravine, and he could see in his mind the ruins on the other side. Odd, he thought, that he could feel so intimate with a place after only a few days walking through it. Perhaps it was because of the trauma, and the experience intensified his time in that place and limned an everlasting memory.

Alberto walked up to Jack and put his hand on his shoulder.

"We'll have to move if we want to make the road before dark." Jack nodded. He raised his camera to take a final shot of the valley and the eastern range. He looked through the viewfinder, focused, and lowered the camera. It wasn't the same through the viewfinder. His finger raised off the shutter button. He turned and joined the others.

Nearly at the bottom of the ravine, the light was fading fast. The group was picking their way through the strewn boulders and llama trails as best they could when finally, Al stopped and swung his pack off his back. "Almost at our old campsite," Al said. "We can either choose our way down using headlamps or bivouac in the rocks tonight. It's not going to rain, so we could forgo the tents and just roll out our sleeping pads."

"About an hour to the campsite?" Casey asked.

"I think so," Al said, "going slowly with headlamps."

Jack and Claire, both tired, waved in the direction of the camp and dug into their backpacks for their headlamps. Alberto nodded and positioned the headlamp on his forehead. To preserve the batteries, he would wait to turn it on until he absolutely needed it to walk. He waited for the others to be ready, and they continued.

Alberto had been correct; they stumbled onto their campsite next to the tiny stream an hour later. From a distance, they would have looked like four fireflies flittering in a line down the ravine. Their hearth and boulder seats were just as they had left them, and the site was only about a hundred yards from the road. With the aid of the headlamps, each traveler set up their tent and unfurled their sleeping pad and bag, and each dove into their tent with little conversation and fell into a fitful sleep.

Casey rolled from side to side in his sleeping bag. He couldn't stop thinking about the Sendero — the boy— who had looked younger than himself. His mind couldn't let go of the sound his stick made when it contacted the boy's skull. Casey had felt a reverberation in his hands from the club when it struck. He held his hands in front of his face and studied them ... he still felt the feeling in his palms.

Alberto worried about Marisol. The female Sendero hit squads were particularly ruthless. He thought about his friend's cousin, who the assassins stoned to death outside Arequipa. He thought *Marisol is such a gentle, artistic, trusting soul, and she doesn't deserve to be placed in danger.*

Claire laid in her bag, thinking everything was her fault. It was she who suggested the trip in the first place and placed them in this situation. She tried to push the dark thoughts, which weighed on her like a gloomy cloud, from her mind. She kept thinking about her lost city; the scientist part of her was a powerful force. Sleep did not come easily.

It wasn't until they were all awake in the morning, when what they had done the day before sunk in. They had hiked well over twenty-two miles (the first third on sheer adrenaline), over two mountain passes — one of them over 15,000 feet — and skipped supper.

They were all feeling better now, at least physically, and they had had time while hiking to collect their thoughts, and they knew they were safe now. Alberto, sitting on a boulder in front of his tent, still had troubling thoughts about being connected to the imminent report of the Sendero camp. He loved his life in Cusco, and he was well respected throughout the Sacred Valley. He worried about Marisol.

Jack could see that Al's mind was racing. He walked over to Alberto and put his hand on his back. "I've got it all worked out," he said. "You and Marisol will be safe. Trust me."

Al looked up at Jack. Even with something so grave, he did trust him. Al nodded.

"I propose that I alone report the Sendero camp," Jack announced to the group, "which I have a plan for pending Al's approval, and that we focus now on the most amazing thing … Claire's discovery of a lost Incan city."

"Here, here!" Alberto said to Claire. Instantly they realized he was right.

"Let's get to town," Jack said, "get a meal and look over what mapping you two were able to do of the ruins. I can't wait." His smiling face and common-sense enthusiasm were infectious. Everyone felt better, especially Alberto.

They struck camp and walked down the hill to the road and turned south toward Choquecancha. "If a truck comes from the north," Al said, "stick out your thumbs. He'll stop if he has room."

Walking down the road, the valley looked completely different from the terrain they had just spent three days in. This was temperate, Andean agricultural country; steep mountainsides terraced with various crops growing at different elevations. Farmsteads punctuated the hillsides here and there. Sparse, silvery-green eucalyptus trees stood tall in the lower elevations, and alongside the road were wild roses and pepper trees and, next to the gully that ran beside the road, were more prickly pear cacti.

Alberto and Casey set a nice, leisurely pace toward town. Jack purposely lagged behind, with Claire a short distance in front. After a few minutes of walking, Jack caught up to Claire and tapped her on the shoulder. She smiled at him, and he gestured for her to wait for him as he re-tied his shoe. That put some distance between them and Casey and Al.

Claire was worried he wanted to discuss relationship things with her, and she wasn't in a good space for that. But he didn't. When they started walking, he said, "My plan for reporting the Sendero camp without Al being involved requires me to fly back home a few days after you and Case. So that he doesn't argue with me, I will use Maria in Cusco as an excuse for my wanting to stay in Peru longer. Casey will be happy about that. We'll sort everything out once I get home. I just want to know if you will be able to go along with that? It's a little deceitful, and it will be my first time deceiving Casey, but it's only to protect Alberto."

Claire thought for a second and said, "I'll have to hear the plan, and if it's seamless, then yes, I can do that."

They walked together for a while, and then Claire said, "This plan of yours — it doesn't involve you actually having sex with Maria, does it … just to protect Alberto?"

Jack said, "We'll have to see how the plan unfolds. Al's safety is important." Claire mustered a slight smile and looked down. Jack noticed how hard it was now to make a joke amidst all the guilt he was feeling. They continued walking down the dirt road, and Jack started wondering if the past five days had changed him forever.

Choquecancha is a town with about 200 souls, and it is a farming community on one of the Machu Picchu hiking circuits, and its women are known for their weaving skills. Days before, the group had not stopped when they passed through, but now, after a three-hour walk, they ambled into town.

Alberto stopped the first person they came to, an old man bent over at the waist carrying an enormous load of sticks for firewood on his back. In faltering Quechua, Alberto greeted him and asked about a car for hire to get to Ollantaytambo. Shaking his head, he did not know of any. Alberto asked two more people as they ventured deeper into town. The people there seemed overtly friendly — like those in Ollanta.

"We need to find the Catholic church," Al said, hustling ahead, "the priest will speak Spanish, probably some English, and he will know who has a car."

It was not hard to find, as it was the tallest building in town. When they walked up to the front of the church, the three students were struck by the beautiful old doors. The sides and the door jams were Incan stone, and there was a great arch above the door made with long, thin red bricks. The doors themselves were works of art; they were also arched, about twelve feet high, and ornately carved with figures of condors, pumas, parrots, llamas, doves, and angels. Alberto knocked on the door. An old woman wearing a lovely black wool dress, an indigo blue sweater, and a many-colored shawl opened the door from within. Al inquired about the priest, and she motioned for the group to wait in the foyer.

A few moments later, the priest arrived.

"*¿Hablas español?*" Alberto asked.

"*Si,*" the Priest offered.

Alberto introduced the three friends and explained they were looking to hire a car for Ollanta.

"Ah, I see," the Priest replied in perfect English. "I know just the person — Juan, but it will be a pick-up truck." Everybody smiled and thanked him and said they would not mind riding in the back of a truck.

"I will get my jacket and inquire for you," the Priest said. "You may sit in the plaza and wait," he held out his hand toward the opposite side of the street, "or, if you are inclined, you may come inside and pray." The cleric smiled and pulled his jacket off a peg.

The padre seemed engaging. Alberto joked with him. "Yes, we must look like we are in need of prayer, Father."

The Priest pushed his arm through his jacket sleeve, cocked his head to the side, and said as he walked out the door, "You haven't seen Juan's truck yet."

The travelers looked at one another and chuckled. Alberto, Casey, and Claire followed him out to the plaza, and Jack said, "I'll catch up." He was still in the church when the Priest walked back to the plaza with the beat-up old Toyota pickup lurching along behind him. Jack coincidentally walked out of the church as the truck stopped next to Casey and Claire.

When Juan put it in park, the truck coughed, spat, and stalled. He did not seem too concerned. The truck had seen better days. Both rear quarter-panels and hood were three different colors, all replaced over the years with whatever part could be found and made to fit. The backup lights were rewired to a house lamp toggle switch mounted next to the hole in the dash where the radio once lived. It was impossible to tell without kneeling in the dirt and spitting on the tire markings to tell, but it appeared there were at least three different tire sizes — although the rear ones matched.

Jack walked up to his friends, who were staring at the truck. "She's a beaut, Clark."

"Find religion in there?" Casey whispered to Jack.

Jack smiled at him, patted him on the chest, and said, "When you find the time, brother, look in King James. Read about the 'Cities of Refuge.'" Then he strangely hugged Case as if to say, *it'll be alright*.

Alberto first argued with Juan about a price to drive them to Ollanta, and then with Claire about her not riding in the truck's bed. In the end, the friends insisted that Al would ride in the passenger seat.

The pick-up bed was bare metal, so Casey and Jack followed Claire's lead and pulled from their packs their sleeping pads to fold and sit on and their sleeping bags stuffed in sacks to pad their backs or heads if they decide to lie down. They leaned against their packs, grasping for any semblance of comfort they might find for the hours-long ride.

After three tries, the truck reluctantly started. Juan had to feather the accelerator and wind the engine up a bit to keep it from stalling, but the Priest smiled at the group and said, "When she gets up to speed, she runs quite well." He then made the Sign of the Cross and chuckled to himself as he turned back for the church.

As the truck pulled away, Alberto yelled back to him, "Father! How is it you speak English so well?"

The Priest turned and waved as he lifted his voice over the engine, "Notre Dame, '67!"

Casey, Claire, and Jack looked at each other and shook their heads. Jack glanced behind them, back toward the mountains they had traversed. He tried to get the group back on track. "Well," he said, holding both arms outstretched, jostling in the truck bed, "we wanted adventure!"

The Priest had been right. Once Juan had the old truck past twenty miles per hour, it ran like a top. Shocks would have been nice, though.

The truck rolled into Ollantaytambo at almost six o'clock in the evening. Juan pulled next to the adobe wall in front of the hostel, and the truck coughed, spat, and stalled. Casey, Claire, and Jack had to peel themselves off the truck bed. Each was sore in more places than they could count. Their butts, hips, and shoulders ached the most.

Each one stretched, moaned, and grunted as they lowered themselves out of the truck bed. "Well, that was fun," said Casey.

"I'm calling dibs on the first shower," Claire said.

"I'm starving," Al said, "but let's all get cleaned up and then get a nice meal somewhere. But remember, if we all take a shower, they can't be long ones, or whoever takes the last one will get cold water. Meet down here in an hour?"

After three weeks of trekking and hiking mountain passes, all four travelers looked fit and trim. The showers, clean clothes, Tylenol, and some stretches worked wonders. The group walked down the dirt road along the adobe wall, past the cornfield, and into town. They walked until Alberto stopped in front of a tiny café and said, "This is a nice place, and they'll have some beers or wine if you want some." Within an hour, everyone was in the courtyard of the hostel.

They found a corner table big enough for them to spread out.

They sat down and ordered chicken and potatoes and Crystal beers as soon as the waitress came with menus. Overall, they were feeling better.

"It has just occurred to me," Alberto said, "that because of all the events in the last forty-eight hours, we haven't even had the chance to look at Claire's notes or maps of what might be an extraordinary archaeologic find." He wore a big grin.

Claire pulled her journal out of her shoulder bag. Casey also placed his journal on the table, along with the map.

"Before we do," Jack said, I'd like to go over my plan for the other thing first — so we can properly get excited about the discovery and have a fun evening.

"Of course," Alberto said. "That would be best."

"Okay," Jack said. "We agree that it needs to be reported." Everyone at the table nodded. "And we've agreed we cannot connect Al with our trip." Again, they nodded.

"I propose that we travel back to Cusco as planned. Claire and Casey take the map and their notes to the university and report the finding. Casey, you and Claire fly back home on the date of your tickets. I'll switch mine to a later date, maybe a week later. I've been thinking about hanging out with Maria anyway — get to know her better." Jack looked at Claire, whose eyes were down. "After you two have flown out of Cusco, I'll take a bus to Ayacucho and report the Sendero camp. I'll tell them the three of us were exploring on our own. We do have the credentials with our climbing history and the Harvard grad programs. They will not question our desire to explore. Then I'll do a little sightseeing for a couple of days."

Everyone digested his plan and could find nothing wrong with it. Jack told them he would seek out Maria to help him change his tickets to be sure it's done correctly.

Alberto looked a little sad.

"Are you sure you can't go with us, Al, to the university?" Claire asked.

"I would love to," Alberto said. "It would be a highlight in my career in adventure travel. I'll have to think about it for a while. But anyway, I believe Jack's plan is a good one."

"Well, we will write to each other," Claire said. "When you think it is safe, we will officially include you in any literature."

"Right," Casey added. "We'll make amendments to any earlier public documents and papers. But when we report the find in Cusco, it won't seem right if you're not there at the university with us."

Alberto nodded.

"Do we all agree on the plan?" Jack asked.

Everyone did, and they left it at that.

Jack and Casey made no further contributions to the conversation. They regarded each other. Only they knew what had happened in that ravine, and they had decided before reuniting with Claire and Alberto at the top of the pass that it would stay that way. Casey insisted on it, and Jack felt obligated to agree.

The rest of the evening was spent going over the now well-worn map and Claire's and Casey's notes and drawings. This was it. This was what all four were born for; exploration, charting lost ruins, education, bringing the past to life. They all toasted the Incan find with Pisco Sours, but each person had heavy thoughts weighing on their minds.

Each person expected the next few days would be bittersweet and exciting.

THIRTY-ONE
Jack's Contrition

The team was packed and ready to leave for Cusco by nine o'clock in the morning. There was an excellent breakfast at the hostel, and Benita said she wished she could travel back to the states with them. They exchanged personal postal addresses and said they hoped to see each other again.

There were no private vans available for hire in the morning, so the group had to catch one of the daily buses. The ride was uneventful except for when a chicken shit on Casey's hiking boot. He was pissed, and Jack saw it and said, "All part of the adventure, Bub. Don't get in a fowl mood."

Rocking down the dusty road, Jack stared through the windows at the flatter, agricultural landscape. He looked off into the mountains, far beyond the fields of corn and potatoes. *How vast that empire was!* he thought. How many more ruins lay hidden? He reminisced about all they had seen in the last month. He revisited his daily re-living of his making love to Claire on that moonlit bank on the Urubamba, which he would be passing by in a short while. When that memory had run its course, he thought about Pedro, the arriero on the Ausangate trip, and wondered whatever happened to the Poles they met there — what were their names? Antoni, Maja, and Jan? He remembered the bakers Gregorio and Beatriz and what a force Gregorio must have been in the old days when he guided archaeologists and anthropologists throughout these mountains. He thought about Jim Bartlett and Eliana and Maria, and young, capable Benita and how much he loved Ollanta and staying at the hostel. Jack also had recurring visions of the boy in the ravine and his extruding eyeballs. And he noticed that with each passing day, he could push the image from his mind just a few seconds quicker.

And he remembered Enrico and his brother-in-law Benito, and Apurimac, the *alcaldes* — the elder and leader of the extended family who lived off the land with no running water or electricity, who had a sixteen-mile hike to the nearest town, and he hoped Enrico's women would stay safe.

He glanced at Casey, who was staring out his window on the opposite side of the bus. Claire had fallen asleep, and her head rested on his friend's shoulder. He loved her more than anything in the world. She looked so beautiful. Her shorts allowed him to see her smooth, athletic calves and thighs. Her reposed head accentuated her straight jawline and her perfect nose, and he could see through her eyelids and visualize her ice-blue eyes.

How strange his world had become ... in a few days, he would give her a hug goodbye at the airport in Cusco and would not be able to kiss her. All he would have to hold him, to cling to, would be their passionate sex under the Pisonay tree, laying on their clothes in the cool grass by the light of a full moon on the banks of the Urubamba. This thought was always followed by a sick feeling in his stomach. His betrayal of Casey was becoming more than he could bear.

That's enough, he said to himself and looked back out his window.

The friends were elated to find rooms available at the Royal Inka Hotel in Cusco, and it didn't take long to find themselves at the Cross Keys pub. It was nice to be back. Casey ordered two large pizzas and three Crystals, and the friends toasted their find once again. Jack was looking at the Manchester United banner on the wall and was contemplating tossing a few darts when Alberto and Marisol entered the room. Marisol was dressed in an emerald vintage evening dress and a fire engine red silk headband. She hugged everyone in the pub and settled down next to Claire at the table.

"I'm surprised to see you two tonight," Casey said. "I thought you'd spend a quiet evening at home after being on the trail so long."

"We will," Alberto said. "We talked for a couple of hours and wanted to stop by for congratulations again and to say we've decided that I won't be going with you to the university."

"Okay," Claire said. "But remember our commitment to including you in our papers when you think the time is right."

"Thank you."

"We're scheduled to make a call to Professor Fitzroy at Harvard tomorrow morning. We want to make sure our T's are crossed." Alberto nodded. He headed for the bar.

Marisol leaned toward Claire. "That was some trip you had. Are you okay?"

Claire raised her eyebrows in affirmation and nodded. She had an expression of exasperation.

Marisol spoke to Jack and Casey. "You should have seen Al's eyes when he was telling me about your trip. Though it was scary, he was in heaven." She thought for a moment and said, "I'm so glad he met you three. He's meant for exploration but spends so much of his time with tourists he misses venturing into the unknown."

All three friends immediately suspected that Al hadn't told his wife about *all* the things they had seen.

"Hiking into new country," Jack said.

Marisol nodded. "Exactly. By the way, Jack, Maria asked when you three would be back. I think she's sweet on you."

"Actually," he responded, "I need to talk to her tomorrow. I hope I still have her number."

"Casey knows where we live," she said. "If you don't have it, come by tomorrow, and we'll find her." Jack nodded appreciatively. Claire pretended to stare at the dartboards at the far end of the room.

The morning was born with a blue sky and lazy clouds rolling along the hilltops above the town. Jack was first down for breakfast. The courtyard was cool and filled with early light, and Hummingbirds flitted in and out of the fuchsias. Claire followed shortly after, and she and Jack had some time together. Over breakfast in the pretty courtyard, they discussed the elephant in the room.

"It's a good plan you have," she said. "You've played along quite well over the last week."

"No choice, really," he said.

She was looking him in the eye, which, as usual, made him melt. In a different world, he would take her then and make love to her again, like he had ten thousand times before in his mind. But this *wasn't* that world.

"What day will you get back?" she asked.

"Depends on flights and availability," he responded. "I'd like to get another week."

"And we'll sort things out when you get home?"

Yes," Jack said. "It'll be sorted."

"I have an incredible urge to kiss you," she said, "... a kiss that would last for hours."

Jack stared at her before glancing in the direction of her and Casey's hotel room. Then he looked back at her and made the subtlest shake of his head. They sat in silence and drank their coffees until Casey came down. When he did, Jack excused himself and said he had to meet Maria to make arrangements for purchasing the new airline tickets.

Being a Sunday, Claire and Casey walked around Cusco for the rest of the day, enjoying the sights, exploring narrow back streets, and shopping. Jack did have Maria's telephone number, and she was happy to help him with the airline tickets, but it would have to wait until Monday morning. She suggested he visit with her, and she would cook him supper. He had felt a connection with her before the Ausangate trek and accepted her invitation.

He did not have trouble finding her. She lived in a cute little flat about three blocks from the Plaza de Armas. It was tastefully furnished and exuded an artsy, stylish form. In a small anteroom was a drafting table. Architectural drawings were hanging everywhere. Jack did not know why, but he felt oddly comfortable. Maria had given him a big hug when he darkened her door, and he had forgotten how strikingly beautiful she was. *Were she to walk down 5th Avenue,* he thought, *she would turn every head — of both men and women.* She was that stunning.

Maria wanted to know all about the trek, but before she could say "welcome back," Jack started asking questions about her career. Here he was with, along with Claire, one of the most beautiful women he had ever seen, and he was in her flat, and she was cooking for him.

Maria went into the kitchen as she answered his questions. "I hope you eat beef," she said, "I should have asked first."

"I do, thank you," Jack replied. *Oh God,* he thought, *she's a grad student. I hope she didn't spend a lot of money on some steak.* Jack sat down on her tiny couch.

"Would you like a beer?" she asked.

"Please."

She brought out a Crystal, handed it to him, put another on the table for herself, and returned to the kitchen. He watched her and could smell her as she walked by, and she exuded an intoxicating combination of sexuality, class, and intelligence.

"I realized you only just got here," she said, "but it seems supper is ready."

"That's nice," Jack said. "I hope you didn't go to much trouble."

"Not at all. It's a simple Peruvian dish I thought you'd like to try. The easier the meal, the easier it will be to get to talk and to know each other."

Normally, in the past few years, that statement from any woman would send him into a nervous spin of dread and non-commitment. First, there had been Rachael, then falling for his best friend's girlfriend; it was all too much. He was more comfortable on his own, and he was better alone. But, for some unfathomable reason, he found his comfort in Maria's presence strangely peaceful.

She brought out two plates, and as he jumped off the couch, she gestured where he could sit. He did. "It is called '*Lomo saltado*," she said.

It was a nice stir-fry with marinated sirloin strips, onions, tomatoes, French fries, garlic, and rice on the side. It was very good. As they ate, Jack asked more about her career, hobbies, and passions. It was not small talk. For some time, he could not figure out how a young woman from Cusco could become such a sophisticated, worldly-wise person. In the conversation, it eventually came out that her mother was a physician and her father a diplomat, so they have been "fortunate to travel to New York and Paris — but only once to each city."

Finally, she was able to ask about the trek, and he told her everything about Ausangate. He told her about Pedro, and the fishing, and the Poles. He described what Alberto was like on the trek.

"He is truly amazing," he told her. "A man of all seasons."

He continued talking, to his amazement, after they'd finished eating and while they did the dishes together. At one point, he paused and thought, *man, I love Cusco, and I love Ollanta.* And before he could stop himself, he blurted out, "You know, I could live here."

"In my apartment?" she said, giving him a mock perturbed look, and then smiling said, "That's quite sudden."

"Oh!" he replied, "in Cusco — or Ollanta."

She had a cute, reserved laugh.

His eyes scanned the kitchen, and he said, "And yes, the apartment is very nice, also."

"I do love Ollanta," she said, "I go there for weekends simply to go for walks and to study the ancient architecture."

After the dishes, they sat together on the tiny couch and talked some more. Maria sat sideways, bent her knees, and pulled her feet up. She asked more questions about himself, and they talked about their families. She asked about the rest of their adventure at Ollanta. He did not know why, but he decided on the fly to tell her everything. This was an educated, worldly, cosmopolitan young woman. He asked if he could trust her. She said yes, and he knew — but he did not know why, exactly — that he could.

"You are singularly beautiful," he started. Maria lowered her head, and her eyes sparkled, and they seemed to humbly say, "thank you." She had heard that many times before, but from Jack, it was different. "But, you should know something about me." She adjusted her legs and tucked her feet under her butt and braced herself.

Jack told her everything about Rachael and then Claire. As he spoke of the love that was untold for so long, a tear rolled down her perfect cheekbone as she imagined the pain he had been through in his young life. Jack wiped it away, and she caught his hand and held onto it, pressing the back of his hand against her breast. He told Maria how he had explained everything to Claire on this trip and felt it was a huge mistake ever since. Maria listened as Jack talked about his problem for an hour, and in the end, they had bonded, and she asked nothing of him. When he finished, he knew in that cathartic moment that beyond trusting her, they had become good friends. That meant a lot to him.

After they each took a breath and opened a bottle of wine, Jack sighed and apologized for talking so much. She leaned forward, gave him a tight hug, and kissed him on the cheek. She leaned back again and smiled at him, and he responded in kind.

She spoke playfully to him, "Is this a date then, Jack?"

"I don't know what this is at this point," he laughed, "It's weird. But, this is the most comfortable I've been with a woman in five years."

"It feels like a date," she said, "and if it is, it is the best one I've ever had. Thank you for opening up to me."

They stared at each other. Maria was special, and he knew it.

Maria reached out and again took his hand. This time, she held it on her lap.

Jack broke the silence, and he told her everything about the newfound ruins, and without going into great detail, he told her they had stumbled onto a possible Sendero Luminoso camp. "There's more about the trip we just finished." He explained that she was sworn to secrecy about the camp and that he alone was going to go to another city to report the operation in an effort to not involve Alberto for his and Marisol's safety.

"After Claire and Casey fly back to Lima," he told her, "I plan on taking a bus to Ayacucho to report the Sendero camp there, with no mention of Al. The worry is, if I were to report it here in Cusco, someone might be able to make the connection between Alberto and us, and we are afraid of a local Sendero retaliation against him. These ancient Incan walls may have ears."

"I understand," she said. "You must have confidence in me to tell me this."

"I do."

"Are you busy tomorrow?" she asked.

"Actually, I meant to ask you about tomorrow. I'm going with Claire and Casey to the university to report the find, and I was hoping you might like to go."

She smiled broadly and said, "Yes, please."

"I don't know what time they are going," he said, "because it depends on what their professor tells them after they call Harvard in the morning." He continued, "I am supposed to go and try to change my airline tickets, but that can wait. Anyway, after stopping at the university, I hoped you would like to go for a walk around the city and maybe get a late lunch."

They talked until one in the morning. There was an awkward moment when Maria looked like she was about to yawn, and he rose from the couch. "I should head back to the hotel."

Maria held his hand as they walked to the door. He could see that she was thinking. Standing in the doorway, she said, "It is not Lima, but

I am still a little worried about you walking back to the hotel at this time of night." But she felt that it would ruin their wonderful evening if she offered to let him spend the night.

He smiled at her. "I'll be just fine. I have some writing I want to do in the morning. What time can I come by tomorrow?

"Any time," she said.

"Great." He leaned down and kissed her on the cheek, and she hugged him again.

He kept his wits about him as he walked the early morning streets of Cusco, but at the same time, he lost his mind. *What the hell was that?* he asked himself. Not since Rachael had he opened up to anyone like that, and not even to Claire. He was unable to stop himself from rubbing his hands on the enormous, smooth, polished stones of the Incan walls he passed.

He was exhausted, and as he made his way to the fresh linens of his hotel bed, the weight of confusion and chaos descended upon him, and he longed for the simplicity of a more solitary life.

THIRTY-TWO

A Report in Cusco

C laire held her journal open on the counter at the Royal Inka Hotel. She had written down the hotel's telephone number, including the country code for Peru.

"Hello … can you hear me? This is Claire Anderson calling for Dr. Fitzroy — I'm calling from Peru."

There was a pause on the line, then, "Hi Claire, Maryanne was just heading to a class, but I caught her. I'm transferring you into her office." There was a click.

"Hello Claire, is everything all right?"

"Yes, yes, everything is fine — more than fine, possibly. We may have found something."

At first, Dr. Fitzroy was worried the friends had gotten into some sort of trouble. It wouldn't have been the first time a student called from abroad seeking advice. But now, she was interested in a different way, the way even the oldest, most experienced archaeologists get giddy with excitement at the promise of a find.

"Just a second, Claire." She heard Dr. Fitzroy call to the receptionist; "Go tell them I'll be a few minutes late."

The professor got her pen and a writing tablet. "All right, Claire…"

Claire gave her just the details she needed. Later, she could fill in the story: "Possible significant Incan or pre-Incan site much farther east than expected, only a few miles from the Manus. Multiple dwellings — more than a dozen. Two buildings over 800 square feet, possibly temple size. Ramparts and walls, irrigation systems … terraced land works. Not on any maps that we can find. Need reporting protocols."

She sounded like a Western Union telegram, but she was focused on brevity.

Dr. Fitzroy was writing. "Have you told anyone yet?"

"No. We have a contact in the Uni here, but we wanted your recommendations."

"Do you have coordinates yet?"

"Yes. Casey and Jack worked them out with a compass, and we think it's accurate. Ready?"

"Yes," said the professor.

"Twelve degrees, forty-two minutes, eighty-six seconds South, and seventy-two degrees, zero-one minutes, fifteen, point fifty-nine seconds West."

Dr. Fitzroy repeated the coordinates back to Claire. "Okay," she said. "When are you supposed to fly back?"

"In three days," Claire replied.

"Good. That gives us time. We have somebody there in Cusco. Give me two hours, and I'll get a message to you. Where can I call?"

Claire gave her the hotel's number.

"All right ... two hours. Talk then." And she hung up.

As they walked back out to the courtyard, Jack said, "I spoke yesterday with Maria about airline tickets. Is it okay if she goes with us to the university? She knows her way around the school, and we can't assume that everyone we contact there can speak English."

"Does Alberto know about this?" Claire asked.

Jack shook his head. "No, but Maria is safe," Jack spoke with an unusual inflection that suggested he did not want to discuss or defend his confidence in Maria. Claire and Casey looked at each other and left it alone.

"That's fine," Claire said, hiding any hint of jealousy. "She might be able to help."

The next day, Maria led the way past the ornate fountain and through the enormous stone-tiled courtyard of the National University of Saint Anthony the Abad. The Baroque architecture of the older school section was fronted by an open arched two-story loggia where students sat in the shade and studied.

"I'm glad the archaeology department is in the old colonial building and not in one of the modern ones," Casey said. "It's fitting."

"This Professor Bache," Jack said. "It's not a Spanish name."

"No," Maria said. "He was born in Switzerland or Germany, I think. But he went to school in the U.S."

All four passed under one of the arches and through the 266-year-old doors which lead into the school's foyer. Maria led them up a short stairway to a mezzanine, where a student sat behind a large, uncluttered old desk.

Maria knew the student. "*Hola, Lucia, estamos aquí para ver al profesor Bache. Tenemos una cita para Andersen.*"

Lucia smiled at Maria. Everyone always smiled at Maria. "*Sí, Maria. Le diré que estás aquí,*" and she rose from her chair and walked down a long hallway.

"Beautiful building," Casey said. He looked at the walls, the stairs, and the ceiling.

"The school was started in 1692," Maria offered, "and this particular building was finished in 1722."

"Have you met the professor?" Claire asked.

"No, but I have attended two of his lectures in which he spoke about pre-Incan architecture."

Lucia returned from the hallway, spoke to Maria, and sat down at the desk.

"We can go," Maria said. Casey, Claire, and Jack followed Maria down the hall as she inspected the numbers on the doors. She knocked on one and tentatively opened the door.

"*Adelante,*" came a voice from within.

All four entered the professor's spacious office. It was furnished with an established archaeologist's accouterment, with bits and pieces of historical importance on every flat surface and tucked into every corner. Casey noticed on the wall the knotted strings of a kipu framed and highlighted amongst the clutter.

The professor was an interesting gentleman. He was a small man with a European manner and intense eyes. His light brown hair was carefully brushed back, but he had a remarkably bushy and unkempt mustache that did not fold down around the corners of his lips but extended straight out to either side toward his cheeks. He wore wrinkled khaki pants and a well-worn casual white shirt, yet he sported an oversized butterfly bowtie.

Maria introduced the three friends in English. The professor shook their hands and told them it was a pleasure to meet them. Maria told Dr. Bache she had accompanied her friends to translate if needed, so she would take her leave. Each said they would be happy if she would like to stay, and she did.

"I received a message from Dr. Fitzroy from Harvard this morning," he said in English, with only a slight German-sounding accent. He pointed to some chairs arranged in a semi-circle in front of his desk, and he pulled another from a corner for Maria.

"Have we met before?" he asked her before offering the chair.

"No, Sir," she said, "but I have attended two of your classes." She held up her hand, "Architecture."

"Ah…" he said. "I see."

"So, you are from Harvard? All of you?"

All three said yes.

Dr. Bache nodded. He sat behind his desk.

The professor held up his hand and smiled. "Columbia." He explained, "I grew up in Germany, in Keil. My parents emigrated to the States during my last year at Gymnasium, and I attended undergraduate school in the U.S., and then Columbia."

Claire felt they were in good hands. "Dr. Fitzroy said you have found something interesting. And she said I should trust that you are accurate."

"That is correct," Claire said. "We have found a site that we believe is unmapped and unknown. As far as accuracy goes, we can give you a fairly detailed description of the site and its coordinates, and we did the best we could with the time we had for a rudimentary site survey. As far as being accurate about it being a discovery, we would defer to you."

"Excellent," the professor said. "Have you come here first?"

"Yes," Claire said. We fly to Lima tomorrow, and we will be reporting to the Ministry of Culture there."

"Good. We should work on a good map and a description. As you undoubtedly know, you legally must report this to the Ministry, but it is an expansive, heavily bureaucratized institution. There is a good chance that once you make the report, nothing will be done about it. I can save you some time because I have the reporting protocol paperwork here, and I can help you."

"Thank you, doctor," Claire said.

"I think you all should call me Franz." He already had the paperwork on his desk.

"Once you have filed with the Ministry of Culture," Franz said, "you will be required to have a Peruvian co-investigator who must sign on as the technical consultant for any investigation or excavation — that'll be me. You should begin writing a permiso requesting permission to survey, map, excavate, etcetera. I will sign on in this reporting form. Once it is approved by the Ministry, that part of the process will likely be rather quick. But there are hoops to jump through, as you say."

"I understand," Claire said. "But, before we proceed, there is one thing you should be aware of."

"Yes?" Franz asked.

Claire, Casey, and Jack exchanged glances. Jack nodded at Claire.

"I suspect this process will take the better part of a year to procure permission and to arrange the logistics — providing you will still want to go do a survey — you have not seen how remote the site is. So, I think there will be time for this other discovery to be addressed."

"Other discovery?" the professor asked.

"Yes," Claire said. "Jack will tell you about it. But first, we want your assurance that there will be no talk of this aspect of the discovery until it is reported in Ayacucho and dealt with. We are attempting to report it officially without endangering our local friend — our *amigo y guía*."

Dr. Bache's eyes became more intense, more penetrating. The friends had his full attention.

Casey unfolded the map on the professor's desk. It was now a well-used map with many notes, compass bearings, smudges, and small tears.

Jack sat forward in his chair. He pointed at a pencil mark where the Sendero camp was. "Sir, the site is located on the eastern slopes of one of the smaller Cordillera. About 1,000 feet down the slope from the ruins is a temporary camp set up not far from a river. It is a bad place. It was heavily guarded. All of the guards we saw were dressed in black and armed."

The professor slumped back in his chair. "*The Sendero!*" he half-whispered.

"Possibly," Jack said. He re-thought that. "Probably. It could be a human trafficking compound. There were women... they were being mistreated."

"No!" Franz exclaimed. He muttered something under his breath in German.

"I'm telling you this in confidence only so that none of your people go there to investigate until it is secure."

"Yes, yes. Of course," Franz promised.

"I believe," Jack said, "that if an aerial helicopter survey of the camp was to be made, those bad people would move out of that area. But, I'm sure the police or military will have a plan once I report it tomorrow."

"You are not flying to Lima tomorrow?" the professor asked.

"No," I am staying to take care of this and to see some more of this beautiful country. I genuinely think that once the military knows, it will be taken care of long before the logistical planning of an excavation can be completed. But it would be best to communicate with the authorities in Ayacucho before going to the site."

Dr. Bache nodded. "That is a good plan, I think. Let us proceed with the discussion of the site and complete the paperwork."

Over the next hour, the friends poured over several other maps of the area that included the site. Casey and Jack reworked the longitude and latitude for the professor's maps. Each chart used a different geodetic datum, and it took some time to agree. They checked their calculations against the original map Jim Bartlett had given them. Casey had become attached to this map, with its numerous notes and markings.

"But," Franz said, bent over one of his maps with Casey and Jack's new mark on it, that is beyond the Incan Empire." He looked up at Claire, who smiled at him.

"Yup."

The professor examined Claire's hand-drawn maps in her journal.

"Impressive," he said. "Did you take photographs?"

"Yes. Between Casey and me, there are probably sixty. When I get the rolls processed at home, I'll make copies and mail them to you."

"How did you make your measurements?"

"We had half of a climbing rope," said Casey, "seventy-five feet long — just under twenty-three meters. That is why all of these measurements are in feet, and we can convert them to meters later."

Dr. Bache looked over the diagrams in Claire's journal. "If these drawings are even close to accurate," he said, "then this is a significant find. This is a city." He pointed to some of the linear drawings. "What are these?" He spun the journal 180 degrees as he looked at the markings around the structures. "Fourteen feet?"

"Ramparts," Claire said. "That is the height."

He read the other measurement. "Two hundred-fifty feet long?"

"Give or take a few feet," Claire said.

The professor looked up from the journal. "A walled city. Maybe a citadel. Well done, everyone. Well done." He smiled at each of them. He tapped the map where Casey and Jack had marked it.

"This is why we do this, no?"

🌴

When the group left the university, they felt good about their reporting. They felt good about Dr. Bache, and they were happy that he had helped them with the Ministry of Culture's paperwork. Maria had kept quiet, observing from the side of the room. As they walked, she said, "You all must be proud of your find."

"It might be a good thing for my career, for sure," Claire said, "but it was traumatic. Especially for Casey and Jack, it seems. It'll take some time to sort everything."

Claire noticed as Maria gave Jack a familiar touch on the shoulder and asked, "Do you still want to do some shopping and have lunch?"

"Absolutely," Jack replied. He looked back at Claire and Casey. "Want to join us for lunch?"

Before Casey could answer, Claire said, "I want to go back to the hotel and drop these papers and maps off. We'll catch up later. Remember, we promised Al and Marisol we would take them out tonight since we're leaving tomorrow."

"I remember. Meet at the Cross Keys at six-thirty and walk from there." He whispered something to Maria, and she nodded. "Maria will come with."

That evening, the group had one of the finest meals and the brightest times of their trip. The friends all hugged, and Claire had a tear in her eye when she embraced Alberto. Before they parted, she said to him, "It's safe to say, I will never forget our treks together, and I will never forget you, my friend. I hope in a year or two, I will be the one to survey the new site for the university, and I hope you are with me." Al looked very proud.

As Jack walked Maria home, she held his hand. Tomorrow he would travel to Ayacucho as planned after seeing Claire and Casey off at the airport.

"Would you like me to go with you to Ayacucho?" she asked.

Jack hesitated. He stopped her and turned to face her as they got to the door of her flat.

"I feel very comfortable with you," he said.

"As do I." She wasn't sure where this conversation was going.

She closed on him and pulled him close. She wrapped her arms around his neck, and he could feel her breasts against his upper abdomen. She looked at him with her big, black, almond-shaped devilish eyes and said, "Jack, Dear. I am only twenty years old. I will wait for you longer than that."

She reached for his hand, held it again, put it to her mouth, and kissed his palm.

"Why don't you stay here tonight and tell me, truly, what your plan is. Then tomorrow you can go to Ayacucho. If you stay with me, I know you will come back."

Maria smiled at him and bit her lower lip as she opened the door. It almost made him light-headed. He followed her up the stairs.

In her apartment, he reiterated what he had told her about Claire and his poor, lost heart.

Maria listened, and when he was finished, all she said was, "I understand, but I also believe the undeniable feelings I have for you already, and I see in your eyes that you feel something too. And Jack, that is enough for me."

She tried to kiss him goodbye, but when she did, she could tell he was uneasy. He didn't know what to say and tried to apologize with his eyes. Maria gave him a conciliatory look and placed the palm of her hand on his chest.

Jack smiled, nodded, and left.

THIRTY-THREE
Walkabout

The ride to Ayacucho was better than he expected. There was hardly any livestock on the bus, and he was able to think about how awkward it had been to see Casey and Claire off at the airport. Claire's long embrace was nice but uncomfortable. And there was Casey's innocence and his weird statement, "When you get back next week, we should drive up to Maine for some salmon fishing." Jack's mind was thousands of miles away.

He thought about Maria and how interested she was in everything, and she asked a lot of questions about fly fishing and trekking. He thought about the bundle of letters she would be posting for him today, and he thought she was someone he could trust with his life — but he did not know why. He thought about Maria staying up with him and translating a letter to accompany his map for the police — or the military, whichever he can find.

He grinned when he thought about her smile, and he closed his eyes and pictured her the night before. He tried to burn the image of her into his mind, how she smelled, and what her kiss was like. He did not want to forget.

Ayacucho was even busier than he thought it would be, and the bustling city life came with the big-city blended sweet smells of garbage, urine, and street vendors. It was much warmer than Cusco.

He wandered through the streets, asking whomever he met where the police station was. But he did not have the walk or aspect of a gringo who had just been robbed, which confused the people. He thought of what Alberto had said when they searched for a driver, "We need to find a church. The priest will probably speak some English, and he will know everything."

I have got to learn the language, he thought. He stopped the first person that walked by and said in terrible half-Spanish, *Donde esta las Iglesia?* It didn't occur to him until the man answered that he did not know enough of the language to understand his directions. So, Jack first pointed in different directions and then made finger-walking motions while asking him, *quantas tiempo?* In the end, he guessed it was a few blocks to the right, then uphill, and he could walk there in about fifteen minutes. It turned out he was spot-on.

Unfortunately, the priest's English was not great, but he found someone who could help after some discussion. One of his altar servers was studying for a translator job at his uncle's bank in Lima.

"I will *teléfono,*" the priest said.

Jack took off his backpack, sat on one of the benches outside the church, and waited. It was warm with a light breeze, and it was very pleasant. He took out a road map of Peru that Maria had given him. It appeared to be a nice town, but it had a dark lining. Alberto had told him that Ayacucho was used as the base of operations for the Sendero Luminoso.

Jack inspected the five major roads leading out of the city. He traced his finger along Highway 35. Then he took out the photocopied map with the Sendero camp marked on it, and the letter for the police that Maria had written for him. He looked around at the pretty street scene and thought how it already seemed like ages ago when he and Alberto were hunkered behind the rock wall, fearing for their lives. How strange that it would feel so long ago.

"Hola," came a voice. Jack looked up. This must be the altar boy the priest called. The teenager held out his hand. "I am Pedro."

Perfect, Jack thought, remembering the Ausangate trek; *I liked the last Pedro.*

"Jack." He shook his hand.

"Father Garcia said you need help with directions."

"Yes," Jack replied. "And maybe with something else. Do you have some time to help me?"

Pedro nodded.

"Good. I have to find a police station to report something I saw recently. Can we walk there from here?"

"Yes. It is not far."

"Bueno. I will pay you for your time." Pedro nodded and held his arm out to the side, indicating the direction. Jack slung his pack over his shoulders, and they walked down the hill from the church.

"How is it that you speak English so well, Pedro?"

"I am a student at the university, studying English. I have a job offer in a bank, but I really want to be a translator for the government someday."

After about twenty minutes of winding through the city streets, they came to a four-way intersection. Pedro pointed across the street to the simple, non-descript police station. Jack looked around in the direction of each road. "Excellent. Now Pedro ... which way to the bus station?"

Pedro pointed. "Straight down this street, on this side."

"And I can get a bus to Cusco from there?"

"Yes, but you do not need to go all the way to the station. If you go back the way we came for two blocks, you will see small buses lined up along a plaza. Some will say 'Cuzco.' It is a few dollars more, but a much more comfortable ride than the buses from the station."

"All right," Jack said. "Now, I want to catch a bus, so I'd like it very much if you would simply drop off this map and letter in the police station. I will give you five U.S. dollars for your time."

"Sir, that is 10,000 Intis."

"I know, Pedro. But you are a student, and you can use a few dollars." Jack gave him the map and the letter."

Pedro took the papers and looked at Jack. "Sir, why did you not just mail this to the police?"

"Two reasons; Because, Pedro, I am a student too, in college, and I have a flight back. I did not want them to see the postage mark and go to Cusco to track me down because I was afraid they would make me miss my return trip home. Also, I wanted to see Ayacucho."

Pedro nodded and smiled.

Jack held out some money. "Here is five dollars. Thank you, and good luck with your studies. Your English is excellent."

Pedro took the papers, waited for traffic, and walked across the intersection. Jack backed into the shadows of the buildings and watched Pedro enter the police station with the copy of his letter. Satisfied that Pedro had made the delivery, Jack walked down the street, past the road that led to the plaza, and continued to the bus station. He purchased a ticket and boarded one of the big buses bound not for Cusco but north, for the city of Huancayo.

He rode the rough, bumpy, unpaved road north along the jade-colored Mantaro River and through the Andean Highlands for twelve hours. It did not bother Jack that the road sometimes dropped off a precipice on one side, and the bus seemed to lean out over the valley below, but many passengers closed their eyes, and some prayed aloud.

From Ayacucho, the city of Cusco was a twelve-hour bus ride to the east. The police now had all the details of what he and Alberto had seen near the border with the Manus. They had the longitude and latitude. They had a description of the south end of the compound and its estimated size. They now knew about the women slaves. But Jack knew the police would also have a description of him from young Pedro, and they would surely want to find him to interview him. But Pedro would tell them the gringo was taking a collectivo to Cusco.

Now on the bus headed north to Huancayo, Jack had given them the slip. His duty was done.

By now, Claire and Casey would have dropped off the report of their find to the Ministry of Culture in Lima and were already in Miami. *Their* duty was done, and they were probably waiting for their connecting flight to Logan Airport.

As the bus rocked back and forth and bumped along the dirt road, Jack was suddenly caught with a wave of melancholy. He thought of Maria. Young, beautiful Maria. It was likely she would not yet have found the letter he left for her on her drafting table, explaining how happy he was to have met her. The letter told her that he was confused — that since telling Claire how much he cared for her, Jack knew he couldn't be with her *or* around Casey, not after tearing them apart, which surely would happen. The letter explained to Maria that he did not know where he was going or what he would do, only that he planned to travel as long as he could until he felt better about himself again ... until he felt better about life again. He will travel, he wrote, as a pilgrim, searching everywhere for beauty and simplicity. He will learn about the people he meets and try to make something useful of what he learns. He will write to her within six months, the letter said. He had no idea if he would be returning to Cusco. He told her he had never met anyone like her and that he was sure he never would again.

The letter said, *whatever happens, I will never forget you and will think of you often.*

He thought *she will probably cry when she reads that.*

Jack stared out the window at the valley below and the river meandering through it. *In the past four weeks,* he thought, *I have lost the only woman I found I could love since Rachael died, probably lost my best friend, killed a dog, knocked out a man — maybe worse, met another perfect woman, and left her alone and crying.*

Well done, Jack.

And he thought more about Casey, whom he had been through so much with. He knew their relationship would be different when he found out his best friend loves his girlfriend, but Casey always looked at relationships differently. Jack knew their relationship would change now more drastically than if they had simply graduated from grad school and moved to other states or countries to work. They might still be friends, but not as close. That made him feel sick again.

Quickly, Jack's thoughts drifted to his family. His mother will always support him in what he decides to do, but his father will struggle with him taking some time from his graduate program. And how will his professors handle him taking time off? How the people back home would accept his decision to travel was up to them. It was done. He had examined his finances. If he lived simply and camped whenever he could, he had enough money to live for a year in a country like Peru, providing he wasn't robbed. And there's Ecuador and Bolivia. *I can work if I need to,* he thought. *Do odd jobs. If I learn the language well enough, I could even teach. As long as there are buses and my legs work, I can go wherever I choose.*

Maria would have already mailed the letters to the university and Casey and Claire. In a couple of weeks, his parents and little sister Lisa would get their letters. As quickly as he felt the melancholy, Jack felt an extraordinary lightness. He felt a freedom he hadn't experienced since before grad school when he had hitchhiked around Utah, Idaho, Wyoming, and Montana, searching for fly-fishing rivers. *I will be all right,* he thought. *When I get to Huancayo, I will find a hostel, and during breakfast, I'll decide where to go next.*

He closed his eyes and put his head back. Visions of Maria, Casey, Claire, and of his mother and father, his brothers, and little Lisa flashed in and out of his brain. He wondered what sort of crazy quest he was on. For the second time in his life, his only direction was straight ahead, down a road. Any road. For the time being, he realized he was homeless.

I will find simplicity, he imagined, *and then I will find the beauty.*

As he tried to sleep, the vision of the women tied by their necks in that cold mountain stream returned. He worried most about those two little girls and the thoughts of them being sold into prostitution in a lawless mining town in the jungle. The same wretched voice rang through his brain; "*Alessa!*"

And then he wept.

THIRTY-FOUR

Revelation

I t took Claire and Casey four days to decompress. The familiarity of their apartment was a comfort, and the anticipation of their photographs being developed was palpable. Still, that anticipation was wiped clean on their seventh day at home when the mail arrived.

Casey picked up the mail and left it unread for most of the day. When he returned to the apartment in the afternoon and looked through the letters, he saw the two beige airmail envelopes with the red and blue hash marks around the borders, one addressed to him and one to Claire. "*Via Aerea*" was written in the front and back, and each had three Peruvian stamps totaling three dollars and fifty cents. Claire walked into the kitchen from the bedroom, toweling her wet hair, and Casey handed her the letter.

"I figured he wouldn't call us," Casey said, "and probably just show up later this week. Maybe these will say when his return flight is."

Claire froze and then took the letter from his hand. This was it. Whatever she had with Casey ends tonight. *Now he will find out what she and Jack had talked about on the banks of the Urubamba River.* She slumped down into a chair and put her letter on the table. Then she folded her hands over the envelope and watched Casey leaning against the kitchen counter open his. She closed her eyes as he started to read. She braced herself.

After only a few lines, he stood erect.

Here it comes, she thought.

But he kept reading, and he did not look upset. Then he scowled. *Oh, God ...* but he reached into the basket on the table and picked up an apple and bit into it as he read.

What the fuck? Thought Claire. She was waiting for the shoe to drop.

Casey sat down at the table opposite her and continued reading. Then, he started shaking his head and winced. He suddenly looked pained, and he checked the backs of the pages and then put the letter down. He sat back and looked at her with a saddened face.

Claire looked at him with tears in her eyes, which he did not notice, and shook her head. "Then she said, "Casey, Honey ..."

"He's lost it," Casey said.

Claire did not finish the sentence.

"He's not coming back. He's staying in South America, but he doesn't know where. Can you fucking believe that?"

Claire felt herself getting lightheaded. "Not — coming back?"

"Nope. He has to take some time to sort some things out. He says he has written to the university and his professors, and he has asked his brothers to come down here to get his truck and his stuff from his apartment. He told them I have a key."

"Do you? Have a key?"

"Yes, but that's not the point. I don't understand what happened. This could ruin Jack's life."

Claire shook her head. "It could do worse than that."

There was a strange moment of silence before Casey said, "Maybe it's Maria. Maybe he has fallen for her and is shacking up with her in Cusco."

"I don't think so."

"No, I could see it," Casey insisted, "she's gorgeous and clever. They seemed to get along, and she was definitely into him."

Claire got up and took the letter, and headed for the bathroom.

"Aren't you going to read yours?"

She continued toweling her hair as she walked. "I will, after my hair's dry. It probably says the same thing as yours." He did not notice the strain in her voice. And he did not see that the towel was wiping tears, not her hair.

A half-hour later, Claire breezed through the living room where Casey was reading and said, "Forgot something at the museum. Be right back."

"I still can't believe about Jack," he called after her as she went through the front door.

"Yeah. Crazy ... talk later."

Claire walked into the warm spring evening and up the road past Divinity Street and into the Yard. The maples and oaks were leafed out now, and the Yard smelled good. She found a park bench that was out of the way. It was lit by a streetlamp, and there was a lilac bush beside it that still had some blossoms on it. She sat for long minutes, staring straight ahead, holding the letter on her lap. Finally, she opened it and found a single sheet of paper.

She drew a deep breath.

Dearest Claire,

It is with the saddest heart that I write to you — or perhaps the fondest heart as I mean to tell you that I will not return to America to be with you. I fell in love with you the moment I laid eyes on you and have had to endure that untold love for two years. Now, I have said the words to you under that full moon, and I knew in the subsequent hour that the pain I would surely cause you, Casey, and others would be more than the happiness I might afford you. And that would be more than I could bear. I wrestled with what is good and right and now realize the better course is for me to allow you and Casey to pursue whatever life offers you. It is better this way.

I am, as you know, a broken man. It would not be fair to ask you to mend me. Instead, enjoy your time with Casey and work well defending your thesis. Focus on your career, and I beg you to continue on as things were. You will understand that it would now be too difficult for me to do the same. But you can. I know it.

You will still be a part of my life daily ... you should not worry about me, for you often come to me in my sleep, and sometimes that is enough for me. My affection for you will never leave me, and that is one of the only things in my life I am sure of.

I am off to see new places and to see what wonders life brings my way. I search for simplicity, and I seek the beauty that is everywhere in nature.

Forever yours,

Jack

Claire burst into tears. She held the letter up again. "That's got to be less than 300 words!" She sat on the bench for a long time, crying, breathing hard, and then sitting in silence. *This is ridiculous,* she thought.

He can't just bail like this. This is wrong. Fuck ... Claire's human feelings were doing battle with her methodic, scientist self. *What are the options here?!*

She thought long and hard about what to do next. If Jack didn't want her, that was one thing. But to leave the program over this? It made no sense.

When she had exhausted herself from thinking, crying, and thinking some more, she got up and walked back to the apartment. She entered the living room, and Casey had a Red Sox game on the television, but he wasn't watching it. He appeared sad. He looked at her with pursed lips and shook his head. He did not ask if she found what she went to the museum for or took so long. He said, "I cannot believe Jack. How could he do this to his career? Or to *us?*"

It didn't help that Casey was losing sleep regularly. The dream always remained the same: He takes a step and swings a bat — in the dream, it was always a real baseball bat — then the sound of the bat hitting a human skull and the sound of the man hitting the ground. He would wake and try to rationalize it. *It was attack, or be killed,* he told himself. Usually, it worked, and he could move on with life ... until the next dream.

Claire and Casey didn't talk much for the next few days and nights, only making short comments about Jack and what he must be thinking or going through.

One evening, a week after receiving their letters, Casey was first in bed, reading when Claire finally came into the bedroom. She took off her pants, shirt, and bra and stood in only black panties at the dresser, looking for a t-shirt to wear to bed. She looked absolutely gorgeous, and that had not changed. With all the trekking over mountains they had done and a month of eating a very healthy diet in Peru, she had toned up. She looked more fit than ever, and her legs looked like a runner's legs. The side view of her breasts, while she slipped the t-shirt over her head, made Casey move a little.

She climbed into the bed and lay on her side, facing away from Casey. Her blonde hair splayed on her pillow made him temporarily forget about his studies and "the problem with Jack." He rolled onto his side facing her, spooning with her. He put his hand gently on her hip. She did not move. He rubbed his hand down the outside of her thigh and back up over the panties where they crossed her hip. She did not move. Then he let his hand slide down over her flat belly — her lower belly and over her panties. She moved. She twitched and leaned back, lifting her head toward his, and said, "No, Casey … just, no." And rolled farther away from him.

"Yeah," was all he said and rolled onto his side, facing away from her.

Four days later, they split up.

They hadn't talked much since getting the letters, and Claire had been looking around for an apartment for a couple of weeks. She found one in Somerville, and she had been secreting her things over there, a piece at a time. When the time was right, she had packed her backpack and put it in the Subaru. She waited for Casey to come home. She was sitting at the kitchen table.

"Hey," he said when he saw her, and he could sense something.

"Hi. I was wondering if we could talk." He dropped his daypack onto the couch and sat down next to her at the table.

"You know things have been weird for us for a while now …' She looked at him, slightly nodding.

"Well, yes. I figured it's school and everything we went through in Peru, and with Jack."

She paused. "I think it has more to do with Jack than him not coming home." There was an awkward pause. "I know it does."

Casey was no dummy. "You and Jack?!"

"No — not really."

"It's real, or it's not. What does that even mean, 'not really?'"

"Not really, because there's nothing real." That gave her pause. "I think."

"Claire. Just tell me, for Christ's sake."

"Case, Honey, apparently Jack loves me and always has."

"Since when? What do you mean always?"

"Since the day you introduced me to him." Casey sat back in the chair. His shoulders slumped. He looked at her with pained eyes, less for himself and for the coming breakup than for Jack.

"Why didn't he tell me?"

"Oh, Case, because he loves you. He didn't want to hurt you or lose you as his best friend." Casey waved her off as if to say, *I know all that.* He went full-on logistical, analytical, let's get our facts right. "I love you too, Claire. What we had was a good thing, but we both knew that we'd probably live in different cities when we graduated. But Jack doesn't love anything partially — I don't love you partially either — but you know what I mean … Jack is Jack."

She nodded. She knew what Casey meant.

"We'll be okay," he continued. "But how sure are you? Did he tell you?"

She nodded again. "He told me the night you and Alberto went to Cusco for the mountaineering food. And in my letter."

Casey looked at her with another pained look. "Did you…?"

Claire immediately dropped her head and her sniffling cry and the tear hitting the hardwood floor told him what he actually didn't want to know.

Not knowing what on Earth to say, he blurted out, "My best fucking friend!"

He started shaking his head. He wanted to comfort Claire but was too hurt. Instead, he simply sat in a chair, breathed deeply, and took some time to calm down. Claire gave him the time, and she offered nothing more.

Finally, Casey spoke. "Is this why he's still in Peru?"

"I think it's a big part of it," Claire said.

"Wait … Maria?"

Claire shook her head and shrugged slightly. "I don't think so. I think he could not handle breaking you and me up, and in the week-and-a-half, after he told me he loved me, he felt it was a terrible mistake. I think he immediately tried to bury his feelings. But, knowing Jack, I'm guessing he's gone walkabout, and he'll eventually figure things out."

Casey got up and started pacing in the dining room, where months before, he and Jack had sorted equipment for the expedition. Then he sat down abruptly at the kitchen table. "I have to go back," he murmured. "I have to find him and tell him it's okay."

Claire reached out and took his hand because he was grasping the edge of the table. "Case, how could you find him? Give him some time. He'll reach out when he's ready."

"But for now," she said, "are you going to be okay?"

Casey nodded. "It hurts," he said. "It all sucks. Where … do you have a place to stay?"

"Near Davis Square," she said.

Casey was processing a great deal. "Did he say anything to you in the letter about where he was going?"

"No. Nothing. He wrote that he is 'seeking simplicity and beauty.'"

Casey shook his head. "Sounds like him."

Then he said, "Promise me you'll let me know if you hear from him. You two were closer; he might reach out to you first. And keep that letter. If we don't hear from him in six months, I'm going to look for him."

"I promise," Claire replied. She was sure he would either turn up, or she would get a letter by then. "By the way, I'm driving to his folks' house tomorrow to tell them about the trip. I called them, and they've received letters also. I might stay for the weekend. Will you be okay?"

Casey nodded. He was digesting a lot of information.

Claire got up, and Casey rose with her. She gave him a firm hug."

"I'd like to still get together once a week for a burger or a coffee," Claire said.

"You bet. Of course."

Claire squeezed his shoulder. She looked back as she walked out the door, and Casey was standing where she left him, with his head down. Then she drove to Somerville. On the way to her new apartment, she marveled at how adroit and calm he had been. *If he truly loved me*, she thought, *he might've fought for me. He's either Superman-tough, or the whole relationship was mostly physical.*

She was almost angry at herself for not crying.

THIRTY-FIVE

Stonington; The Sea & Broken Hearts

Claire pumped the brakes of the old Subaru as she coasted down Tennent's Hill into Stonington. The town looked like the same small, sleepy fishing community when she and Casey had spent a week there two summers earlier. She pulled into the Beals's driveway and backed the Subaru off to the side next to the old cedars. By the time she parked and got out, Jack's mom was in the driveway.

"Hello, Claire!" Karen gave her a big hug. "So glad you called. Let's go inside." Karen looped her arm through Claire's, and they walked through the kitchen door.

"Is Mr. Beal here?" They sat down. The kitchen smelled like homemade bread, just as it had when she visited before, and it brought back a flood of memories of the fun she, Casey, and Jack had that week. She remembered going out on the boat and pulling traps with the winch and measuring the lobsters and banding the "keepers" with rubber bands and how one of them snapped her hand and broke the skin near her thumb. She remembered how Jack cleaned it and put a Band-Aid on it, and she remembered how the locals called lobsters 'bugs.' She looked down at the small scar at the base of her thumb and touched it.

"No," Karen said. "Alton is busy this time of year, but he should come in in about three hours. Coffee?"

"Yes, please."

"This business with Jack — Alton is not too happy about it. Jack's mind ... he's gifted. Alton knows that. We all know that." Claire nodded. "We know he has his Masters and that he would be happy teaching or doing something simpler, but we'd be happy if he finishes his program. It's not like him to quit like this."

"It's interesting that you said he'd be happy doing other things for a living," Claire said. "The reason I came up here is that I may be able to shed some light on why he has chosen to leave the program — let's say temporarily at this point — and perhaps you can gain some clarity. And I hope that if you are able to correspond with him in the next few months or if he shows up here, you'll be better informed."

"I hope it's a temporary leave. Have you talked to any of Jack's professors about this?"

"I have," Claire replied. "They have great affection for Jack. They're willing to give him until next fall to make a declaration, and it might set him back a semester, but they're being quite generous. They will work with him. Harvard is good that way."

"That's all we hoped for. That's good."

"You said on the phone that you got a letter?" Claire asked.

Karen nodded. "We got one, and Lisa got her own. She and Jack are quite close." Karen pulled the letter from her apron pocket, still in its airmail envelope. She offered it to Claire.

"Are you sure?" taking the letter. Claire noticed it was stamped from Cusco.

"You read it," Karen said, "and then tell me what you wanted to say."

Claire opened the letter. It was a single page, and Claire flipped it and saw nothing written on the back. "Good economy of words," she said.

"That's our Jack," Karen responded.

It read:

Dear Mom & Dad,

I just wanted you to know that I have decided to take some time off from school — and America — for a time. We have been on the most amazing journey, one of exploration and discovery, and I find myself now in a state of mind where I want to explore my life, its direction, and this lovely country some more. I do not know where I'm going, but I will try to send letters when I can.

I have plenty of money, and my health is excellent. There is a group of misguided, bad people down here, but I will avoid the areas where they are active. The vagabond community is a good resource for learning where it is safe. So, you must not worry about the troublemakers.

I love how friendly the people are here, and I'm fascinated by the country's history and its culture.

Don't worry about anything, and please tell everyone I miss them. And Dad, please smack Tom for me when he walks by once in a while.

All my love,

Jackson

Claire re-read the letter twice and could not glean anything valuable or telling from it. It was a nice, generic, assuring letter.

"Lisa's letter was what you might expect," Karen said. "Jack told her about some of the interesting things he had seen in Peru and that he was sorry, but his travels meant he wouldn't be home for the summer. She was very bummed out about that, but he said he would be sending her a package soon with some cool presents."

Claire did not respond.

Jack's mother sat down and slid a cup of coffee in front of her. Karen looked at her in a kindly manner and waited for her to speak. When she didn't, Karen prompted her with, "Dear, I think there's something you want to tell me."

Claire breathed in heavily one time. "I suppose what I want to tell you is that Jack staying away might be all my fault, and I wanted to see if there was anything in your letter that might've suggested his frame of mind."

"Your fault? I don't think anyone is to blame here."

"You see," Claire explained, "Jack and I have been very close. We have always connected on many levels; art, history, literature, music … humor. And well, while we were in Peru, Jack told me that he loved me and always has, and I reciprocated, and I told him I felt the same. We planned on going on normally while in Peru and then sorting things out when we returned … I'd break it off with Casey, and Jack and I would be together."

"Oh, Dear," Karen replied with a smile, "we knew he loved you."

"You did?"

"Of course. Anyone with a good eye could see it. Especially his mother." Karen continued to smile at her.

Claire shook her head. "Well, it was over before it got started. After only a day or two, he felt he had made a terrible mistake telling me. He abhorred the idea of breaking Casey and me up, and he was sure he was going to lose his best friend. I think he could handle losing one of us, but after over-thinking the scenario, he worried he would not be able to make me happy, and in the end, he would lose both Casey and me. With Maria in the mix, I think he was ready to explode."

"Maria?" Karen asked.

"Yes. A young Peruvian woman, the most beautiful woman I've ever seen. A student of architecture. They became friendly in the middle of all this. His being in love with me for over two years, his history with Rachael, telling me his feelings, worrying about what that would do to Case, then meeting Maria ... I think it was all more than he could take."

Karen was skeptical about this Maria being so relevant to Jack's decisions. She knew her boy ... he was not one to be frivolous with people's emotions. Plus, she knew he was likely devoted to Claire.

"Rachael. Yes," Karen said, "that was hard on him. Good Lord, I hope he's okay." Now she looked worried.

"I didn't want to scare you," Claire said. "I just wanted you to know why he has taken some time off and where his head might be in case he reaches out."

"You drove over four hours to tell me this," Karen said. "You're very brave." She smiled at Claire. "You do care for him, don't you?" Claire nodded.

Karen sat back in her chair and looked out the kitchen window at the bay, and watched the returning lobster boats maneuvering around the dock and their moorings. Then she finally spoke.

"Do you want my advice?"

"I'd love it."

"Live your life for now. Jack will be fine traveling around. Maybe he'll clear his head. But you're a scientist. Focus on your graduate program. If you two are meant to be — or if he and this Maria are meant to be, it'll happen. Don't fret over it at this point. You can't do a lot about it right now, not if you can't call him, or write him — or go to him. You live your life as you see fit, he'll live his, and hopefully, he'll figure things out by the fall. If he ends up with Maria, then pour yourself into your work. You're smart, fun, gorgeous, and yet you remain a humble, lovely person. Whatever Jack ends up doing, everything will work out."

"It's hard," Claire said.

"I know. Would you like to go for a walk?" Claire nodded and sipped her coffee.

Karen and Claire walked down the lower half of Tennent's Hill toward the waterfront. They walked past William King Art Gallery and Harbor Antiques, and Karen blessed herself as they passed St. Anne's Church. They walked past the Dockside Convenience Store to where Main Street flattens-out, and then out onto the pier where the brokers weighed the lobsters as the fishermen waited and talked about the sea or their wives and girlfriends. They leaned on the railing and watched the dinghies bobbing next to the pier and the seagulls coming and going on their never-ending quest. Karen looked down at the green-grey water, and she could see the remains of old wooden pilings on the bottom from a dock built two hundred years ago when men wrestled a living from the sea from small dories they built themselves.

"The mackerel will be here soon," Karen declared. Claire said nothing. Karen continued to stare into the sea. "It's autumn in Peru now. I wonder what he's doing."

Stonington is on Deer Isle, off of a peninsula in mid-coast Maine. In the morning, on Claire's drive back to Somerville, she first had to drive an hour north, through the villages of Sargentville, Blue Hill, and Bucksport, before turning south toward Boston. She had time to think.

Claire thought about what Karen had said. His mom had been right. There's nothing she could do about the situation. She could either wait for Jack to sort things out or not — and move on. Her choices were few: *If he writes, and if there's a return address, I will write him. Otherwise, I'll talk to him when he returns.*

As Claire negotiated the Subaru wagon through the little villages, she felt glad she had visited Stonington. It gave her a sense of connection to Jack. No closure — but a connection, which felt good. She pondered about how Alton didn't seem too upset or concerned, and he seemed to be taking a 'sow his wild oats' point of view about Jack's decision.

Lisa was a delight. Only eleven, she listened intently as Claire sat on the floor in the living room and told her about the trip.

Lisa's eyes got wide when she heard about the group finding the lost ruins. Both hands covered her cheeks when Claire told her about eating guinea pigs. She was careful to not bring up the Sendero Luminoso and what they had experienced at the edge of the Amazon.

When they parted, she and Karen promised to share any news or correspondence from Jack when it came. Both women wanted to try to keep track of him, and each woman understood the other. They both wished to understand Jack.

Once on Interstate 95 South, Claire zoned out. *Keep marching forward,* she thought. *Jack was looking for simplicity? Then I will keep it simple. Work on my thesis, set up the new apartment, meet Casey for coffee next week, and try not to think about getting something in the mailbox. Simple.*

Casey and Claire together attended several meetings with Dr. Fitzroy. The professor was truly worried about Jack and his decision. Fitzroy understood the unique brainpower he possessed but was confounded by his actions. Of course, she did not know of his pained, wandering heart.

In Fitzroy's office, they examined Casey's homemade map and made new, more detailed ones. They wrote letters to the Ministry of Culture requesting a Peruvian co-Director and co-sponsor, pending approval of the applied-for *permiso*, and a letter to Dr. Bache in Cusco. Professor Bache was quick to reply. He was very professional. He wrote to his contact at the Ministry and helped Dr. Fitzroy write a proposal for the examination of the site. The problem was going to be safety and logistics … there was no road anywhere near that part of Peru. The professors recommended an expedition to examine and map the site and for a good surface scatter analysis, when they could map and scour the ground for artifacts or signs of construction. They would use burros and arrieros to transport equipment and supplies for two weeks. In the last letter from Dr. Bache, he suggested it all could be possible — if his friend at the Ministry could push things along. The professor hoped to be ready for the initial expedition the following January.

Dr. Fitzroy also was told everything about the Sendero camp. She and Dr. Bache talked about that. From Cusco, Franz would call his colleagues at the university in Ayacucho. They contacted the police station where Jack had left the information, and two policemen visited the professor at the college. As far as the police knew, the archaeology department had been aware of potential ruins in the area east of the mountains, and the scientists were inquiring about security. The police swore them to secrecy and proceeded to tell them about "some potential terrorist activity" in the area. It was being dealt with by the military very soon. It was hard for Dr. Bache not to smirk, considering he knew about the Sendero camp long before they did.

In their last meeting, Dr. Fitzroy told Claire and Casey, "At this point, we stay in communication with Franz Bache, and we wait for news about the area being cleared for travel and the permissions from the Ministry. As things develop between now and next fall, we will meet and talk."

The professor suggested, "If this site turns out to be important, Claire, as co-discoverer, I assume you will adjust your work here and be the student from Harvard in charge of this school's involvement."

"Yes," replied Claire.

"Okay," the professor said. "Now, we wait."

Maryanne Fitzroy stared at the map in front of her. "And that boy better come back."

THIRTY-SIX

Lost in Limbo

The rest of April came and went. Rain showers arrived every few days, and the cold, wet month was made more gloomy when there was no word from Jack.

The first communication came on May second. Claire got back to the apartment that evening, and one of the roommates had taped a message on her door. It read *Someone named Karen Beal called.*

Claire grabbed the Beals's number from her desk and could not get downstairs to the telephone quickly enough. *Was he there? Did he show up on their doorstep? Was he sitting at the kitchen table?"*

"Mrs. Beal?"

"Claire?"

"Yes, it's Claire. I got the message that you called."

"I just wanted you to know we got a package from Jack." Claire was silent at first and then said, "Oh, wonderful. Where was it sent from? Did he say anything?"

"It was mailed from a post office in a town called Huaraz. Do you know it?"

"Very well," Claire said. *He's climbing,* she thought.

"It had some gifts in it for Lisa: some textiles, a jade llama, a pendant, some earrings, and a small pan flute. There was a letter filled mostly with travel chit-chat. He said he was going climbing with some people he met."

"I bet she was happy to get something from him," Claire said.

"She was. There's a letter in here for you, Dear, with a note clipped to it asking that we mail it to you. The note said the post office in Huaraz did not have any airmail envelopes."

Claire felt relief. At least he's communicating.

"I don't have your new mailing address, Claire."

She gave the address to Karen.

"I hope you know you're invited to visit Stonington anytime," Karen said, and they said their goodbyes.

The letter took four days to arrive because it came in a three-foot-long box. The letter, a fly rod tube with a note attached, and a smaller package were in the box. The message on the tube was from Karen. It said, "*Jack asked that we send this fly rod to you. Alton sent some flies that were tied by Jack years ago.*" The small package was a reel and the box of flies. The letter was written in Jack's typical neat cursive:

Dearest Claire,

By now you have hopefully received my letter. I hope and pray that you are not too upset with me. That would break my heart.

After a month, I have decided to continue traveling for some time, as I am finding it very affordable. I have learned that if I have only some fruit and coffee in the morning and eat only one meal a day, I can live on practically nothing. But, after only five weeks of living with this diet, I have lost, I think, about eighteen pounds.

I have seen some beautiful places already, Claire. And you were right, the Cordillera Blanca near Huaraz is amazing. I have completed a ten-day trek on which I met a couple of Brits who have invited me on a climb. It is ambitious. I will be unable to write to you for a month or more, I should think.

I hope you are okay. I am so sorry I said what I said to you that night on the Urubamba. Maybe I thought there would be a way to work everything out, some way for us to be together without either of us losing Casey. But within hours, I realized that could never be. I hope you and he are still together.

You'll be happy to know that my Spanish is coming along, and I've picked up quite a few phrases in Quechua. Alberto would be proud, I think. I hope to see him again — I plan on returning there at some point. I'd like to see Macchu Pichu, and as you know, Cusco is the jumping-off spot for the Amazon. I cannot get the image of the Mashco Piro tribe out of my head.

I will write again when I get out of the mountains. I am sorry you cannot contact me, but I genuinely do not know where I will be from day-to-day.

Take care, Claire. I hope by now you have come to terms with me staying here and that you realize it was for the best for you and Casey.

Love always and forever,
Jack

Claire lay on her futon mattress and read the letter twice. Then she let the letter drop onto the floor and said, "Shit! Shit, shit, *shit*! How could such a brilliant guy, so in touch with the world around him — so tuned into everything in the natural world, be so wrong?" *He better come back by fall*, she thought. *Goddamn it.*

Then her basal instincts kicked in. *He wants to get back to Cusco. How stupid of me … it's not Alberto he wants to see there. He has chosen Maria.*

That night she wrote a letter to Alberto explaining everything that had happened. She didn't have his address in Cusco — Casey had that — but she had a receipt from the Cross Keys Pub with its address on it. She found it tucked into her travel journal. She had met Ian, the owner, one of the nights they were there. She sealed the letter to Alberto in a small envelope and would tomorrow put it inside a larger airmail envelope with a note asking Ian to get the letter to Al. She knew he could do it and would do it. Since she would be going to the post office, she wrote a letter to Jim Bartlett at the Explorer's Club. She already had that address in her journal. She doubted Casey had written him, and she knew Jim would be interested in all the adventures and things the group had done and seen.

After posting the letters the following morning, Claire went to the Peabody to work on her thesis. As she walked down the 5th-floor hallway, she ran into Maryanne Fitzroy.

"Good morning, Claire."

"Morning," Claire said. She did not seem herself, and the professor picked up on it.

"Is everything all right?" Dr. Fitzroy stopped next to her.

Claire stopped. "I'm just worried about Jack."

The professor responded, "I've got some time. Let's go into the office." She sat next to Claire in front of her desk, both in the chairs placed for visitors or interviewees.

"Tell me," Dr. Fitzroy said. "At the end of the day, professors are still teachers, and we're supposed to help if it's within our capacity."

Claire explained that Jack might not be simply taking some time off only to travel. She told him what had happened — what he had said to her in the Sacred Valley on the banks of the Urubamba and that he may have a broken heart or at least a confused one. And, she told her that she and Casey were not together because of it. Then she told her about Maria.

Dr. Fitzroy looked at her with widened eyes. "All of that, and the lost ruins, the Sendero Luminoso — you three had an incredible month. The things that must be coursing through your mind. I'm sorry you and Casey broke up. As for Jack, as I see it, you simply have to wait and see how that plays out on his terms, unfortunately. At least until you have a way of reaching him."

Claire's eyes were watering, but she knew she could not cry in front of the professor.

She nodded and thanked her for listening.

"Try to focus on your work for now," Dr. Fitzroy said. She was the second person to tell her that. There was a pregnant pause, and Claire nodded but said nothing.

The professor leaned across her desk and picked up an ancient silver garment pin. She rubbed her hands along the wide, flat, slightly elliptical head and felt the thin, four-inch-long pin protruding from the base of the head. "Here." She placed it in Claire's hand.

"Tell me about it," the professor demanded, who then folded her hands and rested her elbows on her knees, leaning forward in front of Claire.

Claire touched the pin in the same way the professor had, as if invoking something hidden within the object. For Claire, this was basic stuff. "It's a *tupu* — a fabric pin."

Dr. Fitzroy shook her head. "More. This is an exercise. Teach me."

Claire realized the professor was trying to get her focused on archaeology, starting with the pin. *I'll play along*, she thought. She looked again at the pin, and her "high achieving, perfect student" persona kicked in.

"This is a tupu; Quechua for 'pin' and was used to fasten textile garments such as shawls like the *acsu* (sometimes referred to in Spanish as *saya*), a rectangular textile garment made of camelid wool that wraps around the shoulders. They secured the garment at their breast, and the tip of the tupu's stem points upward or is oriented on a diagonal. People in rural communities still tend to wear them, and often they use two tupus at a time in order to fasten the *acsu*.

"It is pre-seventeenth century, either Incan or possibly pre-Incan — maybe the Wari culture from the Middle Horizon Period. That puts it between 400-1,400 years old. It appears to be gilded silver but would need analysis to determine the composition. It is hammered, likely from a thin metal rod, and the metal worker probably had to alternate between annealing and hammering to work the metal. The repeated heating would soften the metal and make it more conducive to hammering. The small perforation at the base of the head would have been made with a punch. It was put there so a thin piece of cord could be passed through to either suspend it or allow it to be tied under the fabric, keeping the pin in place in the shawl. How's that?"

"Excellent!" the professor said. "Wasn't that fun? Think about the person tapping away at this maybe 1,000 years ago. That long ago, it wasn't just artisans who made these things; it was work-a-day men. All the men in each household made their own tools, weapons, utensils, *and* tupus. Some poor bastard probably hammered away at the thing you're holding for his wife, and he put so much care and attention into it — but the memory of that effort is gone. That whole family's history is gone. Even their community's history is gone, wasted away over time. Lost forever, or until someone like you or me digs it up and tells people about them. That guy who made that tupu cared for someone. Probably loved someone, and probably the person he loved pissed him off at some point and maybe even broke his heart. Maybe she even stabbed him with it. And it's your job to tell people about his community. What you do in this job, whether it's in the field or the lab, is opening pages of a book for everyone and saying, 'Look here; look at what this poor bastard had to do to make this shawl pin for his wife.' And by the way, this is what life was like in their community ... not entirely different from our own — not on an emotional level. Sometimes what you teach people about pre-history can help them understand things in their own lives or even give them the desire to not repeat historic deeds.

"What you're feeling right now with Jack hurts you; I can see that. But, if it's meant to be with Jack, then it will happen. If not, you have a job to do, and it's a gift. It's rare. Try to focus on the bigger picture, as hard as it is when you're in pain. Over time, all this stuff with Jack and Casey will be okay. Trust in that." She thought for a moment and said to Claire, "My dad was quite the logophile. He always used to say, 'Time wounds all heels.'"

Claire smiled and said, "Thanks." And handed the tupu back to Maryanne.

As she left, she didn't fully know what the lesson was, but she did feel better. For the few moments she was giving the short oral dissertation about the tupu, she thought of nothing else. As she walked into her lab, she thought, *Fuck it. Back to work.*

Claire stayed at the university into June to catch up on work she had delayed while in Peru. She spent a few weeks writing a grant proposal and then decided to drive to Wisconsin. She had written her mother and father a few times, telling them about her time in Peru, and had sent her sister Sam a card with a small package of Peruvian gifts. She knew her sister liked to dress in different, eclectic clothes and seemed to always pull it off, even in the mid-west. In Cusco, she purchased a beautiful black alpaca poncho with thin, cobalt blue piping along the bottom. Claire was confident her sister would love it.

As she finished packing her car, she noticed that she had forgotten something. She ran upstairs and retrieved the fly rod and reel.

Once she drove onto the Mass Pike heading west, she realized she had been so busy since returning from Peru that she hadn't been to the Museum of Fine Arts once, and she started to cry again, which yet again pissed her off. *The first thing I'm going to do when I get home*, she said to herself, *is go fishing.*

THIRTY-SEVEN
Love Lost & Letters

laire's visit home was a pleasant one. Her mother was very supportive, and when she told them about Jack, her father seemed to understand his decision to travel and said, "Every young man needs to find himself, in any way necessary." It was nice to see her sister, who went with Claire to watch her practice fly fishing.

Claire spent over a month in McFarland reading, fishing, taking long walks with her mother, and going for drives with her sister. She and Sam drove to state parks a few times and went on short hikes. Her sister could not believe what a strong hiker Claire had become — how strong her legs were. It was a good visit.

At a library sale, Claire had found an old book about the fundamentals of fly fishing which mentioned some of the more famous angling destinations in the U.S. On her drive back to Massachusetts, she stopped for a day in New York to fish the Beaver Kill, where she caught her first small trout on a dry fly. Claire was elated. She wished Jack had been with her, and it made her sad, but she did not cry. Everyone was right; her mother, Jack's mother, Dr. Fitzroy ... the passage of time was helping. She still wanted to see Jack, to be with him, but she no longer cried so easily.

⁂

Once she was back in Cambridge, she tried to focus on her work. Near the end of August, Casey stopped by the lab to see her and tell her about his dig during the summer.

"Did you know there were wampum factories on the east coast?" Casey asked. "The colonists made wampum from certain seashells and distributed them to agents of the King to use for barter with the Native American on the frontier. It was part of the industrialized empire-building."

The two conversed for a while about the Red Paint people, and finally, Casey asked if she had heard from Jack. She shook her head.

"Not since the only letter he sent through his parents. I didn't tell you. He asked them to send me one of his fly rods, and they did with a reel. I've been practicing."

"Oh, that's great. We should go fishing sometime in September."

Claire smiled and said. "I'd like that."

"So ... how is he? In the letter?" Casey asked. "I haven't received any word yet."

"Honestly, he sounded okay. I want to think of him as a little lost, but it may be me. He said he met some trekkers in the Cordillera Blanca and was going climbing. That was in May."

Casey nodded. "I hope they're safe climbers." He looked at his hands as if he had a splinter, which he didn't. He seemed a little hurt. "I wish he'd write to me."

"He will when he can figure out what to say," Claire said. "I did write to both Alberto and Jim Bartlett," she added.

"That's good. Maybe one of them will run into Jack and send word."

"I hope so," Claire said. "You know, he and I ... I do know he has given up on us as a couple. But I can tell you his biggest regret is losing you, and he is convinced you'll want nothing to do with him now."

"What?!" Casey's face was pained. "I'd like to think he knows me better than that. He'll always be my brother."

"When you get the chance," Claire said, "give him a hug and tell him that."

Some days later, Casey did get another letter, and so did Claire, this time, both sent to Casey's apartment address. And this time from a city called Huanuco. Casey called Claire in Somerville, and she drove over straight away.

In Casey's letter, Jack explained what he had said to Claire with great honesty. And with lovely prose, and he apologized for it. He wished he'd never said anything. He went on to tell Case about his "epic climb" on Huascaran and how much he would love to climb with him in the Cordillera Blanca someday, "if you'll have me."

Jack wrote his old friend saying he had decided to stay in Peru, but he did not know where. He said there was still much of the country to see, and he wrote about Bolivia and Brazil.

Claire's letter was short. In it, Jack wrote that he hoped she was doing well, that he missed her, and that he was "working with some Campesino families in a remote part of the Andes" but did not give a name or location. He told her that he had an excellent climb with 'the Brits.' He tried to keep it convivial. "I've been fishing almost everywhere I've been," he wrote her, "but with moderate success."

This time he signed it, "Love, Jack."

Claire was starting to worry. School officially opened in two weeks, and there was no sign that Jack would be back. She checked with his professors, who told her confidentially that, from the single letter they had received the previous spring, at this point, they considered him absent from the program and that he would have to reapply to continue. One of them took her aside and said that members of the anthropology department had had a meeting about Jack. The professor told her that since they had such fondness for Jack, they would think of his situation as if a student had a medical emergency, such as a motor vehicle accident, and would consider him favorably if or when he reapplied.

She thought *That was kind of the department, and it was kind of the university.*

Casey and Claire went into their last academic year preparing to defend their theses. In early September, Jim Bartlett sent postcards to both of them saying he would keep a lookout for Jack and that he "would send the word out to his ex-pat friends throughout the country." He asked Claire to send a few photographs of Jack, with and without a beard if possible. She sent him the pictures right away, and she thought that was a good idea and also sent several photos to Alberto.

In the meantime, Alberto also wrote a lovely letter back to Claire.

28 August 1985

Dear Claire,

I'm glad you are well, and I hope Casey is too.

I am concerned about Jack. Not because I worry about his capabilities, he is one of the most competent young men I have met, but because of some of the dangerous current affairs down here right now. People are on edge. But, if I know Jack, he will research which areas are still safe to travel in, and he will make wise decisions.

I would like to see him back in Cusco. I have seen Maria several times, and we have talked. She fairly fell in love with him, I think. She has gotten only a few postcards from him from up north, but he made no hints of his plans. If he returns here, he can stay with Maria or with us. Cusco will always be a home for him.

Claire, if he shows up here, I will write to you — but here is our telephone number: 011 51 84 122451. I think you should call or write with a telephone number for you and Casey.

Besides the Sandinista activity in the south, things are going well here. I recently got a gig translating a book for an American archaeologist. It is good work.

Marisol wants to say hello.

Your friend always,

Al

Casey and Claire shared and discussed the letters and postcards. Casey was uneasy.

"It's been six months," he said, "but it sounds worse if you say he's been on the lam for half a year." And still, there was nothing they could do but wait.

There was no more word from Jack until the middle of December, when it seemed like everyone got letters or cards. Karen Beal called first, and she read their letter to Claire over the phone. Then four days later, Casey called, and the very next day, Claire received one. They all had the same postmark; Ollantaytambo! Finally. He's headed back to Cusco, and maybe he'll either settle there or visit and decide to come home. Casey and Claire were excited that at least he was on ground they were familiar with. It was something.

Each person's card or letter included Jack's typical musings about nature and the wonderful things he had seen. Still, each also offered a more worrisome message; he would be gone again for a couple of months and would be unable to post anything during that time.

"I will be going east," he wrote.

That meant only one thing to Casey. Jack was going into the jungle.

Claire went to Casey's apartment, and together they called Alberto. He was pretty happy to hear from them both and was even more pleased that Jack was in the vicinity. They gave Al two separate phone numbers. He was guiding a group of tourists to Machu Picchu in the next week, he told them, and would try to find him in Ollanta.

"In these recent letters," Casey said, "Jack says he is going east."

There was a short pause on the line before Alberto spoke again. "The Manus?"

"That's what I think," Casey said.

There was another pause. "I wouldn't recommend that — not alone, without a tour company. There are many dangers there."

"Well, keep an eye out for him, please. And if you hear about him or see him, don't hesitate to call here collect."

"I'll certainly ask around," he said, "and I'll stop by and see if Benita at the hostel has seen him or heard anything."

"Thank you so much, Al," Claire said. "Love to Marisol." They hung up.

Claire flew home for Christmas, and Casey went to Salem. Claire mailed the Beals a lovely Christmas card and sent along with it a Harvard sweatshirt for Lisa.

On the second day home, Casey caught his father at home in his office and asked if they could chat. Dr. Feagin sat and listened intently as his son told him everything that had been going on with Jack and Claire, and Casey seemed remarkably undisturbed about their relationship developments.

"It was kind of complicated, Dad. By the end of the month in Peru, having realized he and Claire getting together was too complicated and wasn't going to work, he allowed himself to become close with a student in Cusco named Maria. I don't believe it was romantic — but you could see that they got along great, and it looked like she was sweet on him. But it's obvious now his head wasn't in a good place."

At this point, Case simply missed his friend and was worried about him. His father was attentive and helpful. He liked Jack, and he started asking questions.

"Some of the things I'll ask you will be blunt," his dad said, "just answer them, and we'll have a better picture."

"You and Claire are over?"

"We're no longer 'together,' but we're still friends. Probably because we started that way. And no, I harbor no hard feelings about Jack. Those two were connected in so many ways, everybody could see it. At this point, I don't think they'll ever get together. Jack feels as if he has betrayed me. As I say, I'm just worried about him. You know about the troubles we had down there (he never told his father about the attack on the young Sendero—just about finding the camp), and we had our friend Alberto with us, but since we've been back, there's a lot more violence in the countryside. Last June, the Shining Path blew up electricity transmission towers in Lima. During the blackout, they detonated car bombs near the government palace. Alberto says they're evolving from an armed Maoist insurrection to a corrupt death cult.

"Do you think Jack is 'all right,' as in, he hasn't gone off the deep end?"

"No," Casey said, "he seems fine in his letters, though there have been only a few."

"If it's a matter of money, do you think his folks could get him home?"

"That I don't know."

"Do you think he is in danger down there?"

"Possibly, and he might not be aware of it."

"Could you see him settling down there with this Maria girl?"

Casey nodded slowly. It's possible. "If you could see her dad ... and she's smart and worldly." His father nodded and thought about everything Casey had told him.

"Well," he said, "as far as absolute safety goes, the only answer is to leave the country. If he is inclined to stay there and be with this Maria, then that will be that. All you can do is support his decision, and it's a damned shame about his Ph.D., though."

"Claire thinks the school will work with him if he re-applies within the next year or so."

"Son, if you don't think he has had some sort of psychotic episode or isn't thinking straight, then I'm afraid you have to let him live his life."

Casey nodded.

"If something drastic happens, or he communicates that he is in trouble, of course, I'll help you. But, I won't condone you going back there on a wild goose chase."

Casey's dad thought things over. "Though I'll pay for some help in Peru to find him if his parents can't afford it."

It wasn't something that frequently happened in Casey's family, but he leaned forward and hugged his father.

Dr. Feagin patted his son on the back and said, "Jack's a smart guy. I think he'll be all right, Case."

THIRTY-EIGHT

Back to the Sacred Valley

hristmas Day came and went. Claire's family was a comfort, but her father, ever the activist, went on just a little too long about the newspapers reports about the Shining Path and what they were up to in Peru. There were occasional articles about the Sendero's violence in the stacks of newspapers he received daily. Her father did not notice when every time he read the articles, Claire went into the kitchen or other parts of the house ... but her mother noticed.

Back at Harvard after the holidays, Casey and Claire were hard at work. Casey was teaching a few more classes to undergraduates than he would like, but he did not complain.

None of the people who were missing Jack expected to hear back from him until at least March, and, considering his letter-writing track record since he went on his walk-about, many of them thought it would probably be even later into the spring. When there was no word in May, the friends began to worry in earnest.

Then, on the evening of the eighth of May, Alberto placed a collect call to Casey. "You might want to get a pad of paper," Al told him.

Al explained that he had asked around a good deal and would continue to do so.

"I pinned one of the pictures of Jack that Claire sent to me behind the bar at the Cross Keys in hopes some trekkers had seen him. Last night, Ian, the pub owner — you met him — called and said two blokes saw the photo and said they had been traveling with him for weeks. Marisol and I went straight over. As we left the house, I grabbed a map, just in case. They were Brits who had been climbing in Peru for more than six months. They were real climbers ... even smelled bad. They said they had hooked up with Jack in the Cordillera Blanca, climbed Huascaran and Pisco with Jack, and then traveled to Ollanta, where they split up. They said Jack was a great climber. The Brits said they were on their way to climb Ausangate.

"Anyway, as you know, time in the mountains in little tents and snow caves — people get talking out of boredom when they're not physically climbing. They told me almost everywhere Jack had been, and I marked every place they told me on the map, and when I got home, I highlighted the route. Do you want me to send the map to you?"

"We should each have one. If I send you forty dollars, could you pick up another map and copy the route and mail that to me?" Casey asked.

"Twenty will do it," Alberto said.

"Where has he gone, Al?"

"We were correct before," Alberto said. "He was headed for the Amazon." There was another moment of silence on Al's end of the line until finally, he said, "He is going into the *Antisuyu*."

Immediately Case called Claire and told her everything he and Al had spoken about. Before he hung up, he said, "I forgot what *Antisuyu* is ... the Amazon?"

"It was the fabled name of the scary Amazonian eastern frontier of the old empire," she reminded him...where the warriors of the Incan empire were afraid to go."

At the end of May, Dr. Bache sent a letter to Maryanne Fitzroy, also addressed to Claire. The Ministry's permission to examine the site had been approved. Still, because of the site's remoteness, it came with the stipulation that a small team under Bache first investigate the location with a security team. Claire — and Harvard — would be named in Dr. Bache's excavation project. There were still a lot of loose ends that would have to be tied; an approved Peruvian co-investigator (if not Dr. Bache, then likely someone from his program), and many logistical parts of the puzzle must be pieced together and signed off on.

On the Friday before Memorial Day weekend, Claire met with Dr. Fitzroy to discuss Dr. Bache's letter. "We're a long way off yet," said Maryanne, "but it looks good so far. I'm hoping for next May, which would line up nicely with your dissertation, and it'll be the start of the dry season. I've talked to others in the department, and everyone's excited. We ought to be able to get a grant, and we could set it up for you so that the excavation next season would be post-doctorate work."

"That's very kind of you. I would love that … providing it's safe by then."

"I called Franz the day after we received his letter," Maryanne said. "He is in communication with the police in Ayacucho and Cusco, and he thinks it will be quite safe in a few months. That's all he can say about it, but he promised to write as soon as it is settled."

Claire nodded.

"Has there been any word from Jack?"

"No," Claire said. "In his last correspondence, he said he would not be able to post letters for a couple of months, but that now puts him over a month overdue. Casey has been trying to track him down through our friend Alberto in Peru. Miraculously, Al has figured out exactly where Jack has been over the past year." Claire smiled. "I wonder what Jack would think of that if he knew."

"Do you know where he is now?" the professor asked.

"In the Amazon, we think. East of Cusco."

Dr. Fitzroy settled back in her chair. Her brow furrowed.

On the sixteenth of June, Karen Beal called Claire.

"Hi, Claire … we're checking in. We were just wondering if you've heard anything from Jack."

"No, I'm sorry, Karen. No one down here has heard anything since December."

"Oh. Okay," Jack's mother said. "Should we be worrying now?"

Claire did not want to worry the family. She tried to sound upbeat. "I don't think so. He's probably having the time of his life and feeling relatively carefree."

"I supposed so," Karen said.

"But I'm glad you called," Claire said. "I was about to write you a letter. Our friend in Cusco — Alberto, I told you about him — found some British mountaineers who spent a couple of months with Jack, and they climbed with him. Casey sent Alberto some money to copy a map with all of Jack's travels, and it should be here in a couple of weeks. When it arrives, I'll get a map to make a copy and send it to you."

"We'd love that, Claire. But don't you know where he is now?"

"We think he has gone to the Amazon."

"The jungle?"

"Yes, but you know Jack. He probably heard about some great fishing, or some strange plant, or some rare bird, and he'll want to study it." (She saw no point in frightening Karen by mentioning the Masco Piru or other uncontacted tribes, or the Shining Path who could possibly be hiding in the Amazon, *or* the illegal loggers operating in a lawless frontier).

"Yes, of course, you're right," Karen replied. "He loves birds."

"Karen?"

"Yes?"

"I haven't told anyone about this, but I'm thinking of going back. Not so much because I'm worried about Jack, but I want to try to find him to talk to him. I feel it is my fault that he has dropped out of the program, and I think if I could just sit down and talk to him, he'll come home."

There was a pause on the other end of the phone.

"Well, Claire, Jack has always had a different mind; in fact, we've fostered that. There doesn't seem to be anything in life, especially nature, that doesn't interest him. We love that about him. It doesn't surprise us that a young man like him would kind of 'drop out' and travel around, seeking the beauty in life. The truth is, we've been tickled pink that he even chose to enter the program at Harvard and stick with it for so long. His mind is so ... boundless. But we've been saying if we don't receive word from him by the first of July, a call, or a letter in which he tells us what his actual plan is, Alton will go and try to find him. Maybe both of you could go."

Claire hesitated in her response. That was a lot coming at her in a hurry. "Has he traveled to South America? Or any third-world or developing country?"

"I don't know where Alton was for four years — he was in the Army when he was young but won't talk about it. I do know his old uniform has a Ranger patch on it, so who knows where he's been."

"Okay," Claire said. "Maybe. I had planned on going alone and hooking up with our friend Alberto in Cusco to help find him. Al is a guide, not a detective, but if anyone can find him, he can. I have more than enough money to live and travel in Peru for a month or more when the summer break is here."

"When were you thinking of going?" Karen asked.

"Early July if we don't hear from him. It'll be the dry season and should be good traveling."

"Will you please call a couple of weeks before you go? If Alton decides to go anyway, it would be better if you all worked together — maybe you could cover more ground."

"Of course, I will. Take care, and you let me know if you hear anything also."

No word came from Jack in June. But by the twenty-first, the map did arrive from Alberto. Folded into the map was a letter. Casey called Claire right away, and she walked over from the Peabody Museum to his apartment.

16 May 1986

Dear Casey & Claire,

Here is the map. You can see that I traced the route as told to me by the Brits. Yellow highlighter shows where he went from Cusco a year ago, traveling north to the Cordillera Blanca. From there, in red ink, I offer the route the three climbers (including Jack) took back to Cusco and then east into the Amazon by the normal route. I realize Jack isn't normal, but the 8-hour drive from Cusco to Salvación is the easiest way to get into the Manus Preserve, and I don't see him traveling by any other route. From there, he could find different boats to hire to get farther into the jungle. It's essentially a region closed off to the public and only open to researchers, but with a bit of help from the right guides and being sneaky about it, one can get in there.

I wrote the Brit's contact information on the back of the map.

Yours,

Al

Claire picked up the map and held it, tracing her eyes over the highlighted parts and the dotted red line. Except for a couple of short letters, it was the first tangible evidence of Jack's whereabouts over the last year. She laid it back on the kitchen table and studied it closely.

"He has seen a lot of the country," Casey said.

Claire nodded as she read the names of the towns. She could see that from Ayacucho, he had traveled, probably by bus, north to Huancayo, then probably as far as the town of Jauja before going east to Lima.

"I'm surprised he did not look Jim up when he was in Lima," Claire said.

"Me too."

Penned out in the Pacific Ocean was a note from Al: *The Brits were sure about this section because Jack talked to them about the bus ride from Lima to Huaraz.*

Claire pointed to a spot on the map near the Santa River, about eight miles north of Huaraz. "This is where my dig was three years ago. Huaraz is a neat town, and it's the gateway into the Cordillera Blanca, and you can walk into the mountains from town."

Casey inspected the map, leaning next to Claire. His finger traced the Cordillera Blanca mountain range, slid down the valley of the Llanganuco Lakes, and settled on the city of Huaraz. "He probably met the Brits either in town or up in the mountains," he said.

Their eyes followed the dotted red line back out of the Cordillera and then south back to Lima by the same bus route.

"Again, he didn't look up Jim or visit the Explorer's Club," Casey said, "but I suppose they may have been there only long enough to buy bus tickets."

This time Jack's travels took him down the coastline to the city of Pisco. Another handwritten note was in the Pacific, to the west of Pisco: *I'm sure this route because the Brits were with Jack the whole way. They visited the Incan archaeologic site of Tambo Colorado. Then they caught a bus east to Ayacucho and then to Cusco. It still makes me sad that he traveled to Cusco and then to Ollantaytambo and did not look me up. Or Maria. I suppose it's possible he was only in town for a few hours to catch a bus.*

They hiked around Ollanta and Macchu Pichu, from where they returned to Cusco. There they split up, and Jack traveled to the Madre de Dios. Using the photo of Jack, I am asking drivers and outfitters in Cusco if any of them took him east into the jungle.

Claire had ordered two maps of Peru from the Harvard Coop. She pulled one of them out of her daypack, along with some colored pens. She started copying the marks from Al's map.

When she was done, she folded the map for Karen and put it back into her pack. She pushed the original map across the table and sat back into her chair, and breathed a heavy sigh.

"What are you thinking?" Casey asked. "I've seen that look."

"I don't want you to be pissed at me or try to lecture me."

"Have I ever?" he asked.

Claire thought for a moment. "Well, no, actually."

"When we were in Peru," she continued, "you and Jack were the climbers, so I kind of just trekked along, and you guys made most of the plans and decisions. I was fine with that. But you know I've traveled alone before, and I speak more Spanish than both of you, and I'm a fucking capable woman."

"I know this, Claire! What is it?"

"I'm going back to try to find him."

Casey stared at her. "And you don't want me to go? Do you think it might be awkward when we find him because he told you he loved you? Don't you think I would give you two the space you'd need?"

"I suppose yes, all of that."

"Look at me, Claire. I would not make it awkward. I care about both of you, and I want him to know that. You do know it, I believe, but I want *him* to know it. I think it's why he went AWOL."

There was a long moment of silence.

Then Casey rose from his chair, went across the kitchen to the counter, and picked up an envelope. He returned and dropped it onto the table in front of Claire.

She opened it and looked at it. **"United Airlines: Logan International — Miami INTL 07/09/1986 One."** She did not have to look at the rest of the tickets to know the second would be from Miami to Lima.

"I've already contacted Al and Jim," Casey said. "I'm going to find our friend. You're welcome to come if you want."

Claire jumped up and gave Casey a big hug. She had wanted to go alone but instantly felt a clear comfort that Casey was going, and she suddenly felt a greater affection for the man he was.

"Don't worry," he said. "If we find him, I'll give you space."

THIRTY-NINE

Planning & Logistics ... Again

K aren was happy to get the letter from Claire with the map enclosed. In it, she explained that she and Casey would be going down to Cusco to try to locate Jack — if only to make sure he was okay. She explained they would be with Alberto and did not see any reason for Alton to make the trip. Not at this time. "If they hit a roadblock or could not find him," she wrote, "then Alton could make another trip and try. Of course, it's totally up to you folks."

Claire and Casey communicated as the ninth of July approached but did their packing individually. They were old hands now at the logistics of traveling to Peru and living out of a backpack. Claire was able to book tickets on the same flights as Casey, but their seats were far apart. The trip to Miami and then to Lima had a very different feel than a year ago, but things were much the same when they arrived. It seemed the same cabs and cabbies, beggars, police, and pickpockets lined the street outside the airport. And there were the same VW Beetles everywhere. The scent of street food, aviation fuel, fish, diesel, and urine still hung in the air when they walked out of the terminal.

"Jack liked the different smells," Claire remembered.

And again, there was Jim and his friend Javier and their VW bus, waiting for them. After hugs and greetings, they again drove to the Explorer's Club to talk and decompress from the long flights.

Claire, Jim, and Casey sat at the same table. It was nice to reunite with Eliana when she joined them. Peru seemed so familial. The expression on her face was gracious but lined with concern. In an instant, Claire could sense that Eliana had learned more about her sister's connection with Jack and had her vested interest in finding him. She hadn't thought of that. It gave her a strange feeling, which she suppressed by thinking about how Jack somehow touched everyone he met.

Casey got out the map Alberto had sent. Jim looked at the drawn lines. "Yellow appears to be northbound," he said, "and red lines travel back south and east to Cusco. This is amazing. How do you know all this? From his letters?"

"Hell, no. Alberto put Jack's picture in the Cross Keys and the British climbers I told you about on the phone turned up there a few months ago on their way to Ausangate. Al went and met them. They filled in all the blank spots on the map. They had plenty enough downtime on the climb for Jack to tell them all the places he had seen so far. They told Al that Jack had planned on going to the Amazon. 'There's a lot of the country I haven't seen,' Jack had said to them, and he told the Brits he was interested in the uncontacted tribes living in the Manu Preserve and also that he heard about illegal Brazilian loggers and miners in the Preserve. They said it got Jack angry, and they said he wanted to go there to photograph them if the stories were true."

Jim's eyes got larger. He said nothing — he looked back at the map. He followed the red line east of Cusco, then northeast up the dirt Highway 26 to the river town of Puerto Buena Vista and beyond to the village of Salvación, in the region of the *Madre de Dios*. There the line stopped, and there was a red question mark. Jim looked up at Casey and then at Claire. He tapped the question mark with his finger.

"This is no problem," he told them. "Many tourists and scientists visit Salvación and even fifty miles farther down the Alto Madre de Dios River. Remember, the Manu is considered the most important rainforest preserve in the world. The Cultural Zone in the park is the section of land between the Andes Mountains and the Amazon Rainforest. A year ago, you were close to Manu on the opposite side, the western edge, where no one ever goes. This is probably why the Sendero were camped there. *If* they were Sendero."

Jim contemplated the red line. "The biome in the Manu is incredible, so the native peoples there — all the way to here (Jim pointed at a spot on the map at the confluence of two rivers about forty miles past Salvación) are familiar with visitors. But here, thirty miles north of the highway and up the Alto Madre de Dios River ... this is no place for a gringo. Not traveling alone."

He stopped talking and let it sink in.

Casey stiffened in his chair. "Well, fuck. We have all this, and we still don't really have a clue where he is."

Jim nodded. "You brought photographs of Jack?"

"We did," Claire said.

"Then you show them to villagers up in the Madre de Dios. If he did make it there, you'll find some clues. All you'll have to do is follow them. Hopefully, you'll hit the Jackpot." He winced even as he said that. "Sorry. Bad pun."

Claire and Casey stayed in the same hotel they had just over a year ago. Jim had arranged the room, and it was a single with a double bed. There were personal details Jim wasn't aware of. The only romantic aspects he knew about were those relayed to him by Eliana about Jack and Maria's transient connection. Jim had half-thought Jack might ask Maria to move to Boston with him, but that was before he failed to turn up.

Claire looked at the tiny room and the bed. Casey shrugged but didn't say anything.

"We'll save money, she offered. Will you be okay with this?"

"Claire, I slept with you for over a month without sex. A few more nights on this trip won't kill me."

She scowled at him.

"Seriously ..." he continued, "we're here on a mission. I hope you give me more credit than that, and I think I've earned your trust."

He was right. He had. He certainly had, many times over.

"Of course. You're right. I'm just a little nervous about this trip, what we might find — or not find. I'm not thinking clearly."

They both cleaned up and got into bed, careful not to touch each other.

"Claire," he said, staring at the ceiling, "you're going to *have* to be thinking clearly on this trip. We need to count on each other."

"I know. But honestly, I wasn't worried about you 'putting the moves on me.' I know you wouldn't be so crass, and I was just worried if you would be comfortable with this."

"I'm good," he said. "Does it still sting a little? Sure. Do I miss you?

You bet. But I'm long over the breakup, and I'm more concerned with finding Jackson."

"Good answer," she half-whispered. Her eyelids started to drop. "Good night."

There was less turbulence on the early flight to Cusco than on both of their previous flights. As they glided over the Andes and the brown, desolate highlands, Claire looked out the window. She wondered how much of the land below Jack had seen throughout the year. *Casey's right,* she thought. *I do need to be prepared for any eventuality. What if he's not even happy to see me? Or worse — angry at our presence? We don't know what he has been through, who he's met, or what has gone through his mind. Hopefully, he'll be the same old loveable Jack. But he didn't ask us to come find him. Oh, God! What if we can't find him at all?* She started to cry at the idea but caught herself. *Focus, Claire!*

The airplane landed, and the passengers — and the stewardesses — applauded.

Outside, Alberto's was the first face they saw. He hustled and slid through the crowd of mestizos and Campesinos who were waiting for passengers and gave both Claire and Casey a big hug.

"Marisol is with a taxi," Al said, "let's get your luggage."

Alberto grabbed Claire's backpack and insisted on carrying it to the taxi. "You both packed very light. I love you guys."

As they walked to the taxi, Casey asked Alberto, "Did you get the wire okay?"

"I did," Al said. "Your father is a doctor? I saw the stationary."

"Yup. An orthopaedist."

Claire looked sideways at Casey, and he gave her a look back, suggesting he'd explain later.

They dumped their bags at the Royal Inka Hotel. Al had arranged these accommodations, and he had the foresight to get two single rooms. Al and Marisol left them to run some errands, and the two travelers went for a walk around town. They would meet them later at the Cross Keys Pub to catch up. The walk was pleasant. They did not have to be concerned about acclimatizing this time, for they would be descending in altitude to get to the jungle. As they walked, Casey explained the wire Alberto had mentioned. He told her that his father had wired money, hired Alberto for three weeks, *and* rented a Land Cruiser per Alberto's advice. No buses for this trip. Al had explained they might need to be free and mobile. Besides, the rental was cheap enough.

When they arrived at the pub, Al and Marisol were already there. They all sat at the same rectangular table they did a year ago. Everything looked so familiar. Alberto explained how he had spoken with Maria on the way over, and she confirmed she hadn't heard from Jack since a letter she received before Christmas. "We asked if she'd like to come here to see you, but she's pretty heartbroken. I explained that we were going to look for him, and that seemed to please her. I think she still hopes they will be together someday. You can see it in her eyes. When I speak to her, she's not the same, as if she doesn't want to be around me. In fact, she seems to avoid me now. It's very strange."

Al looked at Claire. "It's complicated, I suppose."

Claire did not respond. She looked around the room, then she got up abruptly and walked to the bar. There was her photograph of Jack behind the bar, one of the pictures she had sent Alberto, with a napkin taped above it that said, "HAVE YOU SEEN THIS MAN?"

She hadn't known which photo Al had put there. It was one she took of him sitting at his makeshift table while on the Ausangate trek when she found him early in the morning staring into his antique microscope. He looked up at her and smiled, and she took the picture. He was beautiful in the photo. He was wearing an old, faded Irish wool sweater with a loose turtleneck, and his Hagstone amulet, which he usually wore against his skin, was visible against the sweater. He was in his fourth day of beard growth, and the early morning mountain light was illuminating his already bright blue eyes. He looked every bit the 1930s Himalayan explorer. She suddenly relived that moment in the shadow of Ausangate when only he and she were awake. Just as suddenly, she remembered that that was one of the early moments — moments she would keep entirely to herself for two more weeks — when she got one of the frightful feelings, those rare twinges when she had a strange, subconscious thought that maybe *he* was the one. Claire understood at that moment — even more than when they made love — that she had always loved Jack and reinforced that all along it was Jack whom she was meant to be with. She stared at the photo. She gazed into that moment in time on the trek and was swiftly flooded with emotions.

God damnit, she thought, beginning to cry.

Casey was sitting at the table back-to her while she stood at the bar, but Al saw Claire crying. She was clutching the edge of the bar with both hands. He went to her, and he put his arm around her shoulders tentatively, and she spun around and buried her face into his chest. She was embarrassed.

With his beautiful, stately Spanish accent, Alberto said, "Don't worry, Claire. We'll find him. He'll be all right." He made her feel better, but she knew he had no way of knowing that. By now, Marisol and Casey had turned and saw she had been crying and rose from the couch.

"I'm okay, I'm okay," she dried her face with a bar napkin. "It was just seeing the photo, and it reminded me of the trek. It felt good ... I hadn't cried in a while."

As she sat down, Casey looked at the photo for the first time. He did not cry because he rarely did, but when he looked at Jack's vivid face and that old microscope, he smiled a little, then grimaced and turned away.

Cusco looked, smelled, and felt the same. In the morning, Alberto met Casey and Claire in the courtyard of their hotel for breakfast. "I've got the Land Cruiser," he said. "How are you fixed for tents?"

"I have one one-person tent," replied Casey.

"Okay, I'll get a couple more from my Belgian supplier-friend."

"Belgian ..." Casey said, remembering, "I thought he was French."

"Close enough. I also got four mosquito nets for sleeping."

"Four?" Casey asked. "You don't think Jack will already have one if we find him."

"He definitely will," Al said, "but since we spoke last, I made a decision. If it's okay with you, I hired a man."

"Okay," Casey said. He looked at Claire.

"Whatever Al thinks," she said.

"You remember Ian Jones, who owns this place? He is a pretty amazing guy," said Al. "He also runs river trips into the Manus and leads birding expeditions. Ian knows what he's doing. He recommended this fellow named Juan Gonzalez, who has lived in the Manus and is part Matsigenka Indian. He was a policeman and was in the military for years as a young man. He will know people where we're going, and he'll be a good man in our corner if we have any trouble. I know him too. He's remarkably loyal. Hell, I think he'd take a bullet for you guys, and he hasn't even met you."

"Let's hope we don't find out," Claire said.

"I paid $300 to retain him for the trip. I can pay him out of my money if you prefer. But I think it'll be wise to hire him. He also can communicate with the tribes if we have to go into the interior."

Casey waved him off. "No. I got it. I'm glad you hired him." Casey took out $300 in twenties from his money belt and gave it to Al.

Alberto took the money and put it in his pocket. "I'll give this to his wife," he said. "That is customary here. You completed the immunization list I sent you?"

Both Claire and Casey nodded.

"Good," Al said. "Everything in the jungle wants to sting, stick, bite, or suck you."

They unfolded the map with the highlighted routes.

"I think the first place to go tomorrow should be to the town of Paucartambo," Alberto said, "and ask around — see if we can dig anything up. From there, we'll go to Salvación and hire someone to take us by boat. They're extending the road past the town, but I don't think it's drivable yet. Unless we get a clue, we will stop at every settlement along the river and inquire about Jack."

Alberto studied the Alto Madre de Dios River course and the little villages lining its banks on the map. "I could see Jack just striking out on his own into the jungle, searching for something."

"Me too," Claire said, "and that's what scares me."

FORTY

The Search

The Land Cruiser was much newer than Casey had expected, and Juan Gonzalez was much older than he expected. Juan was tall, by Peruvian standards. He was in his late fifties but was remarkably fit and still had jet-black hair. He did not have the bearing of someone who had grown up poor. Juan had steely dark eyes with crow's feet at the corners and when he met Casey and Claire, his eyes at once showed kindness and a natural fearlessness. He exuded a quiet confidence. Alberto treated him with great respect.

Al had put three coolers in the back of the Cruiser, and the backpacks were packed around them. There was a plastic bin that had camping and cooking supplies. There was enough room in the front of the vehicle for everyone to stretch out. Juan had some classical Peruvian music on the radio, but it was turned down very low; the wooden, muted sounds of the zampoñas could still be heard in the back seats.

Juan drove east-southeast out of Cusco for forty-five minutes before turning left and north onto Highway 26. *This is it*, thought Casey. *We're on our way.*

About four hours later, the Cruiser pulled into the town of Paucartambo. It was a quaint little village with a petrol station where Casey topped off the tank. It was almost noon, so the group decided to have lunch, and Al found a small cafe where they could get sandwiches. They showed the young woman making the sandwiches Jack's photograph, but she had not seen him. They took the lunches and sat on the stone rampart embankments of the Rio Mapacho, where it flowed through the town. They were a few yards downstream from a tall, arched bridge. Casey sat staring at the bridge and marveled at how much it reminded him of the Ottoman bridge in the city of Mostar in Yugoslavia.

"Years ago," Casey said to whoever was interested, "when I was backpacking through Europe, I visited Yugoslavia. There's a bridge in the ancient city of Mostar, and this looks a lot like that one."

Alberto looked up at the arched stone bridge and said, "This one was built in 1775."

Casey nodded. He looked around. "Incredible. We are going to the jungle, but this countryside looks a lot more like around the Sacred Valley and the mountainous areas just east of Ollanta."

Alberto agreed. "It does. You know, I've lived and guided here for twenty years, and every morning I stand in wonder at the beauty in Peru ... and you know how fast the landscape can change. From here, we drive to Salvación — a few hours farther north. We'll find a place there to stay for the night, and then tomorrow, we drop down into the lower elevations. It becomes a jungle very quickly."

The "highway" into Salvación was narrow and built out of crumbling dirt and crushed shale. There were places where there would not be room for an oncoming vehicle to pass. It took eight hours to get to Salvación from Cusco. The village was not much; a small clump of buildings set back from the riverbank, but it was lovely in its way, the way all frontier towns are because of the freedom and the curiousness they hold. There was one small café where the team could get a bite to eat. At this place, there were no menus. When the owner came to the table, she asked how many people were eating and then turned away. She returned a short time later with four plates of *arroz con pollo*.

"Guess we have chicken and rice," Casey said. They took out the map again and showed her the photo of Jack.

Alberto held up the image. "*¿Recuerdas haber visto a este hombre? Es nuestro amigo y estamos tratando de encontrarlo.*" The lady took the photo, moved it in and out of several focal lengths, and shook her head. "*No señor.*" She hadn't seen him, or perhaps she did not remember him.

"This is the only place in town to eat," Alberto declared. "Maybe he camped outside of town, but here is where he would have rented a boat or paid a fare on a boat."

After eating, Al told Claire and Casey about the region they were headed into. He waved the palm of his hand over the section of the map where the Manu National Park is. "This 1,600 square miles of wilderness was established as a park in 1973," he said, "which combines a core area and a huge buffer zone. It's an ambitious experiment — a rain forest set aside in its natural state. They're building a tourist lodge on the Manu River that should open later this year for eco-tourism. I've also heard talk about the whole Manus park becoming a World Heritage Site."

Al then gave two photos to Juan, who rose from his chair, nodded at Claire and Casey, and left without saying a word.

Casey said, "I don't exactly know what Juan is about, but I'm glad he's with us."

Al just smiled and said, "Casey, we know from what you have said that Jack expressed interest in my photos of the Mascho Piru."

Al continued, "And the British climbers told me he was angry about the stories of illegal Brazilian loggers. And we know about Jack's, shall we say, insatiable interest in nature. So, we have to guess whether he is on a quest, or simply trying to see some wildlife and new country. If it is a quest, is it to find an uncontacted tribe? Or to document and expose the loggers? Each one would point us in a different location, on different sides of the river."

Claire responded, "Our best hope for that would be to find someone who has seen him — or better yet, talked to him. Otherwise, it'll be like finding a needle in a haystack. Maybe worse."

Al took out a pencil. He circled on the map three parts of the Manu. Outside the line of the first circle, he wrote "*Logging*." Next to the second circle, "*Likely Nature Course — Anthropology*." Next to the third, "*Uncontacted*." As he spoke about the tribes, he facetiously said, "And they are all nomadic, so that helps."

"Are there any other reasons you two can think of why he would want to venture off into the Amazon Basin outside of exploring new territory? Casey, you have known him longer, but Claire, I saw and listened to how you and Jack interacted, and you may have known him better."

"I think it's one of those three," Claire said.

Casey thought for a minute. "I know Jack differently. We both look at life a little like Shipton and Tilman — or we like to think we do. Jack is very much an early twentieth-century explorer, but he doesn't realize it. His mother told me that people in his hometown often thought of him as a bit eccentric when he was growing up, and even his brothers did. But, he doesn't know that his remarkable interests and his mind are different than anyone else's."

"So, some of this is my gut, but here's what it's telling me; Jack is simply exploring. He will go as far up the Rio Manu as his finances and food will allow, interacting with as many native people as possible along the way. He'll fill a journal and use up all the camera film he has with him. Jack will play with the children in every village and get drunk with the elders if offered. He'll learn how they collect food. If a native woman sneaks into his tent at night … he probably won't sleep with her, but he'll make her feel special. And if along the way he encounters the Mascho — or any other rarely seen tribe — or if he sees what he thinks are illegal loggers, he'll document them and consider the encounters as a bonus. He won't confront the loggers because he's too smart. He won't contact the Mascho because he knows he could make them sick."

Alberto looked at Claire. "That sounds very reasonable to me. What do you think?"

"Until we get a clue," she said, "at least this gives us a plan to follow from here."

"Okay," Alberto said. "We will rent a boat in the morning and hire a driver. Tomorrow we'll head downriver, and we will stop at every settlement along the way and show the photos. If we don't find anyone who saw him, we'll continue to the village of Boca Manu, where this Alto (Upper) Madre de Dios River meets the Rio Manu flowing down from the north and then follow it upriver. We'll go as far as it is navigable and follow any leads we get along the way."

Claire and Casey agreed that it was a good plan.

"I sent word ahead, and we have a hut to share tonight," Al said, "but before we go there, we should secure a boat for tomorrow."

They left the café and walked through the village and down to the water's edge. Claire and Casey felt the heat, and it was hotter than anything they had experienced on last year's trip. As the afternoon wore on, the insects became voracious. Alberto gave Claire and Casey each a bottle of insect repellent that contained industrial strength DEET.

As they walked down to the river, Claire said, "It's a bigger town than I thought it would be. There must be a thousand people living here."

The Alto Madre de Dios River was running clearer than Casey had imagined. All the photographs he had seen of rivers in the Amazon

Basin appeared muddy. There were dozens of longboats pulled onto the riverbank. Some looked to be forty feet long, and all had a canopy for most of the vessel's length, but there were also small dugout canoes. Men and boys lounged about. Juan came toward them, strolling with purpose up from the water's edge to meet them. He spoke to Alberto. Juan seemed calm and spoke matter-of-factly.

Al turned to Casey and Claire. "Two of the men recognize Jack in the photo."

Claire's heart jumped. *That was quick — in only the second town, they have a clue.*

"Can you take us to them?" Alberto asked Juan.

All three followed Juan down the line of boats. Two men were cleaning some catfish next to their longboat, and they looked to be father and son. They both stood up, Juan introduced them, and they shook Alberto's hand. They acknowledged Casey and Claire with smiles as Al spoke with them. They were shown the photos again to make sure.

The older man pointed at the photograph. "*Sí, sí ... ese era el joven. Vino por aquí alrededor de Navidad. Se veía así, con barba.*"

Al asked the man a few more questions, and he said many things. At one point, he was waving one arm overhead, back and forth. Then Alberto translated, "Jack was here about last Christmas. This man says he had a beard when he was here, and he is positive it was him. He said the man in the picture was fishing here, in the river. He described him waving a stick back and forth — probably fly fishing. He tells me Jack paid for passage with another boatman in town who took him as far as Boca Manu."

"Can you take us to that boatman?" Alberto asked in Spanish.

"*No, él está en Cusco ...*" the man said.

Alberto shook his head and explained that the man who took Jack downriver was in Cusco and would be there for several days. Al thanked the man and his son and asked if there would be anyone they could hire to take four people downriver to Boca Manu. The man responded that he knew of a good man for the job and would introduce him in the morning.

Al turned to Juan, Claire, and Casey. "We are in business. This man will have someone here in the morning who is available. If Juan likes the look of him, we will hire him to take us down the river to Boca Manu. From there, we'll see where any leads may take us."

The group unloaded their backpacks at the rented hut just before the afternoon rains came. Everyone staked out a corner of the hut and laid out their sleeping pads. Everyone except Juan, who stretched a hammock with mosquito netting between wall posts in the corner of the building. It being Casey and Claire's first time in a jungle, Alberto brought in two small tarpaulins to place underneath their sleeping pads to prevent insects from crawling up through the cracks in the floorboards. Then, he helped set up their mosquito nets over them. He knew he would have to help them only once.

"We don't want any leishmaniasis," Alberto stated. He sprayed each bedding area with insecticide.

The rain typically lasts less than an hour, and afterward, Al, Claire, and Casey walked around the town, taking pictures and writing in their journals. Juan said he had "some things to do." Alberto offered that he should meet them for supper around six-thirty, but as they walked through the streets, Al said, "I am told that Juan often fends for himself on trips."

They sat around the picnic table in the center of the hut and read with headlamps — all except Juan — but the lights attracted flying insects, so it wasn't long before each was under their mosquito netting to read.

Claire looked at Casey in the nearest corner. "What book is that?" she asked.

"I brought two," Casey said. "This one is *Into the Heart of Borneo* by Redmond O'Hanlon. It's really good writing. Beau recommended it to me a few months ago. I also have *Lost Trails, Lost Cities* by Percy Fawcett, if you want to read that one."

"I'm good," Claire said. "Fawcett? You're thinking about searching for Paititi someday?"

Casey smiled under his netting. "Of course not. But it's fun to read about this country in the 1930s and '40s."

The lights went out early. Thoughts of Jack swirled around both Claire and Casey's minds. Juan was quiet, as usual, and Alberto's mind was mulling over logistics, traveling in the jungle, and the many dangers it holds. Al felt responsible for Claire and Casey and hoped that he could keep them safe from disease, the rivers, and evil men. He was glad he had Juan with him.

A short time after the lights were turned off, Casey broke the cacophony of nighttime animal sounds. "Al?"

"Yes?"

"I remember reading about leishmaniasis but can't remember what it is."

"It's a parasite," Alberto replied, "from sand flies." Al was staring up into the underside of the thatched roof. "The flies were not always here. I think they arrived here from Brazil during a drought. Stay covered up as much as possible and keep using the bug spray I gave you."

Then, almost as an afterthought, Al said, "Leishmaniasis ... you don't want it."

They would be on the river in the morning and have less than two weeks to find Jack or learn where he might have gone. Casey thought, *this place is beautiful, but it's harsh. I wonder if Jack's even alive?*

FORTY-ONE

Into The Manus

When Casey, Al, and Claire awoke, Juan was already gone, and so was his hammock. The three friends rolled up their sleeping pads, packed their gear, and policed their areas. Then they walked to the Land Cruiser and drove to the waterfront.

Juan was there, sitting on the bow of a boat, dangling his bare feet in the water. The man from the day before and his son were there, along with another young man who looked to be in his early twenties. He could tell by his expressions and the melody of his speech that he was a good sort. You can easily tell people's disposition when they are speaking Spanish, even if the listener cannot speak a word. It is a passionate language. Alberto approached the men introduced himself to the young man, whom he liked right away.

Alberto turned to Casey and Claire. "This is Mario. He is the son of a boatman from Boca Manu, who Juan has known all his life. He says they are a good family, and the father and his sons are very capable. Juan also said Mario has been on the rivers since he was an infant and knows the water very well. He can take us as far as Boca, and from there, we can hire someone to take us wherever the leads tell us to go. I recommend we hire him."

Claire and Case smiled at Mario and said, "Sounds good."

"He knows what we are here to do, and he says he knows who to talk to in Boca Manu—if you remember from the map, that is the little village near where this river meets the Manu River."

"Excellent," Casey said. "Let's do it."

Juan drove the Cruiser to the river's edge, and all the gear was loaded in the boat. Mario packed the gear where he wanted it, and the passengers could keep a fanny pack or a daypack with them. Juan drove the Cruiser back to the hut and parked it where it would be out of the way for nearly two weeks. Casey paid the hut owner thirty dollars to watch over the truck, but the insurance policy was that Juan took the man aside and talked to him before they left. The man seemed compliant with whatever Juan told him. While waiting for Juan to get back from the Cruiser, Casey looked over the boat. The ribs and planking looked no more than a few years old. Just under thirty feet long, there was a canopy of canvas strung for most of its length. Casey could see a spare fifty-horsepower outboard engine near the stern but forward of Mario's feet.

Just as the last piece of gear was stowed, Juan walked down the riverbank carrying one more item; a bundle of four well-used machetes tied together. Mario started the motor and eased the boat out into the current. Juan told Alberto that it usually would take about four hours to get to the village Boca Manu, but stopping at every village would be a long day on the water. Alberto asked Juan and Mario to discuss if they thought every settlement should be investigated for the sightings of Jack. They talked it over. It was a consensus that since boats going to the Manu Reserve did not often stop at many of the villages, they ought to stop only at those where the people would be most likely to have seen Jack.

Alberto agreed.

The first village where they pulled ashore was Shintuya. Located just after a large widening of the river that resembled a lake, Juan pointed downstream when they were 1,000 yards from the thatched huts. A group of ramshackle buildings in a vast clearing hugged the shoreline. Juan said something to Al, whose voice then rose above the whine of the outboard. "He said about 150 people live here. We'll stretch our legs and ask around."

Mario nestled the boat along the muddy undercut bank in front of the village. Juan worked his way to the bow and jumped onto the bank while holding a bowline. He wrapped it around a tree and tied it off. One by one, the others stepped out onto the riverbank. Mario stayed with the boat as Juan greeted the few curious people who had come to see who was visiting.

It was almost noon, and the humidity was palpable, and even resting in the shade, everyone in the party was soaked with salty sweat. The people here were different in their appearance and the way they carried themselves, and they were friendly enough, nodding when Claire waved across the open area between the huts.

"They are from either Amarakaeri or Wachipaeri tribes," Alberto said. "Honestly, I don't know which. They are nice people who cling with pride to their tribal identities."

Juan was walking from person to person showing the photographs of Jack, and they were all quick to shake their heads. In only ten minutes, Juan wanted to get back into the boat. Casey said he wanted to take a pee break, and Claire seconded the motion. She stepped into the forest only a few feet, but Juan walked near to her and turned his back while she went. He knew that she could lose sight of the village in only twenty feet — even of the river. Claire did not question him. Casey had seen so many men and women pee in the river that he figured he would, and he started to urinate a few feet from the boat.

"Careful of the candiru fish," Alberto joked. When he said it, Juan looked up at him quickly and winced at Alberto. "*¡Si! Miedo al candiru.*"

Casey looked down at the stream of urine into the water. "The what-fish? Is that a piranha?"

"No," Alberto said, "The piranha are *piraña*, and the candiru is a much smaller fish but worse. You are okay there, but don't relieve yourself in the water if you go swimming."

"Why? It's attracted to the urine?"

"*Exactamente*," Al said. "It is a tiny little fish, shaped like a toothpick, and it is parasitic and normally lives in the gills of bigger fish. They are attracted to urine — probably the salt or something — but it will swim up the stream and into your *pene*."

"Holy shit," Casey said as Claire and Juan returned to the boat.

"No," Al said, "holy urine. But that's when the trouble just begins." Casey stared at him as he zipped up his pants. "The fish becomes lodged in the penis. It has two rows of backward-facing spines that prevent it from being pulled out of the urethra. It must be cut out of the penis. I'm told it is rather painful."

Probably a cystoscopy, thought Casey.

"What are you guys talking about?" Claire asked. Casey stepped into the boat and shoved away from shore.

"Just don't pee in the water," he replied.

Juan asked Mario in Spanish to wait to start the engine, then he said something to him and Alberto. Al nodded and turned to Claire and Casey.

"Juan suggests we go straight to Boca Manu. We can stay there tonight and show the photos around. He thinks we'll get some feedback because everyone goes through that town whether they are going upriver or down. We will follow any leads. If we strike out in the next week, we can stop at all the tiny settlements on the way back to Salvación. I think that's an efficient plan."

Claire and Casey looked at each other and nodded. They trusted Alberto with their lives. With Jack's life.

As Mario started the motor, Alberto leaned toward his friends and said barely loud enough to be heard, "Juan is taking this trip personally. Just watch him. He's well known as "The Guy." It is a matter of pride with him to find Jack now that we have trusted him. I feel good about this."

Claire responded, "That's excellent. But Al ..." Alberto leaned toward her and cocked his ear, straining to hear over the outboard engine. She continued, *"you're* 'The Guy.'" He smiled and shook his head.

The rest of the boat ride downriver to the confluence of the Manu River was spent watching the green and brown landscape roll past, watching for strange birds, and writing in journals when the ride was smooth enough. Claire watched for caimans but saw none. Being on the water was easier, and the constant breeze helped with the humidity and kept the insects at bay. She waved from the boat when they motored past the tiny settlements of Pantiacolla, Cruz de Mayo, Puerto Definitivo, and Piris, and at some places, the children playing at the water's edge waved back. At others, they only stared in wide wonder.

Mario eased up on the throttle as the Manu River came into view, flowing in from the left. Instantly the complexion of the river changed. The Manu River was coffee-colored from the silty humus and the constantly decaying jungle upstream.

Casey turned to Alberto and hollered over the sound of the outboard, "The colliding currents look tricky."

The village of Boca Manu was on the opposite side of the confluence. Mario quartered the bow into the oncoming Manu River and started inching across the 2,000 feet to the far side. Mario said something to Juan, who then made his way to the front of the boat, stepping between Claire and Casey, where he leaned forward over the bow.

"Mario is taking his time, and Juan is watching for debris," Al said. "Lots of limbs and sometimes whole trees come floating down the channel from illegal logging upriver."

It took some time to cut across the converging currents to the far side. Finally, Mario eased the boat along the banks of Boca Manu. The wooden buildings with thatched roofs were laid out in a grid in an enormous clearing and gave a vague sense of order in the natural chaos of the jungle. This was Mario's home, and a dozen people, mostly children, had recognized the boat and came to the bank to welcome him.

The banks along the village had been lined with hundreds of large, black canvas sacks filled with sand to prevent erosion of the riverbank and allow people to unload the boats without walking in slippery mud. They looked like recycled potato sacks.

Once the gear was unloaded onto the grassy bank, Claire and Casey helped Mario unload the supplies he had picked up in Salvación. He tried to decline their offer with gestures, but Alberto said something to the young boatman, who conceded.

Everyone was hungry, having skipped lunch, but the first order of business was to find a place to sleep and stow their gear. Alberto spoke with Mario, who asked something of one of the children, who replied excitedly in a language other than Spanish.

"Mario said we can camp next to his parent's house if we want to," Al said, "but the lodge in town is empty tonight, and for a few dollars, he's sure we could stay there."

As Alberto spoke, Juan picked up two of the backpacks and started walking across the clearing. Mario watched him and then smiled and said something.

Al translated, "Mario said, 'I guess you're staying at the lodge.'"

As the group walked to follow Juan, some of the children followed. Claire said, "I like this place. It feels comfortable." The children kept close behind Claire. A couple of the boys giggled.

Al spoke up, "They might not see very many blonde women here as pretty as you, Claire." She flinched at that. Al continued, "Maybe only a handful of blonde people, period. If you're uncomfortable, I will move them away."

"Oh, no," Claire said. "They're cute as hell, and this is their home." She reached out quickly and pretended to tickle one little girl under her chin, who giggled and pulled just out of reach.

Boca Manu seemed more orderly than most of the river villages they had seen. The schoolhouse near the back of the grid of homes was a bit larger and had a thatched roof, and all four walls of the building were open at about chest level.

The lodge where they were to stay was a two-minute walk down a trail that led away from the river, farther into the jungle. Wooden planks laid parallel and secured to the damp ground made a narrow walkway. The building was quite large, and it was rustic and pretty. There were eight bedrooms and a common room at one end of the building. The roof over the small sleeping rooms was thatched, and a metal roof covered the common room and its attached screened-in porch. The small twin beds had the customary and obligatory mosquito netting draped over the beds, suspended by rope ridgelines above the mattresses. Next to the lodge, a large cistern, twenty feet off the ground, fed rainwater to the building through a four-inch pipe that apparently resembled a tree limb because a three-foot-long copper-colored snake had wrapped itself around it and was sunning itself.

Claire, Alberto, Casey, and Juan each dropped their packs in a room, and Juan motioned the others to follow him. A screened-in hallway connecting the bedrooms led to the common area, and he pointed to the detached bathroom and shower behind the building. Suddenly, without saying anything, Juan left. Al smiled at Casey and Claire as if to say, *I guess we're following him.* They scrambled to grab their fanny packs with their cameras, money, and journals. Casey grabbed the photographs of Jack, and they caught up to Juan on the wooden walkway.

Juan headed straight to a tiny building that was the closest thing in the village to a café. He knew the middle-aged woman who owned the place, and they started conversing in a pretty, melodic language. Claire looked at Al, who whispered, "*It's Matsigenka.*" Al was listening intently, trying to pick out words to learn. The woman spoke back to Juan, who turned to Casey, "*¿Fotografía?*" Casey handed him the picture of Jack.

The entire time they spoke, the café owner had a small Capuchin monkey perched on her shoulder, and the pet regarded the travelers with quick, jerky, contemptuous movements of its head.

The woman smiled and said several sentences. Juan translated for Alberto, who did so for Claire and Casey. "Juan said he came here because he knows this is the cheapest place to get meals," Al told them. " Juan figures Jack must be low on funds by now. He was right — at least about him eating here. This woman said he was here half a year ago. She thinks it was December. He was in Boca for four or five days and ate here twice a day. She said she liked Jack and that he was going upriver but stayed here a while because he wanted to watch the people process manioc."

Casey and Claire exchanged hopeful glances. "So, he went up the Manu River, not down?" Casey asked.

Al asked Juan, who confirmed with the woman.

"She said when he left here, he went up the Manu. She does not know if on a return trip he kept going downriver, bypassing Boca Manu, to Puerto Maldonado or not."

Juan asked her another question, and again Alberto translated. "She knows who took him upriver. It was her nephew. He owns a boat, and he will be back from Puerto Maldonado tomorrow or the next day."

The group agreed to eat and decide what to do next. The owner of the little open-air restaurant was finally introduced by Juan as Susana. She was half Machiguenga, she told the group, and half Brazilian. She asked Juan if the young man in the photo was all right. Through Al's interpretations, Juan explained that they believed he was, but they were trying to find him to make sure. Susana blessed herself and said something in Machiguenga. Then she went into the kitchen where a young girl was working. Within minutes she returned with plates of food wrapped in leaves, with the monkey still clinging to her back. They had ordered nothing.

Alberto raised his eyes. "*Juane!*" He knew this dish. Juan smiled at Alberto, and it was the first time he had smiled since Claire and Casey met him; he was missing a bicuspid.

Juane, named after John the Baptist, was a classic Amazon dish. Large leaf wrappings were tied at the top with string. "These are macaw-flower leaves," said Alberto. He untied the string and unfolded the leafy ball to expose a cooked mound of rice, meat, olives, hard-boiled egg, and spices. Susana then brought out four side dishes of fried plantains that tasted like sweet potatoes.

After a few moments of eating, Juan spoke to Alberto, who translated for Claire and Casey.

"Juan thinks we should stay here until Susana's nephew returns from downriver. I agree, and we will at least know where he dropped Jack off, and we can go straight there. Maybe we will get lucky."

Claire and Casey approved. For this first time on the trip, tomorrow held real promise.

FORTY-TWO
True Evidence

Claire, predictably, was the first to awaken. It was not quite six o'clock. She went to the baño and took a short, tepid shower. She washed her previous day's underwear and shirt in the sink, wrung them out, and hung them to dry on the bamboo railing next to the short set of stairs that led to her room. Keeping clothes dry in the humidity Amazon was a challenge. She took her journal to the screened porch.

Juan proved to be an early riser also. He walked up the boardwalk and came in through the porch door. He was smiling for the second time.

"*Buenos días*," he said.

"Buenos días," Claire reciprocated.

Juan motioned her to follow.

He said the word *manioc* several times as he gestured for her to follow. She knew what manioc was. *He must know where there's some food,* she thought. *Hotcakes, maybe.* She got up and took her journal with her. She thought about grabbing her camera but decided against making Juan wait. They walked back toward the village. Juan led her to a clearing to the side of the village behind the first buildings they came to. Claire could hear women singing in low voices.

There were five women of various ages in the clearing, sitting on logs or the ground. Two were peeling a pile of roots from a cassava plant. One was washing the peeled tubers, and two others were grating the pale pulp of the roots with homemade metal graters. The snowy white mass of grated cassava root was collected and transferred into long, cylindrical baskets. Juan gestured toward the baskets and said, "*tipitis.*"

Called manioc by many indigenous peoples, Claire realized Juan didn't actually want to feed her; he thought she might like to see the process of transforming the bitter manioc root into a food known to be chock-full of carbohydrates.

Claire and Juan squatted and watched the women hang the baskets from a tree and secure the bottom to the ground with a string. Starting at the top, they squeezed the tipitis to force out the excess water from the washings. They then removed the pulpy mass through a sieve, and it was ready to toast on a flat ceramic griddle or a cooking stone.

I wonder if these were the same women Jack watched six months ago, Claire thought, *in the same clearing?* As she observed the women roll the white mass into four-inch balls and place them in clean baskets, Claire speculated what they might find upriver. Or not find. *Is Jack still up there, somewhere in the Amazon Basin? If so, what has he been doing for half a year? Is he alive? Where in Heaven's name have you gone, Jack?* A year and a half ago, they were simply three best friends whose lives were about academics, art, and adventure, and it seemed like yesterday. But her thoughts gave her pause. She hadn't listed love. Maybe their times together were never simple for Jack. Perhaps life as a vagabond in South America was the simplicity he craved. If so, how will he react to being found? It was too much for her to bear. She rose off her haunches and smiled sadly at Juan, voicelessly thanking him for the educational treat. And she walked back alone to the lodge.

🐜

Susana's nephew arrived at about three o'clock in the afternoon from Puerto Maldonado, downriver. Again, the children ran down to the river's edge as soon as someone said there was a boat approaching. Claire had already been near the water, leaning against a palm tree reading, and Casey was nearby, killing time. Al walked down to the riverbank when he heard the outboard, and Juan just appeared next to them out of nowhere.

Beating against the current of the Rio Madre de Dios, it took some time for the boatman to run the vessel alongside the village loading area. Juan stood by the bank to help catch the boat's bow and tie its bowline to a tree.

Interpreting for Juan, Alberto said, "This is Marco, Susana's nephew." And added, "Juan says we will like him."

Marco shut off the sixty-horse outboard engine, tilted it up and locked it into position with the propeller out of the water, and walked from the stern of the boat to midship. He deftly skipped from the gunwale to the grassy bank and shook Juan's hand. The two men spoke for a few minutes, and then Juan asked Alberto to introduce Marco to Casey and Claire. To their surprise, Marco shook their hands and said, "Juan tells me you're looking for Jack?"

The two Americans were taken aback.

"Yes, we are," Claire said, surprised by his English. "You know him?" Just in case, Claire handed him a photograph of their friend, and Marco looked at it and quickly handed it back to her.

"Jack hired me to take him upriver about a week after Christmas. He has lost some weight since that photo."

Casey and Claire exchanged glances.

Casey asked, "Can you show us on a map where you took him? How was he?"

Alberto, ever mindful of his surroundings and considerate of people, interjected before Marco could happily respond — which he was ready to do. Al gestured to the boat. "Maybe we could help Marco unload his supplies for the village, and then after he has cleaned up and said hello to his family, we could buy him supper and ask him the details." "Of course," Casey said.

"That would be helpful," Marco said. It took forty minutes to unload the boat and stack everything in the center of the clearing near one of the communal picnic tables. Almost as soon as the supplies were stacked, people from the village began unpacking items and hauling them off. Marco seemed uncaring as to who took what. It was an everyday routine. Marco then walked back down to the boat and secured two more lines. He removed the key from the outboard and performed a few more maintenance duties. Then he walked back up the bank.

He looked at Claire, Casey, and Alberto, sitting at one of the picnic tables, patiently waiting. Juan had wandered off, but it felt like he wasn't far.

"Thank you for your help," he said. "So, I can assume Jack did not come back downriver?"

"Not that we know of," Claire said. Marco nodded pensively.

"Then how about we meet in a half-hour at my aunt's café?"

"Yes, that would be good," Alberto said.

⚶

Marco was right on time. It was late afternoon now, and the sweltering, humid heat of the Amazon was letting up a little. Everyone sat around the big wooden table outside the café. Susana appeared from inside the kitchen area with the capuchin still perched on her shoulder like a Jazzbo Jim. Juan reappeared from the jungle but not from the direction of the lodge.

"In the past six months, I've been either here or downriver in Puerto Maldonado," Marco said. "If Jack came through either place, I believe I would have known about it. But of course, it's not 100%."

Casey took out the map. By now, it was becoming cracked along the frequently folded seams. "Can you show us where you took him?" He laid a pencil on the map.

Marco regarded the map. He made three marks near the Manu River, upstream from the village, which he circled. "You must understand — the river, it shifts, and the channel changes, sometimes each year. It (he searched for the correct word) *moves,* like a snake."

He pointed to the pencil mark farthest upriver. "This place here is eighty-five nautical miles from where we sit. But it is about 120 river miles. It is a research station where they study plants and animals." Marco dragged his index finger approximately twenty-five miles back downriver — closer to where they now were.

"This is where I dropped Jack."

To the friends, those words were like a punch in the gut. Casey and Claire were stunned. Alberto sat back and shifted uncomfortably in his plastic chair. In Boca Manu, they felt they were in the middle of nowhere. They were days from any medical help, and there were dangers all around them. As Al said, everything in this jungle wanted to sting, stick, bite, or suck them. They could add "wants to transmit some disease into them" and "swim up their urethra" to the list. The Sendero Luminoso was getting more active, though even they did not want to contend with the searing heat and dangers of the jungle this far into the Amazon Basin.

Now, Marco was indicating a place on the map infinitely more remote. Al looked at Marco. So far on the quest, this young man sitting across from them was the last person to speak to Jack.

"We agreed I'd go back for him in ten days," Marco said, "but he was not there. I didn't know his last name or where he was from. I went back five days later, and still, he was not there. After that, I kept my ears and eyes opened and talked to other boatmen. I told the rangers at the Manu Preserve station also. Speaking with you is the first news I've heard of Jack."

The table was quiet.

Alberto broke the silence. "Okay. I'm going to ask Marco a few questions. We need to gather some information before we decide what to do next, and we all need to be informed." He looked at Casey, who was funding the operation. "Are you okay with that Case?"

Casey nodded.

Al took a small notepad from his shirt pocket. He looked at Marco. "If you can just answer them with short sentences, that will be helpful."

Marco nodded.

Alberto fired away. "How long is the trip upriver to the farthest mark you made on the map?"

"This time of year, three days upriver, two days back," Marco replied.

"Are you and your boat available for hire for the next eight days?"

"I can do seven."

"Do you remember any of the conversations between you and Jack on the three days you took him upriver?"

"I do."

"What is the passenger capacity of your boat, with gear?"

"Eight."

"What is your fee for guiding us for the seven days?"

"In U.S. dollars, I will do it for $250, but you will need to buy some petrol, which will be," he thought for a moment, "about $55."

Alberto looked at Casey, who nodded.

Al asked one more question. "Can we leave tomorrow?"

"As soon as we have food and petrol, we can."

Alberto reached across the table and shook Marco's hand. "Excellent." Everyone was happy with the arrangement.

"Marco," Claire asked, "how is it you speak English so well?"

"I am at school downriver in Puerto Maldonado. There is a Catholic secondary school there that offers a correspondence program through the University in Cusco. I take some classes there, and occasionally I have to travel to the city to take exams. When I do, I always sit in on some classes while I'm there. I have a class next week, which is why I can do only seven days."

"What are you studying?" asked Claire.

"Ecology and Government. I've applied for the Peruvian Diplomatic Academy in Lima for next year. My hope is for a career in Peru's Ministry of Foreign Affairs. I want to work in the diplomatic service."

"I think you'll be great at that," Alberto said. Marco smiled and nodded. There was a lull in the conversation. Casey looked around the table; there was Claire, gorgeous, smart, and capable in all things. By this time next year, she would be a newly minted archaeologist with a Ph.D. And there was Alberto, *The Man*, worldly, competent, and able. Then there was Juan, a walking enigma who it seemed had seen a great deal in his life and was a born protector with high values. Finally, there was Marco, who probably might be President of Peru someday, or should be. All of them sitting around a beat-up picnic table in the middle of the Amazon jungle. Casey was feeling a little outmatched, which he wasn't used to. *I'm just a want-to-be adventurer*, he thought. Without Jack, he felt he was lacking some of the confidence he had on previous travels. He missed his friend.

Juan broke the silence and said something to Alberto, who then asked Marco, "Has there been any Sendero Luminoso activity in the Manu?"

Marco shook his head. "Not this far upriver. I think it's too hot and too buggy." He smiled. "There is a small presence in Puerto Maldonado, but they have taken no action there. I know who they are. If we were to run into them here, I think they would only rob us. But I have heard in some of the cities, the Sendero only want to murder. It's a terrible thing what they are doing to this country."

"Do you think they will have any success in starting a revolution?" Claire asked.

Marco again shook his head. "They are too militant…too dogmatic, and they are killing the peasants — the people they are supposed to be freeing from oppression. They are terrorizing them. The peasants in the rural areas are only uneducated … they're not stupid. Though the government military is also tormenting the locals in some situations. The peasants will not cave into the Sendero and start an armed revolution."

He thought for a moment before continuing. "I believe the military will eventually find the head of the snake and cut it off. But already, there will be much healing to do in Peru. I worry that giving the military carte blanche to try to end the Sendero will lead to even more government corruption than already exists here. We need to be smart, and we need some — what is the word? — *restraint* in our response to the terrorists and to those poor people caught in the middle, the people we're trying to protect."

"Yup," Alberto said, smiling at Marco. "Diplomat."

Marco glanced at Al and said, "Also, if anyone wants to send letters home, now is the time. The mail will go from here to Puerto Maldonado tomorrow. It will take at least two, maybe three weeks to get to Boston from here."

Marco took a drink of Fanta and looked at his plate. "I hope we find your friend."

FORTY-THREE
Science & Seeking Clues

arco's boat was interesting. Casey wasn't surprised to learn that the young man had built it himself. It had more of a sweeping bow than the other boats he'd seen in their few days on the river, and the dark blue canopy was new and attractive. The box lid over the spare outboard engine served as a tabletop for a cookstove or a convenient place to spread out a map.

Claire handed Marco the letters she and Casey had written to their parents, the Beal's, and Dr. Fitzroy since arriving in Peru, along with some cash for postage. Marco called to a teenager who had been watching them with curiosity. He pulled a few Peruvian Intis from his pocket and gave the boy the cash and letters. With his hand on the teenager's shoulder, he gave him instructions. The boy nodded, said something in Matsigenka, and walked up the bank.

"He can be trusted," Marco announced.

By the time the boat was loaded, it was eight o'clock in the morning, and it was already sweltering and humid. Claire's cotton shirt was soaked with sweat as she climbed aboard the boat and chose a seat amidship. Scattered about in the boat were things that vaguely resembled life jackets, which everyone used as seat cushions. Once they were all settled, Marco started the outboard engine and let it idle in neutral. He then cast off the stern rope and let the boat swing around in the current as the bow, which was still tied fast to a tree trunk, hugged the riverbank. Juan untied the bowline and pushed away from the bank. With a kick of his leg, he jumped into the bow. Marco flipped the engine into forwarding gear, and the boat lurched ahead into the Manu's current. They were off.

Marco seemed to move the boat quite fast, considering all the shoals, shallows, floating trees, and other debris in the river's channel. Juan rode in the bow and kept an eye out for flotsam. He kept a long wooden pole nearby to fend off obstacles. Being the dry season, getting upriver was going to be tricky.

Under normal circumstances, Marco would be taking either tourists or researchers upriver, and he would be deftly pointing out wildlife as they motored ahead in the coffee-colored water. He would name the primates they could see in the trees along the banks and would point out and describe the giant river otters, some of the 800 species of birds, or the huge rodents, the capybaras. On two previous excursions, Marco had seen the elusive Giant Anteater. Normally, Marco would poke about conversationally with his group. He'd remind them that the Reserved Zone in Manu National Park, the large swathe of land along the length of the Manu River set aside for scientific research and eco-tourism, has one of the highest concentrations of biodiversity on earth. It is arguably *the* highest. If his passengers were researchers, he would then expound on the natural wonders of the reserve from a local's point of view.

But these were not normal circumstances, and this was a very different sort of trip.

Marco ran the boat into the river's current, expertly reading the water with a seemingly innate knowledge of where the ever-changing channel was. The river's serpentine course slowed travel considerably. The lowland rainforest, towering above the riverbanks, rolled by, and as the boat progressed against the current, hundreds of birds leaped from the trees and flew to new perches. Claire could see monkeys scurrying in the canopy, jumping from limb to limb in the tops of palms and the massive Ceiba trees, some of which were 200 feet tall.

Claire speculated about Jack. *Still odd*, she thought, *that he would just take off and bum around South America, potentially throwing away all that education. What was he really looking for? Was he running from me? Or was he just running for the sake of it?* She looked into the cocoa-colored water as it swirled by and then looked back up at the thick forest and the birds scattering in all directions. *If he's looking for a wild place, this is it.*

Suddenly Juan's voice broke through the drone of the outboard engine. He picked up his wooden pole as he called back to Marco in Spanish, who backed off on the throttle and veered slightly to port. Something was floating in the river. As Marco inched forward against the current, the thing approached the boat on the starboard side. It looked like a body.

"Is it human?" Casey asked. No one answered.

As it drifted closer, Marco slowed the boat even more against the current so that he was almost standing still in the river. As the body floated alongside, they could see that it had fur, and it looked like a bloated cow.

"Tapir," Juan called out. "*Uno grande.*"

When it got to the stern, Marco said, "It looks like 2, maybe 250 kilos. A big one."

The head was pointing upriver, and as it floated past, Claire could see its droopy, flexible trunk and the tiny eyes set far back on the forehead, which were whitish-grey now that it was dead. She looked at Marco, who shrugged and said, "It is beautiful here, but it is easy to die in the jungle. It probably drowned trying to swim across." Then he opened the throttle, and the outboard answered. He had to raise his voice over the engine. "We are here — around the next bend." Alberto, Claire, and Casey all glanced in Marco's direction. He saw the looks on their faces. He had forgotten for a moment that this was a search, not a tour group.

"Sorry, I should have given you more warning. This is a Mastigenka community." Marco was still shouting over the drone of the engine. "This is where I left Jack a few days after last Christmas." Claire and Casey turned their attention back to the riverbank in anticipation. There was a remote possibility that Jack was still there living with the locals. If so, he would have heard the motor and might be standing on the edge of the river, waiting to see who was approaching. Alberto heard Marco and nodded approval. He was all business. Juan was sitting on the bench seat in front of Al, who leaned forward and said something to him. Juan stiffened and trained his eyes on the shoreline.

Claire and Casey could make out some huts built on stilts with their thatched rooftops through the rain forest canopy in the bend. A small tuft of smoke drifted up through the canopy, and both friends momentarily forgot about the oppressive, stifling midday heat.

Marco eased the vessel around to the inside of the river's bend and against the right bank. The boat rounded the bend and was only fifty feet from the edge of the village, which was set in a large clearing. Children were already congregating next to the bank. Some were swimming and stayed in the water as the boat swung toward them. Marco was standing in the stern. He yelled at the kids in the Matsigenka language, and they clambered up onto the bank. Three native men were standing among the children, and one of them waved at Marco.

There was no sign of Jack.

※

Marco let off on the throttle as Juan tossed the bowline to one of the Matsigenka men, who deftly tied it around a tree stump. Once it was secure, he cut the engine. The boat's stern swung against the shore, and Marco jumped out and tied it to a tree.

"*Néga pijáque?*" *Where are you going?* One of the Matsigenka men asked Marco.

"*Naniáquemíni,*" *I am visiting you,* Marco replied.

Marco looked at Casey. "Could you please hand me the blue box?"

Casey handed up an old Inca Cola shipping box filled with processed food. As he did, everyone stepped from the boat. Once on the bank, Claire asked, "*¿Baño?*"

Marco asked something in Matsigenka, and the men pointed toward the north side of the village. "It is there, just beyond the edge of the clearing. Claire…just so you know, it is a trench.."

Claire nodded and walked across the clearing. Several of the small children followed her. Juan, Casey, and Alberto followed Marco up the bank. The three men and the children who hadn't followed Claire to the latrine accompanied them. Casey surveyed the village. The stilted huts were built more crudely than the other Amazon villages they had seen. The dwellings encompassed the village, which extended two hundred yards into the jungle. In the center of the huts was a communal cooking pit, an oval hearth made of stones about ten feet long, with a dozen crude log benches placed around it. There was no litter, as in some of the villages, and the air smelled sweet despite the oppressive heat.

Casey and Alberto sat on a separate bench next to Marco's while Juan strolled the village's perimeter. Marco sat on one of the benches, and the Matsigenka elder men rested opposite him. Marco asked the men if they remembered when he had been there with Jack six months ago, and they did. He asked the elders a few more questions before apprising his passengers.

Marco spoke directly to Casey and Al. "As I mentioned before, when I was here with Jack, we had agreed that I would come back for him in ten days. When I did, Jack was gone. He had left word for me that he had followed the river north — upriver — searching for an illegal logging operation about four days' walk from here. The message said I should not worry and that he would find another boat ride downriver when he returned. I did not mention some of these details earlier because I wanted to check with these people first to see if they had seen Jack since or had heard anything. I wanted the information from this place, the *place last seen*, to be accurate."

"And did they ..." Casey asked, "see him again?"

"They did not," Marco said. No one spoke for a minute.

"Okay," Alberto said. "That's something to work with. We know he's on this side of the river, and he's upriver."

Al gave Marco a stern look. "I think you might have told us that yesterday." Then he let it go. Al was weighing his disappointment with the risk of affecting his relationship with the young man, who was clearly the most capable guy they could have with them right now. He lightened his voice.

"Anything else?"

Marco shook his head.

Alberto patted Marco's shoulder.

Just then, Claire returned, with children still in tow. "So much for privacy," she said. "I don't think they've seen blonde hair like mine too many times."

"Your ponytail is covered with your neckerchief," Casey said. Claire looked at him and winced as she shook her head. "Not that hair." "Oh," Casey said, trying unsuccessfully not to smile.

As she sat down, she said, "Obviously, nudity isn't regarded the same way to these folks. I felt like a stripper. I'm just trying to put it behind me."

"It's *not* regarded the same here," Al said. "You're a seasoned traveler. I'm sure you handled it well. I'll catch you up; Jack left here on foot to hike upriver to try to find an illegal logging operation, presumably to photograph it to report it even though the corrupt government already knows they are in certain areas when they're cutting. Marco had originally left him here so Jack could spend time with these Matsigenka. When he returned for him, he had gone. Jack left a message with these men. They have not seen him since."

Claire lowered her head.

Al spoke to the group. "We can stay here tonight and in the morning continue upriver. See what we can find. I think we should go up at least as far as the Cocha Sacha Research Station. Marco, how far to Cocha?"

"With the river down like this, at least three hours."

Alberto nodded. "Also, many of the indigenous groups living in the Manu are nomadic, as these Matsigenka once were. It's possible we could meet some along the way who might have seen Jack. We can camp along the river for a few nights while we search. Does anyone have some input?"

"Nothing," Casey said, "but perhaps we should ask Juan what he thinks."

"I will ask him," Al said, "but he will go along with any plan unless he sees a real problem."

Marco asked the elders some more questions, and they answered with long, drawn-out responses.

"The people in the Manu are facing the same problems indigenous people have for centuries, all over the world," Marco said. "These men are telling me stories. They talk of new clashes between tribes that haven't occurred since the rape of cultures when the rubber extraction companies were in the Manu a hundred years ago. Now it's the loggers, and in some areas, it's oil workers."

"Does the government try to help?" Alberto asked.

"They do — a little, but the area is so vast and difficult to travel in. The authorities cannot do much."

"Do these men have any guesses where Jack may have gone?" Claire asked.

Marco shook his head. "No. But they mentioned that back in December, the loggers were at the mouth of a tributary river that flows from the east — but it's all a guess. They do not have names for months. They speak of time in moons, and they do not celebrate Christmas.

"These men also expressed concern for us. There have been more and more sightings and interactions with uncontacted tribes lately. They tell me the tribe's territories are on the west bank of the Manu. This time of year, the primitive tribes come down to the beaches to fish and search for turtle eggs. In the last two years, they have been shooting arrows at travelers as they motor up and down the river. These elders tell me it is because the tribes are feeling pressured by the loggers, even though the only loggers I'm aware of are on the east bank. The overharvesting of the forest makes the uncontacted groups move into different territories, like the Matsigenka's. Most of the time, when the tribes are contacted, they run away into the forest. But, increasingly, it is becoming violent. These are not the words these men used, but it was their meaning."

Alberto again nodded. "It is an ageless story. Just like in America or East Africa."

"We all know Jack," Claire said to Casey and Alberto. "He cares about things, and he cares about life. I could see him getting wrapped up in a cause like what the indigenous people are going through. He also will know not to make close contact with the tribes who have built up few immunities."

Casey looked back at her. They all took plates from Marco, heaped with plantains, creamy-white manioc, and fried tiger fish, a type of catfish that was wrapped and roasted in palm leaves along with onions, chilis, and rice.

Claire had to hold the plate aside because as she ate, sweat dripped steadily off the tip of her nose. She liked the manioc. "It's like potatoes," she said, "but with a sweet, nutty taste." Two of the older boys, who had followed her to the latrine and had squatted directly in front of her as she relieved herself, now sat behind her in the shade at the edge of the clearing, staring intently. "And the texture," she continued about the manioc from the pulverized cassava root, "I like the grainy texture."

As they ate lunch, Alberto — speaking through Marco — continued to ask the elders questions.

"They are speaking of the scientists upriver," said Marco. "They think Jack tried to walk there. I am sure they are talking about Cocha Sacha. I do not know how long it would take to walk there because much of the river, you cannot walk alongside it … there are swamps where the river continuously floods that you would have to go around. Some of the swamps would take days to walk around, and it would be very easy to get lost." Marco paused. "The swamps can be dangerous."

"Like snakes?" Casey asked.

"Si, snakes. But also, spiders, piraña, and those tribes — what do you call them — 'the uncontacted?' Those people also have to walk around the swamps, and the trails they make are tempting for people like you and me to follow. It is much easier walking, but there is a higher chance of running into them." Marco saw Claire lower her head. "But, most of them are on the other side of the river."

"Piranha?" Casey asked. "Everyone has told us they won't bite when we wash off or swim in the river."

"That is true," Marco said. "I saw an old black-and-white movie once where men tried to wade across a small jungle stream and suddenly were devoured by piraña. In only a minute, they were only bones. Silly movie. That's just Hollywood. But, you have learned that the rivers flood all the time, sometimes twice in one week. When they flood, they recede quickly, leaving small swamps or pools where there were none. If the river does not flood to that height again for months, hundreds of fish can get trapped in the pools. As the pools evaporate and the fish begin to starve, it can be very dangerous to step into that water. Remember that. You would probably not be devoured unless you completely fell in, but before you could pull your leg out of the water, there could be dozens of deep, oval gouges down to the muscle. In the jungle, it would be almost impossible to keep them from getting infected. If you were walking on the backside of one of these swamps, you could be many days from the proper medicine."

Marco looked at Casey and Claire. "Señorita Claire, do not worry about your friend Jack. Six months ago, Jack and I spoke the same conversation. We talked many hours about signs to watch for and where the dangers lie in the jungle." Marco was as smart as anyone in the group, and he was guessing that for Claire, Jack might be more than just a friend.

"What was that *Cocha* place they think he was headed to?" Casey asked.

"Cocha Sacha," Marco said. "A research ... *instalaciones*?" He looked at Alberto.

"Yes, it is a research facility upriver," Alberto said. "It is located on a small oxbow lake a short distance from the river. The name Cocha Sacha is Quechua and means, I think, 'Wild Lake,' but it's really an ancient, sixty-acre section of the river that was left as a standing body of water when the river changed course many years ago. I have never been to the facility, but I have always wanted to visit. It started as a tiny research campsite about seventeen years ago by a German scientist studying black caimans, which were almost extinct. For the last thirteen years, it has been run by an American who is studying, among other things, ecology and conservation.

"In fact, I was on my way to see the facility when I took the photos of the Mascho Piru that Jack saw in the Explorer's Club in Lima. We were just upriver from here when we saw them. They were on the other side." Alberto looked down at the river. "Right after I snapped the photos, we had engine trouble. We paddled over to this side and tied to the bank while we changed to the spare outboard. Unfortunately, we could not get that one started. It was a nightmare. We had to drift and paddle back to Boca Manu. It took us three days. The whole last day, we were without drinking water."

"You have been there, Marco?" Casey asked.

"Si. A few times to bring scientists. Once to drop off supplies. It's pretty cool."

"Then we should go straight there," Casey said. "This Cocha Sacha place. You said it's three hours upriver?"

"Yes." Marco looked at his watch, as did Alberto.

"I say we finish quickly and mount up," Case said.

For the first time on the trip, Juan spoke up without being asked anything. "*No creo que debamos irnos a Cocha Sacha ahora*".

"No?" replied Alberto, who translated for Casey and Claire; "He thinks we should not go To Cocha now."

Juan shook his head. It was odd to hear him contribute. He, Alberto, and Marco conversed for a few moments, then Al said, "Juan says we shouldn't go to Cocha this late in the afternoon. He said the people there are friendly scientists, but they do not know we are coming, and it might be an inconvenience for them to help us find places to set up our tents. He said even in the jungle, it pays not to be rude. Plus, the facility is a six-minute walk through the forest. He also said that if we were to have any engine trouble, we would be trying to find and set up a camp in the dark. He thinks it would be best to go in the morning."

There was no discussion. Juan had spoken.

The group set their tents up along the edge of the clearing on the opposite side of the latrine. They did not crowd the villagers. The evening was spent walking the jungle trails that extended from the village clearing like spokes on a wagon wheel. Marco took Claire and Casey down one of the trails to a salt lick about a kilometer from the river. As the afternoon light squeezed through the jungle canopy, parrots by the hundreds came to the lick — a rare seam of concentrated minerals on the exposed side of a small hummock that seemed half earth, half wall of forest trees.

Casey stood still, pondering the cackling mass of birds.

Claire drew sketches of the lick in her journal and took a few photographs, but her heart wasn't in the moment. *Fuck*, she thought, *has Jack ruined everything for me?* She had felt disconnected with things over the past year, which she chalked up to Jack's disappearance — even art, the thing in which she most easily found solace. Occasionally, when she saw something interesting or wonderful, like a beautiful salt lick in the Amazon, she would feel ill instead of absorbing the moment and enjoying it. She did not like that. She knew it was because she did not know if Jack was alive or not — or ever coming back. And she knew it was not because she harbored some hope of living her life with him. Claire was past that. She simply wanted to know that he was all right and to tell him she was also. She wanted to talk to him.

After thirty minutes of watching the parrots, the three travelers returned to the village. There was only an hour of daylight left. Marco and Alberto had a campfire going and had set upside-down crates around it as seats. They had prepared a simple meal of fried bread, soup, and plenty of fruit. Juan was late for supper. He had spent the afternoon walking the jungle trails and circling the village's periphery. At opportune moments, he had spoken with the village elders. When he rejoined the group after dark, he was soaked with sweat. Before sitting on one of the crates, he walked to the edge of the clearing with a towel and a large pail of water. He took off his Panama shirt, exposing a sinewy brown torso lined with scars here-and-there. He poured the water over his head. He brushed back his thick, black hair, which, though he was sixty, was without even a touch of grey, and did his best to towel off some of the jungle funk.

Claire removed her gaze from Juan and looked at Casey, who was staring into the small campfire. She noticed Casey had been quiet for quite a while, and then it occurred to her that he had been quiet the entire trip.

"What do you think tomorrow will bring?" she asked.

Casey shook his head slowly. "I fear it will bring no leads. Or maybe worse, *some* leads that only go farther into the jungle. But, who knows … maybe we'll get lucky. Maybe we'll find him."

Casey stared back into the yellow, red, and blue flames. After a moment, he said, "I hope you are prepared for finding him, just in case."

"I want to find him," she shot back.

"I know," he said, "but, you know … if he wanted to come home, he would have. I just worry about you too."

Claire looked away from him into the small, mesmerizing fire. They were close. She could feel it. Close to Jack, or maybe just close to his story, she didn't know which. Hell, he might be only three miles away. It had been a long year, and she was feeling tired. She got up and put her hand on Casey's shoulder as she stepped over her crate. Case touched her hand for only a second. Tomorrow would be a big day.

Then she said goodnight and walked to her tent.

FORTY-FOUR

Two Weeks!

The boat was loaded quickly. In the early morning light, giant otters played in the water eighty feet from the riverbank. The jungle dawn smelled sweet but was already hot and humid. Marco pulled the chord on the outboard, and it coughed once, sputtered and spit, and finally found a nice, smooth idle. Juan kicked the bow off the bank, and they were off. Claire waved at the children who remained fixated on her, and only one of the smallest of them raised his hand slightly.

The river seemed lower, but Marco deftly negotiated the sunken tree snags, tiny islands, and floating debris. Marco hollered up from the stern. He was pointing into the water.

"All these pieces of bark and branches!" Marco called out. "They're logging somewhere upriver."

The boat weaved around the obstructions for an hour. Claire and Casey no longer watched the omnipresent monkeys on the riverbank, nor did they watch for interesting birds. Instead, they scanned the banks for people, those nomadic tribesmen who might have seen or heard about Jack, but they saw no one.

After a while, Al tried to cut the tension. His friends were scientists, after all, and he thought maybe they would like Cocha Sacha. Speaking up over the hum of the engine, he said, "I read recently that four years ago at Cocha Sacha, some ornithologists from the States set a single-day sighting world record, logging 331 species. Amazing."

Casey smiled, and Claire said, "Yes — truly amazing."

Claire dared to think that Jack would get excited about such a place. Maybe enough to stay… then she brushed the thought from her mind.

Focus on what is real, she told herself.

Once again, she thought back over the trip the three had taken the previous year. She went over the incredible sights they had seen in the mountains. She thought about the spirit of Ausangate and of the horrific story of the pathetic women in chains who were forced to wash in the freezing stream and how Jack had told her with tears in his eyes how they were treated worse than cattle. She forced that thought from her head, and flowing in from behind were images of her evening with Jack on the banks of the Urubabmba River near Ollanta. The new thoughts made her feel at once melancholic and warm, but regret followed closely behind, and she wished she'd made love to him that night.

Casey's voice snapped her out of her trance. He had been doing the same thing — thinking of their trip.

"What's the last thing you've heard about your ruins?" he asked. "Did the authorities ever correspond with what they found at the Sendero camp, or whatever it was?"

"They sent a few short notes to Dr. Fitzroy, and she read them to me over the phone. The message said when the military flew there by helicopter, the camp had been moved. But, Jack's photographs got all the way to President Garcia— the images were undisputable. He was so moved he ordered a special task force be made up of commandos to explore the whole eastern side of the range to look for similar camps."

Casey nodded. "Good. But I wish they had caught them. Who knows where those poor girls ended up."

It was too depressing to think about. Casey scanned the riverbanks again. Then he said, "Jack's photos ... they made a difference."

Claire offered a smile, and smiles were rare on this trip. "I wonder if he knows that."

Another hour went by. It was monotonous and getting unbearably hot. Everyone except Juan looked uncomfortable as they shifted their butts on the hard, wooden bench seats while trying to stay in the shade of the boat's blue canvas canopy. Claire watched Casey open his map halfway. His finger traced the lines of the river. It was serpentine ... it resembled the fan-folded loops of intestines. His finger stopped at a guess, halfway through a rare semi-straight section of the river. Then he moved his finger to the east — and then it traced a sharp turn back to the north. He tapped the river on the far side of the loop. He looked at Claire.

"I think we're close."

In less than a minute, Casey pointed to the right bank. There was something manmade.

Marco slowed the motor slightly when they were less than a hundred yards from what could now be seen as a small shed in a tiny clearing and a sign. Juan looked back at Marco, who nodded once. Juan picked up the coiled bowline, and Marco pointed the boat into a small, naturally occurring notch in the bank, big enough to accommodate one boat. Juan jumped ashore and swung the rope around a tree trunk. Marco stabilized the stern with his pole while everyone climbed onto the riverbank. He then disembarked and tied off the stern.

"This is where they store fuel tanks, motors, and other equipment," he said, pointing into the shed. Next to the shed, there was a well-worn trail into the forest. "Please, grab your day packs and water bottles. If there is room for us and they accept us as guests, we will come back for the tents and our food."

Within a minute, they were all hiking down the trail. Already this place seemed different. There were more birds than usual, and it seemed every few feet there were frogs, toads, and tiny snakes scurrying away. In the first 200-yards, Claire saw a half-dozen bird species that were new to her. Five minutes into the walk, the group heard something — certainly, a mammal — crash through the jungle underbrush.

Two minutes later, Marco led the group into another small forest clearing holding several modest, rustic, thatched-roof buildings. To the left was what looked to be the main building which looked out over a small, beautiful, placid lake. A rickety dock jutted out into the water was front of the two-story building. There was another smaller building nearby with a water tower and gas canisters attached to the outside. Across from that building were a small greenhouse and a wall-less structure where plants were hanging from cords and drying on two large tables. There was a large floor space in the center of that building, with an easel surrounded by at least twenty plastic chairs.

There were other small buildings for offices and laboratory work. All the structures were built a few feet off the ground on a foundation of wooden pilings. Laundry hung from several clotheslines stretched between trees.

On the edge of the compound stood a long, thin structure with the only metal roof. There was a small deck surrounding the entire building, and under the roof were six shower stalls with curtains. At one end were two bathrooms; at the other stood two porcelain pedestal sinks.

There was no sign of anyone. The place seemed deserted.

As everyone looked around, Casey walked to the edge of the lake and inspected the dock. Claire peered into the laboratory and offices. In the main building, there was a short-wave radio. The offices had bookshelves and small blackboards. One of the chalkboards had what looked to Claire to be an unfinished proof with the title underneath, *Mathematical Models of Plant Growth for Applications in Agriculture, Forestry, and Ecology.*

Oh, yeah, she thought, *this is Jack's kind of place.*

A voice cracked from the far edge of the clearing. "Well, what have we here, lost pilgrims on the trail for ecological enlightenment?"

A tall, fit, middle-aged man strolled from one of the forest trails emanating from the field station. He was an interesting-looking man who walked with a gentleness and sported a pencil-thin mustache like the kind Errol Flynn wore. Then the tall man recognized Marco and stepped toward him, but Alberto moved forward and held out his hand. The man smiled at Al and grasped it.

"Alberto Sanz Montero, from Cusco."

"Pleased to meet you. I am John Liddell, the director of this facility. How can we help you folks?"

"Well, sir, I think that our quest is not a usual one for you — not your typical visitation here at Cocha Sacha. May we all sit somewhere if you have a moment?"

John raised an eyebrow. His interest was piqued. He gestured toward the main building. "Certainly. This way."

Each climbed the short stairway to the open room in the largest building. One could look out onto the dock and lake from anywhere in the room. Besides the plastic chairs around the perimeter, the room was filled with study materials and plant samples. Various daypacks littered the room where students had left them, apparently after a recent lecture. Everyone pulled up a chair while Al introduced each traveler. He introduced Casey and Claire as graduate students studying archaeology at Harvard.

"You might know Marco, boatman extraordinaire from Boca Manu, who has delivered supplies here before." The director kindly nodded at

Marco, who again smiled back but remained silent. "And this is Juan Gonzales, who is helping us on our journey."

"Well," the professor offered, as I said, I am John Liddell. I am the director here under the auspices of the government of Peru. I am on staff at Princeton," he smiled and looked kindly at Claire and Casey, "but I did both my undergraduate and post-grad studies at Harvard, completing my doctorate in plant physiology in 1963." (It was obvious he only mentioned that out of an academic connection to Claire and Casey.) "I arrived at Cocha in 1973 and have been tied to a chair here ever since."

Alberto, the de facto diplomat and public relations expert, asked how much time they might have to speak with him.

"I have an hour before the students come in out of the field. I hope that will be enough time."

Alberto, his hands folded in front of him on the table, said, "Claire or Casey, do either of you want to fill in the professor?"

"Call me John, please," the professor said.

Claire and Casey looked at each other, hoping the other would volunteer. Finally, Casey spoke up. "A year and a half ago, Claire and I took a month off with our best friend to travel around Peru — mostly the Sacred Valley region — to see ruins and possibly climb a mountain … do a little fly fishing. We sought adventure, and with Al's help, we got it. Unfortunately, we witnessed something wicked. Certain things transpired, and our friend stayed behind in Peru and has been missing for most of the past year. He was in the graduate program with us and has forfeited that. We have had minimal correspondence with him, and his family is worried about him."

Casey hesitated, searching for what else he ought to say. "I figured he was traveling around Peru trying to find himself, or some such thing. Anyway, we've come to try to find him."

John sat back in his chair and placed his hands on his thighs. Everyone at the table was fixated on him. Then he spoke.

"Is his name Jack Beal?"

There was a brief moment of stillness at the table. Al and Casey exchanged looks but said nothing.

Then Claire spoke, trying hard to suppress the emotion in her voice. "Yes, it is."

John weighed his words. "Jack was here for quite some time. He worked for me as a volunteer for almost six months. I fed him, and he researched spider monkeys for me. He's quite brilliant. I must tell you; I became very attached to him and was sad to see him leave."

Casey stiffened in his chair and started to speak, but Alberto beat him to it.

"Where did he go?"

"That's the problem," John replied. "I guess the pull of anthropology hasn't left him. He said he wanted to explore to the north and try to find and photograph some of the uncontacted indigenous people who inhabit the Manu Reserve."

Casey's head bent down, and he stared at the table. Claire looked at Alberto, who asked the obvious questions.

"Did he leave word of exactly where he was headed? How long ago did he leave? Did he go over any maps with you?"

"I'll tell you everything, but being his friends, I fear it will be difficult for you to hear ..." John had a slightly pained look on his face, "... that Jack left here on the 6ᵗʰ."

"Of June?!" Casey asked.

"Yes."

Casey was shocked. "Two weeks ago! He was here at Cocha Sacha two weeks ago!" They had just missed him, but somewhere deep inside, Casey was the rational scientist trying to tell himself that this only meant he couldn't be far away. He was feeling emotional, to say the least.

"I'm very sorry that you missed him. More than you know," John said.

Alberto reached to his left and took Claire's hand in his. A single tear rolled down her cheek. John saw it and folded his hands on the table, and looked down at them.

"We all just need to process this for a second," Al said. Then he took out his notebook.

"Okay, John," he said. "Please fill us in on some of the details so we might be able to make a plan and move forward."

"Surely. We talked about the indigenous peoples' plight many times after the day's research was finished. Jack had maps and made notes. He was appalled at the devastating effect of illegal logging on the tribes. He said if it were to continue, the tribes would be forced out of their traditional territories within twenty years because the logging would decimate their food sources. They would then clash with each other, with the loggers, even with researchers. He said it was a hopeful scenario, for it could be dealt with. He thought it more likely diseases from the proximity of the loggers would wipe them out quickly. Exterminate them. He got it into his head to write a seminal paper on the plight of the 'Uncontacted.' It seemed to me that he felt he had found his calling. So, there was no talking him out of it, which I tried to do."

"I imagine you could not," Claire said. "Not because he is headstrong, but because he truly cares about others more than himself."

John put up an index finger, so no one followed up with any questions for a full thirty seconds. "Let me ask you some things about yourselves. Is that fair enough?"

Alberto leaned back. "Of course, John. Sorry for asking so much so fast. We are anxious for news."

John smiled and nodded once. He opened his hand palm-up toward Casey. "You are best friends? How long have you known each other?"

"Since freshman year of undergraduate. Day one, actually. And yes, Jack is my best friend. The best friend I've ever had."

"And you make the third amigo, Claire?"

"Yes. Jack and I are very close." She looked down as she said that.

"Alberto, you were their guide on the trip a year ago?"

"That is correct. We spent a month together a year ago, but I will say that by the end of the trip, I regarded Claire, Casey, and Jack as friends, not clients."

John nodded. "And the evil you witnessed … it was the Sendero?"

"We think so," Al said. "Northwest of here, on the eastern slopes of the Andes's foothills, on the far side of the Manu. Whether it was them or not, it was human trafficking. Slavery. Likely sex slaves. Jack photographed it and reported it. We've read reports that the military went there, but the camp had been moved. Garcia has ordered a task force to patrol the whole region for any such camps. It has taken a year for us to process it. It didn't help that in the week after that traumatic event, Jack goes missing and drops out of his doctoral program."

For John, everything fit.

The open sides of the building offered 360-degree views of the compound. A young woman wearing a daypack and carrying a large bucket walked from one of the trails into the clearing.

"We still have much to talk about," he said. "My students will be coming in soon, so why don't you all stay here for a couple of days while you formulate a plan. And you're in luck; tonight is pizza night. Join us, and after, we'll meet back here and discuss some more things.

"Now, a couple of rules. No swimming after 6:00 pm, and if you do swim at all, don't venture out more than twenty meters from the dock. We encourage everyone to wash off with filtered water from the lake, but no shampoo or soap. We don't want the phosphates in the water. If you are worried about the piraña or the caiman, there are sun showers beside the bathroom building. In the showers, you may use soap."

John stood up. "I'll show you where you can pitch your tents."

As they walked across the clearing, John waved to the girl on the dock. "First one back, Maria! How was the hunting?"

"Not bad. I found three!" Maria yelled up to him.

"She's collecting basin tree frogs," he said as they walked onto one of the trails.

Every twenty yards was a cleared-out spot in the forest. Some had wooden tent platforms, some did not. Each group member picked out a tent site and started shuffling gear the half-kilometer trip from the boat to the facility. As they did, the newcomers received welcoming smiles and waves from a dozen young researchers who were emerging from the forest. All of them were filthy, sweaty, bug-bitten, and happy as hell.

John noted, "All the researchers here stay in their backpacking tents. It's part of the charm."

As Claire walked through the clearing with her sleeping bag, duffle, and two jugs of water, the professor stopped her. "A moment Claire, if I may?"

Claire set her gear down on the steps of one of the buildings. Then she straightened and looked at him.

John smiled at her and looked like he wanted to put his hands on her shoulders to comfort her, but he did not. "So ... you are Claire. *The* Claire. You're even more beautiful than he said."

At that instant, she felt a swell of emotions building up inside her. Obviously, Jack had not moved on completely, and he hadn't forgotten about her. At least, she now realized, he had talked about her.

"You are more than friends, I suspect."

Claire nodded as another tear rolled down her cheek. *What the fuck?!* she thought. *What is up with these tears? I'm a scientist, for Christ's sake. I've moved on — Jack has moved on — we've all moved on. Except for his family. They haven't. Maybe these stupid tears are for them, or maybe for the friendship Casey has lost. Whatever...*

John saw her pain, and he patted her on one shoulder. He had a paternal, calming influence on people. "I hope our talk after supper will answer some more questions."

"John," she asked, "when you were at Harvard in the late sixties, did you ever hear someone yell, '*Rinehart!*' at gatherings or rallies?"

He looked quizzically at her. It was an odd question at that place and time. "Yes, actually. I had an old professor who used it as a sort of rallying cry when he wanted the students to gather as a group. We students thought it was strange. When one of us — who shall remain nameless — asked him why Rinehart, he said, 'Research it.'"

"Why do you ask?"

"Oh, I was just wondering if Jack was pulling my leg once upon a time. Did you? Research it?"

"You're assuming I was the student," said the professor. "You are correct. I did research the name and found out it was simply the name of a charismatic, gifted student from the turn of the century. Fellow students would yell his name from the dorm windows when they needed his help. It simply caught on, and subsequent classes carried on the tradition as a rallying cry for Harvard alums until after World War Two."

"Hmm," muttered Claire. "Only Jack would latch onto an old tradition like that."

Surprisingly, the pizza wasn't too bad. During supper, John and the students talked about Cocha Sacha, the Manu Biosphere Reserve, and a little about the ongoing studies. John noticeably let the researchers do most of the talking. Though they were from Germany, England, Peru, Venezuela, Canada, Brazil, Korea, and Japan, each spoke excellent English at the table. But now and then, the conversation slipped into Spanish.

"Because there has been no hunting allowed near here for over a generation," John offered, "the forest around Cocha has the most diverse amounts of fish, mammals, amphibians, birds, and flora than perhaps anywhere on earth."

"It is really quite astounding," he continued. "I traveled extensively all through Peru for a decade before landing here, not as a tourist but as a practicing, professional biologist, and in that time, I saw only one spider monkey — that's it. Here, you can see dozens of spider monkeys every day. It's remarkable."

John went on to speak of their place in the biosphere.

"As you can see, Cocha Sacha is charming and rustic. We are constantly trying to limit our impact on the environment here. We are working on acquiring things, like a more reliable power supply and more and better composting toilets. Later this season, we're getting a new longwave/shortwave radio for emergencies. We hope to keep developing our research program while continuously reaching out to schools and research facilities worldwide.

"But we want to keep the charm that is this place. For me, it's home. You see that the researchers live in those little jungle clearings in their tents. They're not just studying nature; they are living it — they are part of nature here. Most of the people who live and work here are profoundly affected by the place. Because they have to live in tents in the deep, dark, Amazonian rainforest with many deprivations, I like to teasingly say, 'their experience at Cocha can be ... *in-tentse*.'"

Most everyone smiled at that.

At the end of the meal, Professor Liddell rose and said to the room, "I'll be available in the office after eight o'clock. Whose night is it to help clean up?" John carried his plate to the kitchen area.

"Jina's," everyone said. The young Korean woman sighed.

"Follow me," he said to the newcomers. "I have something for you."

FORTY-FIVE

Contact

Everyone again sat at the table in the main building. Each traveler had the foresight to hang a headlamp around their neck lest they struggle to find their way back to their tents after dark.

John started the conversation, which felt more like a meeting. "As I said before, I became fond of Jack in the months he stayed with us." He looked over at Claire. "We had numerous late-night conversations about many topics. Most were scientific discussions, but some were about life. And I mentioned that I tried to persuade him not to explore farther upriver on his own. I urged him to contact some anthropologists if and when they might be going there and try to talk them into letting him accompany them. We have had over two hundred scientific papers published out of Cocha Sacha in the past twelve years. I told him there is some weight to that, and perhaps I could help him connect with a reconnaissance expedition. He thanked me but said he could move quicker, quieter, and freer alone.

"You know," the professor said with a hint of admiration, "he built a dug-out canoe while he was here. It's really something. He put an outrigger on it. He attached a sponson to the opposite side, and the outrigger could ingeniously retract against the gunwale. When retracted and latched in place, it matched the other sponson perfectly — the boat is almost unsinkable. I gave him a five-and-a-half horse outboard that we had lying around. He tinkered with it until it ran smoothly."

"I do not know this word, *sponson*," Alberto said.

"It's a protrusion along the side of a boat for most of its length, just below the gunwales to give it more buoyancy," Casey responded. He looked at the professor. "Jack grew up in Stonington, Maine, and they know boats."

John nodded. "That boat is what he took upriver; I suspect there is no other canoe like it in the Amazon. If you find the boat, he probably won't be too far. But I suspect he will hide it, camouflage it somehow so nobody tries to steal it."

John reached down by his feet and retrieved a green and black daypack. It was a "*Lowe*" pack, Jack's preferred brand.

"This is Jack's," the professor explained. "He left it with me with instructions that if he did not return in two months, I was to mail it to his family in Stonington." He unzipped a front panel pocket of the pack. "He also said there were letters for me to post with the next boat that goes out. I have not looked at them. So, I don't know to whom they are addressed." John paused before saying, "There hasn't been a boat yet." He pulled a small stack of five or six letters out.

John held up the letters and dealt them like cards on the table. "His parents," he laid it next to the pack. "*Claire*," –

he slid it in front of her. "*Alberto Montero, Cusco*" –he slid that one to Al. "*Casey*," and handed his across the table. "And to his friend *Maria*?" he held the letter in the air. Casey and Claire both pointed to Alberto.

"They are like family," Casey said.

John gave Maria's letter to Al.

"Since you all have been trying to find him for a year, no doubt you want to search the contents. I have no problem with that. And if you find him upriver, all is well. If you don't, I'm sure you understand I have to hold onto this for another month and a half. He entrusted it to me, and I said I would send it along."

"Of course," each traveler agreed.

Juan had been sitting slightly away from the group. John turned to his left and said in Spanish, "You don't talk much, do you, Juan?"

Juan almost mustered a grin. "*Cuando tengo algo que decir, lo hago.*"

Alberto translated for Claire and Casey; "The Professor suggested Juan doesn't say much, and Juan replied, 'When I have something to say, I do.'"

"Well," John said, still in Spanish, "your friends here are going to go looking for their amigo upriver tomorrow … their friend who two weeks ago left to seek out the Mashco-Piro, uncontacted Matsigenka, the Murunahua, and the Nanti and Yora."

John gave him a moment and said, "Do you have anything to say about *that*?"

Juan stared him down. The professor did not flinch, and Juan's 'almost' grin was gone. Dr. Liddell was not intentionally putting him on the spot; he was fact-finding. He respected people, and he truly wanted to know what Juan thought of the enterprise.

But Juan *was* on the spot, and mincing words, or pandering, or lying never entered into his thinking, even as a small boy. "I do not believe we will find him," he finally said. "If their friend is okay, he will return on his own. We will not find him if something has happened to him, either from the tribes, or by the thieves seeking caoba, or from the jungle. Not in a hundred years." He could feel the weight of his words in the room. "But it is good to try. Maybe we will meet him coming downriver in his strange boat. Maybe I am wrong."

"*Koba?*" Claire asked.

"*Caoba,*" Alberto replied. "Mahogany. It is like gold to the illegal loggers."

John removed everything from the pack, and Claire, Casey, and Al carefully sifted through the contents. There were five rolls of exposed Kodachrome 64 slide film and two filled notebooks with a rubber band around each one. There was nothing unusual; two camera lenses, a candle lantern, insect repellent, a coil of nylon rope, a small tarpaulin, some nick-knacks that looked like gifts or souvenirs, a small rock with the name Huascaran written on it.

John stared at the notebooks and said, "Journals are intensely personal, and I submit that we should not read them at this time."

"I disagree," Alberto said. "At least regarding Jack's last few entries. There could be some information in there that might point us in a different direction, which could make the difference in us finding him or not, and that's too consequential to risk for the sake of *propiedad.*"

Everyone decided Al was right. Propriety wasn't that important at this time. John flipped to the back of the most recent journal, looked at the dates, went back two weeks' worth of entries, and asked who would like to read them aloud. Casey held his hand out for the book and started reading. The pages were filled with poetic, philosophical prose and musings on ecology and the indigenous people he had met. They were enough to make Claire tear up, but there was nothing to point them in any direction. The trip would proceed as planned.

They all agreed to adjourn until morning. The black blanket of night had folded over the jungle, and each person pulled their headlamps to their foreheads and switched them on. As the friends walked to their respective campsites, Claire said, "I'll catch up in a minute." She held up the letter and muttered, "I just want to … you know."

"Okay," Casey said, and he too wanted to read his letter in privacy. "Stay in the clearing."

He left her standing alone. She walked to the edge of the lake, the only place where she could see the stars, and she sat down.

She opened the airmail envelope with Jack's classic, neat cursive; *Claire Anderson, 19 Westminster Street, Somerville, MA 02129.* Inside was a single sheet of paper.

She unfolded it with trembling hands.

Dear Claire,

I hope you are well. By the time you read this, it will have been a year since we saw each other. You must be ready to defend your thesis by now. Congratulations — I know you'll be a great archaeologist.

I'm sorry I have been such a poor correspondent. I've been somewhat incommunicado for much of my travels. I do realize that. I have apparently become a vagabond for adventure or perhaps for seeking the stranger things in life. I suppose I have needed the time to find out my true calling, and I think I have found it. I found a place called Cocha Sacha, a research station far up the Manu River in the Amazon Basin. There I met a fantastic professor who has helped me get my shit together. I will travel in the Amazon for a bit longer and then switch my field of study to conservation ecology. At this point, I do not know if I will study in Peru or the States. I don't really care how long it takes me … the journey is the thing, after all.

Please forgive my foibles. I fear I've hurt you. But I have learned one thing about myself … I would not make a good mate for you. Perhaps not for anyone. You are driven; I am scattered. You are a hard worker, and I am a dreamer.

I remember in the Odyssey Homer wrote, "Of all creatures that breathe and move upon the earth, nothing is bred that is weaker than man."

He was writing about extraordinarily imperfect people like me. Not people like you, Claire.

My only hope left in life is to contribute something worthwhile by helping the wild places that nurture humanity and those people and things who currently have no voice. God willing, I will be able to do that through theory, experimentation, and energy of mind. We are doing terrible things to the rain forests, and I hope to document some of it. I am off to seek a little justice.

Please live your life, Claire, and don't worry about me. Perhaps one day I will find you, and we will go look at some art. Art is all around me here, but I do miss Vincent and Claude.

I will love you always,
Your Jack

She crumpled the paper and held it to her chest. She looked out over the black, shining lake and glanced up at the stars. Jack was right, and she knew it. But still, it hurt. As she looked at the stars, she remembered again how bright they were a year ago over the Sacred Valley when she sat with Jack on the banks of the Urubamba. She remembered their kisses and what it felt like when they made love, and she wanted to always remember him that way. Then and there, looking up at the Milky Way, she made an important decision. Though she knew Jack was correct about them never living a life together and why she wanted to hold onto a part of him for the rest of her life. She wanted something more than fading memories of a love that never was.

Claire's mind started racing. Her fear for Jack's safety pained her, and her throat started to hurt. She decided that if they find Jack alive, she will want more than just talk and kisses. She would again give all of herself to him. She wanted that memory.

As she contemplated this revelation, she slowly began to feel relief from the omnipresent 'funk' she had been in since arriving in Peru this time. The beautiful places, fantastic sights, cultural exchanges, and world-class learning opportunities she had experienced had bounced right off her on this trip. Her brain and her heart had been trying so hard to accept what she hadn't been able to admit to herself.

Through her tears, she smiled bravely up at the stars.

They had a later start in the morning than usual. Juan and Marco had loaded the boat, topped off the outboard's fuel tank, and were ready. After breakfast, Casey spent some time going over his river map with the professor, and Alberto took thirty minutes to speak with most of the researchers and students. It mattered not to Claire; she now felt less burdened than she had in weeks.

John walked with Claire and Casey down to the river to see them off. As Juan and Casey pushed the boat from the bank, Casey said to John, "Five days…"

"Yes," John replied, "see you in five days."

The plan was simple; they would first search the left side of the river where the uncontacted indigenous people would most likely be, and the opposite side coming back. That's where the loggers would be. They would keep their eyes open for anything that looked man-made and for little inlets or lagoons. If they saw a beach, they might explore it. They would camp each night on the east side of the river — the logger's side. That *might* be safer.

They went into search mode immediately. Marco maneuvered the boat, quartering into the current to the far side of the river. Both Juan and Alberto had brought binoculars, and the rest scanned the banks by eye. Marco ran the boat as close to shore as he safely could.

For hours they scanned the shoreline. Nothing. Monotony returned after a while, and the intense heat made it hard to stay vigilant. At about one o'clock, Alberto lowered his binoculars and turned back to Claire, Marco, and Casey. "We can stop for lunch and stretch our legs at the next broad beach." Marco nodded.

Fifteen minutes later, Marco pointed the boat around a bend and saw a beach about 200 yards long. He ran almost past it as everyone scanned it, looking for life. On the upriver end, he drove the bow onto the clay beach. Juan hopped out and tied the bowline to a fallen tree that was half embedded into the soil. Marco started to set up the coolers near the tree to use the log as a bench seat. Juan saw him and said something to him in Spanish. Marco put the coolers back into the boat. This was Mascho country. If they had to leave in a hurry, Juan didn't want to have to load coolers. Juan had a machete in a leather sheath fastened to his back in such a way that he could reach behind his head, over his right shoulder, and draw it out of its scabbard. He looked like a Sarmatian Knight.

Having been stuck in the boat for hours, everyone walked to the edge of the forest. Claire started to step into the brush, and Juan said, "No." She looked at him, and he indicated that the men would turn away from her. His face told her it was far too dangerous here to separate — even by a few yards. There she squatted, in line with the men who had all turned a few degrees away from her. That would be all the privacy each of them would have for the next four days. The group stopped just long enough to eat and stretch their legs while Juan patrolled the beach.

Once finished, they navigated another four miles upriver. As the evening heat intensified, they found an abandoned campsite where they could stay for the night. Again, Juan scouted around while the others cleared spots for the tents. No one spoke for a long while. It was evident that Juan had been correct when the professor had pressed him for input; finding any sign of Jack would be like finding a needle in a haystack. Maybe harder. They were all thinking the same thing; there were too many places to look. Lagoons every few hundred yards, tributaries just as often, and hundreds of islands peppered the river. Some of the river they were seeing now was essentially uncharted. It was a disheartening realization.

As they set up their tents, Casey said to Claire, "I think Juan and Marco are only doing this now to assuage our sadness, and maybe Al is too."

Claire looked in the direction of the others. "I feel that also."

Casey thought for a moment and said, "Look, I've been mulling over what Juan said about our chances. I don't think we should push the guys too hard to find Jack this way. It might be best to just run upriver as far as we can to look for settlements...try to find someone who might have seen Jack on the river somewhere or spent time with him. Maybe we should bring it up at supper."

Claire had tears in her eyes as she nodded in agreement.

Later, at supper, everyone still kept the conversation to a minimum. As they ate reconstituted beef stew, Casey spoke up.

"Claire and I have been thinking. It's pretty obvious Juan is right. This search might be impossible, with so many islands and tiny tributaries — there are hundreds of them, and Jack could've gone up any one of them on a whim."

Al was the only one to look up at them. He looked sad, and he held out little hope of finding Jack — not in this way. "It is true," he said, "one boatload of people looking for one person in the Amazon is a stretch."

Casey continued. "Our best hope is that he is okay and will come out on his own in a few weeks. But we are provisioned for another week, and we are here, so I think we ought to keep going. Perhaps the best thing we can do is run upriver another mile or two. Try to find some Matsigenka, and maybe they will have some information."

In the morning, the expedition was taking on an air of reconciliation. The team probably wouldn't find Jack, but they just might find some information … *something* Claire could take back to Jack's family.

Marco pushed the boat along for a mile of the winding, debris-choked river. Again, the group took a break on a beach on the west side of the river, and again nobody saw anything. After stretching their legs, Claire, Casey, and Alberto found spots near the boat to sit and relax. It felt good to be out of the boat, but the sun was getting intense. They had not been on the beach ten minutes when the three friends heard a strange bird. It was a weird, whistling little chirp, odd enough that all three looked down the beach in its direction. Juan was there, fifty yards away, crouching down. It was he who had made unusual the bird sound. He was looking at the group and held his finger to his lips. Marco had wandered down the beach, farther away from the boat, and having heard strange birdsong, he too squatted and stared in Juan's direction.

Juan reached down and felt the clay soil of the beach. Crouching, he inched closer to the jungle. Suddenly Juan stiffened and took a step back. He looked at Alberto, who fortunately happened to be looking his way. Juan motioned for him to be quiet and push the boat into the water. He then gestured for Marco to walk to the boat. With his eyes trained on the forest line, Juan walked backward toward the boat. Both arms were crossed, and his hands were under his vest. The handle of his machete poked up behind his right shoulder. Once at the boat, he pushed off with one leg and climbed in. Everyone was in their place.

As they paddled off the beach, Casey's eyes, nervously trained on the edge of the forest, flitted over to Juan, who was very tense. Sweat dripped from his chin and nose. Juan's eyes remained riveted on the shoreline as he picked up a crate behind his seat and placed it on the boat's small deck in front of him, using it as a tiny fort. Marco started the engine, put it in reverse, and pulled offshore. When they were forty yards out into the river, Juan yelled something to Marco in Spanish. Marco nodded, and when they were eighty yards out from the beach, Marco cut the engine, and Juan dropped the anchor from the bow. Claire could feel her heart pounding in her chest.

Nobody asked anything, but Juan, scanning the beach, said in Spanish, "Footprints. Very fresh footprints."

"They couldn't have been ours?" Casey asked through Alberto.

"None of us are barefoot and have *callosidades* like the people who made the prints."

Without looking back at Juan, Alberto asked, "What did you see in the forest?"

"Vi ojos humanos, pero estaban rojos," Juan whispered.

Casey leaned close to Alberto, who said, "He saw some eyes, human eyes, but they looked red."

Suddenly Marco, standing in the stern, said, "There!" He was pointing just down the beach from where they had been resting at the forest's edge.

"Juan ..." Casey called out, getting Juan's attention, "Bueno."

Emerging from the forest were seven young men. They were naked, except for a broadcloth wrapped around their abdomens. It was hard to tell from far out in the river, but it looked like their penises were pulled up and tucked under the cloth wrap. All seven had black hair cut into a "Prince Valliant" hairdo. A few had some facial hair, but not much, grown naturally, almost in Fu Manchu style. Their faces were adorned with black tattoos and red paint across their eyes. Through the binoculars, Alberto could see that each man carried two or three seven-foot-long spears with either hardened wood or bone tips and large fletches on the opposite ends.

"Mascho," Marco said.

Al, still looking through the binoculars, said, "Yup. Definitely. Amazing."

"I have lived on the river all my life," Marco said. "I have never seen them."

Casey and Claire stared at the men. Two Mascho had moved to the river's edge while the others stayed near the forest line. The two in front were talking. Some of the speech was clearly directed at the boat, but no one on board could understand what the tribesmen were saying.

The Mascho were not afraid.

"See how they are painted and the way they are moving? Their posture?" asked Juan. "They mean business."

For five minutes, the boat stayed anchored, and the men on the beach walked around and yelled in the direction of the searchers. Claire, Casey, and Al snapped photographs as fast as their fingers could work the winders on the cameras. Finally, the Mascho-Piru returned to the forest. Then Marco started the outboard engine, and Juan pulled up the anchor.

It was frightening but exhilarating. Even Claire, in her emotional state regarding Jack, was quite excited about seeing the uncontacted tribesmen. Everyone chatted with raised voices over the din of the engine about the unique experience, except for Juan. He stayed on the job, vigilant for half-submerged trees and debris that could damage the outboard's propeller. It was late in the afternoon when Marco quartered across the river's current again and pointed the bow to the eastern shore. It took another hour to find a clearing suitable for a campsite.

After supper, sitting on crates and coolers around a campfire, the group discussed the Mascho men. Alberto and Marco were both excited about the experience.

"Juan," Alberto said in Spanish, "thank you for your sharp eyes on the beach. We don't know what they wanted, but it's possible it could have gone badly." Juan nodded. "Remember," Al reminded the group, as he stared into the fire's flames, "we are forbidden to make contact with them."

In the morning, the group broke camp and loaded the boat like a seasoned team. Marco skillfully maneuvered the boat farther upriver, negotiating the twisting, serpentine course of the Manu. Marco often directed the boat from one side of the channel to the other, inspecting small tributaries and lagoons. They found no sign of Jack or his boat, nor any indigenous villages. Only an hour from leaving the previous night's campsite, the team motored around a sweeping bend and saw another good-sized river joining the Manu from the west. Marco pointed the boat to the confluence. "The Rio Sotileja," he announced. It did not take long to see a village next to a beach where the two rivers met. A few hundred yards from the village, Juan could see children playing in the water. He turned back to the crew. "Matsigenka."

This was the largest village the group had visited.

Juan jumped out of the bow and pulled the boat up onto the beach, far enough that it could not float away.

A few Matsigenka men met the group on the beach. Juan, Marco, and Alberto conversed with them for a while, and Alberto relayed the salient points to Claire and Casey.

"This village has about a hundred people in it," Al told them. "They have been living here for about three years. For generations, they lived on the other side of the river, but some loggers came and started harassing them, so they moved over here. These Matsigenka were a hunter-gatherer culture for centuries, but now they practice slash and burn agriculture, though they still hunt some and fish a lot."

Claire studied the villagers. They were shorter and had wider bodies than most of the other tribes they had seen. They were indeed different than the taller, slimmer Mascho-Piro they had just seen. And unlike the Mascho, these people were dressed. They all wore rusty-brown colored tunics made from handspun cloth. Most of the younger men wore their hair short and shaved on the sides. Men and women were tattooed.

Al approached Claire and Casey. "These Matsigenka aren't too happy about us seeing the Mascho so close to their village, but Marco says there are too many people living here, and the Mascho will leave them alone. Still, they don't like it…the Mascho often lurk in the forest."

Casey handed Alberto the photos of Jack, who handed them to Marco. He showed them to the Matsigenka men, who shook their heads. Marco described Jack's canoe. Again, they shook their heads. Marco asked if there was a good place to camp on the other side, and they told him their old village site was just upriver, but they were welcome to stay with them tonight.

Juan, Al, and Marco conferred and asked Claire and Casey their preference.

"I vote for here," Claire said. "Maybe someone else in the village has seen Jack. We could ask around."

Marco shook his head, "If anyone has seen him, these men would know. But it would be safer to stay here in the village. Also, I have never been this far upriver, and there is more *información* I would like to get."

"Settled," Al said.

The Matsigenka men showed Marco where the group could put their tents but offered that they were welcome to sleep in their communal huts with 'the people.' Marco summoned his diplomatic skills and told the men the 'grigos' liked sleeping in their tents, that it was like a game for them. The men shook their heads and laughed. They bought it.

After the tents were erected, Juan came to Claire and said her name. It was the first time he had addressed her directly. She stood up, and Juan turned and walked toward the forest, a hundred feet away. It took her a moment to realize she was meant to follow him. She glanced at Casey and walked after Juan. Juan had hacked a short path into the jungle at the edge of the forest, about twenty feet. The slash he had cut was piled up against the forest interior. The foliage between that barrier and the tents was cut down short enough that her head could be seen from the campsite when she squatted.

"Baño," he said, pointing with his machete, "para mujeres."

"Ah," Claire said, "muchas gracias." He was watching out for her.

Juan nodded. "*De nada.*" He smiled before he turned and walked away. She followed him back to the campsite. *His teeth are beautiful,* she thought, *even with the missing bicuspid.*

At the campsite, Alberto leaned close to Claire. "This far upriver, there are cases of women being stolen when off going to the bathroom. Juan is just making sure it doesn't happen on his watch."

After supper, the friends joined the Matsigenka men around a campfire in the village center. Juan walked around the village for more than an hour. Marco asked what lay ahead, upriver. "More of the same river," they said. But they knew of no more villages. "The people who live upriver are nomadic, and they have no names," the men told him. "They do not come out."

Marco explained who they were searching for. They showed absolutely no emotion when they said, "He is probably dead."

But the men suspected if Jack had been murdered, it would more likely be by the loggers than by "the People." Marco translated for Casey, Claire, and Alberto and it was apparent the loggers were *the loggers*; everyone else in their world, seen or unseen, were "The People."

Marco turned to Claire and Casey with a dour look. "They say we will not find him, and they also say if Jack came upriver this far, they are positive they would have seen him. They fish this water every day…every single day."

Claire stared at Marco. She was starting to believe what the men said could be true.

"What else did they say?" Casey asked.

Marco hated to say it, but explained, "They said if he is dead, we will not find him because if the loggers killed him, they would take his body into the jungle and hide it. If it was The People, or if it was the jungle that killed him and The People found him, then the tradition with all deceased people is to deposit the body into the river."

"Then a body might eventually float to one of the downstream towns or villages, and therefore it would be big news, and we'd hear about it," suggested Casey.

Marco again shook his head. "No, long before the next village the body is …" Marco looked at Alberto. "*Consumada?*"

Al leaned forward on his crate and started to translate for Marco but stopped himself. He did not need to. "Nature takes its course," he offered instead, "and here in the Amazon, Nature is very fast."

"God," said Claire. "He has only been upriver for two weeks. Let's not talk about him as though it was inevitable in that short period of time. He could be anywhere."

Everyone agreed. There was a long, silent period.

"But," she continued, "if he did not go farther upriver than this, and there's no canoe or sign of him between here and Cocha Sacha, perhaps we're pissing in the wind."

Marco looked at Alberto, and whispered, "*No hay posibilidad de encontrarlo.*" Then he looked into the fire. He had taken Jack to Cocha Sacha … strangely, he was feeling directly connected to his disappearance, and he professed that to the group.

"Disappearance?" Casey asked. "Is that what this is already?" Everybody looked at him. "He was on the road for a year, and we didn't know where he was for most of it. He was all right. Shit, he might have been having the time of his life. And Claire's right — he has only been on the river for two weeks. He may paddle back to Cocha Sacha next week or in six weeks. Who knows?"

That made Claire feel better.

"But I think Claire's right about the search also," continued Casey. "We're unlikely to find him in this labyrinth of a river system. I think we should head back to Cocha in the morning — keep our eyes peeled, yes — but maybe spend an extra day in Cusco checking in on Maria and Professor Bache at the university. Find out if they have heard from Jack."

Alberto pursed his lips before saying, "I think you're right."

The group had been on the two rivers for only eight days, and they had each lost some weight. They were filthy and riddled with itchy bug bites — Claire's back had hundreds — and they were feeling the effects of the heat.

They would head down the Manu in the morning.

FORTY-SIX

Capitulation

The first sputter and the subsequent familiar hum of the engine instilled a feeling of resignation in Claire. They were giving up. Jack would either come out on his own, or … *or not*, she thought. Marco pointed the bow downriver. Juan, ever vigilant, sat perched up front again. Riding the current, the flowing air felt good in the early morning heat.

Claire closed her eyes for a moment and stretched her neck forward into the breeze. A sadness set in as she thought about the possibility of never seeing Jack again. Then she caught herself. *It's Jack we're looking for. If anyone can disappear into the jungle and come out again looking somewhat healthy, he can. But at this point, we have to move on.*

At Cocha Sacha, Dr. Liddell was happy to see the group. He was sad that they found no trace of Jack, but he was not surprised. He understood the vastness of the park better than anyone. The group stayed the night again, and each member marveled more at the operation and diversity of wildlife at the research station.

"Jack might be okay," John said to the boat as they prepared to push-off in the morning, "and if he isn't, God forbid, how many of us get to live our life on a knight's errand, laying it on the line to right wrongs or to simply explore?"

Claire reached over the gunwale, and John bent down to take her hand in his. She smiled at his handsome, steely blue eyes and his trimmed, stately thin mustache, and he smiled back at her. "Good luck with your thesis," he said. Marco's engine started, and Juan kicked the riverbank, pushing the bow away from shore, and the boat swung downriver. And just like that, they were off to Cusco.

⚜

Two-and-a-half days later, the group — without Marco or Juan, but with Maria and Marisol — sat in the Cross Keys Pub drinking Crystal beer. Claire, dumbfounded by how life was turning out, caught herself staring at Maria and wondering how things would be for her, and she looked away.

Man, she thought. *Jack gave up her — and me — and his education to explore on his own? Maybe it's not Maria or me. Maybe Casey was right when he said that possibly Jack was out there on the move just to be on the move. Maybe it's just commitment he's uncomfortable with. If that's true, it's a fucking cop-out.*

Still, she knew she had always loved him in one way or another, either as a fantastic friend or wannabe lover. She drank her beer and wished they had found him. She felt strange that she, a pragmatic academic, came away from this trip with one certainty; she *did* love Jack.

Maria told the friends she had not heard from Jack in seven months. She embarrassingly told Alberto she still held out hope Jack would come to her soon and live in Cusco. She cried at the table when Al told her everything they had learned on the Manu River, and both Al and Marisol put their arms around her.

Claire fought back the tears.

Earlier in the day, Claire, Casey, and Alberto had visited Dr. Bache and told him everything.

Dr. Bache said, "I do not think the Sendero Luminoso have been active in that region, but they were becoming so active and violent throughout Peru that I feared for your friend. The Sendero, the native element, the poisonous fauna … Jack will have much to navigate. I hope he is well."

He did fill in the friends on the task force the new President Garcia had set up. "As you know," he told them with his German accent, "the camp you found which Jack photographed was abandoned when they went in there, but they found two others just like it a short distance to the north that were occupied. The commandos went in at night. They were trafficking women for the Sendero, and the soldiers liberated three dozen young women. When you see Jack, can you please tell him?" All three said they would and that Jack would be pleased.

The professor offered, "Jack's photographs may have helped save some lives."

"As did Presidente Garcia," Casey offered.

"*Ja,*" Dr. Bache agreed, "but in other things, I think Garcia is as corrupt as all the others in the country. We will see. At Cocha Sacha, I think they will not find a friend in him. Shortly after being elected last July, Garcia issued a statement saying that the reports of uncontacted tribes in the Amazon were hoaxes made up by environmentalists to block oil exploration on the indigenous people's lands. Ridiculously transparent."

"Wow," Claire said.

"Yes ... wow," echoed Dr. Bache. "I wonder if that angered Jack."

Casey and Al exchanged glances. The professor might be right.

"I doubt Jack knows what Garcia said," Al suggested, "he has been out of touch with the world for half a year."

That night in the pub, the group made a multi-part resolution; they would stay in touch with each other. They would continue to reach out to Jack, and Casey would stay in bi-monthly contact with John at Cocha Sacha. Al would monitor his network of guides and adventurers in Cusco for any word from the Manu. They would continue to correspond with Jim Bartlett in Lima, who always seemed to know the comings and goings of explorer types in Peru. Alberto approached the pub owner, Ian, and asked him to keep the photographs of Jack behind the bar and apprise him of any responses. Ian explained that he was running birding trips up the Manu more frequently and promised to keep asking around. And lastly, it fell to Claire to go to Stonington to tell Jack's family they could not find him, but they had just missed him at Cocha Sacha. "*Give him a few months,*" it was agreed she would tell them, "*he will probably emerge from the jungle with a hero's tale.*" It was also decided that she should tell his family the details about the human trafficking and how Jack's photographs had helped set women free. There were kisses and hugs when they parted, but none were more heartfelt than the embrace Claire gave Alberto.

In the morning, Claire and Casey flew to Lima. That evening they stopped by the Explorer's Club, but Jim was off climbing in the Cordillera Blanca, and Eliana was out of town. They left a package with copies of Jack's photographs, and Casey wrote a letter and clipped it to the photos.

For the friends, the flights to Miami and Boston were somber.

Once Claire was unpacked, she telephoned the Beal's. It was evening, and Alton answered. When Claire started to tell him about the trip and wanted to know if she could drive up the following weekend, his voice sounded different, and he asked Claire if she could talk to Karen about it. "Hold on," he said.

Karen came to the phone and sounded guardedly upbeat. She had a lovely sounding voice, but it could not disguise the disappointment that they had not found Jack.

"Oh, thank the Lord!" Karen exclaimed when she learned that Jack was alive and well only a month earlier. That was something.

"We would love for you to come this weekend," Karen said.

"Yes, I'll be here."

Claire left at four in the morning to drive the five hours to Stonington. She did not want to spend the night, and she wanted to visit for two hours or less and leave. She would head back to Somerville the same afternoon, and if she got tired, she would stay at one of the cheap motels along the way. That was her plan.

Claire's old Subaru turned off the bottom of Tennent's Hill and into the Beal's driveway. She breathed hard a few times and walked to the door. At the second knock on the kitchen screen door, Karen opened it and gave her a big hug.

"Come, come in," said Karen, pulling Claire into the kitchen. "Are you hungry, dear?"

Karen asked her that even before she had noticed Claire looked underweight. Usually fit and athletic looking, she now seemed too thin, and insect bites were visible on her cheeks, forehead, and around her neck. They sat down at the kitchen table.

"Alton is on the water."

"It's okay. I drove up to tell you what we found out. You can relay it to Alton later...I have to drive back this afternoon."

"Oh, you can't spend more time with us? The boys are working, and Lisa is at her friend's camp for the week."

"Afraid not," Claire said. "But I'll come back for a longer visit. Maybe go out on the boat next time."

"Alton would like that."

Claire proceeded to tell her everything. Karen listened intently, at times fighting back the tears. It took almost an hour. She spoke of Jack's newfound conviction in conservation. The last time she visited, Claire had not told her about the Sendero troubles, and this time she left out the sightings of the Mascho-Piru.

She explained the group's resolution and how their friends in Peru would continue looking for Jack and keeping their ears open. She tried to inject into the conversation how Jack's actions had helped rescue some anonymous women who had been held captive by evil people *and* how some people in Peru think that what Jack was doing was noble. Claire told her that there was every indication Jack thought his actions were more in line with a calling or a destiny and that he was doing exactly what he wanted.

"Casey and I wrote out the names and addresses of everyone in Peru who we know are continuing to search for him in case you want to reach out to them yourselves. Alberto Montero's name is at the top of the list. He is our friend." Claire laid the letter on the table.

Karen's face became more distraught as Claire spoke. When she mentioned at the end that Jack had built a boat, she mustered a sad smile and said, "He *is* handy like that."

When Claire stopped speaking, Karen made a sound like a sudden cough and pulled a napkin to her face. She got up quickly, and it startled Claire, who did not know if she should get up or stay seated.

Karen went to the kitchen window that looked out over the harbor. She stared out over the boats swaying at their moorings. Karen looked past Humpkins and Grog Islands, toward Camp Island, the Coot Islands, and out to sea in the direction of the shoals off Hell's Half Acre, where she knew her husband was pulling traps. She wished he would come home. She began to cry.

Claire jumped up and tried to comfort her. She put her hand on

Karen's shoulder, but Jack's mother did not turn around. She only sobbed at the direction of the sea, like thousands of mothers and wives before her.

"He's probably fine," Claire whispered. "Jack is resilient."

Karen spun around and faced Claire. Tears were flowing down her cheeks, and it was apparent her throat was painful as she tried to speak. At first, no sounds came out. Karen swallowed hard, winced, and tried again to say something. Her aspect was one seen only in mothers who have lost a child. It took Karen several excruciating minutes to explain to Claire what she was feeling.

It was the hardest interaction Claire had ever experienced.

Karen pitifully clasped both of her hands over her heart, and when no sound again came through the tears, she swallowed harder, shook her head in frustration, and took a deep breath. Finally, the words came out.

"I ..." she sobbed, "I'm so sorry. I was overcome with a feeling." She wiped her nose. "It was powerful like someone punched me in the stomach and knocked the wind out of me." She blew her nose into the napkin. In a different voice than before, she sobbed, "I feel I have seen my son for the last time. He's gone."

Karen took a deep breath, put her hand on her forehead, and said, "Alton should've gone down there."

Claire started to speak — to say, "*We don't know that he's gone...*" but with only a look, Karen stopped her before she could utter a word. It was a terrifying look that said, *Do not question this feeling.*

Claire backed away. Karen slumped back into her chair and put both hands palm down on the table. She sat there in her apron, staring at the table with her tears dripping unabated. Claire had no idea what to do. The whole thing was overwhelming.

Through her tears, Claire asked if there was anything she could do. Karen shook her head. "No, I'd like to be alone now until my husband comes home."

Claire was very uncomfortable leaving her there alone. But it was Karen's home and her wish. She got up and walked slowly to the door, gently touching Karen's shoulder. When she opened the door and started to step outside, Karen spoke.

"Thank you, Claire."

They turned and looked at each other.

With a soft, tired look, she said, "You were very brave to come here."

Claire mustered a false smile, nodded, and walked out the door. When she had driven down Tennent's Hill less than thirty minutes earlier, she held out great hope that Jack would still walk out of the jungle at some point — maybe after living with some indigenous tribe for months — and back into her life. Now, driving back over the Deer Isle-Stonington Bridge on her way to Massachusetts, she knew it was time to truly move on.

She drove straight through to Somerville, walked upstairs to her apartment room, and leaned back onto her bed. She hadn't noticed the post-it note on her bedroom door a roommate had left.

It read:

Your friend Casey called. Said to tell you if we don't hear anything, he's going back in the spring. He said you'd understand.

She was too tired to eat. She was too tired to dream.

FORTY-SEVEN

Let us forget with generosity
those who cannot love us

•*Pablo Neruda*

For the thirty-four years since Jack motored up the mighty Manu River in his homemade canoe, the Beals, Claire, Casey, and Alberto never gave up hope that someday Jack might be found alive. And as much as they could, they never stopped searching for him. While their hope waxed and waned over the decades, their love for him and their grief did not.

His loss was a devastating blow, not only to the Beals and Claire and Casey but to Harvard and everyone who knew him. The unsolved disappearance of a loved one is excruciating. Especially if the missing is one's child. A grief without closure, with so many unanswered questions, is perpetual and unforgiving. It is more painful than an untold, unrequited love or even news of our own imminent demise. The grief of a missing person presumed dead haunts the survivor's dreams, both day and night.

In 1987, Alton Beal spent three months searching for his son in Peru. In 1989, he went there again for two months. Alton would not let either of his remaining sons accompany him. On the first trip, he visited Cusco and then small villages up and down the Sacred Valley. Alton walked from house to house, interviewing anyone who might have seen Jack. He knocked on doors, delivering flyers with Jack's face printed on them and contact information, along with a notice of a $6000 reward for information leading to Jack's safe return. The Maine towns of Stonington, Blue Hill, Castine, and Ellsworth had fund-raisers to help pay for searches and reward money. Alton developed relationships with local Peruvian police, who sometimes accompanied him on searches. The *policia* all felt Jack had died in the jungle, likely in the first few weeks after leaving Cocha Sacha, but sympathized with Alton and wanted to help him. From the Sacred Valley, he traveled down the Madre de Dios River, stopping at every village. On the 1989 trip, Alton made it up the Manus River all the way to Cocha Sacha, where he met Professor Liddell. The research facility — and Dr. Liddell — became world renown for their work in ecology and conservation. Alton gave John a stack of flyers to hand out to visitors who might stop on their trips up or down the river. The leaflets were printed in English, Spanish, and Portuguese.

Alton and Karen's struggle to find what had happened to their son received little attention from government agencies. It did not take long for them to learn that the Defense Intelligence Agency and State Department in Washington would be of little help — Jack was the son of a fisherman, not a Congressman. Part of the problem was that there was no indication or even rumors of foul play, and Jack was not missing from a planned appointment, departure date, or a rendezvous. He had *purposefully* wandered off into the Amazon Basin.

When he met with the Federales in Lima, a kind and conciliatory Detective Lieutenant speaking perfect English told Alton, "Señor Beal, I am sorry. As you know, we investigated your son's disappearance two years ago. You will remember in my letter that again last year I sent investigators to the Manus, and every indication is that your son *wanted* to be lost."

Jim Bartlett eventually married Eliana, and they had two boys. They settled in Mira Flores, where the Explorer's Clubhouse had been relocated. His guidebook for the Cordillera Blanca became a classic and is still used by climbers from around the world, and it broadened his reach with the international mountaineering community.

Jim kept vigilant and continued to talk about Jack to every climber and adventurer who traveled to Peru. He felt it was his duty to disseminate news about Jack's disappearance. Jim held fast to his hope of finding some resolution. Thirty-two years later, he still asks travelers to seek information, and he still has hope.

Occasionally throughout the years, some hiker or birder, or adventurer would contact Jim and offer an idea about Jack's whereabouts or fate. Jim would send the information along to Alberto, Claire, Casey, and the Beals, depending on its plausibility.

On three occasions, all during the summer of 1996, people who had recently been in the Manus reported to Jim that they had heard unsolicited stories of strange sightings along the west side of the Manu River. "*A white man,*" said the travelers, "*untamed and nearly naked, who runs away at the sight of people.*"

"I don't put much stock in such stories," Jim wrote in letters. "The many inquiries about Jack and the flyers with photos we've taken to villages often serve as tinder for a legend to grow. Remember ... people in the Amazon, they *love* a good legend."

The Sendero Luminoso — the "Shining Path" became more active and violent the year Jack disappeared. Late in 1985, while he was traveling by bus with the two Brits, the Sendero had taken their fight to the streets of Lima, bombing power stations and government buildings. Jack never mentioned the violence in any correspondence. Perhaps he was processing what he had seen in the Sendero camp on the far eastern slopes of the Andes. Maybe he had seen enough.

Because of where Jack went missing, the investigators never seemed to think the Sendero were to blame. "Too far upriver," one policeman in Cusco offered. One federal detective who had accompanied Alton up the Manu went so far as to shake his head and say, "*There are a hundred ways to die in the jungle. If he is not alive somewhere, I think he maybe just got sick.*" He felt terrible when he saw Alton's eyes, but he could not take it back.

Sendero hit squads, sometimes comprised of all women, took flats in the poorest Lima neighborhoods. The killings became more random, and the government under Alan Garcia stepped up the pressure on the terrorists. Things got much worse before they got better. Finally, in 1992, the "head of the snake," the leader of the Shining Path, Manuel Rubén Abimael Guzmán Reynoso — "*Presidente Gonzalo*" was captured by the Peruvian government. After a three-day trial by a court of hooded military judges, he was sentenced to life imprisonment for terrorism and treason.

In the aftermath of the trial, information and documents became public, and the population wanted to understand the government's and the military's true role in the twelve-year internal struggle of Peru. Several investigations were launched. Alan Garcia's presidency was wracked with accusations of corruption and nepotism — even sanctioned murder. His successor, Alberto Fujimori, also endured the same allegations, which escalated to the point where he had to flee the country. Fujimori eventually found himself in a Peruvian prison for treason, embezzlement, and corruption, where he remains to this day.

In 2001, in an effort to heal the country, newly minted Peruvian President Alejandro Toledo established the *Truth and Reconciliation Commission* (TRC) to investigate the human rights abuses committed during the "Internal Conflict" between 1980-1992. The commission's mandate was to record human rights, and international humanitarian law violations committed in Peru between May 1980 and November 2000 and recommend mechanisms to promote and strengthen human rights. The TRC reported on the estimated 70,000 deaths and thousands of assassinations, tortures, disappearances, displacement peoples, employment of terrorist methods, and other human rights violations executed by the State and the Shining Path. Not to mention the Túpac Amaru Revolutionary Movement — another Marxist guerrilla group started in 1980 as an alternative to the more radical Shining Path.

A 2019 Stony Brook University study disputed the casualty figures from the Truth and Reconciliation Commission, estimating instead "a total of 48,000 killings, substantially lower than the TRC estimate, and concluded that "the Peruvian State (the Military) accounts for a significantly larger share of the murders than the Shining Path."

The TRC made public one interview with a former female Shining Path member who was re-named after committing her first murder and transferred to Lima, where she was assigned as a bodyguard for the leadership. "There were four of us girls," said the former terrorist, "and within days, we started losing faith in the movement. Close up, the leaders didn't look so great. They drank and partied every night. They just used us for sex and sent us out for beer."

With the advent of the Internet in the mid-1990s, the research on

Jack's whereabouts intensified. Alton and Karen Beal read everything they could find about the TRC's findings, but they found no information that helped them. Karen daily searched Peruvian news sites and information on Amazonian expeditions and developments. After years of surfing sites and taking a few night courses, she could read Spanish perfectly.

Casey made three trips to Peru seeking answers in 1988, 1990, and 1996, and he found none. On the 1990 trip, Casey's visit coincided with the end of Claire's dig season, and she met him, Al, and Marisol at the Cross Keys Pub and reminisced.

On the 1996 trip — the tenth anniversary of Jack's disappearance — he met with Alberto in Cusco. They compared past investigations, gathered stories, and scrutinized legends of sightings and clues, hoping to piece together scattered information, and they found nothing new.

Casey eventually was awarded a position at Harvard and married a pretty Internist.

Casey struggled to put his experiences in the Andean arroyo with the Sendero terrorist behind him. He couldn't shake the thought that he may have killed him with the club. One sleepless night at home after the 1996 Peruvian trip, Casey remembered what Jack had said to him outside the church in Choquecancha, *"When you find the time, brother, look in King James. Read about the 'Cities of Refuge.'"* In the morning, he visited the Widener Library and found the *King James Version of the Holy Bible,* which he was wholly unfamiliar with.

In time, Casey found passages in the Book of Numbers about the Cities of Refuge. Six cities were listed where perpetrators of accidental manslaughter could claim the right of asylum in Biblical times. He read all the passages he could find. He could find nothing which he could relate specifically to his torment, but for some reason, he found solace in the ministrations offered in the passages. Casey nodded his head when he closed the book. Perhaps eleven years earlier, Jack somehow knew they would comfort him.

In April 1990, Alberto sent a letter to Claire that shocked her. It brought to light the precariousness of the political climate in Peru at the time. Alberto's handwriting showed telltale signs of the stress he bore.

16 April 1990

Dear Claire,

Just a short note —

Nothing new to report on the lookout for Jack but will stay vigilant.

I wanted to let you know the news that has many here in Cuzco upset and very sad. It was reported in the Correo four weeks ago that Maria had been arrested. The newspaper article said that she was suspected of being a Lieutenant in the Sendero Luminoso and that she was responsible for planning two bombings near Arequipa last year.

Our close association with her, and our thoughts about what she knew about our discovery in the east in 1985, has left us unsettled. We don't know how much Jack confided in her, if at all. But if she was spying for the Sendero at the time, she apparently kept that information to herself. It appears she did not tell them about us, for Marisol and I have had no trouble at all. On the other hand, when the military raided the camp a month after you left Peru, the camp had been moved. Could she have tipped them off? I really believe that if any of this is true about Maria's involvement in the Sendero, she would never have condoned or participated in the trafficking of women and girls—no matter the political ideology.

It is very hard to believe, and Marisol is convinced it is a mistake. I found out through a policeman friend of mine that she is being held at a Naval detention center in Lima for interrogation. So, I went there last week to try to visit her. It was a dismal place. The guard we spoke to said she was not accepting visitors, which of course, was a lie.

I had a sick feeling as I left the building. I fear for Maria's life. I just thought you and Casey would want to know, sad and shocking as it is. We're praying for her.

Will write again if we hear anything new.

Love,

Al

Alberto never stopped looking for Jack. His connection with his missing friend carried him through the decades.

Al *lived* the Truth and Reconciliation Committee's investigations.

By 2001, he felt safe speaking with authorities about what he and Jack had seen back in 1985. Al's interviews with TRC investigators became a give-and-take conversation, with Al asking just as many questions as the investigators. Usually, his questions were about the Shining Path's historical presence in the Manu. "Were they ever up the Manu as far as the Cocha Sacha Research Station?" he would press. He was still investigating Jack's disappearance.

Alberto continued to work as a tour guide and professional adventurer. Marisol changed mediums several times throughout the decades and is now a sculptor of some renown.

Starting in 1997, Al began running birding trips up the Manu River for a company owned by Ian Jones, the owner of the Cross Keys Pub (which closed in 2005). Jones, who was born just outside Manchester, England, did well with his birding expeditions and co-authored several guidebooks on Peruvian wildlife. He eventually became the British Counsel in Cusco, and in 2004 was awarded an M.B.E., after which Alberto chided him with, "Ah — there's nothing like a knight in the Amazon."

In early 2001, Al got a freelance translating job for an American anthropologist. It was completely by chance. Alberto met the scientist in the Cross Keys, and they struck up a conversation. From that chance meeting came more translating work.

In 1994, Claire wrote a scientific article for *The American Journal of Archaeology* chronicling the discovery of the "Paititi Site," and she included Alberto's significant contribution to the 1985 expedition. It helped solidify Al's place in Peruvian adventure and exploration lore. She and Al developed an ever-growing relationship over the years, and Claire reached out to him always when there was any logistical work that suited him. Several times, Al visited the site during the excavation seasons. One evening, she followed Al when he went for a walk. He retraced his steps to the rock escarpment that he and Jack had hidden behind more than twenty years before. He meandered down the slope to where the Sendero camp had been. Al stood next to the little stream where the women had been forced to wash. He was gazing down the valley toward the Amazon. She could hear him crying. It appeared to Claire that Al was trying to make peace.

Then, one December day, while she was at work in her office at Columbia University, Claire received an unexpected letter from Alberto.

It read:

Almost Christmas, 2012

Dear Claire,

Well, I find myself in the hospital in Lima, in the cancer ward. (Not my favorite place to be, I must say.) It seems I have a tumor on my liver, which is disconcerting because I've become attached to my liver over the years, and I'm sad that it's letting me down so early.

Marisol is struggling with the prognosis. I fear she will take it hard. But she has her art, thank God.

I am sorry we could not find Jack, know what happened to him, or learn where he went. But I feel confident that someday some information will surface and shed some light on his story. I am sorry I will not be here to know that news. What I have tried to do here, on the Peruvian end, is to tell Jack's story to whoever would listen. Over the years of helplessness, I found it comforting. I try to tell people what he was like ... what kind of a man he was. When I had someone's ear, I tried to tell them that what was interesting about Jack was not that he disappeared into the jungle, but rather how many people he touched in such a short period of time.

He was a lover of art and a romantic visionary, a bold and resourceful solo explorer of the wilderness who sought beauty and knowledge in new lands, new people, and the creatures of the earth.

Anyway, I am sad that I will not see you again, Claire, and I wanted to say what an honor it was to get to know you, Casey, and Jack.

Please don't forget me.

With love and affection,

Al

Claire cursed as her tears fell onto the letter, smearing some of the ink. She dried the paper quickly with a tissue and laid the letter on her desk. She slumped into her chair, extended her head back, closed her eyes, and sighed very deeply.

Alberto died the following April, at home in his basement den on a daybed placed along the ancient stone wall where Incan men and women slept five hundred years ago.

Claire became a tenured archaeologist at Columbia University and for a decade excavated the site of her discovery, which she renamed "the *Antisuyu Site*." The Universities of Wisconsin and Warsaw also worked on the site, with Claire as the co-director with a Peruvian archaeologist.

When she received a letter from Jim in Lima stating that Al had died, Claire decided a visit to Jack's family was overdue.

Stonington eventually held a strange familiarity for her, yet there always seemed some underlying anomaly. She loved the work-a-day atmosphere, the smell of the sea, and Jack's family, but the place often seemed to slap her in the face and remind her of the unfairness of the fact that she never got to communicate with Jack after she and Casey got on the airplane in Cusco.

Once, when she scuffed her foot in the Beal's driveway and upset some of the impacted gravel, it reminded her of Jack on the trail to Ausangate when he told her how he thought the spirits of the local Andean ancestors were in the dust kicked up around his feet. Then Claire looked out onto the town pier, and the seagulls, wind-battered and cold, hunkering on top of the pylons reminded her of when Jack and Pedro warmed up the little sparrows in the frigid shadows of the mountains.

Claire felt this would be her last visit with the Beals. She went on a final walk with Karen. She told Jack's mother that Alberto had died, and Karen said she would have Father Eaton say a mass for him.

"And how is Casey these days?" asked Karen

"Fine, I think. I haven't spoken to him for some time. He's at Harvard, married to an internist at one of the Boston hospitals. The last time we spoke, we talked about therapy that he has undergone over the years. I don't know how much you know about Casey and Jack's contact with the Shining Path back in '85, but Casey has struggled with it for a long time."

Karen was watching the ground where her steps would fall. "I only know what you told us many years ago, that you met up with the thugs, and they chased you all over a mountain pass.

Claire nodded. "Yes, but I think there was more to the story that Casey never told me. He and Jack lagged behind to try to mislead the bad people or slow them down in some way, so Alberto and I could get to the pass safely. Casey has been so secretive about what they saw or did that I've come to assume something happened down the ravine that traumatized him. Jack also never said anything to me before he went missing, but he seemed to be dealing with it better than Casey. In fact, it seemed to me that Casey had more difficulty with whatever it was as the years went on.

"Anyway, when we were talking, I asked if he was better now, and he said he was. Case told me he thought if he could just learn the truth about Jack—what happened to him—he might be able to finally get the closure he needs."

Karen thought for a moment. "Well, if you speak to him again, tell him the way we ended up dealing with the loss is to remind ourselves that Jack lived his life on his own terms, the way he wanted to. And, more importantly, we know that no matter where Jack's travels took him, he always loved us. Alton has always been convinced that Jack passed away early in 1986, somewhere in the jungle.

"If that's true," Karen sighed, "I hope it was in his sleep, from some disease, and in some beautiful place. Someplace that Jack would want to write a poem about."

The two women walked in silence for a while.

Then Karen updated Claire; Wade had followed his father's footsteps and had recently purchased a thirty-two-foot "Ralph Stanley fishin' boat" and was now deeply in debt. Younger brother Tom did not want to fish for a living and became a local policeman. Lisa went to the University of Maine, became a licensed clinical professional counselor, and worked in Bangor.

Then, through tears as fresh as the ones cried in 1986, Karen spoke of the pain of an ambiguous loss and how the not knowing made the grieving harder. Claire held her arm as she cried and walked.

Karen was saddened but not surprised to learn Claire had never married. She was the most beautiful forty-six-year-old woman Karen had ever seen.

"I suppose it's hard to be married as a working scientist," Karen said. After a pause, she continued, "I hope Jack didn't ruin your love life, dear."

Claire shook her head. She hesitated to respond. "No. I don't think so, and I am quite busy with the site and with teaching and writing."

Karen said nothing.

After twenty more steps, Claire remarked, "Oh, I tried a couple of times. Nice men. Handsome men. I genuinely thought I was pursuing real relationships, only to find out they were just flings."

Again, Karen just listened.

"There was this archaeologist, Aleksander, from Poland. He worked on my site with me for years." Claire looked wistful. "He was tall, fit, blonde … he looked a bit like a Viking to me." Both women snickered. They walked a few more steps.

"I thought once we might get married, but he never asked. Oh, we talked about it a few times, but Alek said 'I had too many skel —'" Claire stopped herself and pretended she was trying to remember what he had said. "He said I had too much baggage."

"I tried to joke with him; I said, 'One…I'm living out of *one* duffle bag!' But I knew what, or who, he meant. Alek even offered to go on another expedition with me to try to find Jack. He was a nice guy. He eventually returned to Poland, but we still write to each other."

After a long silence, Claire offered, "I suppose I've had my peccadillos."

Karen smiled and, after hesitating, said, "I feel sad for Casey. Whatever trauma he and Jack went through, I hope hasn't been too much of a burden for him." Claire did not respond.

"You know, Claire," Karen continued, "making a living on the harsh coast of Maine isn't easy. One thing we've learned over generations is that life is hard. We've held on to our family histories, and I've learned in every family—every human life—the one constant is there will always be suffering. Fortunately, there's an antidote; it is to embrace and appreciate the subtle beauty of art and learn to enjoy the simple things in nature. When you talk to Casey again, will you tell him that? And that we're proud of him?"

"I will. I'll reach out to him when I get home. You're very wise, Karen."

Karen Beal shook her head. "Nah…I'm just old." The two tired women walked arm in arm as they entered the driveway.

After promising to keep in touch, Claire left Stonington in her rental car to explore some of the places in Maine that Jack had told her about. In the car, she imagined he was with her.

On the drive back to New York, she decided to visit the Museum of Fine Arts in Boston — something she had put off for far too long. *If I'm visiting 'Jackspots,'* she thought, *I might as well take the plunge.*

At the MFA, the doorman was long gone. She could not remember his name, but she could picture him. He had been replaced with a kiosk and a machine that accepted her debit card for a ticket.

The marble stairs were the same, and some of the statuary had not changed in the twenty years since she last visited. Once she had climbed to the landing, she walked down the hallway where the Sisleys and the Manets still hung. The Impressionists warmed her heart when she got to the large gallery at the end of the hallway. Newly acquired—or borrowed—Monets and Renoirs graced the walls. There were three Van Goghs, that "drama queen," where Claire lingered for some time. She thought about how much Jack loved his work. She remembered that Jack would expound for hours on how misunderstood Vincent was and how treatable the artist's illnesses would be today.

She became lost in the paintings.

Even now, decades after their visit, Claire's eyes filled with tears. She collected herself and walked out of the gallery, across the hall, and into another corridor. Moving along, she stopped in front of a familiar piece. *Of course, I remember this one…*

It was the *"Carmen"* painting by Henri Toulouse-Lautrec, only a few feet from where it was in 1984. She suddenly remembered Jack explaining that Henri had painted himself into the picture. Her memory of his conversation about the painting was vivid, and it thrust her into a strange melancholy. Throughout the years, she had never allowed the time to be overly nostalgic. She was too disciplined for that. But now she felt the emotions welling up inside her. Staring at Jack's interpretation of Henri's tiny self-portrait, she burst into tears. For the second time in two days, she felt like someone had punched her in the gut. She coughed and sniffed hard, and her nose ran as she fumbled for a tissue in her bag.

In her peripheral vision, she could see people watching her. An older woman started to step toward her, but Claire held out her hand like a crossing guard to stop her. She only needed a minute to herself, and the woman halted.

Why did I come here? Claire wondered.

Within a few seconds, she had collected herself. She looked again at the picture and thought, *Maybe Jack wanted me to come, to have one last conversation with me.* She almost laughed at the absurdity of that. Claire felt sad for both people in the picture. For Carmen's hard life, and Henri's constant battle with himself and with whatever disease he had

... Rickets, osteogenesis imperfecta, who knows for sure. Whichever the reason, his life was hard, and perhaps because of that, he allowed many foibles. "Even the greatest artists were fallible and weak," Jack had told her.

What quote had he written in his letter? "*Of all creatures that breathe and move upon the earth, nothing is bred that is weaker than man.*" Was it weaker or fallible? She couldn't remember. Claire vowed to look it up later.

Was the art trying to help her move on from Jack more completely? *Again — absurd*, she thought.

She looked away from the Lautrec painting, and her eyes scanned the Monets on the opposite wall. The soft museum light made the colors sparkle. Claire spoke aloud, "No, Jackson, you were never weak." Then she smiled broadly. "Hell, you're probably living in Argentina somewhere."

And she turned and walked down the hallway and out of the museum.

As evening approached, Claire took a cab to Cambridge to take a walk through Harvard Yard, to revisit old haunts. She strolled past her old Veritas Dig, opposite the statue of Mr. Hoar. In one of her archaeology periodicals, she remembered reading that Harvard was now offering a course called "Digging Veritas," where students excavate different sections of the Yard to study the school's history. Claire looked at the ground where she and Casey had toiled in the trench thirty-five years before, and there was no evidence she had ever dug there.

She took her time walking down Divinity Street to the Peabody Museum. It was closed, but it was nice looking up at the old building. She had to suppress the tears that kept threatening. She could see the windows of the old familiar offices. There was Stephen William's, Maryanne Fitzroy's ... there was the genetics lab. She knew Casey would be home with his wife.

Claire then wandered back to the Yard. She passed Memorial Hall and walked through the wrought-iron gates. Most of the students were gone for the holidays, but there was still a scattering of lit dorm windows. The moon was up, and the straight branches of the ancient maples and oaks crisscrossed each other and looked like a giant, black web waiting to catch anything that might fall from the night sky.

Purely by accident, she happened to look to her left and saw under a streetlamp the bench with a lilac bush beside it where on a warm evening decades ago, she sat and read Jack's first letter. "I search for simplicity," the letter said. She continued across the Yard. *But you made everything more complicated, Jack.*

She stopped halfway through the Yard and pulled closed her collar against the cold air. She held it tight as she turned on her heel and surveyed the Yard one more time. *God, I miss those days*, she thought. *I miss Jackson.*

As she looked diagonally across the Yard, she remembered another walk on a cold December night, when she and Jack were going to meet with Professor Fitzroy about their upcoming trip. She recalled how fervent Jack had been about the loss of many college traditions, and he argued the university experience had suffered for it. Jack and his passion!

Then, she headed for the subway gate to catch the Red Line. After only two steps, she spun around, and still clutching her coat collar, she faced the Yard, smiled, and looked up through the dark branches. She took a deep breath and raised her voice high, and yelled as loud as she could, "*RINE--HART!!*"

She waited, hearing only her warm exhalations into the cold night air.

When no one answered, she breathed deeply and smiled to herself. Then she walked across the street and down the steps to the subway.

When Claire walked into her office at Columbia four days later, she felt fairly at peace. It had been good to see Karen Beal again and Stonington.

Her receptionist poked her head in the office door. "How was Maine?"

Claire smiled up at her. Her desk was covered with correspondence, and she turned on her laptop. "It was lovely, Sandy. You know, I think the sea smells different in Stonington than any other seaport, but I don't know why."

Sandy smiled, nodded, and said, "Well, you have the whole day to catch up on the mail."

Claire was feeling more at peace than she had in years. The trip had done some good, she reckoned. Sifting through the emails from faculty, students, the car rental company, and credit card solicitors, she saw one from Aleksander Chmielewski in Warsaw.

Dear Claire,

Hope you are well.

Last month, I traveled with some students down the Rio alto Madre de Dios to the town of Boca Manu. I know you are familiar with the place. We were on a birding/hiking trip. I ran into a Peruvian archaeologist who took me to a community first aid clinic just off the Plaza de Armas. He wanted to show me some artifacts and some remains that a local had shown him a year earlier. The local fellow wanted the doc to tell him if they were very old bones or not. The man said the box of bones and the few artifacts found with them were shown to local authorities, but the constables never followed up on them. At that time, the sergeant told the local man that the bones surely belonged to an illegal logger or a miner from upriver.

I took a couple of photographs of the box's contents and have attached them for you.

They are not old.

If I can help, please call me,

Love,

Alek

Claire clicked on the attachments and matter-of-factly glanced at the images. The first photo was of a large, flat, plastic box, the kind people might store blankets in, with the lid removed. It was lined with blue cloth, and bones were arranged neatly on the fabric. There was the skull, missing the mandible.

If Alek knew these were not ancient bones — not artifacts — then she knew very well why he sent them to her. She was not worried. These were not Jack's remains — she could tell at first glance. Several teeth were missing in the left maxilla, and she could tell by expanding the image that the teeth were long gone while the individual was alive. Definitely not Jack.

Also, there was a healed skull fracture just lateral to the orbit of his left eye. Again, *not* Jack.

Claire breathed easy and settled in to examine the photo so she could give Alek an assessment. She expanded the image more and scrolled over the bones with her mouse.

Caucasian, perhaps — probably Mestizo. Other than the long-healed fracture and the healed-over maxilla where the teeth were missing, she couldn't find any more signs of trauma. There was no pelvis in the box, but the size of the humerus and tibias suggested they had belonged to a male.

Nothing too interesting, Alek, she thought. *The sergeant was probably right. A logger. Maybe a tree limb had snapped up and whacked the bastard in the head at some point, and it healed, or perhaps he had been in a bar fight.*

She clicked on the second image; a smaller Tupperware container was tucked into the corner of the big box, separating the bones from some artifacts. There was a rubber sole of a tennis shoe. *Not* Jack…he wore only Vasque hiking boots, his favorite footwear. She could see the rotted remains of a wallet that appeared empty, a pen, and a few Peruvian coins. She couldn't identify all of the coins.

Claire zoomed in as far as the resolution would allow. The images were a bit fuzzy. Her eyes were drawn to two of the dirty, medium-size coins. She tilted her head slightly and focused. *Ah,* she said to herself, *five Intis. I'm surprised no one has taken that one.* The coin next to it looked like one of the old, tarnished silver one-half Sols she had seen.

Again, she tilted her head to try and make out any writing. She focused hard, leaned toward the computer screen, and suddenly, without warning, jumped up, sending her chair backward banging loudly into a file cabinet. As she did, a loud guttural gasp came out of her.

Sandy came bursting through the door. "Dr. Anderson! Are you alright?!" The receptionist had a frightened look on her face.

Claire was standing with her right hand over her mouth and with tears in her eyes. Her left arm was outstretched, and she held her shaking hand palm-up in Sandy's face. Claire didn't need to speak — she couldn't talk — but the look in her eyes told Sandy to leave her alone. Now!

Sandy, surprised, muttered, "Oh…!" and quickly backed out of the room, closing the office door behind her.

Claire was shaking all over. She reached her trembling hand behind her, found her chair, and lowered herself into it. She was slumped over to one side. Finally, she had to breathe. If she didn't, she would soon faint. There was a forceful sucking sound as she gasped for air, *"Ahhh…!"* She took several more breaths, slowly now, she thought, *Get some air!*

Thirty years of pain, anguish, and loss overwhelmed her. Thirty years of wondering, waiting, and wishing. When she had caught her breath, still trembling all over, she inched forward in her chair and dared to again look closely at the coin. This time she didn't jump up; this time, she slumped forward and dropped her head into her arms on her desk. She began to weep. Her crying lasted over an hour. Her computer screen had timed out, and when she had cried long enough, she wiped her face, dried her eyes, took a few long, deep breaths and touched her mousepad, and made the image reappear.

Claire closed the image file of the bones without looking at them again. She did not look at the coins. Her eyes were focused only on the second image of the artifacts, and the small, grey Hag stone, with the little "J" embedded in the sandstone. She felt sick to her stomach.

After an hour of collecting her thoughts and laying on her daybed, trying not to dwell on the decades of hope she had held on to for her soul mate, Claire sat back at her desk. She closed out of everything on her computer; she would respond to Alek another day. She called for her receptionist, and Sandy tentatively came into the office.

"Dr. Anderson? Are you okay?"

"I'm so sorry if I frightened you, Sandy. I was frightened myself." This took Sandy by surprise; she knew Dr. Anderson wasn't afraid of *anything*. "You see, I opened an email and discovered a friend—my greatest friend—whom I've been looking for for nearly thirty years. Well, maybe not actively looking, but always thinking and wondering about him. And today, just now, I found out he's deceased."

"I'm so sorry. Is there anything I can do for you?"

"I need to be alone for a while, Sandy, and if anyone calls the rest of the day, I'm out of the office."

"Yes, Sandy responded. "Understood." Again, she closed the door behind her.

Claire's mind raced. *They'll never ship the remains to the States for analysis—someone will have to do it in Lima. DNA...we'll have to procure some. This will be a logistical nightmare...*

Claire was only professionally thinking about protocols with the bones. She knew in her gut they were Jack's remains.

After a few more thoughtful moments, when she felt confidant she would not start crying again, she picked up her cell phone. Claire thought about Karen Beal's words only days before, about suffering being a constant in the human condition, and how the lobsterman's wife's life had taught her the antidote for suffering. *What had Karen said? The beauties in art and finding the splendor in the simplest parts of Nature? Damn, I wish I had memorized it.*

Claire hesitated, with her phone in hand. *How would the others react to this news*, she wondered. *Closure. Maybe this will finely mean some closure*, she thought.

She scrolled through her contacts and touched the screen.

Within seconds, there was an answer on the other end, "Hello?"

"Casey…it's Claire."

ABOUT THE AUTHOR

Denis "Dee" Dauphinee

Dee is an American author of novels, biographies, and essays. His writing has gained a following with readers interested in the out-of-doors, human interest, history, travel, and fly fishing. He has been a mountaineering and fly fishing guide, a photographer, a farmer, an orthopedic physician's assistant, and a semi-pro football wide receiver.

Dee split his time between Jackson Hole, WY, New England, and Vancouver, British Columbia, for nearly two decades. He has led or co-led mountaineering, desert, and jungle expeditions on 5 continents. His guiding and photography took him to El Salvador, Peru, the Arctic, Europe, Nicaragua, Venezuela, Iraq, Israel, Egypt, Ecuador, Jordan, the UK, Panama, Africa, and many places in between doing photographic spec work for several media outlets, including United Press International. Now he writes about those places.

Dee lives in Middle Maine.

OTHER BOOKS BY DEE:

Stoneflies and Turtleheads

The River Home

Highlanders Without Kilts

When You Find My Body:
The Disappearance of Geraldine Largay
on the Appalachian Trail

ENDNOTE REVIEW REQUEST

If you enjoyed reading this, please leave a review on on your social media or news outlets. I read many reviews, and they help new readers discover my books. Also, if you're interested in my giveaways or reading my occasional blog pieces or newsletters, please sign up for correspondence at: https://www.ddauphinee.com/contact.
Many thanks! — Dee

www.ingramcontent.com/pod-product-compliance
Lightning Source LLC
Chambersburg PA
CBHW050108120726
47904CB00004B/1270